You don't even know who you are.

"What language is that your parents speak?" I wanted to know. "Is it Dutch? Are you all going to Holland? Last week we put in our application to go to Shanghai! But we haven't even started learning Chinese yet."

Ruben shook his head in disbelief. "You must have heard Yiddish before."

"Yiddish?" I repeated. "Where would I have heard that? No one in my family knows Yiddish."

"But that's our language, Ziska, it has been for hundreds of years. Your ancestors definitely used to speak Yiddish too."

"How would you know that?"

"Yiddish is a mixture of Hebrew and old German. It's a language Jewish people all over Europe use to communicate."

"Is that true? Then they didn't have to learn English or something like that?"

I was fascinated. Ruben looked at me with compassion. "You're being persecuted and you don't even know who you are," he said.

Other Books You May Enjoy

My Family
for the War

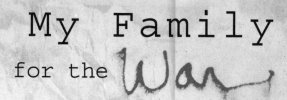

My Family
for the War

by Anne C. Voorhoeve
translated by Tammi Reichel

speak
An Imprint of Penguin Group (USA)

SPEAK
Published by the Penguin Group
Penguin Group (USA) LLC
375 Hudson Street
New York, New York 10014

USA * Canada * UK * Ireland * Australia
New Zealand * India * South Africa * China

penguin.com
A Penguin Random House Company

Originally published in Germany by Ravensburger
Buchverlag under the title *Liverpool Street*, 2007
First published in the United States of America by Dial Books,
an imprint of Penguin Group (USA) Inc., 2012
Published by Speak, an imprint of Penguin Group (USA) LLC, 2015

Text copyright © 2007 by Anne C. Voorhoeve
English translation copyright © 2012 by Tammi Reichel

Edited and published in the English language by arrangement with Ravensburger Buchverlag GmbH

The translation of this work was supported by a grant from the Goethe-Institut
(Goethe-Institut), which is funded by the German Ministry of Foreign Affairs.

THE LIBRARY OF CONGRESS HAS CATALOGED THE DIAL BOOKS EDITION AS FOLLOWS:
Voorhoeve, Anne C.
[Liverpool Street . English]
My family for the war / by Anne C. Voorhoeve ; translated by Tammi Reichel.
p. cm.
Summary: Before the start of World War II, ten-year-old Ziska Mangold, who has Jewish ancestors but
has been raised as a Protestant, is taken out of Nazi Germany on one of the Kindertransport trains, to
live in London with a Jewish family, where she learns about Judaism and endures the hardships of war
while attempting to keep in touch with her parents, who are trying to survive in Holland.
ISBN 978-0-8037-3360-2 (hardcover)
1. World War, 1939–1945—England—Juvenile fiction. [1. World War, 1939–1945—England—
Fiction. 2. Identity—Fiction. 3. Jews—England—Fiction. 4. Refugees—Fiction. 5. Holocaust, Jewish
(1939–1945)—Fiction. 6. Great Britain—History—George VI, 1936–1952—Fiction.] I. Reichel,
Tammi. II. Title.
PZ7.V944My 2012 [Fic]—dc22 2011009350

Speak ISBN 978-0-14-751183-6

Printed in the United States of America

1 3 5 7 9 10 8 6 4 2

For my mother

Table of Contents

My Family
for the War

Book One

Survival Plan

1938–1939

Chapter 1

Jumping

I would never find another friend like Rebekka Liebich. She crouched on the narrow windowsill, one hand holding tight to the frame, and held the other hand stretched out in front of her, as if that would somehow shorten the distance of almost five feet between her and the trunk of the birch tree. I stood in the courtyard three floors below and would have liked to close my eyes, but I couldn't even manage that. I stared up at her, hypnotized.

In a few seconds I would witness my best friend plunging to her death. I could already imagine what my mother would say about that. The beating that Richard and his gang threatened to give Bekka and me if they got hold of us again suddenly seemed harmless compared to what I had coming when Mamu got her hands on me.

My anxiety grew. Bekka was not someone who left things to chance, especially not her survival. She had only climbed up onto the windowsill after she had made sure she could jump five and a half feet from a squat.

I managed to get a little farther than that, at least in the sand pit. But I would have crouched on the windowsill like I was glued there. Ten wild horses couldn't get me to jump into the birch tree! I knew it, and Bekka knew it too. She had offered to go first.

If she falls, I won't have to jump! I thought. Ashamed, I put my hand over my eyes for a moment, as if to shield them from the sun. But on that gray September day in 1938, the sun hadn't even made an appearance.

Bekka rocked gently and took her left hand off the window frame. By then, my heart was pounding so loudly that I heard buzzing in my ears, and for a few seconds I actually thought the approaching drone in the air was the bursting of my own fear-filled heart. Bekka just held tight again, impatiently, and waited.

The airplane moved away, and I saw the small black swastika that clung to its wing like a spider.

Now! Something else flew right over my head: small, with long blond braids, and so quick that it was over in the blink of an eye. A noise, rustling, twigs and dry yellow leaves rained down on me, and there was Bekka, triumphantly perched in the branches of the birch. Perfect!

Oh, help, I thought. *Now it's my turn!*

A window flew open on the second floor. "Have you lost your minds entirely?" Mrs. Bergmann screeched. I had never been so happy to see the old nag hanging out of her kitchen window. "Franziska Mangold and her worthless friend! Running away won't help, I saw you!"

Bekka clambered down from the tree as quick as a squirrel. We knew every little branch on this tree, which would save my life just a few weeks later. Well, almost. In any case, everything would have been different if Bekka hadn't jumped into the birch tree that day.

"Damned Jewish brats!" Mrs. Bergmann's deafening voice bounced off all four walls of the apartment buildings surrounding the courtyard. "I'm calling the police! They think they can just jump into our beautiful tree!" I heard other windows opening. The word *Jewish,* especially when it was shouted, was a sure way to attract attention.

Breathless, Bekka landed on the ground right in front of me. We took off.

"Ziska, wait a minute!" Bekka panted behind me. But I didn't stop until we had taken cover behind the wall of the cemetery. I was the fastest runner, always had been, even in the first grade at my old school. That school had been "Jew-free" since summer, and Monika Bär had taken my place. She won the gold medal in the race, even though I had crossed the finish line first. They couldn't let a Jew win.

"Jew-free" meant that Rebekka Liebich, Ruben Seydensticker, and I, the three Jewish kids in our class, had to get up an hour earlier in the morning and make the long trip to the Jewish school in Charlottenburg. Our former principal was given a commendation and got his picture in the newspaper. We found that rather unfair; after all, we were the ones who had to make our way through half of Berlin twice a day to keep our previous school free of Jews, not him.

"It's just temporary," said Papa.

I didn't tell him that apart from the long trip to school I was actually very happy about the change. In the Jewish school we were left in peace. No one spilled ink on our notebooks or forced us to play "Out with the Jews" during recess, a popular dice game that could also be played with live people. Ruben, especially, with his sidelocks, was a favorite when it came to taunting and beating. The fact that he always knew the right answers didn't help either. Last year the teacher completely ignored him, even when Ruben was the only student who raised his hand. The teacher was more interested in measuring Ruben's long, narrow skull in a lesson about race, to demonstrate the superior anatomy of Aryan children. Bekka and I had made ourselves small and inconspicuous in the last row, even though we both knew that our ordinary skulls weren't in any danger, since they would have ruined the teacher's beloved theory.

We crept into our favorite hiding spot, a cave in the bushes. The homeless man who used to sleep here at night hadn't been around since the spring. "Maybe they . . . *krrrk!*" Bekka made a motion at her throat.

But I didn't believe that. I figured he was working for the Reich somewhere. After all, we constantly heard how the Führer took people from the streets and gave them work. The actual name of the Führer was never spoken at my house. Mamu made sure of that: Anyone who said his name or even the word *Führer* had to put a penny in a glass. That way we could go to Cohn's on Hermannplatz and eat an ice cream at his expense every once in a while. The only trouble was, there were just a few pennies in the glass because Papa and I never wanted to talk about the Führer.

It wasn't until Bekka and I were in the cave and sitting across from each other that I saw that her flight into the birch tree hadn't exactly ended gently. She had scratches on her face and arms, nasty scrapes on both palms, and some twigs had such a firm grip in her hair that we tore out whole tufts when we tried to get them out. Bekka had long, white-blond hair. I, with my unruly mane, not really dark and not really blond, actually no color at all, was secretly envious of it.

Without a care in the world, she licked blood from her arm, turned halfway around, and grinned at me. "The tree is closer than it looks! I didn't need that much momentum!"

"We'd better stay out of the courtyard for a while," I said.

Bekka agreed. "Do you think Bergmann will really call the police?"

"No, she'll just run to Mamu, like always."

"So what if she does? Your mother will take care of her," replied Bekka, who thought the world of Mamu. No wonder, since she didn't have to actually live with her!

"It will more likely be me she takes care of," I predicted darkly. A combination of Mamu and the gentle Mrs. Liebich, I found, would have been ideal.

My friend took off her right shoe, removed the lining, and dug out a well-worn piece of paper—our "survival plan," Bekka called it. She and her parents and brother had been learning English for two years. That's because the Liebichs were going to emigrate to America soon. They were already as good as gone, just waiting for a response from a cousin who had married into money over there and would have no problem at all sponsoring the Liebichs.

I didn't like it when Bekka spoke English, and not only because I couldn't understand a word of it, even though I had been plagued by it at school. No, it was much more because every English word reminded me that I would soon lose my best friend. The ranks of children in the Jewish school were dwindling. Teachers disappeared too, sold all their worldly possessions and emigrated. We never knew who would show up in the coming week, or who would be teaching us which subjects.

Crazy, said my father. You'll see, next year the whole fuss will be over and done with, and they'll be stuck in Cuba and Chile and Argentina and will have lost everything!

But "survival plan" sounded too sophisticated: The crumpled paper inside Bekka's shoe was actually just a tiny, scribbled map of the best hiding places and escape routes in our neighborhood. With her tongue between her teeth, Bekka drew a tree in the appropriate place on the map and wrote "3rd floor, Ziska's room" on it. Then she folded the paper together and stuck it back in her shoe. "Remind me to give you the map when we leave," she added. As if she would ever give up the map, her pride and joy.

I took a long time to make my way back up to our apartment. I studied the ornamental wooden carving on the door to each apartment, the glass paintings on the windows in the hall. But I didn't dare touch the banister with my Jewish hands. I don't even want to think about what would have happened if Bergmann had poked her head around the door just at that moment! Not that I had ever heard that it was expressly forbidden, but you could never be too sure. On Sunday you're happily sitting on the park bench, and on Monday, it's not allowed anymore. "Jews and dogs not allowed." No, I didn't touch the banister.

Christine and her mother came toward me on my way

upstairs. Christine's mother looked away, as if a particularly hideous beggar were stretching out his hand toward her, even though I pressed myself against the wall in order to take up as little of their space as possible. Christine smiled at me, very quickly, so that her mother didn't notice. She still did that, even though we hadn't exchanged a single word with each other since public officials, including their families, had been forbidden to have anything to do with Jews. Before that I had been in her apartment often, or Christine came to ours. She was nice. I smiled back—a little conspiracy.

I opened the door and stepped into safety. Our apartment—spacious, bright—was the place where the outside world ceased to exist. Except for a few small blank spaces on the walls where pictures used to hang, paintings my parents had recently needed to sell, everything looked just the way I had known it my entire life. I took off my shoes so I could tiptoe from carpet to carpet without making any noise on the wood floor. Their voices came from the dining room. That was good—maybe I could slink past them into my room without them noticing. . . .

"We're finished! Through, Margot, do you understand? That was it! It's over, finito!"

Papa's agitated voice rose, and fell again with the last word. I had already covered half of the foyer and was past the kitchen, but I stopped, anchored to the spot. Bergmann had actually gone to the police! Thoughts raced through my head and collided with each other. *We'll lose the apartment! My parents will be taken away! Bekka won't be allowed to go to America! This is it! We're finished!*

"Always be careful how you behave," my father told me.

"Be polite, even if they get rough, and never talk back. Don't speak loudly or thoughtlessly, but you don't want to come across as too refined either—otherwise they might think you feel superior. Always wear clean clothes when you leave the apartment so no one can say we're dirty. A single Jewish child that makes a bad impression reflects badly on all of us! The best thing to do," he added, looking into my shocked and troubled face, overwhelmed with all that responsibility, "is not to attract attention at all, Ziska."

Exactly what would happen if I was noticed or behaved badly he didn't say, because we knew as well as anyone that we couldn't rely on one particular punishment. The Germans could do with us whatever they pleased. But I had never imagined it would come to the point that we were finished, and all because of me.

"Finished? That's ridiculous," Mamu said impatiently. "Your clients weren't paying you anymore anyway."

My father didn't answer. Mamu's voice became more strident. "Let's face the truth, Franz. We're already living entirely from my money now. And it's not so surprising that you've been banned from practicing law. Of our friends, who is still allowed to work? Schumann, of course. But there are always SA standing around in front of his store."

As if led by the strings of a marionette, my feet carried me a few steps to the living room door, which stood ajar. While I pressed my ear to the door I prayed fervently, *Oh Jesus, please only let us be goners if it has nothing to do with me!*

"Maybe we should have tried to get out," Papa said quietly.

Now it was Mamu's turn to not answer. *Uh-oh,* I thought, picturing how she had her lips pressed together. Ever since

I could remember she'd been badgering Papa, *Let's get out of here!* But Papa wouldn't hear of it, even when one country after another started to close their borders to Jewish refugees. "There's still Shanghai," Papa said now.

"How nice that you're finally coming to your senses," Mamu retorted in a frosty tone. "Ziska, you're my witness. Do you think I haven't noticed that you're eavesdropping behind the door?"

Dazed, I entered the room and looked over at my parents. They were sitting at the dining room table underneath the large oil painting of Emperor Wilhelm, and Mamu studied me with one of her scrutinizing gazes through the thick strands of black hair that half covered her right eye.

I was all too familiar with this look, and it made me feel the usual combination of guilt, anxiety, and admiration. My mother was widely considered to be a "beautiful woman," though in my opinion that didn't begin to do her justice. She was tall, dark, and temperamental, with a loud voice and big gestures. And as if her appearance weren't impressive enough, she emphasized it even more with hats and scarves in dramatic colors, wore pants and bright red lipstick. I loved, admired, and feared my mother.

Papa sat in his place, utterly miserable, his back even more hunched than usual, and made a grimace that was supposed to be an attempt at a smile. Whatever it was that he had found out today, it had clearly been a hard blow, and I immediately thought of the photograph hanging in his office. It was of a German soldier looking confident and stern, and it was only recently that I had realized it was a photo of my father! I had never seen him like that; all the troubles that had plagued his life started soon after I was born, slowly but surely wearing him down. My mother seemed to me to grow stronger, the smaller and quieter he became, and she loved him with a devotion that made me jealous.

But my parents had never fought as bitterly as they had lately. Just a week ago, Mamu had bought the *Stürmer* newspaper and brought it home, a repulsive Nazi propaganda rag. Repugnant, dark figures were featured on the front page, supposedly Jews. They didn't resemble anyone I knew. Papa had run out of the room and slammed the door behind him, and I could still hear Mamu's angry cry: "I at least want to know who I'm dealing with!"

"Ziska and her friend jumped out of the third floor today," Mamu said. "And do you know why they do that? It's their survival training in case that stupid group of Hitler Youth running around with Richard Graditz beats them up again. That's how far it's gone, Franz. Our daughter is jumping out of the third floor. The Liebichs, the Todorovskis, the Grüns, all of them already have emigration petitions in the works, everyone except us!"

My mother! Here I had spent the entire afternoon thinking of nothing but the various ways she would let me have it, and now she turned the whole thing around and used our crazy stunt to manipulate my father! All I had to do was play along.

Unfortunately, I glanced at Papa's guilty face and knew I couldn't do it. "But I didn't . . ." I protested. Mamu glared at me so fiercely that I snapped my mouth shut again. She, of course, already knew that it wasn't me who had actually jumped. My mother was the smartest woman I knew, and twisting little details to her advantage was her specialty. If I said that, she probably would have answered, "So what? Why didn't you jump? If you had jumped, I wouldn't have to stretch the truth now!"

"They won't be able to get us anymore," I told Papa instead, by way of encouragement. "We have hideouts and escape routes all over the neighborhood. There are already so many that Bekka has to draw them on a map so we can keep track of all of them."

Strangely, this bit of good news didn't do a thing to erase the worry lines on his forehead. Papa propped up his head in both hands and stared blankly in front of him.

"Well, what do you think of Shanghai, Ziska?" Mamu asked, smiling.

"How would we get there?" I replied, skeptical.

"On a ship, a trip of several weeks."

"Is it as far as America?"

"Even farther, Ziska! Quite a bit farther away than America."

"And when will we go?"

"As soon as I have all the paperwork together. I'll have our names registered tomorrow."

"Don't we need someone who will sponsor us, like the Liebichs?"

"No, sweetie. We can go to Shanghai without a sponsor. We don't even need a visa, just an exit permit and passage for the ship."

Mamu kept glancing over at Papa. Our question-and-answer game was probably intended to point out again how simple it really was—how simple it could have been the entire time. "Of course, we'll have to pay the emigration tax. But with my jewelry and the family porcelain . . . we'll be able to keep enough to live from for a while."

Papa stood up and left the room. His sadness stayed behind and draped itself over me. "What's wrong with him?" I whispered.

Mamu looked off to the side. For a moment I thought I saw her eyes fill with tears, but I must have been mistaken. Mamu didn't cry. Never. Papa maybe, and I definitely did, but not Mamu.

"Papa's license to practice law was revoked today. We knew it was coming, but it's terrible for him anyway, now that it's happened. You know how much he had hoped . . ."

She didn't finish her sentence, but I knew what she meant. My father still believed in the good Germany, the one he fought for in the Great War. In his mind there was a little blockade that held back everything that might have convinced him of the opposite: that his battles on the western front and even his Iron Cross Second Class didn't count anymore; that he was no longer a German, but a Jew, even though the Mangolds had been Protestant for two generations and not one of us had ever stepped foot inside a synagogue. He couldn't understand that we weren't wanted in Germany, or in almost any other country in the world, for that matter.

"Shanghai," I repeated, tasting the name on my tongue. "I think that sounds good."

Chapter 2

Richard and Ruben

As always happened whenever I caught sight of Richard, August, and Eberhard, my scalp and fingertips began to tingle. Had they seen me too? I didn't think so, because as I backed into the nearest doorway I could see them, completely focused on kicking their ratty old soccer ball around.

I tried to stay calm and looked around. I was standing in an entryway near the south end of the Schiller Promenade, which meant we had mapped out four or five escape routes and two hiding places right around here. They wouldn't catch me this time! I pushed myself off from the wall of the house. Leaving my three friends behind me, I leisurely walked back in the direction I had come from.

Right away, I heard that the soccer ball wasn't bouncing on the ground anymore. That didn't have to mean anything. The best thing to do was just continue on my way without turning around. I stuck my hands in the pockets of my jacket and strolled down the street, apparently in no hurry.

But I knew the tragic story of Lot's wife, and that the brain basically ignores orders like "Don't turn around!" I hadn't gone five yards before I risked a tiny peek.

Richard's eyes met mine. He came toward me, grinning, with the ball under his arm, matching my pace with the other two in tow. They were just waiting for me to start running.

I walked a little faster. They picked up their pace too, and they were already catching up. I only had one chance. I stopped and turned around. "Just try to catch me, you cowards!" I screamed.

Then I turned around and fled.

It's a wonderful feeling when you're running and gaining ground. You don't even feel the ground; your legs and feet and the pavement all become one. A few intoxicating leaps transformed what had just been a scared girl into a winged being that couldn't possibly be caught, like Jesse Owens, the black Olympic champion who left all his competitors of the supposedly superior races in the dust two years ago.

I dedicated my run to Jesse Owens, and that gave me luck. Even without looking behind me I could tell that the distance between me and my pursuers was growing. I let out a wild cry of triumph, ran around the church, and nearly knocked over an older man who suddenly stood up from his bench right in my path.

"Grab her! She's a Jew!" Richard screeched. The man actually reacted, spread his arms out, and made a few halfhearted steps toward me. *But Franziska Jesse Mangold can't be stopped! An elegant swerve to the right will do the trick, allowing her to leave her pursuers behind. And it is unbelievable, ladies and gentlemen, but this gifted young runner still has enough energy to step up her pace!*

I turned into the home stretch. The arched entryway I was headed for was at the top right corner of our survival plan, because it was almost outside our neighborhood. Bekka and I had discovered the house in the spring, not long after my first run-in with Richard and his group. The entrance was always open because it led to a butcher's shop in the back of the courtyard. I crossed the street and disappeared into the entrance. "She's over there! Get her!" I heard behind me—in a voice that was out of breath, I noted with satisfaction.

I rushed down the steps to the cellar and found myself in a long, low tunnel. To the right and left of the stairs were passages lined with small niches used as storage space by the people who lived in this building.

Cellar number 8 was way back at the end of the corridor on the left. I ran through the passageway. It smelled like brickwork and mouse droppings. Right when Richard, August, and Eberhard reached the bottom of the basement stairs, I disappeared into the darkness of cellar number 8.

"Now you're trapped, you Jewish pig!" Richard jeered.

I heard steps coming toward me, just one pair of footsteps. Richard had sent his friends in the opposite direction and came alone. A wooden door flew open and banged against a shelf. Glass jars clinked together. There was a brief flash of yellow light when Richard turned on the light in the little storage room and looked around, then a soft click as he turned it off again.

There was no time to lose. I felt my way along the back wall, where the opening was. Sure of the way, I slid my hands along the bricks. There was the cupboard, and right next to it . . .

Ouch! I felt the big, heavy object that stood in my way. It was a storage shelf! I desperately tried to squelch the paralyzing fear that instantly shot from my legs to my head. *Stay calm! You're in the wrong cellar. When Richard looks into the next one, you can slip into number 8.*

I ran back to the door with my heart pounding. Richard had made it to number 4; now he went in and turned on the light there. I took a step out of my shed to dart into the next one down.

But there wasn't another one. I *was* in number 8! Where there should have been an opening into the basement of the neighboring house, some idiot had put up a shelf!

"There she is!" resounded through the basement hallway. I had completely forgotten about August and Eberhard.

Out of my head, I stormed back to the shelving in the darkness, kneeled down, and felt for one of the boards with both hands. Cans, glass jars, bottles, everything I got my hands on I flung to the side and pulled my upper body into the space I had made so I could feel what was at the back with my right hand.

My hand felt nothing. Salvation! The shelves were open at the back! Shoulders first, I crammed myself into the bottom shelf, making so much noise that I couldn't even tell if Richard and his cronies were already in number 8. With one last desperate kick I freed myself and dropped down into the basement of the building next door. I landed on my back, hard, on the cold cement. It was pitch-black, but the scratching coming from the shelves told me that Richard was already working his way through.

With both hands stretched out in front of me, I walked

into the darkness with my eyes wide open. I fell up the first step of the basement stairs, and after several feet came to the door into the neighboring courtyard. With weak knees I tumbled into freedom, slammed the door closed, and I suddenly stood absolutely still, as if I had grown roots on the spot. Richard's soccer ball lay in the middle of the entryway I had just lured the boys through. He had to put it down to have his hands free for me.

How could he? I had never known him to leave it out of his sight. He knew there were children living on this street who would have given anything to have a ball like that. But now the soccer ball lay on the sidewalk because something else had been even more important to him. Richard must hate me fiercely.

Something in me said, "Leave it alone, Ziska!" But instead of doing the only smart thing and getting away as fast as possible, I saw only that ball.

And all at once I was gripped by a rage greater than anything I had ever experienced in my life. That stupid, shabby ball suddenly conjured up everything I absolutely didn't want to think about. The birthday party when Richard had gotten the ball. The game of spin the bottle, where *the next one the bottle points to has to kiss someone!* The bottle turned, turned more slowly, stopped turning, and pointed to Richard. And Richard laughed, stood up without hesitating, walked through the circle of kids toward me, and kissed me right on the mouth. He looked at me so sweetly while he did it.

I hadn't been invited to birthday parties for a long time. But at one time, Richard had been my friend.

"Is it true, Ziska?" he had asked me later in a low voice. "Your parents are . . . you're . . . Jewish?"

"Nah," I had answered. "Papa is a lawyer."

"Are you sure?"

"Of course! You know he is!"

He rumpled his forehead. "But my mother said that you're Jews."

"Should I ask my mother?" I could see how concerned he was about this. "I'll let you know tomorrow."

He planted himself in the schoolyard the next day and listened to me, his face without any expression, as I relayed my mother's explanation. Yes, we actually did have Jewish ancestors, and I had never heard anything about it before because all four of my grandparents had already converted to Protestantism in the last century. So when it was time for religion classes at school, I was part of the Protestant group, I believed in Jesus, and I would be confirmed at the same time as Richard. The other kids stood around us, and no one said anything. Richard shifted from one leg to the other and I noticed that he had just as little clue about what to do with this information as I did. For my part, I couldn't have told you exactly what "Jewish" meant, or why it was of any significance in the schoolyard.

"Eeeew! Richard kissed a Jew!" fat Roland finally screamed.

In the next instant he lay on the ground, crying, because Richard hit him with a perfect right hook. There was a wave of muttering among the other children, who took a step backward just to be safe. Proudly, I lifted my chin and looked around with a challenging gaze. That was much better than a kiss! No one had ever hit someone else for my sake before!

Then he let go of Roland. He fell back in the dust and lifted his arms in front of his face. "Okay, Richard, I get it," he whimpered.

Richard took a step back and looked at me again, and I could not believe what I saw. Everything that was handsome about his face had disappeared; there was nothing there but a hard mask that stared at me, full of accusation, rage, and contempt.

"You should have told me!" he barked at me.

"But Richard . . . why?" I managed to get out.

All I saw then was his jutted chin, his bright eyes, and the quick, hard motion of his shoving me. I lay on my back next to fat Roland, who crawled away from me fast, as if I had a contagious disease. I squinted up at Richard. He gave me a kick and turned away.

"Now we have you, you Jewish pig!"

Richard, who had followed me through the basement, came at me from behind, August and Eberhard from the front. I stood between them with the ball in my hands. Only a few seconds could have passed since I ran out of the cellar, but those were the seconds I needed to escape.

"Drop the ball!" Richard barked. His hands were clenched into fists. The feeling that overcame me was familiar. It was what had led Bekka and me to spend most of the last six months combing our neighborhood for escape routes.

"Come and get it!" They charged me. I wound up my arm as if to throw the ball over Richard's head onto one of the balconies. Startled, he jerked his head up, and raised his arms too. I channeled all my fury into my throw and shot his ball right in the middle of his face.

Where are you, Bekka? We can cross off the entryway at the butcher's, and we definitely need to check the other hiding places to make sure they're still the same as when we found them, so the next time . . . the next time . . . the next time . . .

I lay on my side, and something buzzed on my mouth. A big, fat fly was flitting across my lower lip, tasting a bit here, a bit there. There was certainly enough blood there. Almost dry already. Was there any part of me still whole? I sat up slowly, leaning against the house wall. Someone had watched from the first floor, but whoever it was left me alone.

"Ziska? Can you stand up?" A long, pale face appeared in front of me as if through a fog. It must have taken a lot of guts for him to come into a strange courtyard—Ruben Seydensticker wasn't exactly one of the bravest people I knew. He took hold of both of my limp arms and helped me get up.

I clung to his shoulder, bent over forward, and saw the blood-sprinkled cobblestones in front of me blur. "I'd better take you home with me," Ruben said quietly. "It isn't far."

"Nah, lemme gon," I mumbled through my throbbing, swollen lips, which weren't able to form understandable words anymore. After two yards he stopped us again, leaned me against the building, picked up my shoe, and put it on my foot.

Gradually the other parts of my body sorted themselves out and began to send searing hot messages to my head. Pain rampaged through my left shoulder, my arms, the back of my head, not to mention the entire lower half of my body, and after we had taken three or four steps, I threw up right on Ruben's shoes.

"It doesn't matter. Just keep moving," he said gallantly.

I was so ashamed that I started to cry. And that's how we arrived at his apartment. His parents, who had been sitting at the table, jumped up. "Oy!" escaped from Frau Seydensticker, followed by a wave of strange sounds that sounded like German, but then again not really. *Aha,* I thought dully. *The Seydenstickers want to emigrate too.*

I wondered which language this family was learning. I quietly began listing all the countries I knew of that were still accepting Jews: Argentina, Chile, Uruguay, Paraguay . . . Not that this was really of great interest at the moment, but the whole way to Ruben's I had continuously been checking whether my brain had suffered any damage. *My name is Ziska Mangold, born on February 19, 1928. I live at Hermannstraße 88, front house, third floor . . .* I couldn't have been unconscious for very long, but a small sliver of my life was shrouded in darkness, and that was enough to make me terribly afraid.

Ruben's father laid me carefully on the kitchen bench. His full beard tickled my arm, and perched on his head as if with glue was a perfectly round, flat yarmulke.

"This is Ziska. She's in my class," Ruben said. It was both an introduction and an explanation for my condition, because no one asked so much as a single question. The Seydenstickers were *really* Jewish. They were subjected to attacks on the streets much more often than me, who didn't look the part. For them, going to a Jewish school and getting beaten up apparently fit together somehow.

I lay on the hard kitchen bench with a wet cloth on my forehead. Gentle hands bandaged my arms, my legs. "We have to fix you up a little bit before we call your mama," Frau Seydensticker murmured with a wonderfully rolling *r*. She wore a wide, brown housecoat and had a cloth wrapped around her head that fell down her back. She became embarrassed when she noticed how I was staring at her, and I turned bright red, mortified by my bad behavior and, yes, by the poverty around me.

In fact, the room I found myself in appeared to be not only the kitchen, but also the bedroom and living room for the entire family. The cooking area, the table with a bench and chairs, and a large cupboard took up almost the entire space, but there was still a stack of several mattresses against the wall.

Ruben's little sister shyly brought me some fruit. "My name is Chaja," she whispered, and took two steps backward, gazing at me steadily in astonishment.

"Hello, Chaja," I murmured, and closed my eyes, the apple held in my hand.

It grew quiet. A few ugly pictures still flashed through my memory. I tried to remember the early part of the morning, when I had woken up and still had no idea what this day would bring me. That wasn't so long ago.

I pulled off the wet cloth that covered my entire face and found Ruben, who had made himself comfortable on one of the chairs. "Leave it on," he said. "You look pretty rough. But Richard Graditz does too, if that's any consolation. I think his nose is broken."

On his way home, he had literally run right into the three boys who came shooting out of the entryway without look-

ing left or right. Other than the typical "Bug off, Jew boy!"
they didn't bother him, but to be on the safe side he had still
waited a few minutes before he peeked around the corner
into the courtyard.

I told him what had happened. Since my swollen lip had
already gone down some, I even embellished the heated chase
through the cellar to my advantage a little. The longer I told
my story, the more energetic I got. I had escaped. They only
caught me because there were three of them. If I had been
with Bekka, the story would have ended entirely differently!

"You are completely crazy, Ziska," Ruben announced, as
if I had spoken my last thought out loud. "You can't win
against them. What if Richard's nose is really broken? What
if his parents file a complaint against you?"

"They won't do that. I know them. The most they'll do
is give him another good slap for beating up a girl. Richard is
much worse than his parents."

"May he find a horrible end," Ruben answered ceremoniously.

Half curious and half shy, I looked at him. Ruben sometimes said things that I didn't know how to answer. He was
the only one in his family they sent to school, probably
because he was so clever, they couldn't stand having him at
home all the time.

"What language is that your parents speak?" I wanted to
know. "Is it Dutch? Are you all going to Holland? Last week
we put in our application to go to Shanghai! But we haven't
even started learning Chinese yet."

Ruben shook his head in disbelief. "You must have heard
Yiddish before."

"Yiddish?" I repeated. "Where would I have heard that? No one in my family knows Yiddish."

"But that's our language, Ziska, it has been for hundreds of years. Your ancestors definitely used to speak Yiddish too."

"How would you know that?"

"Yiddish is a mixture of Hebrew and old German. It's a language Jewish people all over Europe use to communicate."

"Is that true? Then they didn't have to learn English or something like that?"

I was fascinated. Ruben looked at me with compassion. "You're being persecuted and you don't even know who you are," he said.

I was about to argue, but Ruben looked genuinely sad at the moment, as if he felt sorry for me. "And? Who are you?" I asked him with a bit of a challenge in my voice.

He smiled. "I was born here, but my family comes from eastern Poland. My mother is Beile, my father is Jakob. My father's father was Herschel and his wife Zeitel . . ."

Ruben told me much more that afternoon while I lay on the bench in the kitchen and waited for my mother to pick me up. He told me about traders who carried heavy handcarts hundreds of miles through the countryside before returning to their families on Fridays to celebrate the Sabbath. About the Black Death, which the Jews were accused of causing. There were smaller attacks and larger massacres.

"They've been murdering us for hundreds of years in Poland," Ruben said. "We came back to Germany when things got better here. Jews from the east don't live particularly well here, but they can get by. Our ancestor who crossed the Elbe River was named Trachim, his wife was Didle. They had one daughter, Shanda, and she married Gerschom . . ."

I didn't hear the ticking of the clock on the wall anymore, I forgot all about my injuries, and I forgot mean, insignificant little Richard Graditz. Each of the names that Ruben recited etched itself deeply in my memory in place of all that. Because I was the one Ruben told his story to.

Not even four weeks later I stood in the Seydenstickers' apartment and there was no one there.

"They're all gone," Bekka whispered, trying to pull me out of the apartment by the arm. "They picked up the Polish people, I told you already. The Polish government revoked Polish citizenship from anyone who has lived outside the country for more than five years, and the Germans don't want them either. They immediately rounded them all up and took them over the border that same night. Ziska, what are you doing?" she asked nervously. "Let's get out of here! I don't think we're allowed to be here, even if the door wasn't locked!"

But in the end she did help me to stack the mattresses against the wall, throw away the leftover food still on the plates, clear the dishes from the table, so obviously left in a rush, and wash them. The Seydenstickers used different plates and silverware to keep milk and meat separate from each other. They were marked with different colors, and we were very careful to put everything back in the right places.

They never returned, but I think Ruben would have been glad.

Chapter 3

Ziska's Flight

The Seydenstickers and all the other families who lived in their building disappeared without a trace. I was aware of my father's fears about the future, and familiar with my parents' endless discussions—they were always about our "survival." I had been beaten and had lost friends. But nothing compared to the shock and helplessness I felt when we pulled the door to the Seydenstickers' apartment closed behind us and stepped onto a street where life went on as usual, as if nothing had happened. Cars honked, horses pulled carts past us, and women carried heavy shopping bags and pushed baby carriages. The baker set a big tray of cake in his display window. I breathed in as deeply as I possibly could, just to feel that I was still there.

At the same time, it was the first experience that I couldn't talk about with my parents, which made me feel even more scared and alone.

Maybe I should have just tried. Maybe Mamu was already sorry about the way she had reacted to my encounter with the Seydenstickers. The rage and accusations she started piling on me in the car struck as if she were beating me with a club.

"Are you crazy, Ziska? Those people and their kind are the reason everyone is always saying 'dirty Jews'! They're the ones who pulled us into this mess with their black coats and their beards! How can you make me go in there?"

My mouth hung open. It was supposed to be the Seydenstickers' fault that we had to be afraid of the Germans? I had only known the family for a few hours, but Mamu's accusations seemed incomprehensible to me, entirely—shockingly—false and unfair. That explained why Mamu had hardly thanked them and hadn't even responded when Mrs. Seydensticker invited us to come Friday night for Shabbat.

"Papa!" I wailed upstairs in the apartment, flinging myself around his neck.

"Ziska, for heaven's sake!" he spluttered.

My mother was completely beside herself. She stormed into the bathroom and turned on the water, then came running back and started to tear the clothes off my body. I screeched at full volume.

"Margot, what are you doing?" Papa called, and tried to push her back. "The child needs to see a doctor!"

"Not before I've scrubbed all the filth off of her! Fleas and lice, most likely! Do you know where I picked her up? Tell him, Ziska!"

"At Ruben Seydensticker's," I sobbed. "Richard beat me up and Ruben helped me."

"You should have seen it." Mamu tried to reach past my wildly flailing hands. "Eight people in one room, chickens on the steps, and my Ziska on the floor holding a stark-naked baby! If I ever catch you over there again!"

Something in my head exploded. "You are so mean! You, you sound like the Germans!" I hurled back at her defiantly.

Mamu staggered back a step. Her enraged face twisted as if she would cry, then she wound up and struck me across the face with the full force of her rage. Then she ran into the bedroom and slammed the door shut behind her.

"They're Jewish, like us," I said to Papa, trembling. I hadn't even felt the blow, but when I thought of the look on Mamu's face it made me go cold.

"You're right," Papa answered thoughtfully. "From the Germans' perspective there's no difference. For us, there are this kind and that kind. Don't you think that people should adapt just a little to the customs of the country where they've chosen to live? That people shouldn't constantly point out that they're different?"

"I think we should stick together," I murmured.

Papa sighed. "It's hard to explain," he admitted. "Why don't you go put on something clean before we take you to the doctor?"

My scratches and scrapes healed quickly, but the split inside of me went deeper. Although we often fought, my mother was the authority figure in my life: big, strong, proud, a lighthouse that Papa and I looked to for guidance. I knew that Mamu made mistakes, and that didn't diminish my admiration of her. It was a new idea to me that she was fallible in a larger context, and it hurt, even more so when she never said a single word about our fight, although she must have noticed how upset I was. My mother waited for me to make the first move. And I was too confused by what had happened to find the right words.

The time when we could have talked about it passed. My world as I had known it fell apart in more ways at the end of the year. There was even something wrong with Bekka, my best friend. She didn't speak English with me anymore. She didn't even want to take the Survival Plan out of her shoe. I only tried a few times to talk with her about all the things going through my head since my encounter with the Seydenstickers and Mamu's violent reaction to it.

"What does Jewish really mean?" I asked. "In the Bible the Jews are a people, but that's much too long ago. For thousands of years they haven't even had their own country."

"That doesn't have anything to do with it. Judaism is a religion," Bekka responded cantankerously.

"But we're Protestant. You can't have two religions at the same time!" I protested.

"Well, it's a race too," Bekka muttered.

"It is not. A race, that's silly! You're blonder than any of the Aryan girls I know. So it can't be a race."

"Ziska, I have to go home now."

She crawled out of our cave on her hands and knees. "What's the matter, Bekka? Stay here! What's wrong?" I called after her.

I sat there for a while with my arms wrapped around my knees. The fall chill in the air wasn't the only thing that made me feel cold.

I don't know if my parents knew about the Seydenstickers' disappearance. I couldn't drum up enough courage to ask them. October drew to a close with that crushing blow. November started out chilly and rainy, and compared to everything that had silently changed for me, it was a remarkably normal time. The foliage that covered our hiding place in the cemetery fell from the trees and was swept away.

My father still put on his hat every morning, slipped a sandwich into his briefcase, and set off for the office, even though he didn't call himself a lawyer anymore, but a consultant, and he only worked with Jewish clients now. The majority of them came to him in desparate situations: emigration petitions that were denied or simply not answered at all, evictions from their apartments without cause, confiscation of their businesses. "Dejudaization," it was called. My father listened to everything, promised to do his best for them, and less and less often tried to reassure them with the phrase "Better times are ahead."

On that evening, a Wednesday, a strange tension filled the air. The embassy secretary in Paris had died following an assassination attempt two days earlier—shot by a seventeen-year-old, who let himself be apprehended, according to witnesses' reports, after he called out, "In the name of the persecuted Jews!" My parents were anxious and glued to the radio. I went to bed early, wrapped up in my own worries. Mamu and I still only talked to each other when absolutely necessary.

It could have been a bad dream. That's what I still thought as I slowly glided from sleep back into waking. Banging, heavy steps of boots, loud voices. It was dark all around me. I would just drink a sip of water, turn over in my bed, and fall back asleep.

I reached for the glass of water on the nightstand when

suddenly light fell through the crack under my bedroom door. A racket followed, a crashing and smashing that struck me like white-hot lightning. I knew immediately that someone had kicked in the door to our apartment.

"DOES THE JEW MANGOLD LIVE HERE?"

I felt my lips on the glass of water, my arm, heavy as lead, holding it, and the liquid running along my chin into the collar of my pajamas. I couldn't swallow.

Another voice answered, calm and quiet. "Who wants to know?"

"HE HAS A SMART MOUTH, THE JEW!"

Again the quiet voice, followed by more smashing and the sound of shattering glass. Papa! The glass fell out of my hand, water flowed over my banket and pajamas. I couldn't think, but I kicked the blankets onto the floor, jumped out of bed, and flew to the door. Papapapapapa! My legs wanted to give out. I turned the door handle with stiff fingers. I heard my fast, shallow breathing.

My father stood with his back toward me. He was wearing his bathrobe and I saw his snow-white feet in slippers.

"HOW ABOUT A BOW BEFORE A GERMAN OFFI-CER?"

These brutes were no officers, even I could see that. They were just common Nazis in their crap-brown uniforms, but after hesitating briefly, my father must have decided it was all the same. He took position and saluted.

"PUT THAT HAND DOWN, JEW! YOU PIG, YOU'RE NO SOLDIER! I SAID BOW!"

"My husband is an officer and fought in the World War. He was awarded the Iron Cross," sounded my mother's voice. There was just a hint of a tremor in it. Only then did I see Mamu, standing in the doorway to their bedroom in her nightgown, flanked by two men holding clubs.

"SHUT UP, BITCH! WHO ASKED YOU?"

My father rocked lightly onto the tip of his toes, then quickly, stiffly, let his upper body bend forward.

"DEEPER, YOU PIG. DO I HAVE TO SHOW YOU WHAT A PROPER BOW LOOKS LIKE?"

The Nazi responsible for the shouting took a step toward Papa, brutally shoved him down toward the floor, and at the same time rammed his knee into Papa's face. There was a sound like when someone steps on a rotten board. Papa bent over forward and sank to the ground silently, pressing a hand to his mouth. Blood dripped through his fingers.

"GET UP! COME WITH US!"

"No, please! Franz! Franz!"

Mamu darted toward Papa with a step or two, but she didn't get any farther. One of the two men who stood next to her held her arm tight and twisted it backward, so hard that she screamed, and threw her against the doorframe.

A gasp escaped from my throat, nothing more. No one could possibly have heard it. But with the heightened alertness of a bloodhound, the man who had hurt Papa lifted his head and our eyes met across the length of the foyer.

"Ah," he said, suddenly very quiet, "you have a little one!"

I stumbled backward, back into my room.

Close the door, close it, shut it, why don't I have a key, why won't Mamu let me have a key, he's coming through the door, he's coming, why isn't he coming, what can I put in front of it, there isn't anything, I can't look at him again, please, no!

Cold night air surrounded me. I crouched on the windowsill. Bekka's voice went through my head: *"The tree is closer than it looks! I didn't need that much momentum!"* I didn't have her courage, I wouldn't make it, I'm about to die, but it's better than looking into those eyes again.

I jumped and didn't feel the impact, didn't hear how branches cracked and limbs broke under my fingers. My bare feet were like claws that dug into the trunk and climbed up. Up, not down. How did I know to do that? When the wolf looked out the window, I was six feet above him, above him and the light that shone out of my room onto the tree. He leaned far out over the windowsill and peered into the dark courtyard, then shook his head slowly, as if with regret, and closed the window. He even pulled the curtains shut.

Outside. Cold, moist air. Somewhere there was a voice calling, laughing, a clatter. Above the roofs in the direction of the city the sky glowed red and gold, lit up and pulsating like a dragon on the loose. The trunk of the birch tree was thin and supple up there, and it gently rocked me. I would never climb down.

The motion behind the curtain was so subtle that I almost missed it. I lifted my face, which I had pressed against the tree trunk, and with a fresh wave of terror stared through the branches at the little white figure in the fourth-story window. There was no question that she had seen me in my hideout. In my light pajamas I was crouched less than six feet away from her.

As soon as I recognized Christine I took off down the tree, fleeing. I didn't stop for a second, even though it felt like my bare feet would split open with every step in the branches;

even though I was moving farther and farther away from my parents with each move. I didn't know what had happened in our apartment in the meantime, but as long as I sat in the tree next to my room, I at least felt like I was close to them. I reached the ground and knew I was the only one left.

It was unbearable. My first impulse was to run right back up the stairs, and to give myself up to them. *You can do what you want with me, but let me be with my parents!*

But then something odd happened. It was as if I were suddenly two different people. The new Ziska moved quickly through the courtyard in a crouch, checked the exit through the front entryway, saw the small crowd of people and cars on the street, and scurried back to climb over the wall to the yard behind the neighboring building. She dragged one of the garbage cans out of its place, slipped into the little niche behind it, crept along behind the garbage cans into the farthest corner of the enclosure, and huddled against the wall.

After a while there were no sounds at all coming from the street directly in front of our building. Way off in the distance I thought I could still hear a dull roar, maybe from the fire I had seen in the sky. Was it really a fire? Shouldn't there have been sirens?

Tears tumbled from my eyes. I was just a ridiculous girl in her pajamas, crouched behind garbage cans, who had abandoned her parents. A coward who had run away to save her own skin.

Sobbing, I wrapped both arms around my knees and buried my face in them. Why did *I* have to be Jewish? It wasn't fair! I hated it! It would have been better never to have been born in the first place!

"Ziska? Ziska, are you in there?"

I startled. A shadow appeared in the gap behind the garbage cans. At first I saw the schoolbag that was pushed forward, then—on all fours—a familiar figure. "I have to go right away so no one notices! Here, wait . . ."

Christine reached into her backpack and pulled out a pair of shoes and her lunchbox. Anxiously, she shoved both of them toward me. Finally, she took off her coat and laid it on the ground in front of me. She was wearing a second one underneath it. Only then did I understand that she was trying to help me.

"Where are my parents?" I whispered.

"I don't know. They took your father away. Your mother might still be in the apartment," Christine said in an unconvincing tone.

"Could you look?" I spluttered.

Christine pulled back a little. "I don't dare, but I'll bring you something to eat and a blanket as soon as I get home from school!"

She crept backward, gave me an encouraging smile, and then disappeared. I reached for the shoes and pulled them onto my feet, which were blue from the cold. I put on the coat. It took a while before it warmed my chilled body. In the lunchbox were two sandwiches and an apple. I devoured everything. I was alive.

I must have held out until about noon in my hiding place. Once someone came and brought out trash. He or she didn't discover me, but the horrifying image of one container after the other being pulled out of the enclosure while I scurried along the back wall like a cornered rat ran through my mind.

The longer I thought about it, the greater my panic became. Finally I couldn't stand it any longer. I pulled Christine's coat tighter around my shoulders and crawled out into the open. I would crawl back over the wall, slip into our building, and find out if Mamu was in our apartment!

But as soon as I was outside I knew I wouldn't be able to do it. My knees trembled, though I couldn't say if it was from fear or the result of crouching motionless for hours in the cold. I would have to go through the building out to the street and enter our building from there. Hopefully no one would notice that I was wearing pajamas under the coat!

Luckily, the door to our apartment building was open. Christine's shoes, which were a size too big for me, made more noise than I would have liked on the stairs, but I couldn't do anything about it.

And as if I had had a premonition, the door to the apartment on the second floor opened. Frau Bergmann, now, of all times! But instead of harassing me like she usually did, she only opened the door a crack, looked at me as if she was seeing a ghost, and slammed the door shut again! Right then I knew I would find something awful upstairs.

The last flight I had to hold on to the banister and pull myself up. My view never wavered from the kicked-in apartment door hanging from one of its hinges.

"Mamu?" I whispered. No answer. Finally I overcame my fear and stretched out my hand to push the door open.

I stood in the middle of the foyer. The world ceased to exist, there was no sound other than the splintering of the glass shards under my shoes. I moved through our rooms step by step and felt nothing, not even fear. I took in the damage, studied each and every room thoroughly, but this ravished apartment was no longer my home.

Papa's office was in chaos: books and papers shredded, the desk overturned, pictures ripped off the walls. The shattered glass cabinet in the living room, Mamu's priceless porcelain—our means to Shanghai on the floor in a thousand pieces. In my parents' bedroom, clothes and bedding were scattered everywhere.

My room. Strange, they hadn't touched anything here. It must have been enough that I had plunged out of the window—they thought—to my death.

I backed out again and stood still, in a daze. In the middle of the foyer was a little pool of congealed blood marking the spot where Papa had been beaten. Red drops made a trail, and I followed it to the door of the apartment. Only then did I glance at the wall. Next to the doorpost, at about my eye level, was a bloody handprint, as if Papa had leaned against it there to support himself.

And that hand on the wall was what abruptly freed me from my frozen state. Papa! Mamu! I dashed back into my room, hurriedly threw on some clothes, and ran out of the apartment.

On that day, when everything that was certain was lost, I followed my familiar route to school down to Bergstraße. This was Mamu's preferred shopping area. People in many of the stores here knew her, and someone would surely have seen her. I started at Krämer's.

"Hello, Herr Manz, has my mother been here today?"

"No, Ziska, not yet."

"When she comes, will you tell her I'm looking for her?"

"Of course, Ziska, I'd be happy to!"

On my way out, I felt the customers looking at me. Was I mistaken, or had someone said ". . . the poor child"?

My next stop, Schumann's gourmet shop, wasn't fifty yards farther along. I could already see from a distance how people were making a wide arc around it, and as I got closer I could see why. The street was full of broken glass. The display window with the Star of David painted on it had been smashed in, and two Nazis stood in the entrance smoking cigarettes. Out of the corner of my eye I saw the Schumanns with broom and dustpan—under the watch of an SA man—cleaning up what the Nazis had destroyed. Broken glasses and bottles lay on the floor and dented tin cans swam in a messy sauce of marmalade, spices, and preserved foods. A small cluster of people had formed in front of the broken display window near the dry goods shop. Women stared at yarn, scissors, and fasteners. The little shop seemed to be intact. Suddenly, one woman made a grab for it, the spell was broken, and there was no holding them back. I saw balls of yarn, buttons, and thimbles flying through the air and heard the clinking and clattering as the rest of the window-pane broke and fell into the display. Hands grabbed over my head as I fought my way through the throng of bodies to the curb. Two boys in Hitler Youth uniforms leaned against a streetlamp and laughed.

I had already figured out that we weren't the only Jews who had been raided during the night. Gradually it dawned on me what else that meant: There probably wasn't a single

Jewish shop on Bergstraße that hadn't been damaged. I definitely wouldn't find my mother here.

And then suddenly it came to me: Bekka! The Liebichs! Of course! Where else would my mother look for me, if not with my best friend?

"Ziska, finally!" She dragged me into the apartment and turned the key in the lock. "Where were you? Your mother is looking everywhere for you!"

"I've been looking for her too!" I wanted to wait until later to tell Bekka that I had spent the entire morning hiding behind garbage cans. "I was on Bergstraße," I added.

"Are you crazy? It could start up again any minute! My mother won't let me go outside at all." She pulled me into her room. As we sat down on her bed, I discovered that Bekka's eyes were red from crying. "They've gone to Hamburger Straße. To see if they can get the men released."

"The men? Your father too?"

Bekka nodded. "My father and my brother."

Bekka's little room, decorated with Shirley Temple posters, spun in circles. Thomas, Bekka's fifteen-year-old brother, was the pride of the family, a talented pianist.

"It was awful," Bekka whispered. "They had to go with them right away. They weren't even allowed to get dressed."

"Did they beat them up?"

"No!" Bekka cried, her eyes widened with fear.

"Ransack your apartment?"

Bekka just shook her head. "Then you can be glad," I said.

"Are you nuts?" She gave me a shove that almost pushed me off the bed.

"Do you want to trade places?" I flared up.

I pressed my lips together and stared down at the tips of my shoes. "On Bergstraße there's broken glass everywhere," I said after a while.

"That's what I heard. And they supposedly burned all the synagogues in the whole city."

"What? The synagogues? All of them?" I was outraged. So that was the fire I had seen during the night. "And what's on Hamburger Straße?"

"The Gestapo prison. Three of them went together, your mother and mine and Frau Grün. They took clothes with them, and some medal of your father's."

"That didn't help any last night," I muttered.

"Ziska, what are they going to do with us?" Bekka asked fearfully.

It was the question everyone was asking themselves. But I had never heard anyone dare to speak it out loud. "We have to get out of here," I said, instead of answering.

"And go where?" Bekka's voice sounded tired and hopeless.

I looked at her with surprise. "But, you're all going to America!"

Bekka started to cry again. She shook her head violently. "No, we're not. I wanted to tell you. Papa's cousin denied us."

"What do you mean, denied you?"

"Last month. She doesn't want to have to sponsor all of us. Papa wrote back that she should just bring Thomas and me over, but she doesn't want to do that either. She wrote that to separate the family was against divine law."

Bekka sobbed. I sat there speechless. The Liebichs weren't going to America, and all their efforts to learn English had been for nothing.

Then suddenly an idea occurred to me that was so wonderful, I forgot everything else going on around me. "Bekka! Come with us to Shanghai! You don't need a visa, just the passage for the ship! We could stay together!"

"Do you think?" Bekka already had the hiccups from crying, but there was a flicker of hope in her eyes.

"Absolutely! No visa, no sponsors! They don't have anything against Jews in China," I assured her excitedly. "Oh, Bekka, just imagine, the two of us in China!"

"Well, I . . . I can talk to my parents!"

Through a veil of tears Bekka could smile again and you could tell she was embarrassed that she had cried in front of me in the first place.

The women did not come back alone. They had Herr Liebich and Thomas with them, and you could tell by looking at the men what they had been through. The left half of Thomas's face was red and swollen; he had been slapped over and over again. Herr Liebich held one arm tightly with the other. His forehead was beaded with sweat and his teeth were clenched together. "Broken," was all he said. With a tremor in her voice, his wife made phone calls to find a doctor who was willing to treat a Jew. Our family doctor, Dr. Fruchtmann, was still locked up on Hamburger Straße, just like my father and Herr Grün.

I was so happy to see my mother that I almost knocked her down with my hug. It was as if our quarrel had never happened. She wrapped me in her arms. "Ziska, my little Ziskele," she murmered tenderly into my hair.

I pressed myself against her, felt the warmth of her skin . . . and all of a sudden happiness and courage and power I never dreamed I had flooded through me, and the terror of the previous night already began to fade.

Mamu and I had each other again, we had survived the worst of it, and everything would be okay! If Thomas and Herr Liebich were released after only half a day, then maybe we could pick up my father tomorrow. Considering how many men they had rounded up, we couldn't expect that they could confirm Papa's innocence in just a few hours!

Before my father came home, Mamu and I would have the apartment cleaned up. I would tape together the torn files, sort all his books. He would never notice that anyone had touched them! The furniture that couldn't be salvaged, we would just throw away. We wouldn't be able to take much with us to Shanghai anyway.

We were together, and that was all that mattered. And we would never be separated again, that much was certain.

Chapter 4

New Plans

"Mama!" Evchen screeched, and swept past me and out of the room like a fat, triumphant dwarf. "Ziska's being mean to me again!"

I rolled my eyes. When the voices in the living room grew louder, I could parrot their words, I had heard this routine so often in the past few weeks.

"Margot, if you can't make sure that your daughter leaves my little one alone, then I'm sorry, but you'll have to leave!"

"If you could manage to occupy the little one for a couple of hours so that Ziska could work in that room . . ."

"In Evchen and Betti's room, mind you! I took you in out of sheer generosity, but this is still my apartment, and if Evchen wants to go into her own room, then I wouldn't think of stopping her!"

I stuck my fingers into my ears so I wouldn't have to hear how Mamu and her sister egged each other on. We had been living under the same roof for exactly twenty-nine days. This was probably just what the Nazis had in mind when they took our apartment. One of the cleverer ones probably had the idea: "Let them move in with their relatives. They'll finish each other off and make less work for us."

There was no chance of concentrating on math homework, at any rate. I sighed and took my fingers out of my ears to figure out how far along they were in their argument.

"I'm not even talking about gratitude anymore! As if you would ever have done anything for me!" my aunt screamed.

Oh, Jesus, I thought in desperation. *It's not that the apartment is gone, or that Papa is still locked up in Sachsenhausen . . . Don't even think about it. The tickets for the ship to Shanghai arrived today. Now they have to let him go. But what have we done to deserve Aunt Ruth?*

The door opened and Mamu came in. She looked distraught and I instantly regretted having fought off Evchen's assault on my math book. I sat down next to Mamu on the mattress where I slept at night, between the beds of my two younger cousins, and put an arm around her. A few days ago she had been forced to turn in all of her jewelry, which I knew had been a hard blow for her.

"I'm sorry," I muttered dejectedly. "I try to control myself, but every time I see Evchen, a switch flips inside me."

"I know the feeling." Mamu rested her head on my shoulder. "Oh, Ziskele. Let's hang on for just a few more days, then Papa will be with us again and we can get out of here."

"Are you totally, completely, a hundred percent sure that you have everything this time?"

With a furrowed brow she counted on her fingers, "Passports, identification cards, the exit permit, a receipt for the emigration taxes, the tickets for the ship. The last time, they turned me away again because I didn't know they wanted to see the exit permit *and* the tickets." She looked at me with a worried expression. "There isn't anything else they could want to see, is there?"

"No, definitely not!" I assured her quickly. But the regulations changed constantly and we usually only found out about it when we got there and were turned away yet again. In the meantime, our three names were not only on the list of Jews wanting to leave for Shanghai, but also for Cuba, Argentina, Palestine, Venezuela, Uruguay, and Paraguay, not to mention the USA, Sweden, and England. Mamu had met more Jews waiting in various lines than in all the rest of her life combined, and had been infected with the widely shared view that we should be on as many lists as possible, just to be on the safe side.

"Please try not to get into an argument while I'm gone," my mother begged me. "These visits to the Gestapo take every ounce of my energy. There's nothing left for Ruth when I get back here."

"It's better if I go to Bekka's," I said, contrite. "Then I don't have to see the three of them at all. Can't you tell Aunt Ruth she should have that ugly wart above her lip taken off?"

"Me, tell her that? Are you crazy?" Mamu replied, but there was a twinkle in her eyes again.

"It wouldn't help much, anyway. I don't think there's anything pretty about Aunt Ruth. It's hard to believe you two are sisters."

"That's the root of the problem," Mamu said. "She was always jealous of me."

In the corner of the room there was a bang, the door of the wardrobe flew against the wall, and my cousin Betti rolled out like a billiard ball. She was five, a year older than Evchen, and had the same thick, sullen face, which at the moment was displaying a mixture of triumph and lust for revenge in the wake of her successful spying. "I'm telling, I'm telling!" she sang, and danced past us out of the room.

"Oh, God," Mamu muttered, "now this too. Come on, Ziska, let's get out of here!"

Surpressing a giggle, I grabbed my jacket.

The one advantage of our arrangement with Aunt Ruth was that I was living practically around the corner from Bekka. Under normal circumstances I would have asked if I could just move in with her, but unfortunately, the mood at Bekka's was also very somber—not as charged as at our place, but not any better. Just bad in a different way.

When I broke the news to Mamu about my fabulous idea that the Liebichs could come with us to Shanghai instead of going to America, she just looked at me sadly and explained, "Ziskele, if no one pays the travel expenses for the Liebichs, they can't go anywhere at all. Bekka's father lost his job at City Hall right after the Nazis took power. That was almost six years ago, and their savings are gone. Don't tell anyone else, but they've been seen in the soup kitchen."

"Then we have to lend them some money!" I asserted.

"Us?" Mamu replied slowly. "We don't have enough for all of us."

"But what can they do, then?" I cried, appalled.

"There are other possibilities, Ziska. It's better if we don't talk about it, but I imagine they have something planned."

Something planned? No matter how much I badgered her,

my mother wouldn't give anything away, and even worse, she made me swear that I wouldn't under any circumstances ask Bekka or anyone else about it. I obeyed her, but my imagination was working overtime. What could the Liebichs have planned? Did they have enough money to escape to another country not so far away? Would they be smuggled across one of the European borders? Did they want to go underground?

A shudder ran down my back, a combination of terror and envy. I had heard of people who had simply disappeared when the Nazis wanted to arrest them. Underground—the very word sounded so promising! The longer I thought about it, the more convinced I was that the Liebichs could go into hiding at any time. It made sense to me that I wasn't allowed to ask Bekka about it. It wouldn't really be going into hiding if other people knew about it!

Like I did every day, I asked myself if they would still be there as I ran around the corner to their block of apartments. But Bekka opened the door immediately after I quietly knocked a certain rhythm and called "Ziska here!" It was better to avoid normal knocking or ringing the bell so as not to scare people to death.

"Our tickets for the ship have finally come. Mamu is already on her way to the Gestapo. And a week from today . . ." I gushed.

I cut myself short. Even if the Liebichs probably had something much more exciting in mind than us, I still felt vaguely uncomfortable around Bekka now that I knew that unlike us, they didn't have enough money to get themselves to safety. But today I was in for a surprise. A relieved, radiant smile lit up Bekka's face, a smile I hadn't seen in a long time, and she pulled me into her room. "Ziska!" she said ceremoniously. "Can you keep a secret?"

But Bekka didn't take the time to let me answer. "Just imagine, Thomas and I are going to England!" she said with a little chuckle in her voice.

"To England? You and Thomas?"

"With a kindertransport! My father found out about it at the Jewish Community Center. They've already moved hundreds of children out of Berlin, Vienna, and Munich! We'll live with foster families and it doesn't cost us anything!"

She looked at me expectantly. "In foster families?" I echoed. "And your parents?"

"When we're in England we'll find jobs for them, and then they can follow us!" Bekka replied with glowing eyes. "You know Silke Weinstein, right? She's already there and she got a domestic permit for her mother!"

Only one thing had reached me loud and clear. "You want to go to England without your parents and live with strangers?" I repeated, horrified. "You can't just go off by yourself to live with people you don't know!"

"Why not? Ziska, they're taking us in, they volunteered to do it! They must be good and nice and absolutely wonderful," Bekka raved.

I listened and tried hard to give the impression that I was happy for her. But a single thought ran through my head the entire time: If Mamu wanted to send me to England alone, I would run away and hide until the train had left without me! Nothing in the world could make me leave without my parents! Bekka's enthusiastic description almost brought tears to my eyes, I felt so sorry for her.

At least she didn't have to leave right away. She would still have enough time to think it over. For now, her parents had only put Thomas's and Bekka's names on the waiting list, and I knew all too well about waiting.

"Bekka is going to England," I announced that evening to distract my mother from the fact that even though she had presented our ship tickets, she still hadn't been able to take my father with her right away. "With a kinder-transport. Just with Thomas and without her parents. Isn't that awful?"

"A kindertransport?" Mamu repeated. Since she had returned from the Gestapo, she had been sitting perfectly still, staring off into the distance, but now she lifted her head and I explained everything to her in detail. Even Aunt Ruth and Uncle Erik listened, though my aunt usually cut me off as soon as I opened my mouth.

We rarely got to see Uncle Erik, Aunt Ruth's heavy, jovial husband, since he had saved himself from being arrested by riding back and forth in streetcars all night. Now he had a monthly ticket and rode around all day, all over Berlin, and found shelter at night wherever he could with different friends. "Kindertransport . . . hmm, I've heard about that," he said.

I enjoyed the attention and answered lots of questions: where to sign up (at the Jewish Community Center), who paid for it (the Refugee Children's Movement, an organization that was founded in England just to help us), how many trains were leaving (one or two each week, from different big cities each time), and how old the children had to be (at least four, no older than sixteen). I was amazed that they wanted such detailed information about everything. When I was done, there was a long silence in the room.

"Might be our only option," Uncle Erik finally said.

Not comprehending, I looked from one adult to the next.

"Evchen and Betti are too little," Aunt Ruth whispered. Her haggard, pale face seemed to fall apart.

"No, Evchen is four," Uncle Erik said softly. "It would be possible."

Another long silence. Gradually I felt the import of his words registering in that part of my brain responsible for putting things together, but I refused to believe what I had just heard.

When Mamu pushed back her chair with a clatter, we all jumped. "We should each discuss this for ourselves," she said. "Ziska, will you step outside with me?"

And as we left she did something completely unexpected: She took Aunt Ruth's chin in her hand and gave her intolerable sister a kiss!

I only found my voice again when we were in the bathroom. "They want to send the girls away with a transport?" I asked, incredulous. "Alone? Have they lost their minds?"

"It may be that Papa can't join us in time, Ziska."

"How can they even think of such a thing, sending their children away? What kind of parents are they?"

"If I hand in the tickets tomorrow, we'll get back part of our money and can try again later."

"You have to talk to them, they can't do that! . . . What did you just say?" My chest suddenly tightened. "Give back the tickets? You mean for the ship to Shanghai?"

"If they don't let Papa go by next Tuesday, we can't leave." Mamu's voice trembled.

"Why wouldn't they let him out?" I cried. "We have all our papers together! They've let everyone who wants to leave the country go!"

Now she was fighting tears. "I did something dumb, Ziska. I said that we have to leave early next week. How could I have been so stupid? The way that man looked at me! 'Whether and when we release your husband is our decision, and ours alone!' Oh, Ziska, I blew it, it's all my fault!"

My mother pressed her hand against her mouth. Her face twitched. I sat motionless and tried to grasp what she was trying to tell me. They wouldn't let Papa go in time. Our emigration to Shanghai had fallen through. The ship would sail without us.

"I'm so, so sorry, Ziskele," Mamu sobbed.

I sat next to her on the edge of the bathtub and leaned against her shoulder. I wanted to cry right along with her, but instead I heard myself saying in a determined tone, "Then we'll just exchange the tickets for places on the next ship, and we'll keep doing that until they let Papa go."

Mamu was already calming down. "Or until we run out of money," she said. "Which could be very soon, the way things look. We'll have to get new exit visas too. But you're right, we won't give up. I just wonder . . ."

She stopped. "What?" I asked.

"Whether we should count entirely on Shanghai or if we shouldn't pursue every single possibility that's available to us."

"That's what we're doing. We're already on every single list there is."

"Well," Mamu said, "except for one."

She hardly dared to look at me. "No," I said weakly. "I won't do that."

"Ziska, you have no idea what it would mean to me to know you were safe."

"But I won't go alone! You can just forget it!" Now I did have tears in my eyes. "You don't want to leave without Papa, but I'm supposed to . . . to . . ."

It was too painful to say it out loud. Mamu turned to me and took my hands. "Papa needs me now, Ziska. He's counting on me, I have to get him out of there. But you're a big girl, a strong girl! A girl who jumped into a tree in the dark! So many times recently, it's been you who's told me what I should do."

I could hardly see her through my tears. "Mamu, no! I'll do anything you want, but please, please, don't send me away!"

"I won't do anything against your will, Ziskele," she said in a tired voice, letting go of my hands. "But when you're making your decision, please also consider what you could do for your parents. You could try to get a work permit in England for Papa and me. Then it wouldn't be long at all and we would be with you again—and all three of us safe."

I panicked. *If only I hadn't said anything! Bekka had wanted me to keep it to myself, but no, I had nothing better to do than broadcast the news right away!*

"We might be able to follow you very soon," Mamu repeated. "Think about it."

The first thing I noticed when we entered the building was that no one was laughing. Dozens of children and their parents stood in a long line. I looked around and recognized several girls I knew, but no one waved to me.

"You see? There are lots of kids here who are younger than you," Mamu said quietly.

I didn't answer. Since she had turned in the ship tickets and I knew there was no way around it, I felt old. Mamu was counting on me. I would get my parents out of Germany. That was the only thing that made the pain tolerable.

Bekka's reaction had made me uneasy. "The two of us, in the same kindertransport? That would be a miracle," was her opinion. "We have to be happy if we get to go at all."

I wouldn't have dreamed that so many parents would send their children away. The sight of the line of people waiting made my throat tighten up.

"You know what would be the best?" Bekka had added with a crooked smile. "If you got my spot!"

"I'd like to travel together with a friend," I said to the man who introduced himself as Herr Weitz and took my application. "Rebekka Liebich. She signed herself up last week already."

"What about your father, Franziska?" he asked. "Is he still in Sachsenhausen?"

"Yes, even though we had tickets to Shanghai at one point. They just won't let him out."

Mamu, who was sitting next to me, nodded at me as if I had given the right answer on a test.

"The fact that your father is in a concentration camp improves your chances of getting a spot," Herr Weitz commented. He had a pale, tired face and deep, dark circles under his eyes.

"If my father weren't in the concentration camp, I wouldn't need to go in the first place," I replied indignantly. Surprisingly, a smile flickered in his exhausted eyes.

Mamu, who hadn't seen it, couldn't stand it anymore. "We are very, very grateful to the Refugee Children's Movement for their efforts!" she interjected.

"It's okay, Frau Mangold," Herr Weitz said. "I know how hard it is. My daughter is on the list too."

How we survived the following weeks, I couldn't say. I was with my mother, and at the same time, I wasn't anymore. In my thoughts I was in England, and yet I couldn't be, since I didn't know what it looked like, nor if I would ever really arrive there. Mamu kept herself perpetually busy, spent much too much money on new clothes for me, and sewed little strips of cloth with my name on them into everything. I felt uncomfortable in her presence and had the impression that she felt the same way. Soon I was just as scared that I wouldn't get a seat on the kindertransport as I was of getting one.

For the first time, I received a letter from my father addressed only to me.

> *Dear Ziskele,*
>
> *It looks like you will soon be on your way to England to try to do for us what you can from there. You'll learn a new language and—I'm sure—meet warm-hearted, wonderful people. Just think, somewhere in the world there are still women and men who don't watch what happens to us indifferently, but instead take us into their own*

*families! I hope that I can thank your host parents
in person someday.*

*Don't forget that we, your mother and I, are
only letting you go to make sure that you are safe.
And don't think that you are alone: We will be with
you in our thoughts, hour by hour, and we know that
you won't forget us either, but will do your utmost so
that the three of us can be together again soon. The
stronger you are, the stronger we will be. I am so
proud of you, my Ziskele.*

*May you be well cared for and blessed always,
that's my wish for you.*

With a thousand kisses, your father,

Franz Mangold

I read the letter over and over again. It was so formal that
I felt very important. From Mamu I knew that Sachsenhausen had a better reputation than the concentration camp at
Buchenwald. I couldn't quite imagine my father working on
a construction site, but he optimistically wrote that this way
he was gaining experience in a practical field.

The thought that my father felt stronger because of me
made me happy. My mother sent him packages, clothes, and
money, and ran around tirelessly trying to have him released.
Soon I would be able to do something for him too.

"On Thursday already!"

"What do you mean, don't bring any valuables? What
about her watch, does that count? She can't travel without
a watch! And here: *Apart from 10 Reichsmark, no money*

should be sent with the children! Am I supposed to send my daughter to England as a beggar?"

The adults all spoke at once in agitated voices. I hadn't been allowed to take more than a brief glance at the letter from the Jewish Community Center myself, as it was immediately snatched out of my hands. Uncle Erik, who was there to do his laundry, read the instructions, which were included on a separate piece of paper, out loud in a booming voice. There was a buzzing in my head like in a beehive.

On Thursday! Only four days! Four days that would stretch out endlessly. I would have preferred to get it over with the very next day. My heart was balled into a fist; I was aware that this was a decisive moment in my life, and I expected to feel something. But there was nothing. Aunt Ruth must be right, something was wrong with me.

My otherwise composed mother, on the other hand, abruptly grabbed the paper out of Uncle Erik's hands while he was still reading from it and started crying loudly. The tears streamed freely over her distorted face and I, who in the last few weeks had wondered about her love for me, should have been pleased by this outburst of emotion. Instead, I resented it, she had no right to it, and I heard myself shouting: "Be quiet! You said I should go and now I am going, no matter how much you cry!"

I left behind three stunned grown-ups when I slammed the door and ran out.

The moment I saw her I could tell something was wrong. Her face was pale and shiny, her smile frozen in place. "You're just in time to celebrate with my family," Bekka greeted me. "Thomas has a seat on the kindertransport."

I followed her into the apartment. It was like going back to the apartment I had just left. The same excited voices came from the living room, reading the same letter. As I walked past, I caught a glimpse of Thomas, who sat silently in the rocking chair and moved back and forth as if it were mechanically controlled.

Bekka closed her bedroom door behind us and we sat on her bed.

"When does the next transport leave?" I asked, more to gain some time than anything else. Already I could feel a separation between Bekka and me growing.

She shrugged her shoulders. "On Thursday, and then again at the beginning of February, I guess. But the chances are getting smaller, I tell you. Word is spreading like wildfire, and suddenly every Jew in Berlin wants to get their children out."

I just wouldn't tell her! On Thursday I would suddenly be gone, and I'd write to her from England that it was a big surprise, and practically at the last minute I was able to take the place of another child in our building who had gotten the mumps!

"It's just plain cruel," Bekka erupted. Her carefully composed good-loser expression collapsed, and her eyes glittered with anger. "Thomas doesn't even want to go! Why did they take him? Because he plays the piano? Crap, I should have told them how well I draw!"

She kicked the wastepaper basket, and its contents emptied onto the floor. I sat next to her like a bundle of misery, choking on the tangle of excuses and lies that were already perched on my tongue. For the first time I realized how many ways there are to divide people from each other, and that the Nazis would tear Bekka and me apart in a way that would never have occurred to me.

An idea flashed through my mind: *What if I offer her my spot?*

I know the old Ziska would have done it. She wouldn't have betrayed anyone, and certainly not her best friend, not at any price.

The new Ziska thought about herself. The new Ziska's voice was strong as she responded: "I have a spot too, Bekka. I leave on Thursday. But I promise you, once I'm in England I'll try to find a family for you so you can come too."

And the new Ziska stood on the street not five minutes later and thought, *Well then, too bad, you dummy. If you're mad that I'm leaving and trying to get my parents out, just like you wanted to do for yours, if you accuse me of something that isn't my fault at all, if your last words to me are that I took the place that should have been yours, then you can't be my friend!*

Chapter 5

The Voyage

There were so many important things to do. The printed packing list needed to be filled out—two pair of pants, two skirts, three sweaters, three blouses, one coat, two pajamas, six underpants, six pairs of socks, two pairs of shoes—and in the line "Name of the emigrant," with a trembling hand, was written Franziska Sara Mangold. My children's identity card also had to be stamped with a large red *J* for *Jewish*.

I wrote to my host parents. We had received their address on the same day as the letter of acceptance. Their names were Marcus and Hermione Winterbottom, and they lived in London. Mamu wrote a much longer letter than mine, and Uncle Erik translated it into English. I chewed on my pencil, but couldn't think of anything to write.

"Dear Mr. and Mrs. Winterbottom," I wrote in my best handwriting. "Thank you that I can come to you. I come Saturday. Yours truly, Ziska."

"But they know that already," was Uncle Erik's opinion.

I was terrified of the parting at the train station. I was relieved when word came: "Please take leave of your children in a room at the Jewish Community Center. The children will be brought to the train station by bus to avoid any interruption of normal activity."

The noise in the big room was deafening. Our departure was set for late evening, probably to spare the general public from the scene that Mamu and I encountered when we arrived shortly after nine, one of the last families to get there. I took one look in the hall and said, "Please, Mamu, we're not going to cry! Otherwise I'll go straight back home again."

"There's no reason to cry," my mother replied with a determined voice. "We're just glad that you were accepted. Do you know how many children would like to be in your shoes right now?"

I know one, I thought to myself. I hadn't told Mamu how Bekka and I had parted ways. It was so awful that I just didn't want to relive it. "Do you think Uncle Erik will keep his word and wave to me from the Wannsee train station?" I asked quickly.

"You can count on it," Mamu said with a smile.

We stood in one corner and pretended I was heading off to summer camp. Someone started calling out names in alphabetical order. As each name was called, a cardboard sign with a number on it was hung around the child's neck, they took their suitcases, and moved toward the group that was waiting near the exit. The names starting with *C* were called, then *D*. Fear filled the air. Parents were reassuring crying children, or broke out in tears themselves, anxiety, tension. I noticed that my entire body had begun to tremble.

"I have something for you." My mother reached into her coat pocket and pulled out a silver chain. A small cross hung from it. "I got this for my confirmation. It will protect you until we see each other again."

She opened the clasp and stepped behind me, gently moving the hair on my neck to the side. "I'll never take it off!" I vowed. "Not even to wash!"

We held hands and waited. Mamu's hands were icy cold.

The letter *L*. Thomas Israel Liebich. Had Bekka come with him to say good-bye? I felt a short, sharp stab of pain and hope too; maybe we could still see each other one more time after all! But I only found the gentle, round face of her mother.

"I have to say good-bye to the Liebichs!" I called, upset, and tore myself away.

"Ziska!" Mamu yelled, and ran after me.

I saw Frau Liebich open her arms as I ran toward her . . . she wasn't angry with me! I broke out in tears. "I am so sorry!" I sobbed into her neck.

"Franziska Sara Mangold!"

"Ziska, come, it's your turn!"

Mamu was behind me and pulled a little too roughly on my arms. I let go of my friend's mother, someone put the sign with my number over my head. Desperately, I slapped away the strange hand that wanted to push me toward the other children and tried to stop crying. I knew I must have hurt Mamu terribly; I couldn't leave before I explained everything to her! But the only thing that came from my mouth was a loud, embarrassing wail.

"God bless you, Ziska!" my mother whispered, briefly put

her arm around me, and pressed the suitcase into my hand. I stood with the others by the door. Cold night air blew in on us, and two buses were already waiting.

It was much worse than I had imagined.

Germany slept. Outside the train windows lay darkness once we had left Berlin, darkness and the regular clickety clack of the wheels crossing wooden railroad ties. It represented terror and comfort at the same time, separating us from our parents and yet bringing us to safety. There could be no greater contradiction.

I saw myself sitting in the train compartment, where out of the throng of children individual faces became distinguishable. Greta, Luise, Vera, Fanny, Gabi, Marion, and Jette. We younger ones smiled at each other shyly. Greta immediately began to write a letter. She had already declared herself the oldest in the compartment, and therefore in charge. Her first move was to usurp the window seat that I had taken in the mad rush onto the train. I hunched over in the seat next to the door, as far from her as possible. My stomach was turning somersaults. I had hugged the wrong mother good-bye. Could there be any mistake more bitter?

In the aisle the young woman in charge of our car of the train walked up and down holding the hands of children who hadn't yet found a seat. Our compartment door opened and I sat at eye level with the fearful faces of the youngest ones.

"Look, Tessa, there's still room, you can sit here."

"And where will my mama sit?"

No one answered, and I pushed the door closed behind

the little girl. Inside, Fanny lifted Tessa onto her lap right away. Luise took a teddy bear out of her backpack and made a funny voice. "Hey, everyone, this is Tessa! She's so brave, she's riding the train all by herself!"

The girl laughed and stretched out her hands for the teddy bear. The rest of us laughed too, even Greta, so we wouldn't have to hear the whistle that meant we were leaving. As the train started to move, only Jette craned her neck and eagerly peered out the window; maybe she had forgotten that our parents hadn't been allowed to come to the platform with us.

The rest of us only looked out the window after we had left the train station behind us. The lights were turned off in the compartments, and we waited for them to go on again. No one was supposed to notice the train taking hundreds of children out of Germany in the middle of the night.

Somewhere out there, our parents were on their way home—without us. I had a sudden, vivid, unbearable image of my mother alone in the subway. It was one of those images that you have to get out of your head immediately.

"Can I look out the window when we get to Wannsee?" I asked Greta politely. "My uncle Erik will be standing at the train station waving."

"But he won't even see you. We're only passing through."

"He knows that, but he'll be there anyway. He promised."

"Then we'll all wave!" That decided, Vera slipped past me out of the compartment and I heard her telling the children next door, "There will be someone waiting and waving to us in Wannsee. Will you wave back?"

The darkened train carried us all away, a hundred and

twenty fearful and curious, sad and excited children from Berlin. We would double our number after a short stop in Hamburg. Germany slept and no one noticed our trip. The only person who waved at our train was a round, good-natured bald man at the train station in Wannsee who had positioned himself under a lamp so that I would be able to see him. He was completely overwhelmed when children appeared at every window of the train rolling past, all of them leaning out, waving their arms and calling to him, "Good-bye! Good-bye, Uncle Erik!"

When I woke up I noticed that we must be close to the Dutch border. There was no other way to explain the restlessness in the train. This was in the early hours of the morning, and a current of fear spread among the older children. "What if they send us back again?"

With my eyes closed, I leaned back against the partition between the aisle and the compartment and listened to Greta and Vera whispering with each other. "We can't move a muscle, that's the most important thing! Just don't even look at them when they come in."

"I've heard they make one of us from each compartment go with them for questioning," Vera replied nervously.

"Then hopefully they'll take her there, with the cross," Greta said spitefully.

It took a moment before I realized she was talking about me. "Ziska is all right," Vera offered, but her brief hesitation was unmistakable.

"How do we know whether she's even Jewish?" Greta retorted.

"Jews aren't the only ones on kindertransports. Some are children of communists, or resistance fighters who are stuck in prison."

"Well, I think they should only take Jews," Greta grumbled.

I opened my eyes. "I am Jewish," I said angrily. "If you don't believe it you can look in my passport."

I could tell that Greta had words on the tip of her tongue, but just then we felt it: The train was slowing down! None of us uttered a single word as we slowly rode into the lighted station, and the tall figures in brown and black uniforms that awaited us came into view. The stiff black caps bearing the death's-head symbol of the SS glided past the window as if in slow motion. The train stopped with a screeching of brakes, lights went on, and we heard the heavy treads of boots in the aisles and the opening and closing of compartment doors. Strangely, there were no voices. It was ghostly—as if they made their way through an empty train.

I was staring at the floor when the door next to me was opened abruptly. A pair of highly polished boots appeared, stood in place, and stopped moving. Several seconds passed. I looked up. The Nazi looked down at me—he had a face that looked like it was chiseled in stone—and made an impatient little gesture with his hand. Two of us at a time had to stay in the compartment while our suitcases were searched, while the others waited outside in the aisle. With stiff knees I squeezed myself past the giant, who practically filled the doorframe. A small, still crowd was already waiting outside the compartment doors. I could hear some of the children's teeth chattering.

"Stay calm," said a boy next to me. "They're just looking for anything valuable. They don't care about us at all."

I looked sideways at him. He was big and strong, probably about the same age as Thomas, but he carried himself almost like an adult already. He noticed my glance and winked at me.

All at once I felt better. "I have a necklace," I whispered. "I hope they don't take it away from me."

The boy whispered back, "You can have a diamond from me. If you put it in your suitcase, right on top, I can guarantee no one will notice your necklace!"

As scared as I was, I had to laugh. The boy didn't look like he had ever even been near a diamond. Lots of the children had been dressed in new clothes from head to toe for the trip, but he definitely wasn't one of them. He was wearing a long, well-worn coat, and boots that had already been mended on the side.

"You're not from Berlin, are you?" I whispered. I couldn't remember having seen him in the meeting room of the Jewish Community Center. Somehow I had the feeling that I would have seen him, if he had been there.

"Walter Glücklich," he answered quietly, "from Hamburg. And before you ask, yes, that's my real name!"

Walter Glücklich, I repeated to myself, remembering that *Glücklich* meant "happy." It was one of the few English words I could remember. It was the most beautiful name I'd ever heard!

The door to our compartment opened. Two SS men pushed their way through the aisle, examining our passports and comparing the smiling children in the photos with the faces that looked up at them now, frozen with fear. One officer stood in front of me, studying me for a long time. I felt an icy cold rise inside of me as if everything that was warm and alive was being sucked into the shadow under his cap.

Jette and I didn't look at each other when it was our turn. The man who searched our belongings just made piles of clothes next to our suitcases, without a word, feeling everything, pressing things down, and gliding his hands into every pants and jacket pocket with practiced motions. I almost passed out when I remembered that Mamu had sewn a 20 Reichsmark bill into the hem of my pants, but the money wasn't noticed. Without comment, instead he took a stamp album out of Jette's suitcase and set it aside. I saw how she couldn't tear her eyes from it. The Nazi clamped it under his arm as he left the compartment; maybe he had a child at home who collected stamps.

Silently, our traveling companions crowded their way back into the compartment. Greta opened a package of cookies and held them out to us, even me. She was probably sorry for saying she wished I would be questioned on top of everything. I took a cookie even though my throat was shut tight, and chewed on the first bite as if it were sand.

It didn't even register when the train started moving again. I didn't understand where the noise came from, a roar that suddenly swelled and rolled from one compartment to the next like a wave. It took me a whole minute to recognize that it was the other children, who were no longer sitting in their places, but hopping wildly around, celebrating, and took turns pulling each other out of the compartments into the aisle.

We were in Holland. We had made it. We were free.

The contrast couldn't have been greater. We had just stood in front of the Nazis, who had managed to spread paralyzing fear without speaking a single word. Fifteen minutes later, the train stopped again at a station beyond the border and smiling women with great big baskets climbed on board, handing out apples, whole bars of chocolate, and hot tea. They had wonderfully kind faces, spoke to us in warm, throaty voices, and took up the younger children in their arms. *Welkom, welkom!* We didn't have to know Dutch to understand that.

The Nazis were the nightmare we had gotten used to. Much more shocking were the Dutch women with their chocolate. None of us could have imagined that such a completely different world began directly across the border from Germany. I finally understood my mother's hopes for me when she sent me on the kindertransport against my will.

The instant I set foot on the lower deck of the *Harwich II*, I started to wish I had stuffed a little less chocolate into my mouth. "I'm going to get some fresh air," I moaned, and was already on my way back above deck.

I managed to reach the upper deck. I leaned far over the railing and took in deep gulps of air; an ice-cold smell of salt and fish reached me and I lost the entire contents of my stomach into the English Channel.

"One of the first rules of sea voyages," said Walter Glücklich, handing me a handkerchief, "is never throw up into the wind."

I took his handkerchief and wiped the tears from my eyes.

He advised me to stay outside. "Look at a point on the horizon, and you'll feel better eventually!"

I followed his advice, and noticed that in a very short time my fingers were frozen solid to the railing, but my legs became functional again and I got my footing. Walter stayed right behind me, just to be on the safe side, a strange but not unpleasant feeling.

"Do you have an address over there?" Walter had to yell to be heard above the wind, waves, and the humming of the engine.

"Yes, and you?" I yelled back, totally thrilled that an older boy was talking with me.

"I'm going to join my father. He's been in London for a year already."

"And your mother?"

"She died two years ago." Before I could be dismayed, he smiled again. He had cheerful eyes and brown curls and leaned toward being plump. "What's your name, anyway?" he wanted to know.

"Ziska Mangold. And I'm going to bring my parents over too!"

"Good luck! There's a coffeehouse in Tottenham Court Road, the Café Vienna. They might be able to help you there."

Café Vienna, I repeated in my thoughts and could hardly believe it. I hadn't even reached England yet, and I'd already found out about a place I could go to get help for my parents!

An especially high wave struck the ship with a loud noise, pressed the bow up, and then it came down so steeply that water sloshed onto the deck. The winter storm on the sea seemed so perfectly fitting, almost comforting, as if God himself were responding powerfully to the turmoil in our lives. When the next wave came, I opened my mouth wide and screamed at it at the top of my lungs.

Soon! Mamu and Papa would come join me soon! In the unfettered wind of freedom that blew from the English coast, everything seemed so wonderfully simple.

Ever since we had received their address, I had been thinking about the Winterbottoms, awaiting my arrival. They were willing to guarantee, with a considerable sum of money, that I wouldn't become a burden to the English government. Who were they? Why were they doing so much for a completely unknown child? Could it be that they were expecting something from me in return—and if so, what?

The closer our first meeting drew, the more nervous I became. After the ferry docked in Harwich, while we waited for hours for the medical examinations and another round of passport and customs controls, the Winterbottoms occupied every cell in my brain. Had they received the letter Mamu and I had written in time, or did they know as little about me as I did about them?

I furtively rubbed the small crucifix at my throat. *Jesus, if you can hear me now, please make sure the Winterbottoms like me. If it's not too late, please let them be wonderful people, like the ones Bekka talked about.*

I had a bit of a bad conscience, because I only prayed when I wanted something from Jesus. I couldn't even be a hundred percent certain that he was responsible for me at all. When I was still allowed to be a Protestant, I was told, "Jesus is always with you and loves you just the way you are." But was that automatically revoked when I was kicked out of religion class? If he really had been by my side up to that point, wouldn't Jesus know better than anyone that I wasn't really Jewish?

Of course! If anyone knew, it was Jesus! That meant he was definitely still looking out for me, even now as our train pulled into an enormous, light-filled, columned hall: Liverpool Street Station, London. In orderly groups of four we walked through the small triumphal archway into the main hall of the station and found ourselves in a kind of warehouse that had been divided in half with rope and tarp. Friendly looking, elegantly dressed women from the local committee for the aid of Jewish refugees were already seated at tables, ready to sign us in and hand us over to the right people. We were directed to the rows of benches that took up one whole side of the hall. On the other side, a haphazardly assembled, colorful crowd of people had gathered.

A wave of expectant murmuring broke out as we entered.

Our foster parents! Most craned their necks, smiling or waving in our direction, immediately setting off a round of whispering, nudging, and guessing games on our side. I envied the children who were going to stay with their own relatives. They had nothing to worry about. Walter had been met by his father right on the train platform. I'd caught a last glimpse of both of them before they were swallowed by the crowd and I was driven along in the stream of children. Thomas Liebich had already boarded a bus in Harwich that was headed for a collection center for children who didn't have a permanent address in England yet.

My heart pounding, I tried to peer over the table from my place on the bench. Which of those people were the Winterbottoms? The noise level in the hall rose as soon as the adults were allowed to come over to us. All manner of sounds were directed questioningly to my face, but no matter how hard I tried, I couldn't make out anything that sounded even vaguely like Franziska.

That is how my stay in England began—with foster parents who changed their minds. I watched as one child after another disappeared through that same door with their English people, and the hall emptied. Marcus and Hermione Winterbottom were nowhere to be seen.

"Go sit with the others, Franziska," one of the volunteers said. When she spoke to me I realized that everyone else was looking straight at me. The ladies from the committee had gathered our guardians around a table to answer a few final questions before they had to return to Germany. There were other children there too—three of them, a girl and two boys, the only ones left waiting with me. With our bundles and suitcases and our bedraggled cardboard signs hung around our necks, we stayed well away from each another. We could have moved closer together long before. But each of us would rather have died than take a single step in that direction.

"At least come down from the bench," she suggested.

With burning cheeks, I jumped down to the floor, filled with shame and the dull, terrifying emptiness of loss. I had been left behind. No one was waiting for me.

For a brief but intense time, the Winterbottoms had been my entire future, the only reality in a fog of "perhaps," the only thing I could rely on. Now I had lost them as well. Maybe my letter had been too short. Maybe Mamu or Uncle Erik had mixed up an important word. Maybe they had simply woken up this morning and decided they would rather take in someone from Vienna or Prague. Maybe they had been here, taken one look at me, and left again.

I would never find out. But I did know one thing for certain: No one would have seen Bekka and left her standing there.

Chapter 6

The Shepards

Three weeks after arriving in London, I felt like someone had created a new planet especially for us Jewish children, one that was far removed from any real life. We couldn't even pronounce the name of our new planet: Satterthwaite Hall. We shared it with the residents of a nursing home in the main wing of the building. We almost never saw them. Now and then a few of them sat out on the balcony in their wheelchairs, never moving, while we were allowed to play on the lawn after our English lessons.

The one thing we all had in common was that we couldn't leave. Satterthwaite Hall, a small, enchanted castle with many little towers and gables of gray stone, was surrounded by a seven-foot-high wall. Beyond the wall lay England. We could hear its noise, smell its odors, and sometimes even sense the footsteps of people walking on the other side. But the longer I was there, the less I could envision that there really was an "outside."

Every afternoon I walked along the wall, to the left, to the right, and all around, missing Bekka like I had never missed anyone before. But Bekka was far away, and the other children came and went. Satterthwaite Hall was just a way station, and all any of us could really do was sit and wait—full of anticipation, hope, and fear—for Sunday to come around.

Sunday was our only chance to get out of there. Clean, well behaved, and with friendly smiles, we sat at our places in the dining room answering future foster parents' questions in our ever-improving English, although anyone could see from across a football field that most of them were only looking for the little ones. How could this young couple, that older woman, or this family know that they weren't making a mistake by taking someone else home with them?

With growing uneasiness I waited day after day for news of my parents. My father had been released from Sachsenhausen in poor health, but my mother didn't write what was wrong with him. That belonged to the category of questions that you instinctively sense should not be asked. "Papa says we should have traveled to Shanghai without him," Mamu wrote. "Now we're waiting for approval of our new exit visas—to anywhere at all."

Anywhere at all? I was horrified. They had sent me to England, so it seemed perfectly clear that they would come here and meet up with me! It weighed on me more and more heavily that our future depended entirely on me. But how could I get them out of Germany when I couldn't even manage to get myself out of Satterthwaite Hall?

Everything at home seemed to be getting worse. My mother complained about how difficult life was without the car and her driver's license, which she had been forced to give up. She wrote about money being tighter and that it was getting harder to buy things. She wrote about Papa's weak heart, so damaged by all these blows that she was making every effort to keep the worst of it from him. He still believed, for example, that our car was parked around the corner in the Meyers' garage.

At the same time, she would entertain me for pages with lively descriptions of her most recent bouts with Aunt Ruth, and I pictured the two of them quarreling over the kitchen table so vividly that it seemed like I was there myself.

As hard as I tried, though, I couldn't imagine Papa in Aunt Ruth's apartment. Whenever I thought of Papa, all I saw were his white feet in slippers and a bloody handprint on the wall, and I had to stop thinking about him at all.

February 19, my eleventh birthday, was coming up. I kept it to myself, not telling anyone. To talk about a birthday was like exposing a raw wound; even worse, admitting to myself that I was completely alone on that day, without a home and with a giant question mark hanging over the coming year of my life.

The fact that everything changed on my birthday could only mean that Jesus—the only one who knew about it— hadn't given up on me after all, despite the disaster with the Winterbottoms and the long series of disappointing Sundays. Since the English people continued to overlook me, I needed to go out and find a family on my own.

The porter at Satterthwaite Hall was a gnarled, elderly man. He was clearly less than thrilled about having to run a refugee hostel on short notice, and we tried our best to stay out of his way. Every Sunday, just past two o'clock, he unlocked the tall, iron gate leading to the street, hoping just as much we did that there would be fewer of us inside by the day's end.

With the key in his hand, he stomped back to the house, passing by the compost heap next to the wall without giving it a glance. How could he know that there was a girl hiding behind it—a girl with a plan? Resolutely, I sneaked behind his back along the wall and slipped out the gate. I was in England!

I decided I would only speak to people who were on their way to Satterthwaite Hall, although at the moment there were no people in sight. Cars pulled up and others drove off. Finally, after I had been leaning against the wall for half an hour or so, a number of visitors arrived all at once, and there I was, unexpectedly confronted with a question I hadn't yet considered. How on earth was I supposed to pick *the* people, out of all these strangers, who were right for me? I had been terrified at the thought of being handed over to the Winterbottoms, people who didn't know me at all. Now I realized that the alternative wasn't any less troubling. I had to make a spontaneous decision about which people I wanted to live with, and for who knows how long?

I was so completely paralyzed by the weight of the decision that lay before me that I let the first visitors pass through the gate without speaking a single word to any of them. Time went by, dragging on endlessly. Then I saw a couple walking toward me along the wall, followed by two elderly women.

This was it! Brashly, I stepped in front of them and blurted out the phrase I'd cobbled together from my dictionary: "Excuse me, you look one child?"

Without changing his expression, the gentleman reached in his pocket and handed me a coin. Not stopping for a second, the couple walked right by me through the gate.

The ones who did stop were the elderly ladies. They looked at me sternly and were more than a little irritated, although I hadn't spoken to them at all. They exchanged a few words, of which I understood just one: *committee*. Then they marched in through the gate. It was clear that I was about to get in big trouble.

I stole a glance around the gateposts and saw that I wouldn't have long to wait. Two minutes later, both women came back out of the house with Miss Werner between them, speaking to her, the only German volunteer at Satterthwaite Hall, authoritatively. Even from this distance I could tell that Miss Werner was extremely angry as she strode across the lawn in my direction.

Survival plan! I dove down behind the nearest car, where my ever-dependable brain cells, well trained in running and hiding, got to work at once. If I could lure Miss Werner away from the gate, I might be able to sneak back in and act as if I'd never been away. I squatted down and ran, all bent over, around the cars, keeping both the gate and Miss Werner in sight. She had started looking underneath the vehicles. I was sure she had no chance of catching me as long as I stayed hidden behind the tires. So I was quite surprised when a loud bang brought my retreat to a sudden and painful end. A passenger door swung open and hit me squarely in the head. The next thing I knew, I was lying facedown on the asphalt with a view of two pairs of big feet in black shoes, and asking myself if that sound was really birds chirping.

The owners of the old Rover were sitting in the car with the motor turned off discussing whether they should look for a younger or older boy. They hadn't yet come to an agreement when they stepped out of the car, only to discover that they had knocked out a girl. Careful hands turned me over onto my back. I opened my eyes and saw the friendly, worried face of a man about Papa's age wearing a big, black hat.

"You look child?" I croaked.

A second face appeared above me. Now I was sure I must have injured my head, because boys this beautiful simply didn't exist. He looked to be sixteen or seventeen, with dark hair, and bright green eyes that looked down at me over a nobly arched nose. I blinked, and blinked again, but he didn't disappear. He was real!

"Ziska, for heaven's sake!" All at once I heard a cry of horror and I saw my two English people disappear left and right from my field of vision as Miss Werner forced herself between them, filling the space above me. "Did they run you over?"

I shook my head. The English people were discussing something. "No, she can't get up," said Miss Werner testily, in German. "She will lie right where she is until the doctor arrives."

"No need doctor," I murmured, heaving myself into a sitting position and leaning against the wheel of the car. There seemed to be something working its way out through my forehead from the middle of my skull. I poked around in the general area and, my heart sinking, discovered a bump the size of an egg. No one would pick me today with this on my forehead!

The older Englishman spoke a sentence directly out of chapter two of our English grammar book. "I am a doctor." He crouched down in front of me, felt my head, and moved his index finger from right to left in front of my face. Finally, he pulled my eyelids open and seemed pleased with the annoyed expression he saw there. "She's much better already," he concluded.

"You look child?" I asked desperately.

Miss Werner looked down at me, enraged, while apologizing to the English people for the trouble I had caused them.

The Englishmen exchanged a glance. "Well," said the older one, "we were indeed . . . looking for a child."

Considering that we had barely exchanged a word, it was unbelievable how quickly we came to an understanding. By the time I had gone to the dormitory and packed my things, they had already taken care of all the necessary formalities. I had only just shaken hands with Miss Werner to say goodbye, and there I was following my saviors, Dr. Shepard and his beautiful son, Gary, to the gate, accompanied by the envious looks of the other children. It was only as we drove through London that I was able to get everything straight in my head: My goal was not to find an English family, but to bring my own family to England! The nice Shepards in the front seat of the car just didn't know it yet.

I saw the famous red double-decker buses that made their way through the streets in such great numbers that London appeared to be colorful, narrow, and entirely chaotic. When we stopped at an intersection, to my dismay, a little boy shouted directly into our window. He wasn't in any danger; he just stuck a newspaper through the opening and was given a coin in exchange.

Soon, we left the lively downtown and drove on far outside the city along tranquil suburban streets lined with rows of identical houses. There was one street with two-story, white duplex houses, and another with three-story brown ones, and a third that seemed to consist of a single, endlessly long building curving its way around a bend. When we finally came to a stop I saw little towers on the roof and tiny front gardens. The space between the houses was so narrow that an adult with both arms outstretched could touch the walls of each building.

"Our house," Gary said proudly. A low step led to the front door, and a small canopy covered the entire entrance area. It looked pretty, like a toy house, but the biggest surprise was the itty-bitty mailbox attached to the doorframe! The glass tube, just six inches long, was decorated with incredibly delicate little ornaments. While they had been away, someone had apparently stuffed a small piece of paper with a message inside it. But instead of taking out the note and reading it, Dr. Shepard and Gary touched it with the fingers of their right hand as they walked by, then brought those fingers to their lips and kissed them.

I was astounded. English people kiss their mail! Right there and then I took the entire country into my heart. What a respectful, fitting gesture to make toward those who had taken the time to write to us!

Inside the house it was warm and smelled good, a mixture of coal fire, fresh-baked bread, and herbs, some of which sat in a vase in the entryway. A narrow, steep staircase led upstairs. The living room was right next to it, but I didn't have a chance to do more than glance at it quickly. We had only just stepped inside when a small, plump woman came toward us, smiling and drying her hands on her apron.

I liked her immediately, although I had not pictured her being quite so old. "Good afternoon, Mrs. Shepard," I greeted her politely, as I had been taught to do.

Dr. Shepard and Gary broke out in ringing laughter. The small, plump lady had a dignified, though somewhat embarrassed, expression on her face. This was Millie, the housekeeper.

"And this is Francesca," said Dr. Shepard.

Who? I thought, baffled.

Millie also looked a little surprised. "That a boy?" she asked.

The Shepards seemed to be a cheerful family, for once again they laughed before replying "No," whereupon Millie, full of anger and loathing, pointed at the bump on my forehead and declared, "Bloody Nazis."

A flood of words followed, of which I was able to extract only one, the word *tea*, not one of my favorite things, after which Millie hurried back through the narrow hallway to the kitchen. Dr. Shepard said something to Gary that included my name. Since Gary then said, "Follow me," I gathered that his father had asked him to show me my room.

I followed Gary up the steps, but soon fell a bit behind. The entire wall next to the stairs was covered with framed photographs. They featured Gary as a baby, as a toddler, in his school uniform, and wearing his yarmulke, in an embroidered prayer shawl and with a thick book in his hand. Gary was obviously the focal point of this household, his parents' pride and joy.

"Are you coming?" he called in English from one of the rooms upstairs. I was just about to take the stairs two steps at a time so that I wouldn't keep him waiting when suddenly, at the top, one more picture caught my eye. It was the kind of image that made you stop and stare. There was Gary, maybe five years old, leaning against a chair with a knowing smile on his face, so thoughtful and deep, extraordinary, especially for a such a young child. His smile was paralleled exactly on the face next to his. That had to be his mother. She had the same eyes, the same nose, and the same beautiful, elegantly proportioned face, framed by dark hair. Her hand, emerging from a white tailored blouse, lay on Gary's arm. A strange shiver went down my neck, as though my own arm could sense that tender touch.

"Francesca?" Gary stood in a doorway looking at me with a questioning expression. I hurried to follow him.

My future room looked out over the front garden. It had light blue walls that were decorated with delicate floral designs, a bed, bookcase, and a child's desk in front of the window, which completely filled the small room. There could be no doubt that the Shepards were expecting a boy: Pictures of ships and airplanes hung on the walls and the bookshelf was full of wooden cars and model boats.

"All my old things," explained Gary. He spoke very loudly, apparently so that I could understand him better.

There I was, standing as if rooted to the floor again. "Letter!" I said, enraptured, pointing at the doorframe, where a little tube hung, exactly like the one I had seen on the front door. This one was made of metal, but no doubt about it, there was already a letter in there for me! I quickly took a step toward it, to turn the little tube around and extract the tiny note that I could just see through the small opening. Then it occurred to me that I had to kiss the container first, though that was a little embarrassing in front of Gary.

Hesitating, I stopped and stood still, with Gary's gaze following mine toward the little tube, and then he started laughing again.

I tried not to show how much that hurt my feelings. Gary stopped laughing, pointed at the tube, and said slowly, "This is a mezuzah. We . . . are Orthodox."

"Orthodox?" I repeated, confused.

Gary laid his hand on the little tube and repeated: "Mezuzah. Inside it are two texts from the Torah. Do you understand?" he asked, seeing the baffled expression on my face. "You'll learn. Do you want Millie . . . your suitcase?" he gestured.

I shook my head and he left the room with a "See you later."

Orthodox! I would have to digest that piece of information. Something told me that my parents wouldn't be overjoyed, although the Shepards wore neither long beards nor sidelocks and probably belonged to an entirely different sect than the Seydenstickers. I decided to wait a few letters before gently filling them in.

Happily, I looked around, taking in every last detail of my room. My room! It seemed like an eternity since I had last had my own room. There was nothing to do but take off my coat, scarf, and shoes and let myself fall back on the bed.

I closed my eyes and unexpectedly felt right at home, embraced by warmth and friendliness. The people who had set up this room must have been very excited about taking in a child. I could hardly believe my luck, even if it was only for a short time, until my parents could follow me to England.

"Francesca, tea is ready!"

Again I heard them call my strange new name. I slowly rolled myself out of bed, went down the stairs, and followed the voices, which came from the living room. Gary was telling a story, interrupting it again and again with his laughter. *"Whaaamm!"* he demonstrated explosively, probably reenacting my encounter with the car door to the amusement of all.

I recognized Mrs. Shepard at once from the photo, although she was visibly older and had cut her long hair into a dull, helmet-like style. She looked serious, almost a little intimidating. Still, when she saw me she let loose a spontaneous, hearty laugh. "What a lovely boy," she said cheerfully. Her voice was warm and dark. Deep laugh lines ran up from the corners of her eyes like rays of sun. I stood frozen in the doorway. Mrs. Shepard was almost too beautiful to be true.

I saw the smile freeze on Mrs. Shepard's face, and the atmosphere grew colder with every step she took toward me. She was staring at something, I didn't know what it could be, but by the time she reached out her hand to me, I was already paralyzed with fear.

"What is that?" she asked, her voice now completely changed, toneless and nearly flat. I felt ice-cold fingers at my throat, and as she turned around to Dr. Shepard and Gary, my tiny silver cross was in her hand. "We wanted to take in a *Jewish* child!" she said, appalled.

Dr. Shepard and Gary stood up as well and came closer to us. My head was pushed back as far as possible from Mrs. Shepard's grip on my chain. Terrified, my eyes begged both of them for help. They were responsible; they were the ones who had taken me home with them in the first place! At the same time, it occurred to me that it wasn't their fault. They couldn't have seen the cross. I had worn my coat and scarf the entire time.

Both of them silently considered the problem that hung around my neck, then began to speak at the same time, Dr. Shepard in a calm and soothing tone, and Gary upset and reproachful. I heard him say something about "Herr Hitler" and it was probably this name more than anything else that forced an immediate reaction from me. A growl rose from my throat, my head shot forward, and my teeth clamped down on the tender cartilage and delicate knuckles of the enemy's fist. My chain came free immediately and I stormed out of the room as if the Furies themselves were chasing me.

Mrs. Shepherd herself was so thoroughly shocked that it was two seconds before she let out a cry of pain. It was echoed in the kitchen, where Millie dropped all her pots and pans as I fled up the staircase. I threw open the door to my room and sprang into the closet. Trembling, I crouched behind the boys' clothing in the darkness and heard my teeth chatter. I tried to pray, but it didn't work. Again and again the same film played in my mind, with a crazed soundtrack playing in the background: *That can't really have happened . . .*

*not Jewish . . . I can't stay here . . . not Jewish . . . something is
wrong with me . . . not Jewish.*

I don't know how long I sat in the closet, but it was long
enough for my entire life to pass before me. Mamu, Papa,
Bekka, the Refugee Committee . . . I had betrayed them all.
The painful departure, the falling out with my best friend,
the cost and effort put into saving me . . . all for nothing. A
feeling of hopeless failure overwhelmed me with such shattering finality that I couldn't even cry.

They would send me back to Germany, that much was
certain. I had had my chance, and I had blown it. A small
voice inside me weighed in with the perspective that it was
all Mrs. Shepard's fault, but that was no comfort. Quite the
opposite: Despite all my brooding about the Winterbottoms,
I had never really been able to imagine what it would be like
to be completely, utterly dependent on the goodwill of my
foster family. They helped save my life, and at the same time
I was entirely at the mercy of their judgment, their charity,
their moods. I suddenly understood just what this meant.

After a while I heard steps. "Francesca?" Gary asked. I
heard him standing in front of the closet, breathing. "Come
out of there!" I didn't answer.

"Please, Francesca!" Now it sounded as if he was sitting
on the floor on the other side of the door. All at once, the
tears began to flow.

"I hate Francesca," I howled.

"That's okay. I'll give you a new name. It's an ancient Jewish tradition. Do you understand? New life—new name?"
He listened. "Do you want a new name?" he asked, tempting

me. I bit my teeth together. A new name—as if that would change anything! He knocked on the door. "Come on now. I always wanted a little sister!"

My resolve to remain in the closet for all eternity began to weaken a little. It occurred to me that Gary, at least, had apparently defended me. He had defended me even against his own mother. If there was anyone at all I could still trust, it was him. I heard him say something about "good-bye," "school," and "supper." Then he sighed softly to himself and said, "What I need is a dictionary."

Gary looked surprised when I opened the closet door. "Hi!" he said in greeting. I crawled past him to my suitcase and took out my dictionary, handing it to him without a word. He took it with great gentleness, as if he had just tamed a small wild animal, which, considering my most recent public performance, wasn't too far off the mark. Beneath my window the front door slammed; Dr. Shepard was probably taking his wife to the hospital.

"Come closer," he said, beckoning me to his side so that we could look at the dictionary together. Hesitating, I moved a little bit nearer. Gary paged through eagerly, looked up a word, and passed the book over to me. I had no choice but to sit down in front of him. "Boarding school" was what I read there, *Internat* in German. I nodded.

It seemed to take forever to piece together all the information, but by the end of the laborious process I had learned that Gary lived at a boarding school and was only home from Friday to Sunday. His father wasn't a real doctor, but a professor of Roman studies, which had something to do with languages, and Gary's mother worked in a Jewish nursing home every Sunday, and that's why she hadn't been able to accompany them to Satterthwaite Hall.

Just my luck, I thought bitterly. If she had been there, the Shepards would certainly never have chosen me and we would all have been spared a lot of trouble.

"So what about your new name?" asked Gary.

I hesitated. I would have liked to say that it didn't make any difference to me, but I was getting tired of leafing through the dictionary. So I nodded. Gary helped me up and laid a hand on my shoulder. "From now on . . . you will be called Frances," he announced ceremoniously.

"Frances," I repeated, awed, and then again, "Frances."

I looked at him in amazement. He had simply taken the other half of my name. Now I had half a name for Germany, and another half for England.

Shyly, I picked up the dictionary and asked, "Will you help me?" I thought about the new school I would have to attend and the language I didn't understand. I thought of helping my parents. I thought of the help I would need with Gary's mother. There were so many things I needed help with that it seemed extremely unlikely to me that anyone would volunteer for the job.

Gary didn't seem to have the slightest idea what he was getting into when he confidently replied, "Of course! I'll stay for supper and show you everything you need to know."

"Everything I need to know?" I repeated silently. What in the world was he talking about?

For the second time that Sunday I stood in the Shepards' living room doorway waiting to be introduced, but this time I didn't stand there alone. Gary laid his hand on my shoulder and said, "Mum, Dad . . . this is my sister, Frances."

Mrs. Shepard's right hand was bandaged and there was a deep crease between her eyebrows. It was clear that Gary's parents had already discussed the question of whether or not they should keep me. I saw his mother swallow hard when he introduced me as his sister.

Apparently, however, the two of them couldn't deny their son anything. I was invited to sit on the long side of the dining room table, directly across from Gary, and told that this would be my place from now on. Gary had brought my dictionary with him and set it down on the table between us, where it lay between the candlesticks, strange dishes, and odd bowls, looking every bit as lost as I was.

The evening meal began with rinsing our hands with water poured from a pitcher into a bowl. We were only allowed to dry them after Dr. Shepard had recited a long prayer in a language that sounded like nothing I had ever heard. Then he began to cut the bread and I thought we would get on with the meal, but instead there was another prayer before he cut each of us a slice. I politely reached out my hand, but he just looked right past it and placed the bread on my plate.

My stomach was all in knots. I was deeply offended. But then Gary picked up the dictionary, paged through, and explained that his father had not placed the bread directly in my hand because that would signify begging or poverty.

I said nothing. Slowly but surely, I began to panic. This must all be a horrible mistake! Completely unknown people had sat me down at their table to take part in their mysterious, complicated rituals. If I didn't do something soon, everyone would think I was one of them!

In the meantime, Dr. Shepard had blessed the vegetables and the wine. Then he sat down, and the meal began. Gary pointed to the plates and bowls, saying that there was vegetable soup, eggs, cheese, and fish, all of which I could eat at the same time. But after eating meat or sausage I'd have to wait six hours.

I didn't belong here! I wanted to go home! I was becoming so foreign even to myself that when Gary put a piece of fish on my plate, it felt like I was literally observing myself sitting there.

My legs twitched violently underneath the table, as if they wanted to run away, but then the strange feeling was gone again. I sat there quietly, glad that no one had noticed the inappropriate thoughts that had been running through my head.

"Just do what I do," Gary advised me.

That was just what I had in mind. Firmly determined not to make any more mistakes, I put the same things on my plate that he did, even though I didn't like fish. I tried to hold my fork just like he did, and when he rinsed out his mouth between the fish and the cheese courses I did the same. I barely noticed Dr. Shepard buttering bread for his wife because she couldn't use her hand.

Then Dr. Shepard turned and spoke to me directly for the first time this evening. "Well, Frances," he said, with help from Gary and the dictionary, "naturally you can't call us Mother and Father because you already have a mother and father. What would you think of calling us Uncle Matthew and Aunt Amanda?"

The food I was swallowing stuck in my throat. I nodded so violently that I knocked my fork to the floor.

"She can also just say Uncle and Aunt, if she wants," Mrs. Shepard said calmly.

Or nothing at all, I thought.

Once this matter had been settled they left me in peace and I could concentrate on making it through the perils of an Orthodox meal. I gradually started to suspect that eating was only the smallest part of the procedure. Gary took his knife and fork in the opposite hands when he switched between hard and soft cheese, and he laid his napkin over his glass while buttering another slice of bread. I bravely soldiered on with him. I noticed in the background that the room was becoming quieter and quieter, until Gary's parents stopped talking altogether and watched the mirror pantomime the two of us were performing in fascination.

The rituals involved in eating fruit were by far the strangest. Gary laid the napkin over his right arm while cutting up an apple, and then laid a small piece from each individual slice in an orderly row next to his plate. I thought this was rather messy on top of the clean tablecloth, but all right, then. I set out my apple pieces in the same way, moving them around a bit to get the spacing just right. Gary waited, friendly and patient, until I was finished. He then pressed his middle finger to his thumb, watched me copy him, and laid his wrist on the table in front of the apple pieces.

Our eyes met across the table and I saw him grin. Before I knew what had happened, he flicked a piece of apple at my arm. My jaw dropped. A full barrage of apple pieces flew across the table until finally it dawned on me: Gary had been pulling my leg the entire time!

My shock lasted for about two seconds, then without a second thought I pushed my plate out of the way and shot back. Gary cackled like a hen and began to crawl under the table to resupply himself with ammunition.

"Gary, that's enough. Sit back down!" His mother tried to put a stop to it, but it was no use. Even Dr. Shepard fired off an apple piece at his wife when one strayed over to his side of the table. Finally, she simply gave up, covering her face with both hands as my first evening meal under their roof came to a close in a suspiciously unorthodox fashion.

After we were finished eating, Dr. Shepard recited prayers of thanks that seemed to go on forever. I wasn't quite sure if that was part of the normal routine or a kind of apology for flinging food around. When it seemed like he was coming to the end of the prayers, Mrs. Shepard looked at me and said that he had forgotten something.

"Right you are," Dr. Shepard answered, and everyone smiled at me as he launched into another prayer. It seemed to be a prayer about me. I blushed bright red, but luckily no one expected me to say anything.

Later, as I was about to go upstairs to my room, Mrs. Shepard asked me if I wanted to come along to bring Gary to his boarding school. She stood at the front door in her coat and waited for her son, who had run upstairs to get his suitcase. I hesitantly shook my head. Of course I wanted nothing more than to go with them—but that would have meant being alone with her on the ride back to their house.

"Then we'll see each other at eight o'clock for breakfast," she said, turning away and looking through the pieces of paper that lay in a flat bowl next to the telephone. That must have been her way of saying "good night." I waited another moment, then turned away too, and went upstairs without a word.

Gary came toward me carrying his small suitcase and patted me warmly on the shoulder as I squeezed past him. "We'll see each other on Friday!"

I forced a bucket of tears down my throat and managed a smile. I watched as he bounded down the stairs and put his arm around his mother, both of them touching the mezuzah with their fingertips and then bringing their fingers to their lips. I ran into my room to watch their car drive away, but the tree right in front of the window kept me from seeing more than a pair of headlights.

Chapter 7

Becoming Frances

A hot, bright flash struck me directly in the eyes. I threw both my arms up to protect my face and screamed at the top of my lungs, "No!" Poor Millie, who had done nothing more than pull aside the curtains to let in the morning sun, was so startled that she jumped backward and smacked into the wall behind her.

"Goodness! Get up!" Millie prompted me as she set something on my nightstand and left. It was an alarm clock, and according to the clock it was half past nine.

Half past nine! Horrified, I instantly forgot about being blinded and jumped out of bed. Mrs. Shepard hadn't said much to me, but the one thing she had said was "breakfast at eight o'clock." I quickly grabbed some clothing, scooted down the hall to the freezing cold bathroom, washed myself quickly, and got dressed. After I had spent about five minutes on the landing, I dared to go downstairs.

At the far back of the house, where it looked like the house ended, was actually the kitchen, where Millie was already busy making me breakfast. She set a cup of tea, two slices of buttered toast, and a fried egg in front of me. It took me longer than one would expect to eat an egg and two pieces of toast. The bread tasted as if she had put pure salt on it! When Millie stood up to get something out of the cupboard, I folded the second slice of toast in half as fast as I could and shoved it under the waistband of my skirt.

The door that led from the kitchen into the backyard opened and Mrs. Shepard came in. "Ah, Frances!" she said when she saw me, and pulled a pair of rubber boots off her feet. "Are you finished?" she asked, peering into my half-full teacup. She held the door open for me and I followed her into the living room, where I stopped and stood in the middle of the carpet while she went to a secretary and opened one of its drawers. "I'm glad you slept so well," she said. "We have a lot to do today. We have to register you at your new school, and of course, you'll want to write to your parents. I'll give you a card with our address that you can send with your letter."

I just stood there and stared at her. Mrs. Shepard had spoken German! At least some kind of German; it was a mixture of Frau Seydensticker's Yiddish and a word here and there of my native tongue. I had understood almost everything! She turned to face me and seemed to be glad that her surprise had been a success. "In the nursing home where I work, lots of the residents only speak Yiddish," she explained. "If you want to talk with them, you have to learn it. You don't talk much, do you?" Mrs. Shepard commented. I lowered my head and shrugged my shoulders.

When I looked down, my gaze fell upon the grease spot on my blouse, as big as the palm of my hand and growing by the second. It seemed to spread farther up my blouse as I stared at it! Unfortunately, Mrs. Shepard had seen it too. I reached under the waistband of my skirt and, with great shame, retrieved the sticky, crumbling remains of my toast.

"Some of my old people are also not fans of salted butter." Mrs. Shepard stretched out her good hand, the one that wasn't bandaged. I placed what was left of the toast in it and wished I could disappear on the spot.

"It would probably be best if you go put on a clean blouse," she suggested, "and then we'll go to your new school."

I hadn't expected that I would have to go to school on my very first day, and a dark foreboding came over me. My school career had so far consisted mainly of pushing, fighting, and being made fun of, but at least that was all in German, and I felt completely unprepared to encounter English children. Shouldn't I at least know my way around the neighborhood first, and have some idea where I could run and hide? I guess there was a certain possibility that they would leave me alone in England, but could I really be sure?

The walk to my future school didn't exactly do anything to boost my confidence. We passed dozens of little houses, turned left here and right there on different streets, but there weren't any courtyards behind the buildings or outbuildings, and at most two or three little paths between houses that probably ended at a wall. My feet rooted themselves to the ground. When Mrs. Shepard noticed that I wasn't coming along, there were already five yards or more between us, and the first words I spoke to her were: "Excuse me, where I hide here?"

Mrs. Shepard didn't say anything for a long time, then slowly came back toward me. "People don't hide here," she said. "You're safe now. That's why you came, after all."

"Right," I mumbled gloomily, and starting walking again. This time it was Mrs. Shepard who stood still for a few seconds longer before she hurried to catch up to me. When she reached me, I got a very strange feeling, as if she was about to take my hand. I quickly made both my hands disappear into the pockets of my coat, and then we reached the school without stopping again.

Classes had started and I only saw a single young boy, who stood sullenly facing the wall outside the door to a classroom. It smelled like old maps and soup and yes, Mrs. Shepard confirmed, I would get a warm meal at school and could even have a kosher diet if I wanted. I answered that kosher would be fine, though I didn't know about the diet part.

We had to wait a while outside the director's office. Then we were called in, and it turned out that the director was a woman. The first thing Mrs. Collins asked about was Gary. I heard the word *war* and saw Mrs. Shepard's smile freeze; puzzled, I thought, *Why war? Gary is just at a boarding school.*

Then Mrs. Collins turned to me and I tried very hard to follow her, but unfortunately I hadn't brought my dictionary and soon had to give up. Mrs. Collins apparently felt the same way, because after less than a minute she told Mrs. Shepard that she would put me in the first grade.

Mrs. Shepard looked at her in disbelief. "Frances is eleven! You can't just put her in the same class with the youngest children!"

But Mrs. Collins would not budge, and so we were back

outside rather quickly and walked the same way we had just come, only quite a bit faster, it seemed to me. "Then we'll just practice at home!" said Mrs. Shepard, after she had let off some steam. "After the summer holiday you'll join the fifth grade, she can count on that."

The first letter from my mother came to my new address, 121 Harrington Grove, Finchley, London, a week later.

Berlin, 27 February 1939. My dear Ziskele, you can't imagine the joy that your letter caused in our entire house. Papa, Aunt Ruth, and Uncle Erik all send their love. Papa will write to you himself, but he's not having a good day today and I'm glad that he is sleeping a little right now.

Your situation sounds so wonderful! We are hearing stories of children who are placed with families that don't even have a toilet in the house. Now I really don't need to worry about you anymore. By now you'll have your first days at school under your belt. By the time we see each other again, maybe you will have learned English really well, and then you have to help Papa and me!

Here things have remained calm for the last few weeks, and we are hopeful that the troubles have reached their peak. We expect news about our departure any day now. Have you been able to find out anything yet? No, of course not, you've only been there a few days! Sweetie, you have to write us more about the Shepards. That's really the only ray of

hope for us at the moment. You already described
Dr. Shepard quite well, and Gary too—do you
maybe have a bit of a crush on him? But you left us
completely in the dark about Mrs. Shepard, and she's
the one who is mainly looking after you.

Is it already springtime there? The sun broke
through the gray today and reminded us just a little
of the good old Berlin that used to be. Do you know
who came to visit me yesterday? Your friend Bekka!
We went to Cohn's for an ice cream and she wanted
to know all about you. Don't you write to each
other? She is an exceptional girl. I was so happy to
have a few hours with her now that you're not here!
When I told her that, she said she would come every
day, if I wanted her to.

So we sit here and wait for better times (ha ha!)
and hopefully not too much longer for more news
from you.

Until then, consider yourself desperately hugged
by your Mamu.

"Well, Frances, what news from your mother?" said Mrs. Shepard, looking at me over the rim of her reading glasses.

I didn't answer.

"Is everything okay at home?"

"Yes!" slipped out a little louder than I intended. I bristled, but she only reached past me, took the book we had been reading together from my hand with friendly insistence, and shut it. "Maybe both of us have something better to do today. It's still nice outside, why don't you go for a little walk?"

She said it, stood up, and left my room. End of the English lesson. I stayed seated at my desk and had the feeling, not for the first time, that there were at least five different Mrs. Shepards running around in this house. I had been here for more than two weeks and still didn't know who I was dealing with at any given time.

First there was the gentle, young Mrs. Shepard in the photograph. Once in a while I looked at her, wondering, as I passed her image on the stairs, but I suspected that she was gone, just like the energetic young man in that other photo in Berlin.

Then there was the Mrs. Shepard who had nearly scared me to death on my first day there. When I helped in the kitchen, she presided over the most rigid rules. Meat had to be soaked, thoroughly salted, and then rinsed three times to remove any traces of blood. Eggs couldn't contain the tiniest dark speck. More than once, Millie, who wasn't Jewish, took home with her in the evening fruit and vegetables that hadn't met the strict standards. There was also Mrs. Shepard the teacher, looking strict with her little teacher's glasses perched on her nose, who pinned me down at the desk every afternoon and studied English with me. Another Mrs. Shepard did the most embarrassing things. My first *Shabbat* began with her pulling me aside, closing the living room door behind us, and saying, "Frances, we've been cooking and getting ready together all day long, but we can't celebrate the Sabbath together while there is something standing between us. The two of us got off to a pretty miserable start. That was my fault, and I want to apologize for it."

Adults never apologized to children! I had never heard

such a thing and was sure there were no rules about how children should behave if it happened to them. The next day it occurred to me that I should have said "I'm sorry I bit you," but she wasn't to going to wait twenty-four hours for my answer. "That's all," she said, and let me go, and later when we sat around the beautifully set table I had the feeling that there was much more standing between us than there had been before.

But it was the fifth Mrs. Shepard who confused me most of all. To watch her as she laid a see-through black cloth on her hair, lit the Shabbat candles, and spoke the blessing over them in Hebrew made a shiver run down my spine. The reflection of the flame on her face, the joy in her voice, her quick, graceful motions—all of these suddenly seemed so unfathomable, so unbearably beautiful, that I wanted nothing more eagerly than to be a part of this mystery.

Indeed, it was and remained a mystery to me, how these people could celebrate being Jewish. What I had learned to hide, even to hate, was a source of joy in my host family's house, surrounded by ceremonies and songs at the table and an entire day of quiet on which the Shepards didn't do any work at all, not even drive a car, and a neighbor who wasn't Jewish came by late in the evening to turn out the lights.

I wasn't really Jewish. But the more I thought about what was appropriate for me in this house, the more confused I became and the less I understood what I actually *was*, if I wasn't Jewish. Because something in me was unfolding, quickly and entirely unexpectedly. It didn't feel foreign to me, but touched me in some inexplicable way: the rituals, candles, and lights, even the Shabbat restrictions, which, if you didn't constantly think about the things you weren't allowed to do, brought an incredible peace.

Part of the Sabbath was Gary too. Throughout the house, the anticipation of his arrival was so tangible you could almost touch it with your hands. The ceremony began with his arrival on Friday evening.

And yet I only needed to think of my own parents to be reminded that all of this wasn't intended for me, that I belonged to someone else, whose sign I wore on a chain around my neck. I wouldn't betray Jesus, Mamu, and Papa for a little candlelight, for all the lovely and wise rituals in this house. And I wouldn't touch the mezuzah, not even secretly, and even if my fingers tingled with desire!

Every time I passed a mezuzah in a doorway recently, I felt guilty because I was the only one in this house who didn't pay my respects to it. Especially now that I knew what was written on the little slip of paper that began: *"You shall love the Lord your God with all your heart, with all your soul, and with all your might."*

I knew that commandment. Jesus had said it too, but did that make it okay for me to pay tribute to a Jewish tube?

Mrs. Shepard was right, it was still lovely outside on this late March afternoon. I started walking as soon as I closed the garden gate behind me. Walking usually cleared my head right away, but today, all the disturbing thoughts that had been gathering in my head over the past weeks were just mixed up more thoroughly. The Café Vienna, which I hadn't yet looked for, the petition on behalf of my parents that I hadn't yet written, Papa sleeping in the middle of the day, Bekka taking my place, Mamu letting it happen, "now that you're not here anymore."

With three great bounds I crossed the street, and if it had been the English Channel itself I probably wouldn't have had any trouble walking across the water. What was I doing here? I had to go home! I raced through Holland, a street with low houses built of red brick, ran across the border, a narrow bridge over train tracks, aimed straight for Berlin, and stopped, gasping for breath.

Train tracks! After two weeks of walking around in the neighborhood, I had assumed there wasn't a train connection leading out of this section of London, but apparently I had been in the wrong area of Finchley. Just after I crossed over the bridge I saw the sign for the Underground to my right. The subway ran aboveground at this station, and even as I stood on my tiptoes to look at the map of the London transportation system, I saw a train arrive and pull away again. It took a while until I found "my" station way up in the north. Only one line stopped here, and there it was in black and white: If I switched trains just once, I would land directly at Tottenham Court Road!

There it was on the map, as if it had been waiting for me. I knew what I had to do next as clearly as if it was also printed on the map.

It seemed to be my fate to be ignored at school. I couldn't really blame the teacher; he had his hands full exploring the mysteries of the alphabet with thirty first graders and had as little clue as I did why I had been assigned to his class, of all places, and what on earth we should do with each other. But after two days of staring into space, I thought to take books from my shelves at the Shepards' to school with me. With the assistance of a dictionary—and the silent acquiescence of the teacher—I read all day.

The little ones soon formed crowds around me during the breaks, fascinated that such a big girl who could hardly speak a word correctly could nonetheless read to them from books. They eagerly gave me tips, outdid each other in sharing vocabulary with me, and hardly left my side until the teacher finally let me walk around during their lessons and help them as they wrote the letters. Receiving such recognition, no, more—elevation to an authority—I noticed after a few days that I actually looked forward to going to school in the mornings!

Mrs. Shepard took me to a store that carried the uniforms for the London schools, and with trembling hands I dressed myself in the various pieces of the ensemble, stepped out from behind the curtain, and viewed the new me.

The new me! Surprised and a little scared, I had discovered that I was listed in the teacher's roll as Frances Shepard. My English wasn't good enough to convince the teacher that Shepard should be erased, but at least I got him to pencil in my real name behind it. And so instead of Ziska Sara Mangold, it was now Frances Shepard Mangold who faced the world, wearing a blue skirt, a neck scarf, and a straw hat.

It wasn't easy to free myself of my crowd of admirers and sneak off to the Underground unnoticed during the break. But when I turned the corner onto the next street I held on to my straw hat and started running, filled with irrepressible anticipation of adventure and destiny.

With my heart pounding, I asked for a ticket, and rode on a narrow, rumbling subway car into a dark hole. As soon as we reached daylight again, surrounded by honking cars and scurrying pedestrians, I felt entirely at home, as if I were back in Berlin! I quickly found the street sign I was looking for. I hurried along the street, my eyes raised to read the signs on each storefront, and stood as if paralyzed for at least two minutes in the middle of the sidewalk when I actually did see the words I had been longing for. Café Vienna.

A soft, sweet music began to play in my mind and accompanied me through the door, which opened with the tinkling of a bell and revealed a surprise: The music was real! An actual violinist and a live piano player were playing in the middle of the hustle and bustle, tables crowded close together, men in hats and women in clouds of perfume, plates with huge pieces of Sacher torte and Black Forest cake, cups topped with towering crowns of whipped cream. The scent of chocolate, coffee, cigarettes, and baking overcame me, and if I hadn't been in a trance of shock and delight already, the smell alone would have instantly robbed me of my senses.

It wasn't until an older man pulled out a chair at his table and looked at me with a questioning expression that I noticed that they could see me too, and I wasn't the only living creature in the midst of a fairy tale. "Na, what may I offer you?" he asked with a wink. "Hot chocolate, perhaps? With lots of cream?"

That's when I realized that all these people spoke German! A weak "Ohhh . . ." was all I could manage, but it was answer enough. Less than a minute later, one of the fragrant cups floated down from the waitress's tray and was set before me. I dipped my spoon in the whipped cream, licked and sipped and closed my eyes as I savored the last drops.

"Playing hooky, are you?" The gentleman grinned.

I leaned back in my chair and ran my tongue along every surface in my mouth, hoping to find a little bit more whipped cream. "Only from school," I said. "I'll be back in time and my host family won't notice."

"Your host family?"

"My parents are still in Berlin. I have to bring them over. That's why I'm here." I suddenly had the feeling I was doing something wrong, something illegal. I bent over forward. "Someone told me that people here could help me," I whispered.

"Ach," murmured the older man.

"I came with one of the kindertransports," I added, to avoid any silence. "From Berlin. My mother is a cook and a seamstress—now. My father is a lawyer, but he can also work as a butler or gardener."

The elderly man leaned back, where several newspapers hung from a coatrack under the coats and hats. He unhooked one, laid it out on the table in front of us, and leafed through it. "Can you read English?" he asked.

"A little," I answered hopefully.

After a while he found what he was looking for and pushed the newspaper over toward me, without saying a word. It was half a page, at least. I read and read; there was no end. And the older gentleman just sat there the entire time and watched me.

Who will sponsor Jewish sisters from a good family, 14 and 16 years old?

Unmarried Jewish woman, 34, teacher, seeking any household position, gardening, child care, in exchange for room and board.

Urgent! Married couple, Jewish, mid-40s, academics, still in Vienna, seeking any kind of work.

Who will make it possible for a young man, 22, to emigrate to England . . .

And on and on and on.

When I had finished reading, I didn't have to ask anything else. "Those are notices that land on English breakfast tables every morning," said the older man. "I'm sorry I had to show them to you, but I think it's better if you know what you're dealing with."

"But," I started, but my voice faded. My hand lifted in an almost accusing gesture that took in the room, the piano player, the violinist, the fancy cakes, all the people at the tables. I stood up. Suddenly I was filled with so much rage that I just wanted to get out. It was as if I could see directly into the rooms of the people who had placed the announcements, people who were trapped, like my parents and Bekka's parents, like Aunt Ruth and Uncle Eric, and waited desperately for help.

"Go to the Jewish Refugee Committee," said the man. "To the Red Cross. To the church. To the prime minister. Knock on the doors of the biggest houses, maybe someone there needs help. But you should speak good English if you do that. You have to make a very good impression; they'll judge your family by what they see of you. You know," he said, suddenly smiling, "I think you might just manage it."

"Thank you for the hot chocolate," I muttered.

"Come by again! I'm Professor Julius Schueler, and you'll always find me at this table at about this time of day."

Back through the streets. It seemed to take all my energy to set one foot in front of the other. Had I been unfair to the old professor? I turned on my heels and ran back. Professor Schueler was just paying and putting on his coat. He smiled when he saw me.

"The addresses," I panted, "of the Red Cross. Of the prime minister. Do you have them?"

"Of course," he said calmly. "We all do."

"Mum says you're working really hard at learning English," Gary said. We sat by my window and searched the dark night sky for the first three stars, which meant the end of Shabbat. "She's very impressed by your progress."

"And you?" I asked sassily.

"Me? I have great hopes! Now we only have to look up every third word. Soon it will be a real pleasure to have a conversation with you!"

"Do you want to know a secret?" I asked. "I wrote to the prime minister this week."

"You wrote . . . you mean Mr. Chamberlain?"

Now he was amazed! "Yes, that's his name," I answered with satisfaction. "He should help me get visas for my parents. But don't tell anyone!"

Gary said, "I have a secret too. And this you really can't tell anyone else, otherwise there'll be a disaster. My parents think I'm going to the university this summer. But I'm not going. I'm taking the entrance exam for the Royal Navy."

I looked at him questioningly. He reached for one of the little model ships on the shelf next to the desk. "If they take me, then I'll be a soldier on a ship. If there's a war, I want to fight Hitler. He should pay for everything he's done to the Jews." His face took on a hard look.

"War?" I repeated, shocked. There it was again, that word that had already been mentioned in Mrs. Collins's office.

"Yes, don't you know? This week the Germans marched into Czechoslovakia. First Austria, then Czechoslovakia, and what will be next? Poland, maybe? Holland? Belgium? Jews live everywhere over there. The world will pull together and help them. Soon they won't have any choice. And then there will be war."

I was speechless. I had never thought of it that way. I had always thought of war as something terrible, frightening, something my father didn't want to talk about even twenty years later. But what Gary said made me see it in an entirely different light. Suddenly I could see the whole world before me, setting itself into motion to help the Jews. Little black troops marched like ants from every direction over a big, round globe like the one that had stood in Papa's office and met in Germany, until there was nothing visible but a united, determined, seething mass that suffocated Hitler beneath it.

And then we could all go back: Professor Schueler, Thomas and me, Walter Glücklich and the Seydenstickers. My father wouldn't have to work as a butler and my mother wouldn't have to be a cook. We would get our apartment back and no one, no one, would have to be afraid of a knocking at the door in the night.

A thought raced through my mind: Why would all these

countries that didn't want to take in Jews who were in desperate need come to our aid?

But just as quickly it occurred to me that if they conquered Hitler, they wouldn't have to take us in. They wouldn't even have to be inconvenienced by all our letters and emigration petitions anymore, because we could just stay in Germany! It was best for everyone that Hitler disappear. Of course they would help us.

And Gary, my brother Gary, would be part of it!

"One, two, three!" he counted, pointing to the stars that all of a sudden blinked from the heavens. "Let's go! Time for the havdalah!"

I already knew that I played a not unimportant role in the havdalah ceremony that marked the end of Shabbat. As the youngest child in the family, I held the candle with a certain pride as the blessing was said over it. And just as the Sabbath had begun with the greeting "Shabbat shalom," I knew the words used to wish each other a good week as it ended: "Shavua tov!" I had the feeling I was going to have a special need for that blessing in the coming week. On Monday, right after the lunch break at school, I wanted to start knocking on doors and asking about positions for my parents.

I was glad when Gary leaned over and whispered something in my ear that immediately distracted me: "There's another secret!"

"What?" I whispered eagerly, stealing a glance at his parents.

Gary placed a finger on his lips and pulled me up the stairs to his room. On the way he pulled a small book from the living room bookshelves. When he opened it, I looked at the countless Hebrew characters, bewildered. "This is a Haggadah, the Pessach ritual," he explained. "Passover is celebrated about the same time of year that you celebrate Easter, because it's the ritual that Jesus conducted the night before his death."

"Jesus?" I repeated. "What does Jesus have to do with a Jewish holiday?"

Now it was Gary's turn to be dumbfounded. "What else should he have celebrated, as a Jewish man?" I was thunderstruck. "Do you mean you don't know that Jesus was Jewish?" Gary asked. "He was a rabbi from Galilea and did a lot of good things. We Jews just don't believe that he's the Messiah we're waiting for."

All I could do was silently shake my head. I couldn't believe it. Jesus, a Jew! Even my religion teacher in Berlin surely didn't know that, otherwise he would have mentioned it at some point! I'd heard often enough that the Jews had killed Jesus, but never that he had been one of them, *of us.* "You mean he did all these things that you do?" I asked excitedly. "And what's this Hagga thing?" I asked eagerly.

"With this Hagga thing you'll learn your part for the Seder. You have exactly two weeks."

"For what?"

He grinned. "For a huge surprise. Your first official solo in Hebrew!"

Chapter 8

A Cinema Surprise

I listened for my letter as it fell through the slot, slid down, and landed in the big red mailbox with a soft thud. It had taken me a whole week to write. The letters to the prime minister, the Refugee Committee, the Red Cross, and the Anglican Church asking for help for my parents practically wrote themselves, but the first letter to Mamu since she told me about the situation with Bekka turned out to be really hard. What I put in the mailbox must have been the seventh or eighth version, and it had so many pages that I had to use double the usual postage. And still, as soon as the envelope disappeared through the letter slot, I had the feeling that I'd made yet another mistake.

The first two pages consisted of a glowing, enthusiastic description of my life in London: how comfortable my room was, that I looked forward to school every morning, got to wear a uniform, and was practically the teacher's right hand; that in England, Jews were not only allowed to go to the movies, but the Shepards actually owned a movie theater called the Elysee, *and* had equipment to set up a portable theater too! I had even thought to slip in a word of English here and there, as if I was already starting to forget German.

But the part that I hoped would get under Mamu's skin the most were the pages about my host mother.

> You asked me to describe Mrs. Shepard. That's impossible! I could write that she has brown hair, green eyes, and a pretty face, but that doesn't mean much, does it? Imagine someone who's just extraordinary, speaks English, Hebrew, and Yiddish, and has an answer for everything because she knows more than 600 laws. I already mentioned that the Shepards are Orthodox, didn't I? [I knew full well I had done no such thing!] And even though Orthodox life is so complicated, Mrs. Shepard always has time for me.
>
> Last week, for example, we were downtown because the things I brought with me from Berlin are getting so worn out already. I was allowed to pick out what I wanted myself, and Mrs. Shepard really enjoyed shopping for me. My English lessons are fun too. We are reading a book together, out loud, so I learn the words and the sound of them. I hope I'll have as pretty a voice as hers someday.
>
> Mrs. Shepard wants to ask if it would be okay with you if she says a Jewish bedtime prayer with me at night. It's a lovely prayer to keep away bad dreams and ugly thoughts, and it really helps! I haven't had any bad dreams for weeks now! I told

*Mrs. Shepard you definitely wouldn't have anything
against the prayer when I wrote you that Jesus
was Jewish! You didn't know that either, right?
Otherwise you would have told me that we actually
belong to Jesus twice, even more than ordinary
Christians.*

*Please say yes! It's so lovely when Mrs. Shepard
sits on my bed, lays her hand on mine, and says the
prayer.*

That was a lie. Mrs. Shepard had never placed her hand
on mine, only on the bedspread once.

My letter ended with the news that Gary was teaching me *the questions,* the ones the youngest child in every
Jewish family asked at the Passover Seder supper. I would
practice every day for the next two weeks so nothing would
go wrong. Gary's grandparents were coming for Pesach,
and they were supposed to be very strict. And now Mrs.
Shepard and I were going to a café together, just like Mamu
and Bekka.

Mrs. Shepard had no idea she was supposed to have
invited me to a café with her. Sunday and Monday were
her nursing home days, and she wouldn't even notice that I
got home from school late because I had been scouring the
neighborhood for work for my parents.

As I stood in front of the mailbox and had already put
my letter in, and it was too late to take it back, it occurred
to me that I hadn't mentioned even a single word about the
petition letters I had written and the door-to-door campaign
I was about to begin for them! And I had completely forgot-

ten Papa. I hadn't even asked how he was doing, not once.
He would be so disappointed in me! And Mamu wouldn't be
jealous, just angry, when she read my letter.

I clenched my teeth as I stepped through the first garden
gate. The house had a large front yard that might offer something for a gardener, and looked more well-to-do than the
houses in Harrington Grove. An impressive car was parked
at the curb. The heavy, melodious sounds of the doorbell
sounded elegant. I was intimidated even before the door
opened.

But the young woman wearing a white kitchen apron
who stood before me looked quite friendly. I took a deep
breath and recited my memorized speech: "Excuse me, need
you a help in the house? My mother is very good cook and
sewer and my father a servant or gardenman or . . ." Thinking
on my feet, I pointed toward the car in front of the house
and improvised, "carman. You can buy them without money,
only for bed and food."

The young woman smiled, shook her head, tapped herself
on the chest, and said something I didn't understand. I was
so confused, I forgot my next lines, and had to pull the paper
from my coat pocket and read from it. "My parents are in
Germany. They are very clean and educationed."

The young woman shook her head again, spoke, and
tapped on her own chest again. Suddenly I understood:
She was the cook in this house! I looked at my paper, said
"Thank you for your time," and ran away as fast as my feet
could carry me.

I didn't stop until I reached the end of the street. I looked back and, despite the rejection, I felt triumph well inside me. Ha! I had actually done it! My first house! That hadn't been so bad. Just two months ago I had pressed myself against walls and hidden in entryways—now I could just go up to a stranger's door and ring the bell! I could hardly wait to go to the next house.

Everything went unexpectedly quickly. I said, "Excuse me," and the door was already shut again. I didn't even have time to find out if a man or a woman had opened it! I decided the next time someone opened a door for me, I would smile at them in a friendly way for a few seconds before I said anything.

I practiced the smile as I walked. Someone smiled back. With this encouragement, I rang the bell at the next house. The door was opened by an older man in slippers, and before I had uttered a single word I was invited in: "Come in, dear! Have a cup of tea!"

This was getting better and better! I was already in the house, and now the people would surely listen to what I had to say! Excited, I looked around me. The living room was small and dark, stuffed full of furniture, books, and at least a dozen cats. There were blankets, pillows, and baskets every-where, and used dishes and cups too. In short: The house was perfect! A housekeeper was desperately needed! The old man busied himself with the teapot.

"My name is Frances," I introduced myself, but only when I held a cup in my hand. "Need you a help in the house?"

The gentleman lowered himself into a wing chair. Cats came from all directions to crawl onto his lap or chest, and I watched as he almost disappeared under purring cat fur, all the while answering my question. He talked, called, and coughed, occasionally waved his arms about, pounded on the arms of his chair, and laughed in a croaking voice.

After about two minutes I started to think about Professor Schueler. "Wait with your visits until you understand more English," he had advised me, and if I had been smart enough to listen to him, I would have at least understood what I had done to launch this man into such a state of excitement!

It was when the old man stood up, went to a cupboard, and pulled out a photo album that I realized he hadn't understood a word of what I was trying to say to him.

"My mother is cook!" I tried once more.

"You hungry?" he yelled, and fell back onto the couch next to me with the album.

"No! My parents look work!"

It was pointless. The poor old man was deaf as a stone. We bent over the photo album together and all the cats came over to join us on the sofa.

Professor Schueler thought that for a beginner, I had done quite well. Although I hadn't managed to get a *domestic permit* for my parents yet, I was gaining a lot of experience in knocking at strangers' doors.

"But since then I've been to so many doors," I protested, "and all of them either have someone or don't want anyone. My mother could have a job as a cleaning lady right away, but only for a few hours a week, and that's not enough to get a visa. I just have to find bigger houses. Really wealthy houses!"

"I don't understand why you don't ask your host family

for help," Professor Schueler remarked. "They're very good to you, aren't they?"

That's just the point, I thought gloomily.

"You say they own a movie theater? That means they come into contact with a lot of people. Surely they could keep their ears open for you."

"It's a pretty small theater," I muttered.

But Professor Schueler, who sat at his usual place at the window and had already ordered me another cup of hot chocolate, just continued to brainstorm all kinds of ways the Shepards could do something for my parents. But I was too timid to ask the Shepards, who were already doing so much for me, to do even more.

The last two days had made it abundantly clear to me that I wouldn't be able to do it. All the houses near my school had already been canvassed. I would have to expand my search, but how could I do that without anyone noticing? So I had gathered all my courage and asked Mrs. Shepard, "Do you have a bicycle?"

"Of course! We have Gary's old bike!" she answered immediately. "Come, let's go right now and look!"

The bicycle stood in the shed, slightly rusted and with flat tires, but otherwise perfect. And when I came home from school the next day, there it was in front of the house waiting for me, cleaned up and repaired and with a new bell. I tried it out under Mrs. Shepard's watchful eyes, riding in a circle, then without hands, then in some wild curves, showing off my skills, and found her all the more worried when I stopped in front of the gate. "You have to promise that you'll ride carefully," she warned. "We've only borrowed you from your parents and we have to be absolutely certain that they get you back in one piece."

Borrowed! What was she trying to say? I had only borrowed a few things myself, but all of them had been things I had been curious about and would have liked to have owned myself. Valuable things. How could anyone want to borrow me?

Borrowed! Congratulations, you've been borrowed! You're valuable!

Even Professor Schueler's warning that I would someday regret not asking my foster parents for more help was drowned out by that tempting word. But I let my daydream go and came back to our conversation.

"By the way, I'm going to the movies tomorrow," I said. "Dr. Shepard shows children's films at a cinema in the East End and I get to go and tear the tickets!"

Professor Schueler went right along with the change of subject and told me about a theater in Munich he had visited often before the Nazis contaminated it with their disgusting propaganda films. The next time we met I would have to tell him everything I experienced, and all about the film too, of course!

While he talked I observed the normal business of the Café Vienna unfolding. This was already my third secret visit, and by now I had noticed that people came for more than just hot chocolate. People came to Café Vienna to exchange the latest news about events in Germany and Austria, and newly arrived refugees came to get practical advice. You could even leave your name and address, in case an acquaintance also came to London.

I wrote my name in the book, my real name—Ziska Mangold, daughter of Franz and Margot Mangold from Berlin-Neukölln. To my disappointment, I didn't find the name Glücklich, even thought it had been Walter who first told me about the Café Vienna.

"There are lovely moments in the life of a refugee too," Professor Schueler remarked as he observed my excitement about the address book. But he looked incredibly sad and wouldn't tell me who he had been thinking of when he had entered his own name more than three years earlier. He was old; maybe there wasn't anyone anymore who belonged to him. Suddenly I felt terribly guilty about my enthusiasm and quickly put the book back in its place.

I tried to hide my excitement about my trip to the cinema too. "I have to tear the tickets, you know." I minimized the upcoming experience. "When it starts, I'm sure I'll only be able to find a seat way in the back and won't be able to see much of the film at all."

It felt strange and somewhat uncomfortable to be alone with Dr. Shepard—the member of my foster family I knew the least so far. All I knew about him was that he had been in France during the war and since then had been a great fan of all things French. In addition to running his cinema, he wrote film reviews for newspapers, and there was even a book on the shelves in the living room that had his name on the cover: *The Early French Movie Theatre*, by Matthew G. Shepard. The film he wanted to show came from America and was called *The Kid*, and in order to show it we had to take along the portable equipment that just barely fit into the car. Dr. Shepard groaned under its weight.

I stood there while he struggled, holding the cash box containing some change and the tickets I was supposed to tear off the roll and hand out to the children. There wouldn't be anyone standing at the entrance to check their tickets, but Dr. Shepard thought children should receive a genuine entrance ticket for the penny they paid. There would also be children there who had no money. I was supposed to send them to him without making a fuss so they could get a penny from him and get in line with the others.

"You're paying for them to go to the movies?" I was shocked.

A mischievous expression flitted across Dr. Shepard's face. "No, why? They give me the money right back." I studied him furtively from the side while we drove. He looked gentle and compassionate, and suddenly I didn't find it strange at all to ride along with him.

We were driving right through London toward the Thames and the harbor area, and the city took on a whole new look. The houses were lower, the streets narrower, there were fewer cars and taxis and buses, but more pedestrians. Cranes and factory smokestacks towered just behind the low roofs and wafted a biting smell in our direction. There were clotheslines hung from many of the houses, from which sad, worn clothing hung.

"The poor district of London," Dr. Shepard said regretfully.

In one street with low buildings that all seemed to house little tailor shops, to my great excitement, I suddenly saw Jewish men with beards and black coats who looked like Herr Seydensticker! Hasidics, Dr. Shepard explained. They spoke only Yiddish and had almost no contact with English people. And their children didn't go to school, but had to work all day in factories or little shops in back courtyards.

The children who were already waiting for us in front of a flat, gray hall with dingy windows looked quite cheerful. Many curious eyes followed me as I carried my cash box through the door behind Dr. Shepard. Once we were inside I recognized that it was a gymnasium, where we still had to set out chairs and put up the screen at the speed of light. My cashier's table was set up directly next to the entrance. Dr. Shepard and two boys lugged the projector inside, set it up, and placed dark cardboard in the windows. The audience was already pressing into the foyer and eagerly held out their pennies toward me. My hands trembled a little at the sheer unbelievability of the situation as I tore off the tickets. I was scared of kids I didn't know—and had little hope that would ever change—and yet here I was sitting at the table selling movie tickets to a crowd of a hundred. I heard them say "Thank you" to me and saw their respectful glances. I wished my parents could be there and see me!

"Hallo, Ziska! With this crowd today it looks like I'll have to save you a seat," someone suddenly said in German, and it took me a few seconds to notice that these words weren't part of my brief daydream of Mamu and Papa. The boy who stood before me in a worn-out coat with a shiny penny in his hand and a wide grin on his face was none other than Walter Glücklich.

Dr. Shepard sat on a stool next to his film projector and waved at me after I had closed the box office. He had probably saved a place for me too, and was dumbfounded when

I waved back and then continued up the center aisle, as if it was the most normal thing in the world, toward the front where an older boy eagerly gestured to the seat next to him.

"Mensch, Ziska, what are you doing here?" Walter gave me an excited little shove in the side.

The light went out, a quiet murmur swept through the rows, and a crackling came from the loudspeakers. "Dr. Shepard is my foster father," I whispered to Walter. "The Winterbottoms didn't come to get me. Maybe I should write them a letter thanking them for it!"

"Definitely! To luck into a cinema, unbelievable!" Walter agreed.

"And you?" I asked. Loud music began and names scrolled across the movie screen.

"Not so fun, unfortunately," he replied. "I work in the same tailor shop as my father, twelve hours a day. I dream about zippers! I'll never learn English at this rate."

"Hey, you two!" A boy sitting behind us tapped me on the shoulder. "Could you stop putting your heads together? I can't see anything!"

Walter and I jumped apart, and my cheeks got hot. Putting our heads together! What an idiot! If I had known the right words, I would have rained them down on his dumb head!

And of course, that was the moment when all the hundreds of things occurred to me that I would have loved to ask Walter: whether he believed there would be war against Hitler, what he thought of England. It was odd to be friends with someone you didn't really know at all yet. But even in the dark and without talking, it was lovely to sit next to him.

"Well, how was the film?" Dr. Shepard asked an hour and a half later, while the other children streamed out of the gym talking and laughing. He placed the film rolls back in their silver cases and glanced at Walter, who stood behind me, with curiosity. Dr. Shepard smiled at me as he took in my amazed look, and it was a few moments before I recovered enough to say, "Dr. Shepard, this is Walter Glücklich. He was on my kindertransport."

Walter and Dr. Shepard shook hands. "You must visit us sometime, Walter!" Dr. Shepard said in a friendly tone. He pronounced the name the English way, like "Wolter." "Any friends of Frances's are always welcome!"

Walter looked a little confused. Either he understood English much worse than I did, or he was wondering who Frances might be. "Well, I guess I'll be going . . ." Walter said awkwardly in German.

"Wait!" I held him tight by the sleeve. Something like panic was rising in me. We had only just found each other again, and that was it already? "Give me your address! How can I invite you if I don't know where you live?"

Dr. Shepard gave me a pencil and one of the papers announcing the next movie showing. But Walter hesitated to write down his address for me. "Where do you live, anyway? I'm sure it's too far away for me. Why don't we just say we'll see each other in two weeks at the next movie?"

"In two weeks? And what if something happens in the meantime? No, I have to have your address! You haven't even left it at the Café Vienna."

"At the Café Vienna?" Walter suddenly had to grin. "Don't tell me you actually went there?"

"I'm a regular," I answered with a quick glance at Dr. Shepard, but since he didn't understand any German, my little secret wasn't in danger of being revealed.

Walter thought for a moment, then laughed and wrote his address on the back of the cinema flyer. But when Dr. Shepard offered to take him with us and drop him off at home, he politely refused, even though it had started raining hard outside.

"I suppose I don't have to ask you if you'll come with me the next time," Dr. Shepard said in the car with a wink.

But I wasn't in the mood to talk anymore. I sensed what Walter had really wanted to say to me: That even if I didn't care that he lived in London's poorhouse, it bothered him, and I could understand that too.

We drove through the darkness and suddenly it was as if Walter was sitting behind us on the backseat observing us as we left behind the East End with its filth and the stink of factories, how the streets became brighter and livelier, and as we arrived at clean, orderly Harrington Grove, where in this weather everyone sat contentedly in their living rooms, ate supper, and listened to the radio. It was as if he watched us step into the warm, comfortable house, where it already smelled like the pancakes we were having for dinner.

Dr. Shepard greeted his wife with the words: "Amanda, just imagine, Frances met a friend from the kindertransport. A nice young man named Walter Glücklich!"

Mrs. Shepard's face lit up in a spontaneous smile so warm and beautiful that it hurt to look at her. "Walter Glücklich . . . ?" she repeated, enchanted. "That is the loveliest name I've ever heard!"

Tears welled in my eyes, and I ran up the stairs to my room and threw myself on the bed. How I wished that I didn't have pancakes to eat, a soft bed to sleep in, and nice foster parents. I wished, with all the misery out there, the struggles of Mamu and Papa, of Bekka, and Walter, who sewed zippers all day long and still wore a tattered coat, that I at least had the decency to be poor too.

After a while there was a knock at my door and Mrs. Shepard came in. I had expected her to come see me; she wasn't the kind to let someone go to bed without supper and be sad for reasons she hadn't yet uncovered. There was even a little pamphlet in Mrs. Shepard's secretary with the title: *How Do I Take Care of a Refugee Child?*

Mrs. Shepard placed a plate with two pancakes on my knees and a cup of milk on the nightstand. I reacted by pushing away the plate and grumbling, "I haven't washed my hands." With greatly exaggerated gestures I pantomimed the motions of the Shepards' ritual, tipping a pitcher of water over the lower arms. Instinctively I held my breath, because my gestures came across as more insulting than I had intended. But Mrs. Shepard's refugee pamphlet must have included a bit about unjustified attacks too, and she stayed totally calm.

"It doesn't matter," she said, and put the plate back on my knees. "You walked through the rain, and that counts too."

"I don't have to wash my hands anyway," I responded, tearing off a big piece of pancake and stuffing it in my mouth. "I'm not even properly Jewish!"

"You're right, I had almost forgotten," replied Mrs. Shepard. "Would you like to invite someone to Passover anyway? Pesach is a holiday that no one can celebrate alone."

"I can invite Walter, but he definitely won't come," I said haughtily, and without any explanation of what I meant by it.

Mrs. Shepard apparently wasn't as interested in Walter as I thought, because she just asked, "And you don't know anyone else? Someone who might be alone otherwise?"

My food suddenly stuck in my throat. I did indeed know someone who was all alone, but unfortunately it was someone that no one could find out about. "I don't know anyone else here who's Jewish," I replied, thinking to myself, *I'm sorry, Professor Schueler . . .*

"They don't have to be Jewish."

Mrs. Shepard just wouldn't give up. Other than Mamu, I didn't know anyone who was so persistent.

"The others aren't interested in Passover," I said with disdain.

Mrs. Shepard raised one eyebrow. "Now listen. You can't mean to say that you don't find us entertaining!"

And without any warning, a grin began to spread from within to my face, and I had to fight hard to keep the corners of my mouth from turning upward. "I do! Especially all the fuss at the table and the macken in the kitchen, or how the men in the synagogue all sway at different speeds."

"Go ahead," said Mrs. Shepard. "Let me have it. Although I should point out that you just used the word *macken*, a revealing and very Yiddish word."

"I just want to make sure you understand what I mean."

"Do you now! That's not as hard as you might think."

"Not if you read the right pamphlets. *How Do I Take Care of a Refugee Child?*. . . . What's written in there?" I asked suspiciously.

"Among other things, it says that you need contact with other children," Mrs. Shepard said, taking my empty plate. "We would be very happy if your friend 'Wolter' came to visit. It isn't good for you to only be with the younger children in school."

"Walter won't come. It's too far."

"Then we'll have him picked up. There's always a way."

"He won't come because he's poor," I said glumly.

"You mean because he's proud," Mrs. Shepard corrected me.

I sighed. "All right then, I'll invite him," I replied. "Let him decide for himself what he is."

But of course I was right. Walter didn't come, even though we extended the invitation to include his father. He didn't even answer my short, awkward letter. Instead, I received a letter from Mamu in the days before Passover. Her letter didn't make a single reference to the carefully formulated little warning I had sent her the last time.

"Apparently you haven't had a chance to do anything for us yet," she wrote. "But Papa felt much better when he could read how much fun you're having in England."

Chapter 9

Pesach

The little tube in the doorway to my room looked harmless enough, but I still waited until I was the only one upstairs. What was the big deal? I boldly stretched out my hand and just for a split second tapped the mezuzah. Then I raced triumphantly downstairs, plunked myself down in my usual spot at the table with a loud "Good morning," downed a glass of orange juice in one gulp, and took a deep breath.

Millie and Mrs. Shepard looked at me with surprise. They had no idea what had just happened! I briefly thought about telling them, but I would have had to explain too much that I barely understood myself. So I concentrated on eating my breakfast as fast as possible so that I could watch the sale of our food before school.

The night before, I was convinced the whole thing was a joke, but one look around the kitchen made it clear that I had understood correctly. A basket with bread, cake, and a box of flour stood on the sideboard. As soon as I finished eating, Millie would buy all of these things from the Shepards, along with the rest of my breakfast, so she could take them home with her and keep them for a week. Then the Shepards would buy back their own food for the same price. When I came home from school at midday, there wouldn't be a single crumb of anything leavened in the house anymore.

We had made sure of that the night before. Armed with candles, Mrs. Shepard sent me and her husband off in search of anything leavened, which she had hidden around the house just for us to find. There were exactly ten little pieces of bread, and after we finally found all of them, Mrs. Shepard put them in a paper bag to be burned later. I giggled the whole time, but Dr. Shepard took it very seriously. "This is a test, I have no idea what there is to laugh about," he said. "If we miss even one piece, we might have bad luck . . . or worse, my mother could find it!"

He said that with a quick, wry smile, and for a moment I thought I saw a shadow pass over Mrs. Shepard's face. But I must have been mistaken, because she answered lightly, "I'm sorry, I can't remember where I hid that tenth piece! You'll just have to keep looking until you find it, Matthew."

Then Dr. Shepard said a prayer and we swore to banish everything leavened or fermented from our thoughts for the next seven days. That was the end of my giggling for a while, because I knew that this vow was about more than just food! For me, it meant my negative thoughts, my secret grudges against Mamu, and the unanswered questions between Jesus, my parents, and me about how Jewish I wanted to be. And so I woke up that morning knowing that I had until noon, when everything leavened had to be out of the house, to make my peace with the mezuzah.

I had been so scared of it, but it seemed as if someone was whispering the answers to all my questions.

You don't have to kiss it, you can just touch it, and then you'll remember every time that you all belong to the same God, Jews and Christians, and that he's there.

There was a sudden brightness in me, a light and floating sensation, as if I was happy to be me. I was convinced other people must be able to see a change in me, but Mrs. Shepard and Millie were so busy with their preparations, they didn't even notice!

"Now, Millie," said Mrs. Shepard. "Shall we say two shillings, like last year?"

When I came home from school that day, a fat envelope lay next to the telephone, and Mrs. Shepard and Millie shot out of the kitchen as if they had been awaiting my arrival for hours. "Frances! You have mail from the prime minister!"

They stood so close that I felt like I was completely surrounded. "I know," I said as indifferently as possible, but secretly I was weighing the letter in my hands and trying to figure out what its heft revealed about its contents.

The responses I had received from the Refugee Committee and the church had been very friendly.

Dear Franziska,

We are so pleased for you that you were given a place on a kindertransport and are allowed to live with a British family. We understand that you

> *miss your parents very much, and you are surely*
> *aware that the Refugee Committee/the Protestant*
> *Church is already making great efforts to relieve*
> *the situation of the Jews still living in Germany.*
> *Obtaining visas and permits for individual persons*
> *is unfortunately not in our power, but perhaps there*
> *are possibilities in your current situation. Have you*
> *heard of a domestic permit? That allows women and*
> *men to enter into private service agreements that do*
> *not burden the British labor market, for example*
> *a position as a married couple with cooking and*
> *housework for the wife and a role as gardener and*
> *butler for the husband . . .*

And so on. Nothing that I didn't already know. But the prime minister's letter was so thick and so heavy that my heart began to pound painfully. The envelope felt just like the one Mamu had used for all our papers for Shanghai. Maybe it had identification cards inside!

Just holding the envelope in my hand released such a storm of hope that it made me dizzy, like coming into contact with something holy. I ripped open the envelope with a trembling hand.

But it was only a single, heavy sheet of paper.

> *Dear Frances,*
>
> *The prime minister was deeply moved to learn of*
> *your family's concerns. He would like you to know*
> *that he is so pleased that you were given a place on*
> *a kindertransport and are now living with a British*

family. He understands that you are homesick for
your parents, but unfortunately it is not possible for
him to arrange visas for individual persons . . .

The sheet slipped through my fingers, and Mrs. Shepard caught it before it fell to the floor. She glanced at me questioningly and started to read. When she finally raised her eyes and looked at me with concern, I said, "I knew it wouldn't work anyway," took the letter from her hand, and threw it into the wastebasket. Then I went into the kitchen as if nothing special had happened, and as I turned the corner into the kitchen took a quick glance at Millie, who retrieved the letter from the trash and smoothed it out with both hands, almost worshipfully.

Mrs. Shepard followed me. *Go ahead and ask,* I thought, and sat down.

The loudest silence I had ever heard filled the kitchen. Mrs. Shepard went to the counter and mixed matzoh and water, kneaded it into a dough, rolled it out thin, and pricked it with a fork.

Now that Mrs. Shepard had read much more than I had, I wanted to look at the letter again. Why had the prime minister written that I was *homesick,* when I hadn't even used that word? Now Mrs. Shepard must think I was unhappy with them!

After a few minutes I couldn't stand it anymore. "Can I help?" I asked in a shaky voice.

"No, I'm just going to put this in the oven." Mrs. Shepard reached for her baking sheet.

But I was faster. Hastily I jumped to the oven, opened the

door, lit a match, and turned the gas knob like I had seen her do dozens of times. "Leave that alone, Frances," were her last words before there was a hiss and a boom. Shocked, I let go of the gas knob, it spit out the flame, and as I fell backward I saw a little fireball shooting toward Mrs. Shepard.

I swear my heart stood still. She threw the baking sheet aside and turned her head, but it was too late. The flame went right to her hair and instantly she was on fire. What happened next I will never forget as long as I live. Mrs. Shepard reached up to her head, pulled her hair off, threw it to the ground, and trampled on it!

I started to wail, a high, piercing sound that I never knew I could make. I crawled out of the kitchen on my hands and knees screaming, ran up the stairs, and jumped into the cupboard in my room, all without taking a single breath. I sat there with my teeth chattering as the entire cupboard shook with me.

Not a minute later there was a hammering on the door of the cupboard. "Frances? Can I come in?"

The cupboard door opened. I buried my face in both arms. I didn't dare imagine what she looked like now, burned and disfigured, and it was my fault! I could hear her kneel down in front of the cupboard . . .

"Frances, nothing happened!"

I had so loved to look at her. Her thoughtful smile, the sunshine around her eyes. She could make her eyes laugh without moving her mouth, as if she were lit up inside. She would never look like that again.

"Frances, dear, open your eyes. Please!"

Well. The least I could do was look at what I had done!

After what seemed like an eternity I opened one eye first, then the second. In front of me on the floor sat an even more beautiful Mrs. Shepard. Her hair was short and dark, her face younger, and her eyes bigger and more glowing than I had ever seen them.

It's a dream, flashed through my mind. Mrs. Shepard had emerged from the fire so unbelievably beautiful that there could be only one explanation: The whole thing was my fantasy image of her, which my subconscious made me see to protect me from the reality.

"Sweetie, I thought you knew that I wear a wig."

"A wig?" I mouthed, without making a sound.

She nodded. "A sheitel, a wig for married Jewish women. You poor thing, this on top of everything else. By now you must think we're complete aliens."

The lump in my throat rode into the open on a wave of tears. I myself fell forward into Mrs. Shepard's arms—exactly where I had been trying *not* to fall since I had first seen her kneeling there unscathed. At the last second I tried thinking of the train station in Berlin, but it was useless; it was as if I hadn't learned anything from that experience. There I was, not three months later, hugging the wrong mother again!

But the worst thing about it was that it didn't feel wrong at all. It was just as soft, warm, and comforting as I had feared, and at the same time strangely familiar, like something I had imagined so often that I recognized it.

Mrs. Shepard, who smelled a bit singed, held me so lightly in her arms that I could have slipped away at any moment: slipped away to race to my desk and write a long letter to Mamu. All the things I had wanted to say to her the whole

time but couldn't put into words came together into clear
sentences in those few seconds: *I love you, Mamu, you are
the one and only, if I had only one wish in the whole world it
would be to have you with me . . . I'm not having fun, Mamu, I
have the wrong name and the wrong life, and why does everything take so long?*

But I stayed and allowed what I had feared the most to
happen: Someone made their way between me and Mamu,
someone who was happier and more generous, whose love
would mean joy, rather than pain.

"There's been a little accident," Mrs. Shepard explained when
Gary came home. She sat at the vanity table and worked on
an old, long-haired wig with a brush and scissors. I was disappointed that she didn't just leave her much prettier natural
hair, but she told me that wouldn't be appropriate.

Gary stared at the scraggly old wig with distaste. "I thought
I might be able to cut it off," his mother said halfheartedly.

Only then did I see how exhausted she was. For her and
Millie, the past several days had been filled with cleaning,
cooking, and baking. There were potato dumplings, cheese
dumplings, marrow dumplings, matzoh dumplings and little
liver balls, various soups, chicken, a roast with a delicious
filling, a cake made with matzoh flour, and all the ingredients
for the Seder supper. The stove and oven had been heated to
a very high temperature to make sure that not the slightest
bit of food was left, and the Pesach dishes and silverware,
which were used only for this occasion, had been cleaned
according to Kosher laws.

Even the dining room gleamed: the best tablecloth, the

best dishes, twenty-five wine glasses, four for each guest and one for the prophet Elijah. Everything was perfect, except for the *little incident*.

"I give up," Mrs. Shepard said, scornfully snatching the wig from its stand and throwing it to me. "I'll wear a hat. Here, Frances, you can wear this for a costume at Purim." To my dismay, I saw tears in her eyes. "Come here. I'm afraid you won't escape either," she added, and hesitantly reached out her hand toward me.

She carefully took my little cross pendant and stuck it through the space between the two top buttons of my blouse, so that only the chain was visible. "It would be better to wear that out of sight. Gary's grandparents are very strict, you know."

"I can't take it off. It's from my mother," I murmured, staring at her hand.

She said, "You don't need to take it off. But they don't need to see it right away."

"I have that blouse with a high collar," I suggested. "I'll wear that, then you won't see anything, not even the chain."

"Good idea," my foster mother agreed with a forced, narrow-lipped smile that I didn't quite understand.

I had already figured out that Gary's grandparents only came to visit once a year, for Pesach, even though they lived in Sussex, which wasn't far away. When they visited the Shepards, they didn't stay at their house, but in a hotel.

As we waited for them to arrive, there was a strange tension in the air; I looked into the spotless dining room and noticed that I was getting more nervous every minute.

How could I possibly sing the part Gary had taught me and take on such an important role when I wasn't even really Jewish? Something would go wrong, something had to go wrong, even if I wore five shirts at once to hide my cross! Suddenly I was hot. I pulled on Gary's sleeve. "I can't do it," I whispered.

But he didn't hear me anymore, because right then a car pulled up outside and he called, "They're here!" At that cue all the Shepards tried out variations of a welcoming smile, giving the impression that the king was paying them a visit, or the prime minister.

As the guests approached, I recognized with amazement that Dr. Shepard's parents must be very wealthy. They didn't just enter a house, they made an *entrance,* and the kiss Dr. Shepard exchanged with his mother was so respectful that they didn't even touch each other. Mrs. Shepard senior— Julia—was a birdlike, delicate lady with perfectly styled hair (I couldn't tell if it was real or not) and, despite her age, almost perfectly smooth skin so thoroughly powdered that we could smell it. Her husband, Marcus Shepard, wore an impressive, full white beard. He growled, "Good evening, son!" and that was the last we heard from him for the next several hours.

We had all dressed up for the occasion. Gary wore a blue suit and Dr. Shepard a black one, both with a tie and matching kippah; Mrs. Shepard wore a dark red dress and pearl earrings. Her hat looked very elegant, as if she had never intended to wear anything else that evening, and as for me, all I could think about was that one of my knee socks had slipped down. Dr. Shepard took coats and hats from both his parents and Julia Shepard repeated the genteel air kiss with her grandson, who politely said "Grandmother!" as she did.

I slid a little behind Mrs. Shepard so that I could pull up my sock unnoticed. She stretched a hand out and said, "Good evening, Mother," and what happened next was so fast that I needed a moment to be sure I had really seen right.

With a quick, almost dancing motion, Julia Shepard turned to her son and took the heavy coats he had draped over his arm from him; it looked like she might disappear beneath them. In a sweet voice she said, "Amanda," and with a force that one wouldn't think possible of such a fragile person, she threw her load over her daughter-in-law's arm, still outstretched in greeting.

There was no time to be stunned. In the same movement, Julia Shepard turned to me and I was met with a look so contemptuous and hateful that my arms and legs turned to stone on the spot.

I remembered that look well. It was the look of my teachers and the other students in Berlin, the look of the men who had broken into our apartment and taken my father away. I had never, ever thought I would be confronted with that look again in England—and on the face of a Jewish woman! A woman who leaned toward me and said in a soft voice, "And this is your little refugee? I am pleased to meet you, my child. What is your name?"

She gave me a cool, bony hand, and as I watched the friendliness return to her eyes, I realized that the look hadn't been intended for me, but that I had just been in the line of fire.

She doesn't mean me! The relief was so great that I wasn't able to say my name; I didn't know it. Ziska? Francesca? But at least my knees knew what to do; they executed a perfect curtsy. "Hello," I whispered gratefully. The look wasn't for me. In that moment nothing else mattered.

Mrs. Shepard silently hung up the two coats and went to the kitchen to get the welcome drink she wanted to offer before we went to the synagogue. And suddenly I caught myself wishing she wouldn't come back, that for her sake and ours she would just stay there.

I didn't want to have anything more to do with that look.

Two weeks ago, when Gary had given me the Haggadah, it had been clear to me that Pesach would be a more complicated affair than Shabbat. I already knew some things: the kiddush blessing over the wine in a special little silver cup, the hand washing, the prayers over the parts of the meal. But this time there were really strange things. There was an egg as a symbol of life, a lamb bone representing the sacrificed animal, and parsley that was dipped in a bowl of salt water and eaten to remind us of the tears shed by the people of Israel. Three pieces of matzoh, thin flatbread made from unleavened flour, lay under a cloth. Dr. Shepard uncovered them, broke the middle piece in two, and set one half aside. *"See, children, this is the bread of affliction that our fathers ate in the land of Egypt . . ."*

I looked nervously in my Haggadah to see when it would be my turn. Why had I let myself be talked into this? How was I supposed to utter even a single word with the strict older Shepards right in front of me? What if they noticed that something wasn't right about me too? In the synagogue, I had sat between Mrs. Shepard and her mother-in-law like I was frozen, hardly daring to move.

Gary sat next to me that evening, his parents at the short ends of the table. But Mrs. Shepard blended into the background and I didn't dare look over at her.

"And now, Gary?" Dr. Shepard asked encouragingly.

But Gary made an amused face. "I'm not the youngest one at the table, Dad, have you forgotten?"

Then everyone looked at me and it was just as I had feared: The words, which I had been able to recite in my sleep for days, escaped me entirely! It grew quiet and everyone was waiting. I opened my mouth and nothing happened.

But then a hand rested on mine and Gary started to sing! I joined in, held tight to his hand, and didn't even notice that he stopped singing after a few words. My voice grew stronger as I sang alone; the song drove the older Shepards from my mind, and I thought about my parents, about Bekka, about Ruben.

What makes this night different from all the other nights? Why is it that on all other nights we eat leavened bread or matzoh, but on this night we eat only matzoh? Why is it that on all other nights we eat all kinds of herbs, but on this night we eat only bitter herbs? Why . . .

When I finished, the room remained so quiet that you could have heard a pin fall. I leaned back, suddenly exhausted.

"Wow," Gary said later. "That was eerie. What happened?"

How could I have explained it to him? I had thought of some of my favorite people and entrusted them to Jesus and his Father.

*Wasn't this the Passover feast, the meal celebrating the res-
cue of the people of Israel? Aren't the people of Israel God's
people? Aren't they in trouble again?*

And for one inconceivable, unforgettable second, I felt
that my prayer had been heard.

Dr. Shepard told the story of the departure of the Isra-
elites from the land of exile, and we sang and ate matzoh,
radish, and a sweet mixture of apples and nuts. After all that,
the actual meal began. Mrs. Shepard and Gary carried the
food in from the kitchen.

Gary's grandmother turned to me. "If you're from Berlin,
you must find it exceptionally dull here."

And the way she said it! Her look was condescending and
conspiratorial at the same time, as if I knew exactly what she
meant! I didn't dare contradict her, but *not agreeing* with her
was something else—I hoped. So I swallowed the "No" and
answered, "Actually, I think it's very nice here."

"Nice? Aha . . ." Her tone became overly sweet and made
me think of Kaa, the snake in *The Jungle Book.* "And what
exactly do you find *nice,* my child?"

"The family," I replied awkwardly. "I learn English," I
added more confidently, "and many more things. It is nice to
be in an Orthodox family."

I added that last bit to make her happy, because Mrs.
Shepard and Gary had joined us again and I felt responsible
for keeping the grandmother in a good mood.

But Julia Shepard smiled coolly. "You are not with an
Orthodox family," she said.

That left me completely speechless. Gary's grandmother
lost all interest in me on the spot, turned away, and criti-

cally examined the chicken soup that Dr. Shepard ladled into the bowls. Neither he nor Gary commented on that last remark, and Mrs. Shepard, who was still making herself invisible, certainly didn't. I must have misunderstood again.

Hours later, when the older Shepards got into their car, Dr. Shepard took his wife by the hand to take a little walk. Gary and I stayed behind by ourselves. I finally felt like I could take a deep breath.

"Well?" Gary asked after a brief silence. "What do you think?"

"Well . . ." I said. While I was still pondering whether I could honestly tell Gary that I thought his grandmother was the second-most evil woman I had ever met (right after our old neighbor Frau Bergmann), he had already interpreted my "well" correctly and replied, "Once a year it's tolerable."

"I hope your other grandparents are nicer," I muttered.

"The O'Learys?" He gave me a sad sideways glance. "I don't even know them. They don't want to have anything to do with us."

There was no way around it. I thought about what he had just said, turned the sentences this way and that, but there was nothing good to be found. This time, I knew I had understood correctly.

"There's something about my mum that you should know," Gary said.

When he was little, his mother sat down with him and together they wrote two letters. One of them, to the O'Learys in Dublin, came back unopened. The other one resulted in a visit from his Shepard grandparents, who reluctantly decided to get acquainted with their only grandchild. At that point, Gary didn't yet know that in their eyes, he had no right to be alive.

The annual visit was established. Gary and his parents were never invited to Sussex, to the big house on the ocean his father told him about. But still, he felt that he must mean something to them, and that they wanted to love him, but didn't know how.

"At least they keep coming, even though it's hard for them," he said bitterly. "The others don't even give us a chance."

The O'Learys had thoroughly planned their oldest daughter's life. Amanda was allowed to attend school until she was sixteen, then go to London for a year to serve the war effort as a telecommunications assistant, and when she got back she would be introduced to suitable young men. The O'Learys didn't have anything against Jews. They had never thought about Jews; after all, they didn't know any. But when Amanda returned from London and introduced Matthew Shepard to them, they must have instinctively sensed that something was terribly wrong. After a single evening, which had been very pleasant and friendly, they made it clear to their daughter that she would under no circumstances be allowed to see this young man again.

And even when they noticed they were being disobeyed, they hadn't immediately lost their cool. They trusted that their daughter would come to her senses on her own and choose someone from her own cultural background. A Protestant would have been a big enough catastrophe, but a Jew! Insecure, the O'Learys turned to their priest, who recommended more drastic measures. Amanda was shut up in her room.

"Mum jumped from the second-story bathroom window," Gary explained. "She didn't notice until the next day that she had broken her foot, but by then she was already in London. Dad had arranged for her to stay with friends, because his rabbi didn't want to help them."

"Are you meshugeh?" the rabbi had ranted. "I should hide a goy?" a derogatory word for non-Jews that I had never heard before.

"She will convert to Judaism," came the answer.

"But not under my roof! A Catholic cannot become Jewish. Never. She will never be anything but a converted goy . . ."

They found another rabbi who taught Amanda, and a year and a half after she had fled from her home, she formally converted to Judaism. Then they had a wedding according to the Jewish rituals, under a chuppah, including stomping on a glass, dancing and singing, but without even a single relative. The newlyweds moved to Camden, into a large apartment, because they wanted to have lots of children, and lived strictly according to the kashrut, Jewish dietary laws, and the halakhah, the entire body of rituals.

It took two years until a doctor suspected that the halakhah itself might be the reason why the children the Shepards so longed for weren't forthcoming. "As long as a woman bleeds plus seven days," Gary explained awkwardly, "a man can't touch his wife. That's usually two weeks, but sometimes longer, and then the fertile days can already be over."

I leafed furiously through my dictionary. Gary turned red.

"I'll just say that my parents broke a law in order to have me. They were almost banished from the congregation. Today only a few people know about it, but still, I always have the feeling that they're looking at me strangely because I should never have been born. And in their opinion, I'm not even Jewish, because for them, only people whose mothers are Jewish are true Jews."

"I didn't know you could *convert* to Judaism," I said, amazed. "Before I came here I didn't even know there were people who are happy to be Jewish!"

"What do you think?" he replied. "Is my mother Jewish? Am I?"

He looked at me with a smile and I could tell how anxiously he awaited my answer.

"I think so," I said thoughtfully. "Anyway, I've only wanted to be Jewish since I met you. You're contagious, you and your mother, and no one can pass something on to others that they don't have themselves. Of course you're Jewish," I said triumphantly. "I'm the proof!"

I surprised myself as I heard what I said, and even before I had finished I knew that for once I had said exactly the right thing. So I wasn't entirely unprepared when Gary leaned forward and gave me a kiss, my first *real* kiss; just on the cheek, but still, my first sweet, respectful kiss from a young man! It felt like I must be fourteen, at least.

I went to bed sure that I was in love with Gary, and certain that I had all the answers. And confused that there were people who gave up everything and broke off contact with their families, taking on hate and scorn, only to become what I had never wanted to be.

While the Seder meal consisted of very simple foods, the actual day of Pesach was celebrated with a feast. I had never eaten anything more delicious than Mrs. Shepard's roast, but of course her parents-in-law didn't say a single word about it. I sank my eyes, ashamed. In my excitement following the conversation with Gary, I had completely forgotten that I let her be made invisible, and avoided her for the entire evening. Me, who knew all too well how painful that was!

I thought about the time at school when the other children started to treat us differently. There were some who stood apart when Ruben, Bekka, or I were abused, who didn't attack, but whose faces clearly showed that they didn't approve. Had they been on our side? They hadn't had the courage to help us, and it didn't take long before they just kept their distance so they didn't have to see what was happening in the first place.

I had despised those children. And last night I had done exactly the same thing. I had looked away. With burning eyes I looked up at Mrs. Shepard, so long that she got nervous and it was hard for her to pretend that she didn't notice me looking at her.

I'll make it up to you!

No one said anything during the meal. How could I come to her aid if nothing happened? As the main course was coming to an end, it became clear that there wouldn't be any further harsh words, only an icy, silent meal, then the grandparents would drive away. I could have helped the night before, with a glance or a smile. I wouldn't get a second chance.

It was my darkest hour in that house. With every bite from my plate, I thought of more good things I had experienced with Mrs. Shepard, and how I had betrayed her with my cowardice. By the time dessert was brought in, I was so desperate that I wanted to smash my little glass bowl against the wall. Dr. Shepard lifted the bowl with the dessert and said the blessing. *Dear God, forget the stupid dessert and help me instead!* I pleaded quietly.

And then it came to me!

"Excuse me," I murmured. My knees felt like jelly when I stood up. I dashed to the foyer, to the wardrobe mirror. My fingers trembled. I could have done it at the table, but I wanted to see it, I wanted to see myself, before and after. I must have looked at myself in the mirror for a full minute before I returned to the dining room.

Julia Shepard uttered a little gasp of dismay even before I sat down across from her. By the time the others looked up from their food, she had already grasped everything. There it was again, that look, with all that belonged to it, that I had hated and feared for years.

And I felt—nothing. No rage, no fear, I just stared back at her and noticed that the look couldn't affect me anymore. Because that was ME.

"What is that?" Julia Shepard asked hoarsely.

"That is a cross, Mother," Dr. Shepard answered quietly. "The Nazis persecute assimilated Jews too, didn't you know?"

"You took in a Christian?" she hissed. "From all the thousands of Jewish refugee children that are coming into our country, you chose a Christian?" She turned to face her daughter-in-law in rage. "Surely we have *you* to thank for this!"

"Mum wasn't even with us," Gary protested.

Mrs. Shepard sat up straight to utter her first words in this round and declared firmly, "If I *had* been there, I would have chosen her." And even though I remembered perfectly well that it had been very different between us at the beginning, I knew she wasn't lying, but confirming something I had long since known: Now that we had gotten to know each other, she would *borrow* me again anytime.

Gary's grandparents looked at each other silently.

"Marcus," his grandmother said, putting down her napkin, "I believe we're leaving."

The two elderly people stood up. I could see how Julia Shepard was trembling, and at that moment I almost felt sorry for her. Dr. Shepard and Gary accompanied them to the door.

"Don't feel too sorry for her," Mrs. Shepard said to me. "A little setback won't hurt them. They've made our lives very difficult."

"I saw that," I answered sheepishly. "I'm sorry about last night."

"It's all right. I should have told you the truth right from the start. Are you very lonely with us?"

"Oh, not anymore. I was just a little . . ."

"Confused?" She laughed quietly, bent over the table, and I thought she wanted to take my hand, but instead she only ran her finger very lightly over it. "Believe me, it was just the same for me at the beginning. But you learned so fast, much faster than me!"

Dr. Shepard and Gary came back and sat down. Several seconds passed. Then Gary gave me a satisfied little kick under the table and Dr. Shepard raised his glass. "Blessed are You, Lord our God, King of the universe, who has granted us life, sustained us, and brought us to this moment . . ."

It was the Shehecheyanu, the blessing for everything new that he had prayed on the day of my arrival. Back then it had been nothing more than a gesture, but now I really felt it.

I had arrived. I was no longer Ziska. From now on I was Frances, and would never want to be anyone else again.

Book Two

Blackout

1939–1940

Chapter 10

News

When I lay on my back next to the lilac bush and gazed up through the twigs and blossoms at the blue-gray spring sky, I didn't have the energy to get up again. I thought I might just close my eyes and let my fingers grow ever so slowly into the earth. The ground under the bush was still hard from the winter cold, and I'd have to scratch and dig a little, but not too fast! Plants wilted if they weren't given enough time to take root, Amanda said; she kept a sort of logbook for her garden, so she must know what she was talking about. She carefully recorded which plants would grow together, where in the garden they did best, and how much space and time they needed to get strong enough to flower.

She made sure I understood that the winter rest was vitally important. By now I was convinced that my exhaustion was because I'd had no time to rest this year. My departure from Germany, Satterthwaite Hall, moving in with the Shepards, my new school, the new language, Café Vienna, my secret door-to-door solicitations, not to mention the Jewish questions, had all been crammed into just three months. And as the pages of Amanda's logbook would testify, roots that shoot out in every direction at once don't hold.

Fortunately, all was not lost. There are also late bloomers, plants that take their time in spring. I was quite confident that I would get back to normal if I didn't do anything for a while. Nothing tiring, at least: no secrets, no door-to-door visits, nothing that had the slightest connection to Germany. I would start again soon, I would help my parents any way I could—but at the moment I just wasn't able to stay away from home any longer than absolutely necessary for school and my twice-weekly Hebrew lessons.

After school I pedaled home as fast as I could, and even before I turned the corner into Harrington Grove I felt joy—a joy that grew and filled me with warmth as I neared our little house. I'd throw my schoolbag next to the stairs and find Amanda and Millie in the kitchen, preparing afternoon tea or supper (depending on what time I arrived) ready with a welcome kiss and the inevitable question, "How was school?"

We took tea right in the kitchen, with plenty of sugar in mine, and Amanda's shoulder so close that I could lean on it and moan that I had had a difficult day. I still needed this excuse—I wasn't used to spontaneous displays of affection. Apart from the miserable weeks at Aunt Ruth's, Mamu and I had never cuddled, and I was quite certain that we wouldn't suddenly start when we were together again.

I really couldn't say why it was different with Amanda. Maybe it was because she had wanted many children, but had only been able to have one, and all that unused love stirred a need I never knew I had. That the affection was mutual was even more confusing. The way things looked, she was going to have to take the place of not only Mamu, but also Bekka until further notice. She was able to occupy several empty spaces in my life at the same time: mother, aunt, sister, friend.

The week before we had had an extensive talk about Walter. I told Amanda that Walter meant a lot to me, but of course I was in love with Gary. Suddenly, to my horror, I remembered that I was talking to Gary's mother. But she simply replied that she considered herself lucky never to have had feelings for two men at the same time, but she could imagine what a great dilemma that must be for me.

In my entire life, I had never felt like I had been taken so seriously.

It was also Amanda's wonderful idea to invite "Wolter" to a specific occasion, namely Gary's birthday in June. And I could hardly believe it when his answer came in the mail: He would be happy to come.

"Frances, come take a look at what I've bought!" Amanda's voice tore me out of my daydream.

She was taking off her hat as I slipped through the garden door and into the kitchen. Her own hair peeked out from under the hat; she had been letting it grow since Pesach. Apparently Matthew had always been opposed to the idea of a wig! After that revelation, she wore a hat or a fairly unusual knitted cap. At home, she didn't cover her head at all.

Along with several bags and smaller boxes, the taxi driver had deposited a large package in the hall, which she and

I brought into the kitchen. We removed the paper and admired the finely made gray suitcase.

"It will be so odd, Gary being at Oxford," Amanda murmured as she ran her hand over the soft leather. "At least he'll come home during the holidays. "

Uh-oh, I thought. *He still hasn't told them!*

"But that's exactly what we want from our children." Amanda sighed. "We raise them to be adults, to go off into the world and break our hearts."

She glanced at me and startled. At first I was afraid that Gary's secret was somehow written across my forehead, but luckily she had only misread my unhappy expression.

"Goodness, I'm so sorry! How could I say such a stupid thing? It's of course completely different with your parents!"

"It's okay," I said, embarrassed.

"Have you written them, by the way?" inquired Amanda. "Frances, they're waiting to hear from you!"

"I don't think so. They have other things to worry about. Mamu's letters always sound like she hasn't even read mine."

"That's the silliest thing I've ever heard!" Amanda replied angrily. "You can rest assured, your mother is constantly thinking about how and what you're doing. And that's why you'll go straight to your room now and write home."

That was the other side of my foster mother: She could become very strict all of a sudden, and then it was pointless to argue. Not that I intended to; I hoped she was right. My spirits renewed, I sat down at my desk, gazed into the fresh green of the tree before the window, and started writing.

It was about time for one of us to start telling the truth!

London, 29 May 1939

Dearest Mamu, dearest Papa,

I've been in England for four months now, it's almost summer, and I still don't have any good news for you. Unfortunately, I haven't been able to make door-to-door visits for the last six weeks, but I'll be starting again soon. There are still lots of streets in Finchley!

I want to tell you honestly how I'm really doing.

Papa, I don't like it that you never write to me. You always just sign Mamu's letters. Are you not able to write for some reason? Are you really doing that poorly?

If that's the case, then I want you to tell me. But I hope you are well, Papa, and that there's some other reason for your silence.

Mamu, I would like to know what you think about what I write. I know it's nothing special, but when you don't respond to what I say, I don't know what to write anymore. I also want to let you know that Bekka and I are not speaking. Maybe you should ask her what she said to me and why we don't write each other. Then you'll certainly find her less exceptional.

I only hugged Frau Liebich because Bekka and I had such a terrible row.

I miss you. Come soon!

A thousand kisses,
Your daughter Ziska (Frances)

It would be a small birthday party—Gary, his parents and me, and Walter—and on top of that, it would take place several days late. But the magnificent weather that arrived on the third Sunday in June gave my foster parents the idea to pack a picnic basket and head to Regent's Park.

Walter was waiting for us at the "theater," as he called the old gymnasium. He had dressed up quite a bit, wearing a slightly too-big suit and a plaid shirt, and he turned beet red as he shook hands with each of the Shepards. Then he climbed in the back with Gary and me, and I sat blissfully between my two beaus.

"Happy birthday," said Walter shyly. Poor Walter was so bashful he didn't know where to look. His eyes darted across the narrow car several times, here and there, finally colliding with Amanda's smile, and an entire minute passed before I heard him breathe again.

This is not going to work, I thought with apprehension. Later, when we were spreading out our blanket in the park and Walter took a few steps away toward the water's edge, I whispered to the Shepards, "Don't be so nice! Just act as if he wasn't there!"

They were utterly baffled. "But he's our guest, Frances!" Amanda said.

"That may be," I answered, frowning, "but someone who's been starving for a long time can't eat a whole cake in one sitting."

The Shepards looked at each other and simultaneously broke out in suppressed laughter. By the time Walter returned, though, they seemed to have understood my point, because Gary asked, "Would *anyone* care to come with me to rent a boat?" and after a little hesitation, Walter set off with him across the grass of his own accord.

"Don't you want to go with them?" asked Amanda in surprise.

"Actually, I would," I admitted. "But I think it's better if they go by themselves."

I lay on the blanket with my foster parents, arranged my straw hat, and felt disappointed and magnanimous at the same time. In less than ten minutes their boat approached, stopping at the shore a few yards from us. "Come on, Mum! Frances! A short round before lunch!" called Gary, who shared the oars with Walter.

I jumped up. "Don't you want to go?" Uncle Matthew asked his wife.

"Oh . . ." Amanda stretched lazily and gave me a meaningful glance. "Yes, actually. But I think it's better if she goes by herself."

Sitting in the bow of the boat—being warmed by the sun and rowed around by my two best friends—the day came pretty close to how I imagined bliss. I sat up straight and smiled at the rowers, as I imagined would be expected of the only lady on board.

There was a lot going on along the shore. Swarms of Londoners had come to the park; there were children standing in line at the ice cream cart while adults played cricket, and a few brave souls joined the swans in the water.

Walter and Gary sat next to each other in the middle of the boat, rowing at a leisurely pace and conversing with some effort. I helped several times by contributing German or English words, until Gary suddenly interrupted himself mid-sentence and observed, "My gosh, Frances, it's hard to believe how good your English has gotten."

"I've been in England for almost five months," I answered modestly.

"Me too," said Walter. "But where I am, I'll never really learn it."

"We've got to get you out of that sweatshop!" determined Gary. "Let's talk to my parents. Maybe you could work at the theater."

Walter shook his head. "My father would never allow it."

"How old are you? Sixteen? Fifteen? Parents need to accept that children make their own decisions at some point," Gary said with a fierce determination that could only mean that Walter's problems were not the only ones on his mind.

"Have you heard from the navy?" I asked.

"I have!" A broad grin spread over his face.

"And? Are you in?"

"Well, what do you think?" Gary responded with pleasure. "Everything starts in six weeks. I'm just starting to realize what a great honor it is. The Royal Navy only takes the best, and I'm one of them!" His satisfied gaze wandered over the lake, but when it landed on Amanda and Uncle Matthew, it clouded over immediately. "But I hate to do this to them," he muttered.

We looked over at the Shepards again, who had caught sight of us and were waving happily. Walter whistled quietly through his teeth. The boys pulled in the oars, letting the boat glide sideways to the landing, and Gary grabbed the hitch so I could climb out first.

"Well, what are you waiting for?" he asked.

I didn't move. All at once, every fiber of my being resisted leaving the boat. It felt like—with this one small step—the summer that had just begun might actually come to an end.

Amanda and Uncle Matthew had already set out plates and cups on the picnic blanket. There were sandwiches, cold chicken, fruit, and cake, but no ants, thankfully. Before we ate, we each took a small lit candle in our hands and made a wish for Gary for this next year of his life. Walter wished, "May you never fall in the water," and everyone laughed, including Uncle Matthew and Amanda, because they had no idea what he meant.

It was difficult for me to come up with the right wish for Gary without giving away what he had yet to confess. "I wish that you always find the right words," I finally said, and the others applauded.

Then Gary wanted to hold the candle himself, because he had a wish too: "I wish," he said, looking earnestly at Amanda and Uncle Matthew, "that you will always remain my wonderful parents, even if I sometimes disappoint you."

We were all quiet, and I had to think about how Amanda's and Uncle Matthew's parents had abandoned their own children when they were not much older than Gary.

Apparently it was nothing unusual for adults to play blind man's bluff and hide-and-seek in English parks. I, who had mastered the art of hiding in my earlier life, was surprised to discover how much fun it was to be *found*! My hiding places were so easy that at first, the others intentionally overlooked me so I wouldn't feel stupid. Soon, though, Amanda and Uncle Matthew saw through my game; they snuck up so conspicuously that I roared with laughter as they grabbed me and dragged me back to the starting point.

When it was Walter's turn to find us, I was standing behind a tree peering at him, when out of nowhere someone grabbed me from behind and a dark flash streaked before my eyes. Instantly I saw the world in black and white, something raced through my body like a strange energy and exploded. Someone was holding on to me by my jacket. They ran two or three steps with me, and then I was loose, running past the pond, jumping over other people's picnics, dashing across the cricket field.

I didn't come to my senses until I reached the entrance to the zoo. I had bolted across half of the park, and my jacket was gone. Panting, I looked around and tried to remember where I had come from. The memory only returned slowly. Gary's birthday. Hide-and-seek. The tree. What on earth had happened to me?

Confused, I crossed back over the lawn. The Shepards met me halfway across, Gary holding my jacket in his hand. "Frances, I'm sorry, I didn't mean to scare you, I wasn't thinking . . ."

Gary was white as a sheet. He gave me my jacket back, and I saw that the buttons had been ripped off. Bewildered, I turned the jacket over and over in my hands, inspecting it, until Amanda draped it around my shoulders and led me back to our blanket.

Walter, who had kept watch over our things, pressed the buttons he had gathered into my hand. "This never would have happened with a zipper," he said, and I laughed so loud that the Shepards went another shade paler.

"This has got to stop!" Gary declared in a strange voice that didn't sound like his own. "Being afraid all the time, running away, waiting for everything to calm down by itself. We have to start defending ourselves! I'll probably never find a better time to tell you this. Mum, Dad . . . I'm not going to Oxford. I'm enlisting in the Royal Navy—this summer."

I held my breath. Gary's parents stood utterly still, thunderstruck. Then Uncle Matthew said, "Now, I can understand how a young man might have such thoughts. But I hope I don't have to tell you, Gary, that spur-of-the-moment decisions seldom make for good results in the long term."

"This isn't a spur-of-the-moment decision. I've passed the entrance exam."

"Entrance exam? Are you saying that you've already arranged everything behind our backs?" Uncle Matthew asked quietly.

I watched Amanda with growing concern. Several emotions crossed her face in rapid succession—disbelief, shock, fear, rage. "There's no need to even discuss this!" she gasped.

"Like your parents, Mum? I have different plans for my life than you do, and we don't even need to discuss it?" Gary countered. Amanda flinched. "Come on, I know you won't do that to me," said Gary nervously. "Of course I don't expect you to say yes, but I do expect you to support me, because *you know* what it's like!"

"And what if there's a war?" Amanda snapped at him.

"Then I'll go to war, and then I'll come back, and then I'll go to university, Mum," Gary added emphatically. "I wouldn't enlist if I thought I could *die!*"

She lurched as if someone had hit her, turned around as she staggered backward, and ran off across the lawn. "Dammit!" Gary cursed in despair and ran after her, followed by Uncle Matthew. Walter and I stayed alone with the picnic basket, the blanket, and a handful of buttons.

In the distance, we could see Gary and his parents arguing. "He's a bit naïve, isn't he?" Walter said, shaking his head. "He doesn't know much about war, and nothing about death."

"We hope you'll visit us at home soon, Walter." Amanda was the last to offer him her hand as we dropped him off in front of the theater. She sounded tired. In the three hours since Gary's announcement, mother and son had tried so hard to interact normally that they were completely drained, and I began to find that worse than the argument itself. Gary didn't stick around very long after we got home either. He packed his things in the beautiful new suitcase, and Uncle Matthew drove him back to school.

I closed the front door behind them and started upstairs to my room. My heart felt like a heavy weight I was dragging around.

"Frances?" I turned around. Amanda stood in the doorway to my room. "You knew about it, didn't you?"

Suddenly I was scared. "Gary knows a secret about me too," I whispered. "I'll tell you if you want."

I sat on the bed. Amanda smiled weakly. "Not necessary. We have a treaty with Germany—there won't be any war. Hitler has high regard for England, and Chamberlain has no intention of provoking the Germans. Hard to believe, isn't it? Suddenly we're counting on Hitler."

I didn't answer. The pressure to tell her about my secret afternoon missions mounted and urgently wanted to be told, but the moment passed.

"Excuse me, do you need a cook or gardener? Any kind of domestic help?"

I thought back to the speech full of mistakes that I had recited mechanically in the spring, and was surprised at how different it felt to stand on strangers' doorsteps now. Friendly and confident, I looked the lady of the house in the eyes and realized immediately that she was impressed.

"Are you Jewish?" she asked.

"Yes. I'm asking for my parents, who are still in Berlin. I arrived in January on one of the kindertransports."

The word *kindertransport* always made a good impression. Many people had read about them or heard about them on the radio. "Goodness. How old are you? Do you go to school here? Of course you do, my children wore the same uniform! Would you like to join me for a cup of tea?"

"That would be nice." I followed her into a large, bright house, and we sat in the kitchen.

"I'm Mrs. March," said the lady. "I already have help, of course, but I do know someone . . ."

"You do?" I asked excitedly.

"Mrs. Soderbergh. The poor thing just had a stroke. She can't afford a nurse, but I've heard that her maid Grace is quite overwhelmed."

I set down my teacup.

"I don't know if she would mind if I sent you to her, but if you were to tell me where I can contact you, I could find out myself," Mrs. March suggested.

"That would be . . . that would be . . ." My voice failed. I tore a piece of paper out of a notebook, wrote my address with a trembling hand, and gave it to Mrs. March.

She studied it for some time and then looked at me with surprise. "You're staying with the Shepards?" she asked.

"Um . . . yes," I admitted after a brief pause.

Suddenly I realized she was scrutinizing me more closely and, I thought, more sternly. "Does Amanda know what you do during school time?"

My head sank. "No," I confessed meekly.

"Good heavens," Mrs. March mumbled. "And she always seemed to have her household in such good order. Aren't the houses that take you children in screened?"

"There are too many of us—they haven't been everywhere yet!" I was beginning to find Mrs. March not very nice at all anymore.

"Well, Frances"—she threw a reevaluating glance at my address—"I will see what I can do. You will hear from me!"

A moment later I was standing on the street. I didn't know if I should be happy or afraid. What would she do—help my parents, or betray my secret to the Shepards? At any rate, I certainly didn't want to visit any more houses. I had to talk to Amanda before Mrs. March did!

I had hardly pushed my bicycle into the front yard when my foster mother approached me. *Oh no!* I thought, horrified, when I saw how pale she was. *She knows already!*

"It wasn't like that at all!" I implored.

And then I saw that she had a letter in her hands—in

both hands, as if it were too heavy for just one. "Frances, dear, something arrived for you . . ."

But she made no move to give me the letter. Finally I simply took it from her, and was about to open it when I realized that I knew the envelope. It had my own handwriting on it.

My most recent letter to Mamu and Papa. But the address had been crossed out and a stranger's hand had written something next to it. It said "Addressee unknown."

I remember a few things about the following sixteen hours: me lying in bed shivering, Amanda cradling me like a baby, Uncle Matthew on the phone to Germany, trying to reach Theodor Todorovski, a friend of my parents' who had still had a telephone when I left. The Liebichs hadn't had one for ages, Aunt Ruth and Uncle Erik had never had one—and even if they had, it would have been of little use to us, since they must have disappeared with my parents. Otherwise they would have accepted my letter.

Disappeared. My head, my chest, my stomach—everything consisted of just this one word.

The letter came the next morning. Mamu's handwriting, a foreign stamp. "They're in Shanghai," I whispered. "In Shanghai, and they didn't tell me!"

"That's not Shanghai, that's Holland!" Amanda hastily tore open the envelope and showed me two pages filled with writing that immediately blurred before my eyes. "Oh, Frances, how wonderful! They made it—they got out!"

I looked at the pages in my hand and tried to push away the memory of the previous night to make room for what

172

the letter meant. My parents hadn't disappeared. They were safe. They were in the place where newcomers were welcomed with baskets full of chocolate.

And: They were only letting me know now. They hadn't waited to come to me. They were in a different country.

Groningen, 27 June 1939

Ziskele, my darling, by the time you read this letter, you'll already have discovered our surprise: Papa and I, Aunt Ruth, Uncle Erik, and the children are in Holland! I can't tell you now exactly how it happened—just this: We crossed the border in the night.

We have been staying in a hotel for three days, five people in one room. Yesterday Papa was admitted to a sanatorium, where he was immediately given a bed and medical attention. The Dutch don't send escaped Jews back to Germany. We can still hardly believe it. Our financial situation is precarious— people who smuggle Jews across the border charge a steep price! But Erik and I hope we can get jobs this summer with some fruit farmers.

I'll also write down Papa's address. Please write him often! He needs our support to get healthy again. I'm convinced he'll be able to in this wonderful country.

Ziskele, our plans to see each other again soon will have to wait. Considering our situation, you're better off with your foster parents, who can surely be persuaded to keep you a little longer. But in the

meantime, we can tell ourselves that we're only
separated by a few miles, and that's almost as good
as being together! One day!

> *Hugs and kisses,*
> *Your very happy Mamu*

Amanda was sitting with a lady in the living room. I heard their voices in the hall and thought twice about going in, but they had already heard me.

"Frances? Would you come here . . . ?"

If Amanda's bolt-upright posture was any indicator, this couldn't be all too pleasant a visit. "Hello, Franziska," the lady greeted me. "I am Mrs. Lewis, from the Refugee Committee."

"Good morning," I answered, surprised that the committee would make an unannounced visit before noon, as I would normally have been in school at this time.

"You look so pale," observed Mrs. Lewis. "Are you all right?"

"Frances received a letter today from her parents. They've fled to Holland," Amanda said nervously. "But otherwise you're quite well, aren't you Frances?"

Disconcerted, I kept silent.

"There's been something of a misunderstanding," she continued. "Mrs. Lewis believes that, instead of being in school, you spend the afternoons calling at strangers' houses hoping to find positions for your parents. I've already assured her that she must have you mixed up with another girl."

She looked at me with an expression that said: "Please say she has you mixed up with another girl!"

"It wasn't every afternoon," I whispered.

That backstabbing Mrs. March! She didn't call Amanda

with her news—she ran straight to the committee!

Before my eyes, my foster mother seemed to turn to stone. "It was only a few weeks in March and the last three days!" I cried in despair. "I couldn't tell you because . . ."

"Why didn't the school notice anything?" Mrs. Lewis demanded.

"I don't really go to school," I defended myself. "Until the summer holidays, I've been placed in the first grade, where I help some with the little ones. But the teacher doesn't mind if I leave early." I looked to Amanda again, who had begun to breathe deeply, in and out. "I couldn't tell you," I repeated mournfully. "At first because I didn't know you, and then because it was too late."

"Was that the secret?"

I nodded.

Amanda slumped against my arm. "If you plan to take Frances away from me, I will have to go into hiding with her," she said dully to Mrs. Lewis.

"Take me away!" I was horrified.

Mrs. Lewis smiled reassuringly. "I don't think that will be necessary. You're not the only girl who has been trying to do something like this for her parents. But no more secrets, understood? Your parents in Germany are relying on us to make sure you're all right."

"My parents in Holland," I corrected her, and was surprised at how nice that sounded. Amanda showed her to the door.

When she returned, I was still sitting on the armrest.

"Honestly now," she said seriously. "Is that it, as far as secrets are concerned?"

"Well," I said hesitantly, "there's also Professor Schueler..."

"Oh, Frances."

"... but only once a week, and not at his house, but at the Café Vienna, on Tottenham Court Road," I quickly admitted, trying to play it down.

"Wait just a moment. You're telling me that you've been riding into the city all this time, to a pub, and I haven't noticed anything?"

"On Mondays," I affirmed, noticeably quieter. "That's when you're..."

"At the nursing home."

"And it's not really a pub, it's a café," I hastened to add.

Amanda grabbed me by the arms and shook me. "Frances, I trusted you!"

"I'm sorry! I didn't want this to happen," I cried. "I didn't know they'd send somebody here."

"No, you didn't," Amanda said grimly. "But Iris March, that scheming old witch! Don't cry, it's not your fault. Tell me instead why you gave her our address."

"She knows someone who needs help," I moaned. "A sick lady named Mrs. Soderbergh."

"Wilma Soderbergh? I know her too. I was at her funeral just yesterday," my foster mother answered coolly.

I wiped my hand across my face. "It's too late anyway," I said with a trembling voice. "My parents are in Holland. They like it there. They don't want to come to England anymore."

"What did they write, then?" Amanda asked, more friendly now.

I gave her the letter. "You can keep me," I answered, and burst into tears.

Chapter 11

Evacuation

One day, about three weeks before the summer holidays, the teachers didn't call us back into the building after recess like they normally did. Instead, they had us gather in groups around them and after a few minutes, Mrs. Collins came out on the front steps and called for silence.

"Today we're going to have a little drill," announced Mrs. Collins. "We are going to line up by twos holding hands. And once we're all in order, we will march in line to the Underground station, like a crocodile!"

I couldn't help but laugh. In Germany, we only had fire drills occasionally, always accompanied by a lot of noise and sirens. Here we marched blithely, hand in hand, through the neighborhood. It was strange, though, how the people on the street stood still, regarding us earnestly and mournfully as we cheerfully trotted past them.

My mother seemed to be enjoying the summer. She had found work at a gigantic strawberry farm, and the letters she sent me were covered with reddish stains. Her letters even smelled faintly of strawberries. At first I thought I was imagining it, but when I held out a letter to Amanda, she smelled it too!

The letters from my father, though—two or three sentences scrawled in a thin, shaky hand—worried me. Four days after he went to the sanatorium, he was taken to the hospital for an emergency operation. It seemed my mother had gotten my father to Holland just in the nick of time, and by now I was very happy that they hadn't waited any longer for my help.

Mine were not the only letters Mamu received these days. Amanda asked to borrow my dictionary. She disappeared for two hours, and when she returned, she handed me a densely written page. "Could you read this through and tell me what needs to be corrected?"

Eagerly, I threw myself down on the armchair and read aloud:

> Dear Frau Mangold,
>
> Now that you and your husband happy in Holland are, want my husband and I write to say that you for Frances not worry. She is a very sweet girl and every day with us a great joy to have.
>
> She has accustomed very bravely, although she missed you painfully and of her parents talks without end. Frances has for much tried to do, so you very proud of her must be, so is Frances proud that you got out of Germany your husband!
>
> Mine husband and I have asked in the summer to visit Holland with Frances, but there is a problem with visa: When Frances leaves England, it can

be that she is not allowed to come back. So if you
agreement, we rather not risk. But Frau Mangold,
I very want to say that I everything do for you to
have Frances back safe and healthy, as soon as all
madness past.

We enclose some photographs that we in our
garden made, where how well Frances goes you see,
and how she has already grown in great deal. Now
you want all your energy to concentrate on not to
worry, but rather in Holland to settle, and prays our
whole family for your husband fast to get well.

Faithfully yours,
Amanda Shepard

I put the letter down. "Don't you dare change a single word!" I said.

Amanda grinned. "You mean it will at least give your poor mother a good laugh? Well, that's fine by me!"

I got up to give her the letter back, and suddenly found myself in her arms again. I held Amanda so tightly that she gasped for air. "My mother would drop everything and come get me if she had any idea how much I love you!" I declared without thinking about it. Amanda didn't say anything, but when I let her go, I could see her reply in her eyes.

If I thought we would see Gary off on a pier, or that he would stand, dressed in a white-and-blue uniform, on the deck of a magnificent ship, saluting as it majestically steamed out of the harbor accompanied by fanfares, then I was to be deeply disappointed. We gathered at an ordinary train station in the south of London, which shimmered in the summer heat. Gary wasn't even wearing a uniform. "A few months' basic training," he joyfully proclaimed, "and then we board ship."

He gave me a brotherly punch. "Will you get a uniform then?" I inquired.

"Of course! Take a good look—you'll never see me like this again!" he cheerfully ordered, a remark that didn't improve his parents' mood. Although they'd had six weeks to get used to the idea, I was still the only one who was happy about Gary joining the navy. Worse, Amanda's dogged refusal to talk about it, even now, baffled me.

"I never found anything wrong with your appearance," was her curt response.

"Oh, Mum!" Gary said quietly and put his arm around her shoulders. Even if she still didn't answer, she tolerated Gary's gesture, and after they had walked a few steps, she hesitantly wrapped her arm around his hip. I felt like a great weight had been lifted.

When it was time, dozens of future sailors stormed the train. "See you in December!" Gary yelled before the train started to roll, enveloping my brother and the other boys in a white cloud. That was it. No uniform, no tears, not a single grand moment. He was simply gone.

We drove back into the city in silence. I stared out the window and let the blurred landscape flit past. *Now I'm an only child again,* I thought, feeling depressed and pleasantly tragic at the same time.

But as the bridge over the Thames became visible, I

leaned forward eagerly. "Look," I exclaimed. "What's that?"

High above the city floated several silvery objects, moored to steel cables. They looked like giant inflatable animals. "Is there a holiday? A festival? A sporting event?" I wondered. In England, there were a lot of peculiar traditions, and I would have hardly been surprised at an inflatable animal race!

"Those are barrage balloons," Uncle Matthew explained. "They must have started installing them this afternoon. If there's an air raid, they'll force the enemy planes to fly at a higher altitude, and that makes them less accurate."

I almost asked, "Less accurate at what?" But it occurred to me that my foster parents weren't in the mood to explain anything about war. So instead I said, "Or else the pilots will laugh themselves silly and crash in the Thames!" which to my delight elicited a little smile from Amanda.

Not that there was any getting around the topic of war. The newspapers were full of headlines like "Will There Be War?" and when we returned home from the station, a little brochure was hanging out of the letterbox. "I have three of those now," Amanda said impatiently, and laid the pamphlet next to the telephone.

As I walked past, I glanced at the cryptic title: *Public Information Leaflet No. 3—Evacuation Why and How?* I made a note to myself to look up the new word *evacuation* in my dictionary later. That same evening, I was going to my room when I passed Amanda sitting on Gary's bed, lost in thought. "Matthew and I have been thinking about something," she said hesitantly. "I wonder, Frances, if you could imagine sharing our home with another child."

Another child? At first I thought she wanted to have a baby, and I felt a pang of jealousy, but Amanda continued talking. "Gary's room is free now, and the Refugee Committee is still frantically looking for foster parents for children from the kindertransport."

I couldn't speak. A dreadful roaring began in my ears, and Amanda's silhouette began to flicker, as if she were about to dissolve into thin air.

"Frances, what's the matter?" Her voice sounded distant and hollow.

"I have a friend," I enunciated with great effort.

"A friend . . . ? But of course! Is she still in Berlin? What's her name?"

"Her name is Bekka . . . and I took her place."

It's a strange feeling, seeing the floor come up at you. A sharp pain shot through my right arm, and then I was sitting on the rug, without the faintest idea how I'd gotten there. Amanda knelt down next to me and screamed for Uncle Matthew, and I cried loudly because I hurt my wrist when I fell.

Later, when I was lying in bed, I mulled over how the Shepards—after all the shocks and frights I had already put them through—could possibly be interested in taking in another unpredictable refugee child. In the middle of the night I got up, took a pen and pad, and for the first time in six months wrote the words *Dear Bekka*. They looked so wonderful that I got goose bumps, and I had to mutter the words out loud several times before I finally grasped that what I was writing to tell her wasn't a dream.

London, 28 July 1939

Dear Bekka,

Do you still have that Mickey Mouse suitcase? You'd better get it out, because you'll need it soon! As of today, there's an extra room in our house, and we thought you might like to have it!

It's true, Bekka—my foster parents, Amanda and Matthew Shepard, are inviting you to come live with us in London! I told them about you and about our quarrel, and I can hardly believe that we might have a chance to make up.

I'm so excited, Bekka! I hope you're not cross with me anymore. I want to tell you that it was just as horrible for me as it was for you when you didn't get a spot on the kindertransport. I have no idea why they took me. That wasn't fair. Maybe they drew names. But now you have a place, and not with just anyone, but with the dearest people in the world. They are just as you imagined back then, do you remember? You were right!

The Shepards will start arranging everything tomorrow, and they think you could be here by the end of August. They say you sound like a strong, brave girl, and they don't dare imagine all the mischief we'll get into together . . .

• • •

Berlin, 3 August 1939

Dear Ziska,

*I cried like a baby when I read your letter. I've been
so sorry about what I said to you, but I was too
much of a coward to write. And now you've found a
place for me. When I think that we'll see each other
in a few weeks, I get all giddy!*

*But Ziska, I'm so worried about my parents.
They're trapped—the Germans don't want them
here, but they won't let them leave either. I don't
understand it! When I get to England, I'll start
looking for a sponsor for them right away. I'm
excited about the Shepards, but I don't think I'll
really be happy until my parents are safe too.
Sometimes I'm so happy when I think that I'll
finally be able to leave, but then other times I can't
stop crying.*

My mother sends her love and is so grateful.

•••

London, 16 August 1939

Dear Bekka,

*Today I'm sending a picture of us so you can start
getting used to us. It was taken this weekend in the
yard. The boy in the picture isn't Gary, but Walter,
my friend from the kindertransport, who spent
the Sabbath with us. The older man is Professor
Julius Schueler, from Munich. And the beautiful
flowers won't be around much longer, because the*

government is distributing corrugated sheet-metal bunkers that everyone has to build in their yard.

Nobody talks about anything but war. We also had to get gas masks this week. They stink so horribly of rubber that I feel sick when I put it on, and I wonder what's the point of a gas mask if it makes you sick just to put it on?

The radio is on all day, and Amanda and our housekeeper, Millie, are trying to stock up on anything that was rationed or that they couldn't get during the last war. But don't think that it's dangerous here! These are only security measures, and no matter what, it's still a thousand times better than everything we experienced in Germany.

• • •

Berlin, 24 August 1939

Dear Ziska,

Today I got the date for my kindertransport! I leave the evening of Saturday, 2 September, and on Monday, the 4th of September, I will arrive at the Liverpool Street station.

My mother hums to herself while she looks over my things. That's something I haven't heard for a long time, but she probably just wants to calm herself.

Your preparations for the war sound exciting. Don't think for a minute that I'm scared! My father says that war is the only thing that can still save us Jews, so as far as I'm concerned, it can start whenever it likes!

Give my regards to everyone—the Shepards
look so sweet in the photo. But what made me
happiest of all was seeing a picture of my best
friend, Ziska!

"News from Bekka!" With these words I stormed into the parlor, where Amanda was sitting at the secretary, reading her own mail. "She's coming on September fourth!"

Overjoyed, I came up behind her and wrapped my arms around her.

Amanda stroked my hand without taking her eyes from the letter that lay before her. "Wonderful! But I'm afraid you have something else first." She sighed. "You've been summoned to school tomorrow afternoon."

"During the holiday? Have I done something wrong?"

"No, it's just a drill for the evacuation. You're to bring your gas mask and a light travel bag, what you would need for an emergency."

I remembered the pamphlet I had seen in the mail, along with the word I had meant to look up. "What is . . . *evacuation?*"

Amanda looked at me, astonished. "But I thought . . . it says in the letter that you already had a drill before the holiday!"

"A drill? They took us to the tube station and back again. That was evacuation?"

Amanda hesitated. "Not exactly," she replied. "Evacuation means that you're to be brought to safety. You've already been evacuated once—from Germany. Now there's a plan to send the children of London to the countryside in case the Germans . . . are serious."

"The children?" I could feel my face turning red. "Without their parents? But . . . why?" I blurted.

My foster mother sat up a little straighter, adopted a firm tone, and became matter-of-fact. "Because no one can say what's going to happen. England is an island; if the Germans cut off our sea routes, they can cause all kinds of shortages and starve us out. Not to mention the fact that if they attack London, it will be hell. You'd be spared that ordeal in the country, Frances. I remember very well living through the war in the city, and believe me, you do not want to go through that!"

"But I only just found you!" I exclaimed. "And what about Bekka?"

"If it comes to that, you two will go together. This time you wouldn't be alone!"

"Can they make us go?"

Amanda looked past me. "Yes," she answered.

I took a step backward. "You're lying! I can see it!" I yelled.

"No, dear. The Refugee Committee makes that decision. There's nothing we can do."

"We'll see about that! I'm going to write to my mother! If she tells the committee that I'm to stay with you, there's nothing *they* can do about it!" I cried.

My hands were trembling so much that I could hardly write the short note to Mamu.

London, 28 August 1939

Dearest Mamu,

You've got to help me! If there's war, they want to take me away from the Shepards and send me off into the countryside. Please send me the following

*note immediately: "Dear Refugee Committee, I
hereby request that my daughter, Frances Ziska
Shepard Mangold, not be evacuated, but rather
be permitted to stay with the Shepard family in
London." Please do it as soon as you can, Mamu,
so I've got something to show them! I'll also write
to Frau Liebich so she gives Bekka the same letter.
Bekka is coming September 4. More soon—I have
to post this before the mailbox is emptied!*

I ran as if my life depended on it. I reached the mailbox two streets away at the same time as the post office van, and gasping for breath, I gave the mailman my letter.

"Why don't you have your gas mask with you?" he shouted at me. "If you're outside, you have to carry it with you. That's the rule! Make sure you get off the streets, now!"

Up the street, three small girls were playing hopscotch, holding on to the gas masks that hung around their necks. They had become an integral part of an English child's wardrobe, like shoes and socks.

A stupid school drill during the summer holiday—what did it matter?

On Friday, the first of September, I awoke to the sun shining warmly through my window, and my first thought was the same as it had been on the previous three mornings: "I hope they'll let me come with them to pick up Bekka on Monday!"

The radio was on in the kitchen—a very loud, excited voice. I could already hear it at the top of the stairs. The telephone rang too, and I picked up the receiver as I walked past. "Is that you, Franziska?" I heard. "This is Mrs. Lewis. Do you remember me? I'd like to speak to Mrs. Shepard."

I continued on into the kitchen. "Amanda, the Refugee Committee is on the telephone."

Amanda sat at the breakfast table with Uncle Matthew, who normally should have been at work by then. Amanda stood up and walked past me; one look at her nervous expression and I knew immediately what had happened.

"Has the war begun?" Uncle Matthew put a finger to his lips so as not to miss any of the report. It appeared that German troops had attacked Poland in the early-morning hours. Poland was one of our allies—that meant war.

Poland! I thought, dismayed. Ruben!

The report was still in progress when Amanda reappeared in the doorway, and my heart froze. All color was drained from her face. "It's time, Frances," she said.

"Evacuation?" I heard my own voice like a faint wind.

She nodded. "We have four hours. You meet at the school-yard, as planned."

She took her seat, and I noticed the hasty glances she exchanged with Uncle Matthew. It was as if he were posing a mute question, to which she gave him a wordless answer— a negative answer. His shoulders sank. I saw it clearly.

"And Bekka?" I asked.

Amanda started to answer, but her voice failed, and then I finally understood.

"No," I whispered.

"They let one last train out." Tears appeared in my foster mother's eyes. "But now Germany is at war, and that means the end of the kindertransports. Bekka's not coming, Frances. She's not coming."

I realized that in four hours, our time together would be over.

"I'll send your winter things as soon as I know where your school is being evacuated. They'll send a postcard with your address, in your case they'd of course send the card to your mother, but perhaps it would be better if they sent the address to us, and I could forward it, and then we'll know where you are too, and if it's not too far, I can visit you, as long as they haven't requisitioned the trains for the war effort, although people have to be able to travel in their own country."

Until now, I had known my foster mother to be an exceptionally poised person who never spoke an unnecessary word, but now she was talking nonstop, like a radio that couldn't be turned off. I didn't tell Amanda that I would be back home that evening. The fewer people who knew about my plan, the better.

"Here, perhaps you'd like to take this, it's Matthew's travel candle. He had that with him in France. Would you like it?" She wrapped a richly ornamented candleholder in a cloth and placed it in the suitcase along with several extra candles, not even waiting for my answer.

"Oh, that's lovely, I'd love to take it," I said anyway. I was surprised to see how calm I suddenly was. Ziska Mangold, the champion of the survival plan. Three days, I thought. I only have to stall for three or four days, and then the letter from Mamu will arrive and I'll be able to stay!

All at once Amanda stopped packing and, with a deep sigh, sat on the bed next to my suitcase. "I'm relieved you're taking this so well, Frances," she said. "But we're going to find it much too quiet here without you around." She laughed abruptly. "Do you remember your first night here? Gary's nonsense at the table, and how you soldiered on, trying to imitate his every move?"

"And how I bit you and set you on fire—I remember that much better!"

I sat down next to her. She looked at me, full of warmth. "I also remember what I thought that first evening. I thought somewhere in Germany, there's a mother who sent her child alone on this long journey and has entrusted her to strangers because right now she can't take care of her as she would like. Anyone who can do what your mother has done, Frances, must love her child very, very much."

I looked at her, wide eyed. I hoped I would never forget a single word of what she had just said.

"And that's why," Amanda concluded, "she would certainly want you to be evacuated to the country!" .

I'm not going! I *knew* it, clearly and without any doubt now. I would not go! I had made this mistake once and lost my family. I wasn't about to give up my new family. I would stay with the Shepards, because I would rather die with them than survive without them.

My first thought when we arrived at the school was that well over half the children were late; it was almost one o'clock, and there couldn't have been more than forty students and their families there. Maybe we would all miss the train!

But as we lined up in pairs, it occurred to me that the others wouldn't be coming. Their families were exercising their legal right not to participate in the evacuation. Everyone except the Shepards and me had this right. Hot rage surged within me—anger that I was yet again the exception, someone whose fate was determined by strangers.

Now that things were getting serious, not even the teachers were coming with us. Only the headmistress, Mrs. Collins, was carrying a suitcase and seemed to be saying good-bye to relatives. All around me there was quiet whispering and sniffling. Only a few were openly crying, among them a giant man in a white turban who was sobbing into his sleeve. Uncle Matthew had put his arm around Amanda, just like the other children's parents. If I hadn't already known that we belonged together, it would finally have been clear.

"It's time, children!" called Mrs. Collins, and, waving, set herself at the front of the line. "Stay in your places and stay on the sidewalk!"

The younger children began to cry when they realized their mothers and fathers wouldn't be going to the station with them. I turned and caught one last encouraging look from my foster parents, and then I didn't turn around again, but instead focused on what lay ahead. I was holding hands with a strange girl, and carrying a not-so-light suitcase. And the stupid gas mask hanging around my neck was swinging back and forth. All in all, much too heavy for an escape. I would have to leave the suitcase behind at the station.

"My name is Hazel," whispered my neighbor, and gave my hand a squeeze.

"Uh-huh," I grunted.

"I'm sick," Hazel informed me.

What business was that of mine? If she was sick, then she should have stayed at home! I quickly removed my hand from hers and said, "It's nothing personal, but getting sick is the last thing I need right now."

Hazel looked at me, puzzled, and then she smiled. She was the most beautiful person I had ever seen—delicate, almost fragile, and with skin of a color that reminded me of toffees. "I am a Sikh," she repeated, and now I understood that she wasn't sick, but was from India, and belonged to the giant in the turban.

I decided not to speak another word to Hazel.

We crossed the street—I was being driven away from home for the second time. But we had left Germany by night and in a darkened train. Here, the doors of many houses opened as we passed. I saw strangers coming to the edge of the road to offer words of encouragement: "Chin up! It's not so bad! Our boys'll show the Huns, and you'll be back with your mums before you know it!"

In Germany it had been winter. In Germany, I had cried. Here, the sun was shining, as it had every day of that last week of peace. Birds were singing, the post office van drove past, around me was the steady tramping of feet . . . and I was filled with a peculiar satisfaction, like a liberation from a long wait.

Now Hitler's demonic deeds weren't affecting only us Jews anymore! The world was finally going to wake up!

As soon as we left the Underground and entered the train station, a bustling commotion greeted us. A vast, unmanageable swarm of children from every part of North London crowded around their teachers and the women from the WVS—the *Women's Voluntary Service*—who were accompanying the evacuees. A cardboard sign bearing my assigned number dangled next to the box containing my gas mask, and Hazel was dangling from my sleeve.

"You'll be fine. They have everything under control, as you can see," I said as I tried to free myself from her grasp. But Hazel made a face that couldn't have been more fearful if we had been about to be pushed off a cliff into the sea, and she clung to me even more tightly.

"Listen, Hazel," I said. "I've got to go to the loo, but I'll be right back!"

Resolutely I slipped between some adults so as to first lose myself among unfamiliar children. The art of fleeing consists of taking advantage of unexpected situations. But I didn't get very far.

"Where do you belong, dear?" One of the WVS women stopped me.

"Camden Elementary School," I replied, hoping that this school actually existed.

"That must be platform five. I'll take you there!" She cut a path through the crowd for us, gave Hazel a sympathetic look, and stretched her hand out to her. "Don't be frightened, darling, I'll put you right onto the train!"

When Hazel saw her uniform, she immediately let go of my coat and trustingly took the woman's hand. They walked in front of me, I in the rear. I wouldn't have a better opportunity. Leaving Hazel alone on the platform wouldn't have bothered my conscience, but I hadn't intended for her to be put on the wrong train! I wavered for three valuable seconds. Just as I finally decided to put my own welfare first, I heard the plaintive cry, "But I'm from Finchley!"

There wasn't enough room to make a dash for it. I collided with three or four people, then two WVS women came from the front, and that was that. "Frances Shepard, have you lost your mind?" snarled Mrs. Collins as I was handed over to her.

"We wanted to use the loo!" I claimed, trying to release my arm from her talon-like fingers that were digging into my flesh. "Just ask Hazel!"

Half a dozen children said they also needed the bathroom, and there was no question of fleeing now. Sitting on the toilet, I saw Mrs. Collins's shoes through the crack in the door. The right foot tapped impatiently. "Well, what's taking so long? I thought it was an emergency!" she sneered.

After a minute I gave up and left the stall with my head hanging.

My schoolmates swarmed, screaming and shoving, into the train. I heaved my suitcase onto the luggage rack, kept my coat on, and took the seat next to the aisle. Hazel had become wary and sat in the compartment farthest from mine.

Finally the doors were closed, and the whistle sounded. I heard the loud hissing of the locomotive as we slowly started moving.

NOW! I sprang out of my seat. Within a fraction of a second I was at the exit, turned the handle with all my strength, threw all my weight against the door, and felt it fly open. The ground below my feet was moving, white steam flew in my face, a black hole opened up between the platform and the train. For one moment it took my breath away, then I closed my eyes and jumped . . .

. . . and I was out! I felt a powerful blow and flew through the air, not knowing where, floated as if weightless in the dark space between two seconds that stretched out much longer. In a flash I thought I was dead, crushed between the train and the platform, but I was lying on my stomach, feeling no pain, only a strange, heavy weight on my back that was squeezing the air out of me.

Mrs. Collins climbed off of me, flipped me onto my back and gave me three or four slaps in rapid succession. I was lying in the narrow, dirty space outside the compartment and between two cars, while outside, the landscape rushed by and someone struggled to close the door as the train gathered speed.

They certainly hadn't imagined that I would try again. I heard Mrs. Collins scream as I tore away from her and threw myself against the door again.

This time there were three of them: Mrs. Collins, the other teacher, and a WVS woman. They dragged me down the aisle, a shrieking, flailing bundle of arms and legs, and Mrs. Collins screeched—not at me, but at the pale, horrified faces crowding the compartment door: "Take a good look, children. This is what it's like when you come from Germany, and don't know any better!"

Chapter 12

Tail's End

I lost all sense of time. Were we in the train for two, four, five hours? My own clock seemed to be running backward—I saw Amanda and Uncle Matthew as we said good-bye in front of the school, the pattern of the sunlight on my bedspread when I had woken up that morning; I saw myself writing my first letter to Bekka, over and over. *My foster parents are inviting you to come live with us in London.*

I had no doubt the train was going in circles. It was clear that we could only arrive back in London, and this time I wouldn't spend one minute sitting on the bench. I would walk straight past the tables with the ladies from the committee—I beg your pardon, but my foster parents are waiting, and I'm going home now!

Even when we stopped at a tiny platform in the middle of nowhere and got off, I refused to believe I had been evacuated. And so, on Friday evening, the first of September 1939, we arrived as unexpected guests in Tail's End. A series of volunteer aid workers swarmed out immediately with Mrs.

Collins to find additional places for us to spend the night. Three hours later I was standing at the front door of the only Jewish family in the village.

Tail's End. Two dozen houses of rough brick on either side of the one street, an Anglican church, a tiny school. There was a marketplace with a village well and a pub, the Hound and Horn. There was also a post office, a baker, a butcher, and a general store. After walking around for five minutes, you'd seen it all.

"You'll sleep here," Mrs. Stone had said, opening the door to a tube-like room containing two cots and a changing table. The room was so narrow that even the gaunt Mrs. Stone brushed against the wall as she walked alongside the cots and the thin mattress leaning there. "When you close the door at night, you can lay the mattress crossways in front of it. You'll be sleeping with Rachel and Luke, our two youngest. Show me what you've brought with you."

She reached for my suitcase, and I was so taken aback that I immediately handed it over. With a critical look, she laid it on the changing table and started unpacking it, carelessly mixing up my clothing, and felt the travel candle. Finally, she found what she had apparently been looking for: the metal box with my collected letters, photographs, and purse. With a satisfied look she shook the coins into her hand, and I saw my meager savings disappear into her apron.

"They pay me six shillings eight pence a week for your room and board," she said. "You know, of course, that that doesn't come close to covering the cost."

I nodded, ashamed. I had no idea how much six shillings

198

and eight pence would buy, but I did know that the Shepards hadn't been paid at all.

"Ooh, that's nice," Mrs. Stone said. She reached for the travel candle and took hold of . . . thin air.

"It was lent to me! It belongs to my foster parents in London," I cried, held the candlestick behind my back, and stared appalled into her resentful face.

"Just so it's perfectly clear from the start," she snapped at me. "We are not your foster parents, we are your hosts, and you will behave accordingly, understood?"

"Of course," I murmured.

"You can put your suitcase under the bed. And now come with me."

I closed my suitcase and hurried to follow her. I had seen children in the kitchen as I had arrived, and now I was expecting to be introduced to them, but Mrs. Stone led me directly into the washroom. "Here," she said, pressing an iron into my hand, adding nastily, "What is it?" when she saw my embarrassed expression. "I suppose you didn't have to work with your posh London family?"

I swallowed. "It's Shabbat! We're not allowed to iron," I answered feebly.

"I don't believe I need a child to tell me how to practice my own religion," Mrs. Stone retorted, and slammed the door behind her.

I am *not* going to cry! I ordered myself. Not because of a couple of days. Not because of a beast like Mrs. Stone! Thief! Breaker of Shabbat! She doesn't deserve to be cried over!

Soothing contempt spread through me. The two hours

that passed before Mrs. Stone let me out of the washroom went by in a flash. I only wavered in my resolve for a very brief moment—when she discovered two burn holes in the bedclothes and gave me a resounding slap.

"How stupid can you be? You have no trouble opening your mouth for insolent backtalk, but to admit that you don't know how to iron, well, that's too much to manage!" she screamed at me. With my head bowed, I sat at the dinner table between her children, whose looks might just as well have burned holes into me.

"Can we trade her in? I don't like her." The boy next to me must have been about eight years old. "Shut your mouth, Herbert," his father answered.

Mr. Stone possessed a not-unfriendly face that for a split second even curled into a smile when he gave me his hand. But one look from Mrs. Stone had put him in his place, and all evening he only spoke that one sentence: "Shut your mouth, Herbert."

At least now I knew the names of three of the children. The four-year-old must have been Rachel, the baby was Luke—my two roommates. Herbert's older sister was ten or eleven and didn't think to introduce herself; I found out the next day that her name was Pearl.

But to be honest, the Stone children didn't interest me in the slightest. I was so hungry I could hardly think about anything other than the soup that was simmering on the stove. The smell steaming from the pot made me so weak I had to hold on to my bowl with both hands.

But not for long. "So, here you are," said Mrs. Stone as she detached my right hand from the plate and set Luke in my lap. She placed a bowl of babies' porridge in my soup bowl and handed me a spoon, and as I watched the Stones pass the soup, bread, and butter around, I slowly realized that I was responsible for feeding the baby.

And I will *not* cry! I reminded myself with some effort, and dipped the spoon in the porridge.

Unfortunately, I had no experience with babies. I couldn't be sure if they generally ate so slowly, or if Luke was merely the slowest baby in England. As the Stones filled their bowls for the second time, he was still on my lap, and I had the growing suspicion that he spat out more than I had managed to get in him. Mrs. Stone finally caught on and freed her son from my arms. "You are really the clumsiest child I've ever met," she said, shaking her head, and shoved the pot of soup toward me.

At last! I eagerly reached for the ladle, tried to dip it—and hit metal. I slowly tilted the pot and looked inside. It was as good as empty. As I looked up in disbelief, my eyes met the spiteful sneers of the two older children.

"Dump the rest in your bowl," Mrs. Stone said indifferently.

I did as I was told and got ten spoonfuls of cold soup and the handful of crumbs that were left in the breadbasket, which I shook into the bowl as well. As I ate, I smiled at the Stones. This is certainly a joke, I thought. They must have hidden my real dinner in the pantry!

"And now you can clean up with me," Mrs. Stone ordered. "Mind you, remember where everything goes. Starting tomorrow I won't be helping you anymore."

Two hours later, as I laid my mattress crossways in front

of the door, I was still expecting someone to come and bring me my dinner. But one after the other, the Stones brushed their teeth at the tiny sink in the washroom and went to bed. In spite of my hopefulness, it became quiet, quieter, and finally completely silent outside the door.

Only Rachel whined in her bed. "I want a story!"

"I don't know any," I said, now indeed close to tears. "I'm too hungry."

"But Mum said you have to tell us our stories now! I'll call Mum if you don't!"

I was starting to understand how things worked in this house.

After about four days, Mrs. Collins began to wonder why I came to school with my suitcase every day. "Surely you're not so bold as to try another escape right under my nose?" she asked distrustfully.

"I can't leave the suitcase unguarded, or the Stones will steal my things," I explained truthfully.

Mrs. Collins sighed. "I've seldom met a child so prone to exaggeration," she remarked, and just seeing me drawing breath, she cut me off before I could say anything else. "I know you'd say anything to get back to London, but I can't do anything about it, do you understand?" she asked irritably. "You're here now, and until an authorized person turns up and convinces me otherwise, you will stay here!"

The local teachers had decided that their school was too small to house another class. And so we met on the village green, the other children sitting on blankets and I on my suitcase, and Mrs. Collins looking anxiously at the heavens whenever even the tiniest cloud appeared. She had to teach outdoors and she wasn't in the mood for any more problems.

"But I'm not lying!" I defended myself with a trembling voice, to which she didn't respond. She did tolerate my carrying all my possessions around with me after that, though.

If there was anyone in the Stone household who ranked lower than me, it was Dolf, the dog. The large, shaggy mutt was shoved and ordered around and even kicked if he didn't get out of the way. Even little Rachel called to him disdainfully, "Ey, Dolf!" He and I became friends almost immediately.

"May I take Dolf for a walk?" I asked during the midday break.

Mrs. Stone decided that I could have the afternoon free between washing up after lunch and setting the dinner table. Four hours for me, four hours without the Stones! I didn't even have to take Luke with me.

"Ey, Dolf doesn't go for walks," answered Mr. Stone, whom I had asked. "Well, all right," he added when he saw my disappointment. "Have a try. Maybe he'll even like it."

By the time I had convinced Dolf of my plan, I had lost twenty valuable minutes of my free time. I pulled on his leash, but he pulled back with bulging eyes. Pearl, Herbert, and Rachel stood by the fence, cheering him on. "Good, ey, Dolf! Don't go with her! Sit, ey, Dolf! Attack! Sit! Get her!"

Maybe it was their noise that unnerved him; at any rate, he suddenly gave up and resigned himself to trotting off with me.

The Stones lived at the far end of the village street, and just past their garden began the open country, immediately rising to a hill. When I reached the top, I looked out over the distance. The landscape was a warm, fragrant painting, caressed by a light summer breeze. There were trees of all shades, from lush green to light yellow; there were gently rolling hills and pastures bounded by stone walls as far as the eye could see. Beyond the forest, I could see a light gray strip that disappeared into the horizon . . . the sea! My heart began to beat faster. We must be very near the channel!

Even Dolf seemed to be enjoying himself, and he ran with me down the hill, his tongue hanging out of his mouth. His nose swayed close to the ground; he was picking up scents with relish. Now I was the one being pulled by the leash. Reaching the edge of the forest, we could already hear the sea; we ran up the last sandy hill, ready to reach the summit and then plunge into the delights below . . . and nearly collided with a coil of barbed wire! We stood there catching our breath. Even the dog seemed bewildered. The barbed wire stretched the entire length of the beach. We walked a few paces to the left, and then to the right, but we couldn't find a way through.

Disappointed, I placed my hand above my eyes and peered into the distance. Out on the water there were considerably more boats than I had seen before: a few small freighters and fishing boats, but also patrol boats and a large gray ship from which multiple narrow torpedo tubes extended, which appeared to be cruising slowly up the coast.

And then I understood what the barbed wire meant. It

was set up to defend against a German landing—in case the destroyer in the bay didn't stop the invaders.

"Come on, Dolf, we're going!" I whispered, and the dog seemed to understand. We ran back through the woods as quickly as we could.

I hadn't realized that the war had already come so close to us.

"But you have to tell Mrs. Collins how the Stones treat you!" Hazel whispered to me on the Friday before our second weekend in Tail's End.

"I tried. She thinks I'm lying!" I answered hopelessly.

Hazel had had good luck with her host family. And unlike the other children, who still called me the "crazy Hun," Hazel was kind to me. Every morning, she slipped me one of her two sandwiches. And she was the one who had pointed out the apple trees behind the church, where I stocked up every day.

"What about your mother?" she asked sympathetically. "Has anything come in the mail?"

I silently shook my head and tried to suppress the tears that welled up as soon as I heard the word *mail*. Whereas all the other children had long since heard from home, some even twice, I remained the only one without a letter. That mail delivery to and from Holland took longer now was understandable, but I simply couldn't believe that Amanda had deserted me.

And yet I had already been here an entire, endless week, and slowly it was starting to look like she had.

"Maybe you can visit me on Sunday afternoon," Hazel

suggested hesitantly. "We always have plenty left over from lunch . . ."

Although no one in Tail's End locked their door, I was only allowed to enter the Stones' house after I had knocked and was officially granted access. I sat in the rocking chair next to the door while I waited for someone to deign to let me in.

After about five minutes, the door opened and Mrs. Stone looked out. "There you are," she said indifferently. "Come on, we've already started."

I'll bet you have, I thought, and asked anxiously, "Is there any mail for me?"

The usual answer—"No"—followed by the sudden, sharp, pain in my stomach that worsened daily. I shoved my suitcase under Rachel's bed, lay down for a few minutes on her mattress, and silently doubled up.

An impatient yell sounded from the kitchen: "Frances! Where are you?" I dried my tears, rolled myself off the bed, and joined them downstairs.

Apart from Mr. Stone, who worked in a sawmill, the family was already gathered at the large kitchen table, where they were enjoying tea and cake. "Once you've cut the vegetables for the cholent," said Mrs. Stone, who held Luke on her lap, "you can have a piece of cake."

She cut off a hard piece of crust without even a trace of the cake's fruit topping and put it on a plate for me. What would be left of supper remained to be seen. I had a glimmer of hope that the coming Sabbath that evening would put her in a more generous mood.

About six o'clock Mr. Stone came home from work,

Mrs. Stone lit the candles, and we sat at the table. There was no synagogue in the area, and so keeping the Sabbath was limited to a prayer over the bread and wine, and two songs. "Shabbat shalom," we wished one another—the first time that the Stone children had stooped to offer me their hands—and the meal began.

"So, here you are," said Mrs. Stone as she set Luke on my lap.

I looked away as they filled their plates with roast, carrots, and potatoes. When Luke had finally had his mush, two potatoes in a little sauce were left in the bottom of the bowl.

"Hope you enjoy it," said Mrs. Stone as she dumped them onto my plate.

After dinner they left the washing up to me and moved to the living room to spin the dreidel. I heard their laughter over the splashing of the dishwater. That was about all I could take, and I would have wept bitterly, except there at the sink stood poor Dolf, who had an even worse time of it than I. He stared at me as if it had been his potatoes I had just eaten, and my suspicion probably wasn't far off.

"Let me see if I can't find a slice of bread for you, Dolf!" I murmured conspiratorially, and—as if he had understood—he followed me as if on tiptoe toward the pantry.

But hardly had I turned the key in the lock when a knife-sharp voice demanded, "And might I ask what you're doing?"

I spun around and saw the entire Stone family standing in the kitchen doorway.

"Dolf is hungry," I said and pointed at the dog, who immediately folded back his ears, pulled in his tail, and denied any responsibility.

"This is the thanks we get?" asked Mrs. Stone, trembling with rage. "We take you in, give you food and shelter, and you steal from us?" She grabbed me roughly by the ear and dragged me to the staircase. "Get upstairs! I was going to give you an apple and your letters after the washing up was finished, but now you'll have to wait a while longer for that!"

She shoved me up the first few steps, but I froze. "My letters . . . ?"

Mrs. Stone smiled nastily. She pulled out three envelopes from the dresser and held them up triumphantly, and she was still holding the letters when something happened that the Stones would never forget. Every time they thought about the war, they would see a small person standing in the middle of their staircase, and it wouldn't matter that it was only an eleven-year-old girl. They would remember the coldness as she looked down on them, and the calm voice in which she said: "When Hitler invades England, he will persecute the British Jews too. Then your husband will be put in a concentration camp, Mrs. Stone, and you will lose everything you own. And if you ever have to send your children away to save their lives, like my parents have, then they'll end up living with people who will throw them their table scraps, and hide the letters you write to them!"

Mrs. Stone put her hand to her throat, and fear and horror flickered across her face like a shadow, but then I turned around and continued up the steps. Behind me, no one moved. I wondered if I might have just cursed them, but I felt no pity. As far as I was concerned, they could stand there all night if they wanted to.

208

When I came into the children's room later, the three letters were lying on Rachel's bed. From now on they would
neither steal from me nor let me starve. They would never
again be able to forget why I was there.

> *Hello Sweetheart,*
>
> *Today is Sunday, the third of September, and a few
> hours ago we heard the news: England and France
> have declared war on Germany, and mobilization
> is under way. A small comfort for us—Gary would
> have been drafted anyway!—but a source of endless
> worry for all our friends and neighbors whose sons
> will be affected. Millie came yesterday to say good-
> bye, as she is going to her daughter in Kent, and
> she cried when she found out that you were already
> gone. But how are you, dear? We think of you all the
> time. The house is so quiet. Hopefully this will all be
> over soon. I'm impatiently waiting for the postcard
> with your address so that I can mail this letter—
> where might you have landed? Nothing has come
> from your Mamu yet, but of course I'll let you know
> the moment something does arrive.*
>
> > *Hugs and kisses,*
> > *Your "Aunt" Amanda*

• • •

London, 7 September

Dear Ziska,

Yesterday Dr. Shepard brought your new address
to the theater for me. What a load of rubbish, you
having to go away! Lots of kids from the East End
have been evacuated too, as we noticed at the last
movie showing—the hall was half empty. If things
get serious here, the movies will be discontinued,
at least for a while. The last three days, there were
air-raid warnings during the day. At first everyone
ran around like they were crazy, but then nothing
happened! Yesterday we just stayed at our sewing
machines and kept working.

   If it was up to me, I'd enlist, but at sixteen
(well, in November!) they won't take me yet. Gary
is lucky! His ship, the HMS Newcastle, set off the
day before yesterday and might already be at the
base in Gibraltar. The Shepards were at the harbor
when Gary set sail, but that's all I could find out. I'll
keep you informed. It must be awfully boring in the
country if you don't hear anything about the war!
But write me anyway!

Best wishes,
Walter

• • •

London, 7 September

Frances, love, word from your mother arrived today,
and I hope you don't mind that I opened the letter.

If the note you were waiting for had been enclosed, I could have sent it to the Refugee Committee more quickly. But now you can see for yourself what she has written, and to be honest, I didn't expect anything else. I hope you're not too disappointed. Above all you must not be angry with her. In her position, I think I would have made exactly the same decision.

I'm certain you'll soon feel at home in Tail's End. I looked for it on the map—it's right next to the sea! Is it nice where you're staying? Have you made any friends? Please write us soon about your new family, and how your first week with them has been.

Gary sends his love. We watched him set sail for Gibraltar two days ago, as proud as can be. I've enclosed a picture of him in uniform—I know you'll find him very handsome! Now you can write letters to Midshipman Gary Shepard, which I hope you'll do often. We'll put a shilling in every letter so you can buy stamps, and so you have no excuse to forget the good old Shepards. If you should need anything else, please let us know, and we'll try to get it for you.

We do hope we'll see you again soon.

Your loving,
Amanda and Matthew S.

Mamu's letter was in the same envelope—two pages that destroyed my hopes of returning once and for all:

Groningen, 30 August 1939

Dear Ziskele,

I'm sure your anxiety about the evacuation has calmed down, and that you don't seriously expect me to send permission for you to be exposed to the front line of war! Papa and I didn't send you to England only to lose you in a bombing raid. It's a great comfort to know that you two are out in the country, just in case. Please be reasonable and don't cause any trouble!

By the time you receive this letter, Bekka will already have arrived in England. That will make it easier for you to leave the Shepards—and your stay with them was never supposed to be permanent anyway, was it?

One more thing: If Germany and England do go to war, there won't be any more mail between the two countries! So if Bekka wants to write to her parents, she should send me the letter and I'll forward it for her. You see, yet another reason we're lucky to have ended up in neutral Holland!

Papa sends his love—he is resting on the North Sea coast, and I am laboring away with Ruth and Erik on an apple plantation. The girls have gotten places at the preschool and can already speak some Dutch. It is just incredible how we are being helped from all sides.

More soon!
Your Mamu

When Mrs. Stone pushed Rachel and Luke into the room, they found me on the floor in front of the changing table, filling page after page of my writing pad. But I was writing neither to Mamu, who I felt had betrayed me, nor to Amanda, who hadn't put up the least bit of a fight on my behalf. I wrote to Bekka, a friend like no other I would ever find, and I wrote as if this were my very last chance to do so.

I told her what had happened over the last few days, described the evacuation, my attempted escape, the Stones. I comforted both of us with the knowledge that our wonderful life with the Shepards wouldn't have lasted anyway, and at least Bekka would never have to meet the Stones. I told her about Hazel, about the lessons on the village green, and about my walk with Dolf.

But I also told her what I had been doing ever since I'd arrived in England, and what I would continue to do whenever I had an important decision to make: I thought about what Bekka would have done—and then did just that!

I don't remember whether I wrote to her that I considered her to be the other half of myself—the braver, smarter, more loveable side. Maybe I just wish I had written that. Whatever the case, I have thought so ever since.

My mother forwarded my letter from Holland, and it wasn't returned to her. So Bekka must have gotten it. What happened after that, I'll probably never find out. Maybe she lost the envelope with Mamu's address, and so she wasn't able to reach me anymore.

Not a day went by that I didn't wait for her reply.

Chapter 13

Enemies and Friends

The more the war turned in favor of the Germans, the more hostile my classmates' glares became. The Red Army marched into Poland, and Warsaw fell before September was over. At the beginning of October the news of Poland's final surrender reached us. In my personal war in Tail's End, there were five children in particular I avoided: four boys and a girl named Karen.

I had given up wondering why anything was happening to me. In Germany I was hated for being Jewish, in England I wasn't Jewish enough, and now that all my connections to Germany had been severed, I was suddenly supposed to be what the Nazis had denied me my whole life: German! At least my new schoolmates didn't dare bother me during lessons, or in the presence of Mrs. Collins. It was on the way home that I had to be careful, and as October wore on and the looks from my classmates became more intense, I understood very clearly that I better be the first to leave once school was over.

By then, we were being taught in a side room of the

church, where chairs and a few tables had been organized. I usually sat next to Hazel, who was still the only one who would let me. Once during a gas mask drill I did sit next to Karen for two hours, but only because she didn't recognize me.

The battered box for the gas mask dangled from my neck on the day that my strategy didn't work. Mrs. Collins had instituted a rotating classroom duty, and it was bound to be my turn at some point. After I had wiped the blackboard, emptied the trash bin, and arranged the chairs, I already knew what would be waiting for me when I left. The Five, as I called them in secret, were sitting on the edge of the village well. From there they could keep watch over the entire street down to the fork that led to Tail's Mews, and all they had to do was wait for me to walk into their trap.

Survival plan, I thought . . . and was surprised by my hesitation.

I certainly hadn't neglected to scout out a couple of escape routes and hiding places! My practiced eye had automatically sought out hedges and piles of wood whenever I walked past them, but on this afternoon I didn't even attempt to escape. Instead of the hiding places I had discovered over the past few weeks, there was just one thought in my head: *If I run now, I'll never stop running away.*

The Five were just as surprised as I was when I marched straight toward them. But then Jeremy jumped threateningly from the well.

"Hey, Nazi! Stop right there!"

"My name is Frances," I retorted in a voice that was a little too high.

He stood directly in front of me, but I noticed that he wasn't quite so sure of himself. "If you want to beat me up, then kindly pick just one of you to do it," I said with a bit more courage. "Five against one—only Nazis do that."

I could already tell from the looks they exchanged that they wouldn't do anything to me. "Search her," ordered Carl, their tall leader. I readily handed over my schoolbag, jacket, and the box with the gas mask to Jeremy. Jeremy passed the items on to the others, who inspected them silently. It was obvious that they felt rather stupid as they did so.

"There are pictures in the gas mask too," I informed Karen, who had opened the little tin that held my photographs.

"Shut up," she countered roughly, but nevertheless looked at what I had hidden in the rubber vent inside my mask.

"Who's that?" she asked, frowning.

"My brother, Gary. He's in the navy . . . but you can see that."

"Quick—give her the bag!"

The hasty command came from Carl, and as we looked up we saw Mrs. Collins stroll across the square. Schoolbag, tin, gas mask, its empty box, and my jacket were all simultaneously shoved into my hands, and I stood there looking like I had just raided a secondhand store.

"We're not done with you!" hissed Carl. "Be at the bunker in an hour!"

"I'll try," I said. "But when I get home, I have to work for my host family."

"Fine, we'll wait until five. But you better show up, or we'll have another chat after school tomorrow, and that won't be so pleasant."

216

I watched them as they took off across the square, then ran back to the Stones' house. Dishes from breakfast and lunch, two bedrooms to clean, maybe a little ironing and chopping vegetables . . . I could have it done by four at the latest. All of a sudden, I could hardly wait to meet the others at the bunker!

The bunker was in the woods in between Tail's End and Tail's Mews. It was a relic from the Great War, and so well hidden that from a distance it might have been mistaken for a normal hill. But when I came running with Dolf shortly after four, no one was around. "Hello? Anyone here?" I yelled, walking around and then to the top of the hill, and looked around, disappointed. "Where are you, then? You said you'd wait until five!"

My voice echoed through the trees, and the woods answered with a silence like I had never heard before. There wasn't the slightest whisper from the dry leaves of the trees; not a single bird sang. Only a tiny rustling noise behind me, and it stopped so abruptly that it could only mean one thing: Whoever made the noise had frozen in mid-step. I stopped breathing. My body was seized by a force over which I had no control. The hairs on Dolf's neck stood on end like a ragged gray brush, and although he didn't make a sound, I could see him baring his fangs.

The invasion!

A twig snapped, sounding like a shot from a pistol. "Ey, Dolf! Run!" I screamed as I let go of his leash. Branches struck my face, and I collided with something large, soft, and loud. I tried to scramble onward, and was thrown onto my back.

"Watch out, you idiot!" screamed Karen, whom I had pulled to the ground with me.

I opened my eyes and realized they were all there—the Five who had told me to meet them there, as well as half a dozen others. Carl's group and the gang led by Lesley and Wesley, the Howard twins, stood around me as if I were a wild animal they had just trapped.

"Get up!" snarled Wesley, and gave me a light kick. I jumped up quickly.

"Hey!" Carl butt in. "She's ours! We're the ones who brought her!"

"So you are, you git . . . A brother in the navy—rubbish! That could be a picture of anyone. And did you hear what she called her dog?"

"What then?" Distrustful looks wandered back and forth between Dolf and me, and I obediently opened my mouth to call him, "Ey, Dolf . . ."

Then it struck me like lightning. After more than four weeks with the Stones, I finally understood the poor dog's name. "Only Nazis name their dogs Adolf," asserted Wesley.

"Nonsense," I said reflexively. "They wouldn't dare. What do you think would happen if they went around in public calling, 'Sit, Adolf! Stay, Adolf! Get lost, Adolf!'"

Some of my captors snickered. "Only enemies of the Nazis think that's funny," I continued, feeling bolder. What was the point of this strange meeting? Somewhere in my belly I had the feeling there wouldn't be much of that boldness left if this lasted too much longer.

"Say something in German," Wesley's sister Lesley ordered.

"How do you get to the beach, please?" I asked politely in German.

"No, *real* German! Loud!"

I thought for a moment, then yelled with all my strength, "You stupid morons with your rotten old bunker! Scaring girls and dogs, that's all you know how to do!"

They were delighted. "What does that mean?" asked Lesley eagerly.

"It means 'Everyone gather at the bunker for the attack,'" I answered, and then wanted to go home even more urgently, because Wesley, Lesley, and Carl signaled to each other, then stepped aside and had a whispered conversation.

"I think I'd better be going now," I announced as casually as I could and reached for Adolf's leash.

A boot appeared and stomped down on the leash. My eyes slowly made their way up Wesley's leg. "As of today," he said, "you're a German spy. Sometimes for us, sometimes for the others. When you get captured, your side will try to free you before your enemies have gotten you to confess your secrets. Understand?"

What could I do? There were twelve of them. They slapped me playfully on the back and immediately started arguing about which of the two gangs would be the first to capture and tie me up the next day! I comforted myself with the thought that being a German spy was better than having no friends at all.

The situation between the Stones and me was more than a truce and less than genuine peace, but at least it was some kind of an agreement. They still expected me to work hard for them, but now they took care to treat me decently—as if their own fate was intertwined with mine. I got plenty to eat, was allowed to take my mattress into the larger bedroom shared by Herbert and Pearl, and always had the afternoon off as soon as the work was done.

Sometimes there was even conversation. "How's your brother faring in the navy?" asked Mr. Stone.

"He's in a Merchant Marine convoy, making sure the German U-boats don't sink our supply ships," I answered with pride. "Two months of war and still no attack on London! Three children from Finchley are already back with their families."

Mr. Stone shook his head. "Funny war, this! Britons under French command—unbelievable—and everyone's sitting patiently behind the Maginot Line and watching the Germans as they build their fortifications."

It was true. The "Sitzkrieg" on the French border wasn't exactly inspiring for our war games.

Walter was delighted to receive mail from "the underground," as he called it, and reciprocated with lively descriptions of his attempts to find his way home after dark. The blackout was in effect in London—streetlights weren't turned on and every household was required to hang blackout curtains over their windows. In an attempt to confuse any invading Germans, all street and place-name signs were removed as well, a measure that so far had only caused exasperation for the British. I tried to imagine how they wandered without direction through the darkness of their cities, falling victim to the cars whose headlights could not be turned on. "Add to that the fog," wrote Walter, "and the best you can do is to crouch in a corner and communicate by calls as soon as you hear footsteps."

But the most surprising message from Walter arrived in November.

> *As you know, Dr. Shepard is going to France to*
> *entertain the soldiers with his portable cinema.*
> *But did they tell you who's going to hold down the*
> *fort while he's gone? None other than yours truly!*
> *The Shepards' offer was so good my father couldn't*
> *say no. Now I'll sleep in the room behind the*
> *ticket office, and share it during the day with Mrs.*
> *Shepard. Officially I'm supposed to help her, but*
> *don't tell anyone—I think it will rather be the other*
> *way round. She's so angry with him, they hardly*
> *speak to each other anymore. Men don't want to*
> *just experience the war on the radio! And since Dr.*
> *Shepard is too old to enlist, this is his only chance.*

I had to read that paragraph several times before I grasped his words. "As you know," Walter had written, but I hadn't known—this was the first I'd heard about Uncle Matthew going to France, even though I got mail every week from Amanda! She hadn't said anything to me about it.

Why did she write me at all if she only wrote lies all the time? Because keeping secrets is also lying—she had to know that! I would have been one hundred percent on her side. I was so angry with Uncle Matthew for leaving Amanda alone that I could hardly sleep that night. But by the next morning, my fury at Amanda took the upper hand, and I decided not to answer her again until she finally told me the truth.

Which she did a week later. In a cheerful tone, she described her struggles with the film projector, which behaved completely differently with Walter than it did for her! Uncle Matthew was already on the Continent, "following that call to which the average female ear is obviously completely deaf."

It was this bitter little half sentence in her letter that immediately dispelled my anger. Amanda was without Gary and Uncle Matthew, without Millie, without her flower garden. She must have felt like I did whenever I started thinking about my earlier life.

For several days after receiving that letter, I sensed the closeness that had meant so much to me in London, and I longed to return. But other things forced themselves into the foreground: life with the Stones, which was sorting itself out; school, which was becoming more and more fun; my first little circle of friends. More children returned to London at Christmastime, since a German attack had failed to occur. I didn't even ask if I was allowed to go with them. I had only been with the Shepards for half a year, and now they were gradually fading into memory.

The situation was much the same with my parents. I could still picture Papa when he was arrested, but wasn't able to imagine him in his spotless, white bed at the sanatorium. And when I thought about my mother I thought about fields of strawberries, as if all the other, more recent reports from her simply hadn't reached me.

In addition to the three subjects Mrs. Collins taught us in Tail's End—English, math, and geography—we girls picked up a fourth that winter that became an addiction in no time: knitting. We tirelessly made scarves at first, and then as we improved we knitted socks and mittens for the soldiers. And we mailed them off with personal Christmas greetings.

We were infinitely pleased when the greetings were returned several weeks later, and it wasn't long before each of us had her own soldier. Mine was named Frank Duffy, a twenty-two-year-old from Cornwall, and I tried as hard as I could to look serious and grown-up in the photo I sent him. On one wall of the classroom, Mrs. Collins hung a map of the world so we could keep track of our soldiers' movements. But Gary was the only one who moved: I pushed the flag with his name across the Atlantic, between Europe and the USA, while all the others remained in France.

For Hanukkah, Gary sent me a necklace made from tiny, smooth, white shells. "I hope you're still learning Hebrew and not neglecting your prayers!" he wrote on the accompanying card.

That remark put a serious damper on my joy about the necklace. My Hebrew book had been in the things Amanda sent with me to Tail's End, but I hadn't opened it since I had been here. While I had lived with the Shepards, it had been my greatest desire to be entirely Jewish. How could it have lost its importance for me so quickly? Whatever it was, the mystery I had experienced before was gone. The Stones' relaxed Judaism, which recognized no laws and only the most important of festivals, was enough for me now.

That evening I took out my tin box and buried Gary's necklace deep beneath my letters and photos. I wasn't worthy of wearing it.

January 26 arrived, the one-year anniversary of the day I had left home. It upset me a little that Mamu didn't mention it, but to my surprise I received a letter from Papa! We had been separated since November 9—I hadn't seen my father for fifteen months.

> *Dear Ziska!*
>
> *Who would have thought that we'd have to spend such a long time apart? I am so proud of you, and how well you're finding your way in a foreign country! But next year I don't want to have to write you on January 26, as I hope we'll all be together again by that time.*
>
> *I'm doing much better. Every day I take a one-hour walk—very slowly—and I look out over the sea toward England. On your birthday, at eleven in the morning, I plan to be standing there. Will you come to the beach too? I hope you'll come, so our thoughts can meet out over the water.*

At first Hazel cheerfully accepted my invitation to walk to the beach with me on my twelfth birthday, but when the day arrived, I was in for a surprise. With a conspiratorial smile, she took me aside before school started and whispered, "I'm glad to come with you, but you should know that someone else would be even happier to go!"

She gave a significant half nod over her shoulder, and I saw Wesley Howard, beet red, leaning against the wall. "Wesley?" I asked, puzzled. "Why him?"

"I guess he has something to tell you," responded Hazel knowingly.

The walk with Wesley seemed interminable. If he had something important to tell me, he must have forgotten it. At the Stones', where we picked up Adolf, he did manage a "Good day," but then he just marched along next to me in silence, driving me to exasperation.

"Just imagine if the Germans landed on the beach at the very moment we got there! What would you do?"

"Uh . . ."

"We'd be sure to hear guns firing if they did, don't you think?"

"Hmm . . . yeah . . ."

"Personally, I don't think they would try to land without taking out our fleet first. In that case we'd have plenty of time to run back to the village . . . or would it be better to hide in the woods?"

"Well . . . er . . ."

Disappointed and angry, I shoved my hands in my coat pockets and gave up. After a while I called, "Come, Adolf, let's run a bit!" and simply ran away from him.

Wasn't this my birthday? Wasn't this my walk to the beach?

If the Germans were planning to land on our beach, my birthday wasn't the day they had chosen. The sea stretched out pale and gray before me, and only one ship—a tiny bright spot far, far out—was visible. The pebbles crunched with the cold as the waves quietly rolled up and broke on them. I thought about my previous birthday, when I had resolved to find a foster family myself. In that sense, the Shepards had been my birthday present. That one wish had been fulfilled in a most beautiful way.

Would I be granted another wish? I didn't dare say it out loud as I looked over the sea in the direction where Holland had to be. Somewhere over there, my father was standing on the beach and thinking of me, making the same wish as me, and I simply thought, "Jesus, you know."

I hadn't completed this thought when it happened. It was as if the sea was so close I could feel the moisture on its surface. I could see my father waiting on the other side, a thin figure in a brown overcoat that I had never seen him wearing, and there was no barbed wire between us. He looked over at me without moving, and I saw his eyes, ringed in shadows and the deep wrinkles around his mouth, but also his smile, his familiar, loving smile.

An excruciating pain shot through me, so terrible I couldn't have endured it any longer than that one moment, before it disappeared along with the image of my father. Then the sea lay there as it had before, cold and calm.

I didn't even have a second to collect myself before the next confusing incident. Out of the blue, someone grabbed me, spun me around, and something cold and wet attached itself to my lips. My eyes, wide with horror, stared into an equally panicked pair of eyes only an inch away!

Wesley and I flew apart like a bomb had exploded between us, he in terrified flight back over the hill, I backward into the coil of barbed wire. By the time I had regained my composure enough to yell indignantly, "Are you completely daft, you idiot?" he was probably already halfway back to Tail's End.

Tears welled in my eyes. I rubbed my mouth with my sleeve as if possessed, rubbed and spat; I was tempted to use sand to remove all traces of that kiss. That jerk! He had ruined my birthday, defiled that precious moment with my father. And if he dared to tell anyone, I'd murder him!

Ashamed, I stumbled home, and the next few days were completely dominated by two rapidly alternating impulses: either to bore holes into Wesley with my eyes, or to not have anything to do with him. Wesley's inner voice seemed to have given him the same advice. I attributed his apparent dejection not so much to the fact that I hadn't responded well to his advances, but rather that he had so unnecessarily complicated our lives.

"But what did he *say*, then?" Hazel tormented me for the rest of the week, until I made her take an oath of silence and through gritted teeth admitted to her that Wesley hadn't said anything at all, but instead had tried to kiss me.

My own feelings about this matter were briefly, most satisfyingly reflected in Hazel's shocked face, then she covered her mouth with her hands and passionately whispered, "Tried? Just tried? Thank God!"

I stared at her. I had led her to the farthest corner of the churchyard to tell her about Wesley's ambush, and skeletons rattling out of their graves couldn't have made a more sinister impression than Hazel's words. "What do you mean?" I asked.

"But don't you know . . . ? It all starts with kissing—you could have had a baby because of that!"

I heard myself swallow hard. "Are you sure he only tried?" pressed Hazel.

"Yes, of course, it was only two seconds, and I wiped my mouth off right afterward!"

Hazel's eyes were as wide as saucers. "You won't know for sure," she said ominously, "for another few months."

Horrified, I pushed it out of my mind, acted like nothing was wrong, and before long Hazel had obviously forgotten about her suspicion. I tried not to imagine the most horrible consequence: Having to marry Wesley and spend the rest of my days being kissed by him!

At last, two months after that fateful morning on the beach, the string I had tied around my belly to monitor any change in size wasn't any tighter, so I let myself relax. I cut it off, happy that I hadn't betrayed my embarrassing ordeal to anyone.

Chapter 14

Moving Again

The Germans did not attack the British coast. On April 9, they occupied Denmark and Norway without even declaring war, an announcement that required extensive repositioning of the flags on our classroom map. British and French units were shipped off to Norway, but resistance there was brief.

For my parents, who had placed all their hopes in the assumption that Hitler would respect Holland's neutrality, the invasion of two peaceful neighbors must have been a heavy blow, so I immediately sent them encouraging letters. But the English were also becoming increasingly nervous. The Certificate of Good Standing that the Shepards had acquired for Walter was no longer enough, and he was called for a personal interview to determine if he was a friendly or hostile foreigner.

> *I tried to explain to them that I'm Jewish, but that doesn't interest them at all. Will they send us back to Germany? All Germans and Austrians between*

*the ages of sixteen and sixty-five living in England
are affected, women and men alike, and also many
of the children from the kindertransport.*

*Public opinion of us has changed. Sometimes
people insult me at the theater when they hear my
German accent. Mrs. Shepard doesn't want me
to spend the night at the theater alone, so starting
tonight I'll go home with her. My short-lived
independence is already coming to an end!*

*My hopes for a quick resolution are fading.
The free world looks on helplessly as the Germans
expand farther and farther. Where are the
Americans? How much longer are they going to
wait? I'm sorry, I don't want to be so negative,
but I'm starting to lose my patience with the
whole business. Luckily Holland is still hanging
on—good thing your parents fled there and not to
Scandinavia!*

Our lives in Tail's End seemed far removed from everything going on in the war. After my housework at the Stones',
I met Hazel and the other girls at the village well to talk and
make fun of the boys, who had picked the cemetery wall for
their meeting place. Our joint escapades at the bunker the
previous year had ceased, an unspoken agreement by both
sides. Although we were always staunchly separated, we constantly kept an eye on each other.

The idea that another girl would take her place as my best
friend once the war was over didn't bother Hazel. "My father
says the way to survive war is by adapting to the out of the

ordinary," she informed me. "So why shouldn't I be your best friend for the rest of the war?"

On one of the first warm spring days in the middle of April, seven or eight of us were sitting at the village well as usual. By then, only twenty-three of the original forty evacuated children were still in Tail's End, and that morning Mrs. Collins had shocked us with a totally unexpected bit of news: Plans were under way to evacuate us farther from the threatening coast to the safety of the interior!

This affected not only those of us from London, but all the children of Tail's End as well, and for days no one spoke of anything else at the Stones'. It had already been decided that Pearl and Herbert would go with us, but Mrs. Stone didn't want to be separated from Rachel and Luke.

I had never expected to feel sorry for Mrs. Stone, but when I saw her red, bleary eyes, I couldn't help it. "It's not so bad," I told her. "And this will be my third evacuation, so I should know!"

But nothing could comfort her or make the decision any easier.

"This time things will run more smoothly than the evacuation from London," decided Lesley. "We should give Mrs. Collins a list of which of us want to be placed together in a new family."

"Good idea," said Hazel, moving closer to me.

She and I were among the first to be recorded on Lesley's list. We turned to look at each other contentedly, and at the same time, my glance rested briefly on the distant figure of a solitary woman climbing the road from Tail's Mews. She had obviously gone into the city with the train, which only stopped twice a day at the neighboring station since the war. This was clear because she had a hat and an umbrella— unusual for our little village.

"If the younger Stone children are coming, we have to take Luke too. Luke Stone," I dictated to Lesley. "He's much more used to me than to his older siblings."

"Oh, yes! Luke is so sweet!" raved Hazel.

"And a dog," I added. "Adolf Stone."

Lesley stopped writing. "You're joking," she said, to which I replied, "In certain circumstances, dogs are allowed to come along!" which was a bald-faced lie. In truth, I was convinced I'd be able to house Adolf if I had him with me. Shrugging her shoulders, Lesley wrote, "Adolf Stone, dog." But she added a question mark next to it.

Meanwhile, several of us had noticed the woman walking toward us. In Tail's End, with its sixty or so inhabitants, anything unusual on the village's one street aroused interest. "Is that Mrs. Caine?" asked Brigid.

"No. Maybe it's Mrs. Tingle," answered Karen, and turned her attention back to the list.

"Frances? Are you all right?" Hazel's puzzled voice reached my ear.

I slid down from the edge of the well, reeling with shock. I stared at the woman, who was still quite far away. I whispered, "It can't be!" although I already knew it was true. Maybe I was just afraid that she would vanish before my eyes, like the vision of my father on the beach.

"Is that her mother?" someone muttered, and Hazel answered, "No, she's in . . ." But I didn't hear the rest. I was running down the street, faster and faster, until my feet barely touched the ground. It felt like I was running backward through time: spring, winter, fall, summer. By the time I reached her, I had never been away.

"I thought I'd never see you again!" I said breathlessly.

How had I thought for even a second that I could forget her? She held me at arm's length, while in a wave of happiness I rediscovered everything that was familiar to me—her wonderful, radiant smile, her warm green eyes, her cheerful, loving look. I could see in the way she looked at me how much I must have changed in the eight months since we had last seen each other. "Good heavens, Frances, is it really you?" she said, and laughed, her voice full of tears.

Amanda Shepard walked up the street into Tail's End and back into my life—she was simply there again.

"Is there anywhere nearby where we could talk undisturbed?" Amanda asked me.

"Talk?" I echoed, shocked. The thought that her sudden appearance could have a specific purpose hadn't occurred to me, and suddenly I saw what I had failed to notice in my joy at seeing Amanda again: She looked tense. Her face was pale, her cheekbones stood out, and I saw fine lines under them that definitely hadn't been there last summer. I thought about how worrisome the last few months must have been for her, but there was something else in her face, and it scared me.

All at once I became very calm. "We can go into our classroom."

We walked through the nave and into the side room that housed our little school. "Look!" I led Amanda to the world map. "This flag is Gary! And down here is Frank Duffy." And I watched her pretend to read the names. "It's about Papa, isn't it?"

"Yes, dear," she said quietly. "I've brought you a letter from your mother."

"She asked you to bring me a letter?"

"Yes. She probably thought it would comfort you a little."

I looked at her attentively. "She was right," I said.

Amanda looked away. "Did she say anything else?" I wanted to know.

"That . . . is also in your letter."

Groningen, 12 April 1940

My dear Ziskele,

When Papa and I recently talked about how best to get word to you if something should happen to one of us, we agreed right away that we would ask your Mrs. Shepard. So I hope that she's with you now when you read what I have to tell you today.

Ziska, your Papa died the day before yesterday, sometime between three and six in the morning. Apparently, he had a heart attack in his sleep—or if he woke up, he didn't ring for the nurse. It was the day after the German invasion of Norway, and as I gather from the letters you sent us right afterward, you immediately grasped what that means for us.

My darling, Papa never received your last letter. But I keep thinking about what he told me on one

of my last visits with him—that you two had a date
on your birthday, and how he felt so clearly that
you were truly with him that day. I wish I had come
up with such a wonderful idea, but you and Papa
always had a special connection, didn't you? I have
one more thing to tell you, and you can make of it
whatever you like. When you asked me in August to
allow you to stay in London, I made the decision on
my own that you should be evacuated. I was certain
Papa would agree with me, but on the contrary, he
was very upset when he heard about it. He said,
"Our daughter has found people who love her. Isn't
that worth more than a sense of safety that doesn't
exist anyway?"

    Now that he's gone, I know he was right. So I'm
sending you a note of permission—in Papa's name
and mine—to return to London with Mrs. Shepard,
if that's still what you want. I will also write to her
and explain everything . . .

Amanda, who had stood quietly looking out the window while I read and reread Mamu's letter, came over and sat next to me on the edge of the table. "I can't tell you how sorry I am, Frances."

But I didn't know what to say about Papa yet.

"Is London safe?" I asked.

"No!" answered Amanda decisively.

I looked down again at the piece of paper with the signature, and of all the possible steps I could take, the only one that I could even fathom.

"The train leaves at seven?"

"You shouldn't rush things. Perhaps I can find a room for the night."

"No. Let's go."

The Stones stood in the hall, bewildered, while I packed my few belongings.

"We don't live in luxury here, as you can see," Mrs. Stone remarked to Amanda. "Four children, the smallest still in nappies, and then a fifth on top of that . . . it wasn't easy!"

Ever since my foster mother from London had crossed the threshold, fear had been all over Mrs. Stone's face. Her refugee, her servant girl, the lowest of all, was being collected by this beautiful, well-dressed lady who spoke with a quiet, cultivated voice, and who lovingly called her Frances "dear." Mrs. Stone couldn't know that I had never told Amanda about the horrible beginning of my stay in Tail's End, but she doubtless experienced this fairy-tale ending from the perspective of the terrified stepmother who knows she is about to be exposed!

"There's one other thing . . ." I said to Amanda. "What about Adolf?"

"We'll take good care of him," promised Mrs. Stone.

"He likes to be rubbed under the chin," I said. "Right here. And maybe he didn't go for walks before, but now . . ." I pulled him toward me urgently and buried my face in his coat.

This couldn't be happening! I had just learned of Papa's death and felt nothing, absolutely nothing, and now I was crying about a dog!

"Don't worry, we'll do everything for him!" said Mrs. Stone, who was obviously ready to promise me anything I wanted. "Please excuse me for a moment!"

She rushed off importantly. I let go of Adolf and didn't look at him again. "We still have to see Mrs. Collins," I reminded Amanda.

She snapped my suitcase shut. When we reached the bottom of the stairs, a beaming Mrs. Stone was already waiting for us with a bag bursting with food from her pantry. I didn't get the satisfaction of refusing her peace offering. Amanda accepted the bag without the slightest hesitation.

"Many, many thanks, Mrs. Stone! Fresh butter! Eggs . . . and such a tremendous piece of cheese! I can't imagine how many stamps I would need . . ."

"Don't mention it," Mrs. Stone modestly replied, but it was impossible not to see that her pangs of conscience had already subsided, and that the elegant lady from London had sunk to the level of a normal city-dweller who couldn't eat her fill of eggs! The rest went quickly. The Stones shook my hand—there were no embraces. We'd had an arrangement and gotten used to each other over time, but there had never been any doubt that when the time came, they would be happy to see me go.

The news of Amanda's arrival had already reached Mrs. Collins, who was waiting for us in her room at the Hound and Horn.

"Are you sure you want to go back?" she asked, holding the letter Mamu had sent. "You've made some nice friends . . . little Hazel . . ."

"I should never have left in the first place," I countered. "My father says so too."

Mrs. Collins turned to Amanda. "It appears that our group will soon be leaving for Wales. You can find out more at school, if you should happen to change your mind."

Amanda nodded after taking a quick sidelong glance at me.

"Well then, best of luck, Frances," said Mrs. Collins. "Let's hope the war is over before we start to get used to all this!"

If by "all this" she meant good-byes, horrible news, or hundreds of thousands of parentless children wandering throughout England, she didn't say.

Outside, my friends were still sitting on the edge of the well and Amanda said, "We have plenty of time for you to say good-bye to everyone."

But I simply shook hands with each of them, and if I had had a choice I would have skipped even that. I wanted to remember the lovely feeling of having belonged rather than a farewell.

That evening on the road to Tail's Mews, I suspected for the first time that I wouldn't see my mother again for a very, very long time, and that Amanda and her family were the only home I had left.

It's difficult to mourn someone you haven't seen in almost a year and a half—even more so if you only learn of his death in a letter. The shock, the pain, the sadness for my father had occurred after the pogrom when I lost him; now that I was sitting in a train to London, I didn't know how I could bring myself to feel that loss again.

But I could have cried for Mamu. Papa had been her life. She had never stopped fighting for him, hoping for him. Suddenly I was terrified at the thought of having to write to her when I returned. No words from me could do justice to her loss; no tears from me could match her pain. What on earth could I ever say to her again?

Through the window, the colors flitted by into gray twilight. The dim lighting on the train made me sleepy. Amanda took bread and cheese from Mrs. Stone's bag as the other passengers looked on and cut some for us. She laid the food on my leg without a word; I took it and ate obediently, now happy that we had something for supper.

Walter's amusing descriptions may have prepared me, but what we saw as we left King's Cross station can only be described as shocking. I had never experienced Euston Road or the square in front of the station as anything but lively and colorful, with pedestrians rushing by, taxis honking their horns, buses sluggishly pushing forward during the day, and at night a steady stream of lights whizzing past. Now, once we got outside, there was nothing but gloomy, numbing darkness.

"Blast!" muttered Amanda. "Fog—tonight of all nights, when we have to take a taxi. Give me your hand, Frances!"

I don't know why she thought it necessary to ask, since I instinctively grabbed her coat with our first step into nothingness. And now I knew why my blackout-experienced foster mother had brought an umbrella: Like a blind person, she tapped the ground to the left and right as we moved forward, making a *clack-clack* that was somewhat reassuring.

We made our way along the station's outer wall and quickly reached the taxi stand.

I was quite dazed as we got off the train, but if I had needed anything more than the eerie scene at our arrival to wake me up, this taxi ride was it. I stared straight ahead with my eyes wide open, every fiber of my body alert, while Amanda and the driver debated—in the middle of the pitch-black hole that had swallowed us—whether we were passing this or that street.

It was half past one when we finally arrived at Harrington Grove. We felt our way through the garden, I heard the searching scratch of a key on wood, then we stood bathed in light, and a voice with an unmistakable German accent enthusiastically exclaimed, "I knew you would make it back tonight!"

Until that moment, I had totally forgotten that Walter would be at our house! After a few seconds of confusion it occurred to me that as of a few weeks ago, he lived here too. This surprise, along with the almost blinding light awaiting us inside, left me standing in the middle of the foyer, disoriented and blinking. "Hey, Ziska, I'm really sorry about your father," said Walter awkwardly as he gave me his hand.

He was wearing pants and a cardigan that had been Gary's, and I remembered him being shy during his last visit to the house, but that had changed so drastically that I hardly recognized him. We went into the kitchen, where a small but complete evening meal was waiting, and for the first time in months I heard a blessing in Hebrew again. *I'm back!* I told myself, stunned, and let my eyes wander as we ate. Meanwhile, Walter told Amanda how his day at the movie theater had gone, and although I didn't much feel like talking, I didn't like it one bit that these two had obviously shared experiences that didn't include me!

It seemed like ages until Amanda finally noticed that I was at the table too, and said, "Poor Frances must think she's invisible by now! Children, let's go upstairs and sleep for a few hours."

"We can unpack tomorrow . . . and call Mrs. Lewis from the Refugee Committee. But first we'll have to get you a ration book," said Amanda as she climbed the stairs. "So, here we are. Do you remember it?"

Apart from the heavy blackout curtains covering the window, this was indeed my old, beloved room. My mezuzah, my books, Gary's model ships, the familiar bedspread, and the mobile hanging from the ceiling—all of it was still there. It looked like I had never left, as if the evacuation, Tail's End, the last eight months, and even Papa's death had never happened.

I felt a wave of panic, a feeling like I had somehow fallen out of time. "Perhaps you'd rather . . . after all that's happened . . . like to sleep with me tonight?" Amanda asked hesitantly.

"May I?" I whispered, ashamed. I pictured how lovingly she had kept the room just as it had been so that I would feel right at home if I should ever return. Why was everything always more complicated with me than for other people?

A few minutes later I was lying on Uncle Matthew's side of the bed, filled with a pleasant mixture of unfamiliarity and closeness. Amanda slid under the covers next to me and turned out the light. I heard her sigh. "I don't want to talk yet," I said immediately.

She rested her light, warm hand on my shoulder and left it there. That was all. Maybe she had understood.

I closed my eyes. She quietly began our evening prayer, but my thoughts had already moved on. Where was Mamu right now? Where had she buried Papa? Once more I saw him as he had come to the beach on my birthday, in the brown overcoat that I now recognized, and with a smile on his face.

But this time it didn't just last a second. This time I could hold on to that image as long as I wanted! And I knew that in the future, whenever I thought about Papa, I wouldn't see him as he had been the night he was arrested, his white feet, the bloody hand on the wall. From now on, he would always be standing on the beach in a country that had treated him decently, waiting for our thoughts to meet over the water.

So that had been my birthday present: a different picture, a different moment with my father that was more powerful than everything the Nazis had destroyed.

Unusually for me, I was the first to wake up the next morning. I opened the curtains to let Amanda know that it was time for breakfast, but she only mumbled and disappeared deeper beneath the covers.

But someone else was already up and about. Walter had made tea and sliced some bread along with the last of Mrs. Stone's cheese. The radio was on, and he sat at the kitchen table, reading the paper. It was almost scary.

"Since when can you read English?" I asked suspiciously as I sat down across from him.

He smiled. "It only looks that way. I'm still practicing."

"Aha," I murmured, hoping that other words would attach themselves to these meaningless syllables, but none did me the favor. There sat Walter, who had sent me such wonderful letters at Tail's End, and I had no idea what to say to him! He had grown considerably taller and thinner, enough that he would have caused a stir among my girl-friends in Tail's End.

"Why don't we have breakfast in the garden?" I asked at last.

"In the garden?" repeated Walter. "Come with me!"

"Oh, no!" I gasped as he opened the kitchen door. "Oh no, no, no!"

Finding bomb craters directly in front of me couldn't have shaken me more deeply. I had left a blossoming, fragrant paradise in September, and now I stood on a wobbly stone slab in the midst of a desolate field dotted with small white paper flags displaying the rain-washed labels of the plants beneath them. The depressing impression was reinforced by a corrugated metal object the size of a goat pen that was sunk two feet into the ground and full of standing water. "Allow me to introduce our Anderson shelter!" proclaimed Walter. "It doesn't look like much, but it will protect us from all but a direct hit."

Skeptically, I peered inside our private bunker. I wouldn't have expected such a thing to look inviting, but I would have counted on a little more than four frighteningly nar-row plank beds screwed into a metal frame with a small lake at the bottom! "Has anyone tried it out yet?" I asked gloomily.

"No, we thought when the alarm comes would be soon enough!" said Walter cheerfully. "The neighbors' children play in theirs . . . but I think theirs is sealed better."

I stood on tiptoe to look over the wooden fence and spied identical vegetable gardens and corrugated metal roofs as far as the eye could see. "Dig for victory!" explained Walter with pride. "Even Hyde Park is a vegetable garden now! Isn't it fantastic how the English can make a collective sport out of the worst adversity?"

We went back into the house, where the sound of Amanda's voice reached us from the hall. The telephone must have woken her; in any case, she said little more than "Hmm," and "Aha." When she hung up and came into the kitchen in her dressing gown I could see from her angry red cheeks that the call must have been from Mrs. Lewis of the Refugee Committee.

"I'll tell you something!" Amanda said grimly. "Your mother no longer has a say in what happens to you. At least that's Mrs. Lewis's opinion. She came very close to accusing me of kidnapping you! If I had told her of my plans before I left, you would certainly not be here this morning."

"And now?" I asked, frightened.

"We will get you a ration book and set you up in the family business."

"And school?"

"Reduced to a minimum. Many schoolteachers are in the army, or are doing important strategic work. In some parts of London there's no school at all anymore. I don't want you alone in the house, so you'll come join us in the city every day after school. We'll eat there, you can do your school-work in the office, and you can help us at the Elysée. And after the last show, we'll all drive home together."

"Work at the theater? Me? And school only in the mornings?"

"Not so bad, this war, is it?" said Walter.

Chapter 15

Divided and United

Apart from the fact that people were only allowed to shop in stores where they were registered as customers, I didn't find the rationing all that bad. Butter, sugar, meat, cheese, and sweets could only be gotten with coupons, and eggs and milk weren't always available. With full shopping bags we made our way back along Camden High Street and almost forgot that we were at war. During the day everything looked just as it always had: cars, taxis, buses, people were shopping, and store windows were full of lovely things. At most there were lines outside the supermarkets—and in front of our movie theater, the Elysée!

Just catching a glimpse of the theater from a distance filled me with pride. I loved the wide red carpet in the foyer and how your feet sank into it without a sound when you walked, and the mirror and crystal light fixtures along the way to the theater itself. The ticket booth was Amanda's territory, where she sold tickets and candy when she wasn't busy in the office leafing through lending catalogs.

My task was to sweep the theater between shows and

check under the seats to see if anyone had forgotten anything. When I was done, I took my place at the entrance to tear tickets for the next film. The first sound that reached my ears was always the melody of the weekly newsreel: The Home Guard built tank barriers to the sound of cheerful music, a famous diva made a guest appearance in the West End, and the princesses visited a children's hospital. As soon as the first images of the main film flickered on the screen I closed the door; anyone who came later was led to an empty seat with a flashlight.

All of that was fine, but after several weeks I felt ready for more important responsibilities. What could be so hard about winding a strip of celluloid around two or three little wheels in the projector? Granted, the machine was big and I would have to stand on a chair to put the top film roll on its peg. But there was a chair there. The problem wasn't my size; the problem was Walter. He wouldn't let me so much as touch the film rolls, as if the movie theater belonged to him!

Did he have to be such a showoff? He wouldn't even let me get on the ladder to change the letters in the marquee above the entrance when the new films came.

FRED ASTAIRE IN BROADWAY MELODY
VIVIEN LEIGH AND CLARK CABLE IN
GONE WITH THE WIND
JUDY GARLAND IN THE WIZARD OF OZ

I was supposed to stay on the ground and tell him if the spaces between the letters were even. The spaces between the letters! I wouldn't even think of it. I hoped he would make some embarrassing spelling mistake, but he never did.

I had become one of the most sought-after people in my new class after word spread that I owned a movie theater! Almost every afternoon kids I knew showed up, and I let them in for free. "Everyone at school wants to be friends with me now," I wrote to Mamu in delight.

"Would they want to even without the movies?" she wrote back.

I liked to think they would.

It was my second summer in England, and apart from being irritated by Walter, the loveliest time of my life. Only a quiet, reproachful voice seemed to want to make itself heard sometimes, one I was inexplicably convinced belonged to Bekka.

Your father is dead, your mother in a different country, and you laugh!

"My mother wants me to laugh," I defended myself. "She writes that her only pleasure is knowing that I'm doing well!"

But I bet she doesn't have any idea how well!

I tried to explain to Bekka that I could have the most wonderful day and still shed tears for my mother at night. *Is it okay to enjoy life without one's parents, Ziska?*

Fridays and Saturdays the Elysée was closed because of Shabbat. Walter visited his father while Amanda and I went for walks, read, listened to records, and of course the radio. Was I mistaken, or was she less strict than she used to be? It could have been because of rationing that things were more relaxed in the kitchen. After all, you had to eat what there was, even if the lettuce wasn't quite so clean. We turned off the electric lights ourselves too.

I continued to sleep in Uncle Matthew's bed, and wondered if she had told him about that. They wrote to each other, but Amanda didn't talk about it. We never talked about these things, and yet "it" was always there.

And when it finally happened, that event we had been reckoning with for a long time, I was too confused to respond by changing the routine I followed every day. On May 10, Germany invaded Holland, Belgium, Luxembourg, and France, and I didn't have enough imagination to recognize anything but the immediate consequences: the end of exchanging letters with Mamu, and worries that Uncle Matthew's portable cinema would now actually be at the front.

How could I have known what else it would mean? I went to school, then rode to the Elysée. The newsreel we showed that day hadn't been updated yet. That was reassuring: Anything we couldn't see couldn't be so terrible!

That very day we got a new prime minister and a few days later heard for the first time the voice that would accompany us throughout the rest of the war: "I have nothing to offer but blood, toil, tears, and sweat . . . You ask, what is our policy? I can say: It is to wage war, by sea, land, and air, with all our might and with all the strength that God can give us; to wage war against a monstrous tyranny, never surpassed in the dark, lamentable catalog of human crime."

"Praise be to God," Amanda said softly with her ear pressed to the radio.

"I feel sure," said Winston Churchill, and I believed him on the spot, "that our cause will not be suffered to fail among men."

I recognized the pale, big man immediately, even though I had only seen Walter's father once before. From my spot at the entrance to the theater I watched him pacing back and forth on the sidewalk outside the glass entrance door before he finally decided to come in.

"Thank you . . . Enjoy the film . . ." Automatically I tore tickets and said my phrases, keeping an eye on the foyer. Walter's father handed Amanda an envelope in the ticket booth, leaned forward awkwardly, and tilted his head as if he was listening to her. Then he lifted both arms in a broad gesture of resignation and let them fall again.

The door to the ticket booth opened and Amanda came out, her face white as chalk. "This must be a mistake," I heard her say, not once, but twice, then three times, as if it would only really be so if she repeated it often enough. She approached me with the envelope in her hands, but her gaze went right through me, and even before I saw her climbing the stairs to the projection room I understood that it must have something to do with Walter.

When the newsreel began, Amanda came down the stairs with Walter. Walter held the envelope, looking completely stunned.

"It's true, my boy," his father said awkwardly in German. "We're being deported."

"I just can't believe it!" Amanda murmured. "Please wait, Mr. Glücklich. I'm sure we can clear this up quickly." She took the letter from Walter and ran into the office. The people who were waiting at the ticket booth exchanged concerned looks. Apparently they too had noticed that something wasn't right. The Glücklichs stood there with sagging shoulders and looked at each other hopelessly. "What's going on?" I asked anxiously. But no one answered. Finally, I couldn't stand it anymore and followed Amanda into the office, where I expected to find her on the phone, energetically sorting out the matter, solving every problem, as always.

But my foster mother stood like a statue next to her desk, one hand on the receiver she had just put back in its cradle. It was the first time I had seen her cry, and the sight made a deeper impression on me than anything that had happened to us in the previous months. "I am so sorry, Frances," she whispered, and hugged me with a force that belied sheer desperation. "I apologize for my country . . ."

Shortly thereafter, Walter and his father arrived at the train station with their meager belongings, where they joined a crowd of German and Austrian men, women, and children already climbing into waiting passenger trains. All across the country, these trains were headed for internment camps such as Huyton, Douglas, and Port Erin on the Isle of Man, but also to the pier in Liverpool, where the "enemy aliens" were crammed into the stifling cargo areas of ships. After torturous months at sea they reached Australia, Newfoundland, or Canada.

At least the Glücklichs were spared that particular torture. On the Isle of Man they encountered conditions that must have seemed luxurious to Walter's father by comparison to his lodgings in the East End. True, they had to work in a tailor's shop there as well, but soon there was a small library, music, and art, and since there were quite a few intellectuals among the refugees, there were even lectures. The people held in the camps were allowed to receive packages and write two letters per week. If it hadn't been for the high barbed-wire fence that held them captive side by side with some steadfast Nazis, the interned Jews might have been able to convince themselves that they were in some kind of sanatorium.

For Amanda, Walter's internment was a turning point— not only of the war, but in her entire life up to that point as an obedient Orthodox housewife. She hadn't been able to prevent her son from going off to war, nor her husband from setting off on an adventure that had recently become life-threatening. But the fact that a sixteen-year-old boy who had been entrusted to her care was torn away from her and suspected of espionage was the final straw. Literally over-night, my foster mother came to the conclusion that she had held her peace long enough.

"We are not going to accept this. We're going to get him out of there, you'll see."

"Get him out? You have no idea! Ask my mother what it's like trying to get someone released from a camp!"

"This isn't a concentration camp, love. We're not in Nazi Germany. There's a certain amount of hysteria in the air at the moment, but when the public grasps who they've locked up there, Walter will certainly be freed!"

In the following weeks, my foster mother discovered a new activity: protest. She wrote to the government and to individual officials, wrote letters to the editors of every news-paper and radio station—and through her efforts learned that she wasn't the only one fighting against the internment of foreigners. Various groups and individuals had dedicated themselves to the same goal. They even banded together for a demonstration.

Almost unchecked, the Germans were marching toward the English Channel, cutting off our troops fighting in Belgium and northern France from the units stationed farther south. The momentum of the German blitzkrieg overran everything in its path, and two weeks after the invasion began, we had no indication at all where Uncle Matthew and his frontline theater might be.

The uncertainty about Uncle Matthew caused Amanda to step up her efforts on Walter's behalf. It distracted her from brooding and helplessly waiting. More than once I woke up during the night and noticed that she lay next to me sleepless, staring at the ceiling. I had inferred from some comment of hers that my foster parents had exchanged harsh words as they parted, and the thought that she might not be able to take them back tortured Amanda.

Now I had her all to myself—and I couldn't have been more depressed. Afternoons in the theater I wished for nothing more fervently than to be able to get annoyed about Walter jealously guarding the projector. With a heavy heart, I stared at the movie posters on the walls of the projector room, the bits of dust caught in the projector's light, or the humming reels as they turned. The fact that after watching how it was done several times I could, indeed, exchange the reels without the film being projected crookedly or catching on fire wasn't the slightest consolation.

While Uncle Matthew had only recently been exposed to immediate danger, that had been the case for Gary since the beginning of the war. Day and night, German U-boats hunted the ships of the Merchant Navy that supplied England with provisions and items essential to the war effort. Gary served in one of their convoys, and ever since I had seen images of the impressively threatening convoys in the newsreels, all illusions about the romance of life at sea had vanished.

The enemy lurked especially along the most important route of the British merchant ships, in the Atlantic between North America and Europe, and while the British Expeditionary Forces were hopelessly surrounded in France, the navy lost many ships to torpedoes and U-boats. We listened, tormented, as yet more attacks on convoys were announced on the radio.

Had I really thought the war wouldn't be all that bad? Sometimes I asked myself whether my presence was a relief for Amanda, or a burden—whether she was happy not to be alone, or if it was an additional strain on her nerves to stay in control for my sake. "Stop staring at me like that!" she blurted out, and once she even locked herself in her room for hours. But I couldn't stop myself—with every new report I nervously scanned her face, looking for signs that would tell me whether it was a small, medium, or big catastrophe this time. A small catastrophe was good news. It didn't get any better than that.

What, for example, should I make of the news that so many British soldiers had been taken as prisoners of war? For the captured soldiers, it was probably only a medium catastrophe; they wouldn't see their families for a long time, but they were still alive, and the war was over for them. There were strict regulations about the treatment of POWs that even the Germans had to adhere to. But what if the prisoner was a Jew?

And what should I think about the Royal Air Force bombing German cities? Did I really want my former hometown to go up in flames? For Bekka to be in danger, and Christine?

Weeks passed before it occurred to me that I had a clever friend I could ask about the war. I had been wanting to visit him for a while, and wasn't even sure I would still find him.

"This is the first happy day in a long time!" Professor Schueler told the waiter as he ordered my hot chocolate. "My young friend is back!" Meanwhile, I furtively scanned the room and tried not to show my dismay. I remembered the Café Vienna as a loud, lively place, and I couldn't have imagined it any other way. But now lots of the tables were empty. No one I saw was younger than Professor Schueler.

"It's quite a change, isn't it?" the professor commented with a bitter smile. "Let's not talk about that. So you are back from your evacuation, I see. Did it go well for you? What news is there from your family?"

I told him everything about Tail's End, the Stones, Hazel, and Adolf. "And your family?" he repeated.

I hesitated. Did he really want to hear that Papa was no longer alive, Uncle Matthew was missing in France and Walter imprisoned on the Isle of Man, that Gary was being hunted down by U-boats in the Atlantic, and that I hadn't heard anything from Mamu in weeks? "Mrs. Shepard and I are running the theater by ourselves now!" I dodged his question.

Professor Schueler's face clouded over immediately. "Oh, dear," he murmured. "What has happened?"

After just a few words I realized how good it felt to finally talk about everything. I didn't even have to cry. When I was finished, it was quiet for a moment.

"I often think that my mother could be here if I had tried harder knocking on doors," I admitted with a heavy heart.

But Professor Schueler shook his head energetically. "You are not responsible for your mother, Ziska! It's the grown-ups who have to make the decisions. At one point, your parents made what seems to have been a bad decision, to stay in Germany. But the wonderful thing is that they also made another, very good decision—they were able to save you! Now it's your job to do everything in your power to make sure the good decision prevails."

"How?"

"Live!" he said. "And live well! That is the only thing you can do for them."

Someone turned the radio up. I heard an agitated voice speaking English and a quiet murmuring in German: "What's he saying? What was that?"

"Do you speak English, child?" someone called, and suddenly everyone turned toward me.

"She speaks beautiful English!" said Professor Schueler proudly. Obediently, I stood up and walked over to the radio. The old men got very quiet and looked at me eagerly. It didn't take long for me to understand the news—but a full, dreadful minute passed before I found my voice again.

"Our troops are pulling out of France," I finally heard myself say. "The units are retreating from the entire country toward Dunkirk on the Belgian coast. The navy is gathering every available ship in the English Channel to rescue the soldiers. Thousands of British and French troops are lined up on the beach, and they're sitting targets for the German fighter pilots."

The men groaned in horror. "The RAF is in the air as well . . . appalling scenes are unfolding," I continued to translate, now simultaneously with the voice on the radio. "The ships that were able to depart are being shot at by U-boats and low-flying planes as they make their way across the channel. They had calculated evacuating about fifty thousand soldiers, but the extent of this rescue effort is clearly much larger . . . will likely last several days . . . and I'd like to go now, please! I have to get home right away!"

"Thank you!" several of them called after me. I waved to Professor Schueler, burst onto the street, and ran to the subway station. The news was spreading like wildfire: The Brits are retreating from France! Now all that was left was to defend England. But I had just one thought: Was Uncle Matthew among those being saved?

It was Saturday, just before the end of Shabbat, and when I didn't find Amanda at home I knew she had heard the news too, and decided to go to the synagogue. The women in the balcony made room for me to get through to her. I hadn't genuinely prayed in a long time, but that night I learned that you can always take it up again, in any language.

Dear God, please spare Uncle Matthew, who is a good person and loves you, and is missed and needed. Give him back

to us, especially Amanda, who still needs to make peace with
him. I won't complain about anything ever again, and I'll go
back to Hebrew school too.

"School is canceled until further notice," Mrs. Holly greeted
us on Wednesday morning. "The classrooms are temporarily
needed for the war effort. Please go back home and take all
your belongings with you."

Somewhere in the school building I heard younger children cheering; they had probably just heard the same news.
Unlike them, we older students exchanged worried looks.

On my way home, I saw something else across the
courtyard: a big military vehicle driving up to the gym. Boy
Scouts jumped out and began to unload it. They handed
each other what looked like blankets, and there were some
tables, and large metal canisters. I stood rooted to the
spot. "Soldiers from Dunkirk are going to be brought here,
right?" I asked.

"We can't talk about it," said one of the boys dismissively.

"But I'm waiting for someone . . . please!"

"Your father?"

"Yes!" I affirmed.

"Sorry. Only Frenchies are being brought here, almost a
thousand French soldiers." Disappointed, I left.

Your father, eh? Are you out of your mind, Ziska? I ran
home without answering Bekka. It was the fifth day of the
retreat from Dunkirk. When would the last train arrive? The
first two days I had been very optimistic and expected to see
Uncle Matthew any minute, but with every hour that passed,
I lost a little more hope.

Amanda was in the yard wearing pants and an old jacket, hacking at the earth and energetically pulling weeds from the vegetable patch. She had a cotton cloth wrapped around her head and used the end of it to wipe the sweat from her forehead. When I stepped out of the kitchen door, she sat up, surprised to see me.

"School is closed, they need it to put up soldiers. No, no!" I added quickly as she startled. "I already asked! It's only French soldiers."

"French," she said. Her eyes shone in a peculiar way. "I think that's exactly where he might be!"

If the scouts had seriously believed they could quarter a thousand Frenchmen in the school without the public getting involved, they certainly knew better by now. The schoolyard was abuzz with people. Boy Scouts, teachers, housewives who had brought teapots, and men from the Home Guard greeted the overwhelmed soldiers, offered them something to drink, and handed out blankets. Children wandered around and marveled at the foreigners, giggling about their language. But most of the soldiers just stood around, confused and exhausted, as if they couldn't grasp what was happening to them.

We ran alongside the buses, Amanda on the right side, me on the left, trying to spot Uncle Matthew. Amanda talked to some of the soldiers in the courtyard, but no one seemed to know anything about my foster father. I pressed on, peering into unfamiliar faces, and felt Amanda's disappointment creeping into my heart, even though I hadn't for a second seriously believed we would find him here.

Next to the entrance to the gym a cluster of soldiers was gathered around two bearded men, who offered them paper and pens so they could write a few lines to their relatives. The pens were practically being torn out of their hands, and as I went by I recognized one of them vaguely, probably from the synagogue. He spoke French with the soldiers as I made my way past them into the gym.

Inside, the Boy Scouts were ladling soup from enormous kettles, served with bread and coffee or tea. The soldiers slurped loudly right from the bowls, greedily tearing off huge chunks of bread and dunking them in the soup as if they hadn't eaten in days.

"Ask your mum for some old clothes of your dad's," one woman told me, "and best bring them right away."

"I will," I replied, and hurried out, energized by the desire to make a useful contribution too. I was so intent on my errand that I didn't look left or right and didn't know at first from which direction someone suddenly called my name.

"Frances? Frances! Frances!"

I stopped dead in my tracks and looked around breathlessly. Uncle Matthew . . . ? But I couldn't spot him anywhere, only the bearded man from the synagogue gave his stack of paper and pens to his colleague and rushed toward me with long strides.

And I, now that I had finally recognized him, was so shocked that I turned right around and ran away! "Amanda!" I screamed at the top of my lungs. Ziska and Frances, masters of the inappropriate response, champions of flight.

But my response didn't matter anymore. Amanda saw

me coming, Uncle Matthew right behind me, and I saw right away that the fight they had had before his departure was a thing of the past. They threw themselves into each other's arms, disbelieving, joyous, shaken, and then tried to do everything all at once: laugh, cry, kiss, whisper. I stood next to them, torn between fascination and deep embarrassment—the moment when a film would have cut to the next scene was long past!

"I'll head home, then, and put on the tea," I finally said. But it didn't seem to interest anyone in the least that I was still there.

So I started off, thinking about how unsettling and difficult it was to be at the mercy of love, and thoroughly convinced that it would be better to do without it during wartime.

Uncle Matthew and the man who sold stationery in Finchley, whose idea it had been, made sure that the soldiers' letters were sent off quickly. Then he came home, slept almost twenty-four hours straight, shaved off the beard that had made him seem so unfamiliar, and was finally "back" for me too.

"Say, what would you think of a little walk, Frances?" he suggested the next morning.

"Alone?" I asked, astonished and a little unnerved, because I had assumed he and Amanda wouldn't want to be apart for even a minute! But Uncle Matthew said, "You and I haven't seen each other for so long—I think there are a few things we should talk about."

It took an unexpectedly long time to make our way down the street. Every few yards someone came out of their house to greet Uncle Matthew and ask him the same questions: Had he really been there at the beach and in the boats, was it true that the British had been forced to leave all their military equipment in France, and why had the Germans been able to beat us in the first place? Uncle Matthew patiently explained to each of them that he had stood belly deep in the English Channel while bullets splashed into the water all around him, that they had been shot at from planes for sixteen hours a day prior to that without any British fighters appearing in the sky, and that in his opinion, England had entered this war woefully inadequately prepared.

The more often I heard it, the more horrified I was, because only then did I understand what a miracle it was that Uncle Matthew had come home unharmed! I was glad when we finally reached the next street, where no one knew us and no one asked questions.

"Frances, I want to tell you how deeply sorry I am that you've lost your father," Uncle Matthew began, and he looked at me with such sadness that much to my chagrin, tears welled up in my eyes. To not be able to cry for Papa and then to tear up because someone expressed sympathy for *me*—that was absurd!

"I've seen a lot of men die in the past few days," he continued, "and believe me, it's something I'll never forget. But I also saw many, many men praying—to God, to Jesus, to Mary, to the saints. God is so much greater than we can ever imagine. So why shouldn't he appear to different people in different forms? Your father was a Christian, but he was also a Jew. He was one of us. We want to ask you if it would offend your parents in any way if we prayed a kaddish for him."

"Oh, Uncle Matthew, definitely not! That would be so wonderful . . . and I couldn't be at the funeral in Holland, you know . . ."

"Exactly," he said kindly. "So that's settled."

I hooked my arm into his. "I'm so glad you're back!"

"So am I, with my whole heart! I heard the most amazing things about you—you being here was the only thing that kept Amanda from total despair. I should never have left against her will. But one word—*la France!*—and there was no stopping me." He shook his head remorsefully. "And now look what I've done! My expensive equipment is gone, I barely escaped with my life, and am more than grateful that my wife will have me back at all."

"And now?" I asked, letting go of his arm again.

"We're still at war. I'll help take care of the Frenchmen and then sign up for the Home Guard. And Amanda wants to go back to helping her old people at the nursing home at least once a week in addition to working at the Elysée. We'll have to see how we manage everything. While we're at it, do you have any wishes?"

"No!" I replied, and laughed. "I just want to stay with you. Otherwise I don't care about anything."

"That would be my next point," Uncle Matthew continued in a serious tone. "We're facing a power that will go to any lengths—I hardly need to tell you that! Over in France they ran right over us, and if they should attack here in the next days or weeks, we don't have much left to fight them off with. Frances . . ." He hesitated a moment and then decided to speak openly. "There's no reason to think they'll spare the Jews in this country. Under the circumstances, it would be better for you not to be staying with a Jewish family."

I stood still in disbelief. Uncle Matthew didn't notice it because he was looking at the ground as he walked on. "In a different family you might be able to . . . hide. No one would ever need to know who you are!"

When he turned around there were five paces between us, but it seemed like an entire vast ocean. "As far as I'm concerned, the whole world can know who I am," I said. "I'm starting to feel quite content with it, actually! You can't just send me away anymore, Uncle Matthew, because my home is with you!"

"Send you away?! We're worried about your safety . . ."

"I know. You want to give me back to my mother unharmed, if she comes. You know, I can hardly stand to hear that anymore." Suddenly I screamed at him, "Maybe my mother isn't coming back! Maybe she's already dead! Maybe I don't have anyone else left except for you!"

"I'll be darned," murmured Uncle Matthew. "I messed it up. Calm down, Frances, no one wants to send you away. Just forget what I said, okay? It was a long night. Maybe we didn't think it through carefully."

"Apparently not!" I shot back, and started to tremble— not because I was seriously afraid of being sent away, but because I could hardly believe what I had just said.

My mother might not be coming back.

And Uncle Matthew hadn't contradicted me. So he and Amanda had already thought of that possibility.

Exhausted, I lay on my bed, where I had started sleeping again two nights ago, and stared at the ceiling, searching inside of me for some glimmer of hope, a prayer, to undo that terrible sentence. But there was none.

Maybe she won't come back.

It wasn't a new thought, and I had known for a long time that it was the truth. But I should never, ever have spoken it aloud. It felt as if by speaking the words out loud, I had set something unstoppable into motion.

You can't do anything more for your mother.

Live! And live well!

My home is with you now.

One thought followed to its end. A new one begun.

Chapter 16

Leave

Herr Mittenbaum had a weakness for folk songs. At first it seemed so inappropriate to be singing German songs in a Jewish retirement home. But after several nurses had poked their heads into the room and remarked that it was just the right medicine for the residents' homesickness, and did I happen to know "*Ich weiß nicht, was soll es bedeuten*," I went home and practiced everything the music teacher in Berlin had ever taught us.

This was my second visit with Herr Mittenbaum, and I boldly made my way through all the verses of "*Lorelei*." The other elderly men who shared the room sat on their beds and quietly hummed along. But I knew Herr Becher was only putting up with it until I finally started translating the newspaper for them.

The sharp, bright tone of the sirens cut right through the song, and right through my chest. I sat with my mouth open, mute, without breathing—my first air raid! In school, I didn't want to admit that I hadn't been through one yet; secretly I actually wanted to get it over with soon so I could finally be in the know.

But that wish flew out the window the instant the siren started screeching, up and down in a spine-chilling wail. "W-what do we do now?" I stuttered, frozen with fear.

"We wait," said Herr Becher. "Go ahead and start the first page!"

I reached for the newspaper as if hypnotized and whispered in German: "President Roosevelt intends to increase material support of France following Italy's declaration of war, but is opposed to the United States entering the war."

The door opened and a small army of nurses came in pushing wheelchairs in front of them. "Let's go, into the wheelchairs, gentlemen!" one of them called. "Time for a trip to the cellar!"

"Is everything okay, dear?" Amanda asked, and touched my cheek lightly before she helped Herr Mittenbaum into a wheelchair. I nodded weakly and followed them down a long hallway with a gleaming linoleum floor, where it smelled like the cabbage soup that had been served for lunch.

At the end of the corridor, four more nurses came out of the elevator with empty wheelchairs to go collect more of the residents. Amanda took my hands and placed them on the handle of Herr Mittenbaum's wheelchair. "You ride down with him, Frances. I'll take the stairs," she said.

"*Ein Märchen aus uralten Zeiten . . .*" Herr Mittenbaum sang happily.

The elevator door opened and there was Amanda, who had gotten to the cellar even faster than us. I stumbled out past her.

"Would you like to push Herr Mittenbaum into the shelter, Frances?" she asked.

I grasped the left handle of the wheelchair as she took the right one. Together we steered Herr Mittenbaum through the basement.

It was warmer and brighter down here than I had expected—not the dim, damp room where, in my imagination, the bomb raids played themselves out. There were a radio and gramophone, plenty of blankets, and even beds, which were already occupied by the weaker residents. The wailing sirens only came through quietly and from far away, as if it couldn't possibly be meant for us. "I'll help get the rest of the people and then I'll come be with you," Amanda said softly.

"*Muss i denn, muss i denn zum Städtele hinaus?*" Herr Mittenbaum started to croon. But Herr Becher immediately pressed the newspaper into my hand: "Enough singing, it's time for the news!"

It was almost two hours before the single, sustained note of the all-clear signal released us from the cellar, and it was another hour before all the old people had been transported back to their rooms and I could catch my first glimpse outside. To my astonishment, absolutely nothing had changed. Nothing had been damaged, and people walked through the streets perfectly calmly, as if they were coming out of a department store instead of air-raid shelters. "Is that it?" I asked, puzzled.

"Well, of course that's it!" Amanda lifted one eyebrow. "Did you think anything would happen to us now, two days before Gary's furlough? God's ways may be infathomable, but I can't imagine that his timing would be so awful!"

I had missed Gary's first two visits when I was in Tail's

End, and even this third home leave wasn't a sure thing. After Italy declared war on us, an attack on the British bases in the Mediterranean was to be expected. "Now they'll never let him go!" Amanda had fretted.

But just a day later a telegram arrived from Gary: His well-deserved vacation would take place as planned! He would come, even if it would only be for a week.

Impulsively, I let out a shout of joy that chased away the last bits of fear. Gary, Mamu, Amanda, Uncle Matthew, Walter . . . there were so many reasons to survive this war!

For a woman in wartime, there is nothing more wonderful than to be able to meet her soldier at the train station. The melancholy record albums Amanda and I listened to every evening had convinced me of that, and I also knew just how to prepare for such an important event.

"Will you lend me a hat?" I asked my foster mother.

"Of course I'll lend you a hat. But first you have to decide what you'll wear, so everything goes together," she instructed me.

I spent hours roaming back and forth between my room and hers, where there was a large mirror, as I took an increasingly hopeless inventory of my closet. That morning I made several disturbing discoveries. First, I didn't have a single outfit that went together. Secondly, there wasn't a single piece of clothing that genuinely looked flattering. And thirdly, I looked rather awful in general, something I had never noticed before. Amanda found me dissolved in tears, with her room and mine looking like battlefields. "You can go to the train station without me!" I wailed.

"Dear God," she said grimly, looking around. I pushed some clothes on the floor and threw myself on her bed sobbing.

"Leave me alone!" Experience had taught me that this was usually a good tactic for getting comfort and attention. But Amanda was not her usual self today.

"Every free minute," she said in a quaking voice, "that isn't spent with bookkeeping and showing films and selling tickets, I'm cleaning, cooking, and washing in this damned house. I don't expect you to help with the housework. You're a child. BUT DAMMIT, I DO EXPECT YOU TO NOT MAKE THINGS EVEN HARDER ON ME THAN THEY ALREADY ARE!"

My jaw fell open and I stared at her. Amanda had never yelled at me before, and she had certainly never said "damn" twice in a row.

"In fifteen minutes," she said in a shaky voice, "every single thing will be hanging in its proper place and this room will be NEAT. Do you understand me?"

I nodded silently. Amanda rushed out and was only halfway down the stairs by the time I gathered up a pile of clothes and stepped out into the hallway. Her cry as the front door opened made me drop my armful of clothing on the spot. I stormed down the stairs, but after a few steps stood still as if rooted to the spot. A marine officer in white and blue carried Amanda through the foyer to the sounds of his own triumphant cries and her muffled, halfhearted protest: "Why are you here so early? We wanted to meet you! Dad isn't even home yet!"

The sailor set Amanda back down on her feet, and I,

watching from the stairs, was spellbound by the similarity between the two of them, which I had forgotten in the eleven months since I had last seen Gary.

"If I had known that," he said with a grin, "of course I would have waited half the day for you at the train station, but silly me, I thought you'd be happy for every extra minute I'm at home!" It must have been the word *home* that made him look around at his surroundings for a moment, and in that moment he found me! "Hey!" he called softly. "Don't tell me that's my little sister!"

Just seeing him step toward the bottom of the staircase sent cold shivers down my spine. I couldn't have said which was more wonderful, and at the same time harder to bear: looking at Gary, or noticing the way he looked at me!

He had changed a lot. His face had grown thinner, almost angular, and he seemed much older than his nineteen years. A suntan brought out his green eyes, and they had a different sheen to them than they had had before. More serious, wiser. As if no one could remain the same in this war, even my carefree, invulnerable brother.

As always, it was Gary who broke the spell and made the first step toward me. I finally jumped up and threw myself around his neck. "You came at just the right time!" I cried. "Mum and I just had a terrible row!"

I suppose I had wanted to say "*your* mum," but I hadn't thought about it at all. Amanda and I were both stunned to hear me say it.

But not Gary. "What was it about?" he immediately wanted to know.

"Actually," Amanda replied as we led him into the kitchen, "it was only about a hat."

"A hat, seriously? Look at her, Mum, she's growing up!" Gary tossed his kit bag into the corner.

"Come sit down and have some cake," Amanda said.

We sat across from him and watched him eat. "How is it that you're here already?" Amanda asked.

"I didn't take the train. A medical officer drove me and two others from Plymouth," he explained. Amanda leaned forward to serve Gary more cake, and the odd sensation that had come over me as I listened to him intensified. Something wasn't right. He talked a little too fast, a bit too loud, and in the moments that passed as he waited for his second slice of cake, I understood why he had eaten so quickly. His right hand trembled—just a little, but still enough to want to distract us from it. Our eyes met, and when he realized that I had seen it, he gave a slight shake of his head and asked me in an almost warning tone, "Heard anything from Walter?"

"No," I responded, trying not to lower my gaze. "But he is doing well and I send him half my ration of sweets every week."

"Good girl. Nothing lifts the morale like a package with sweets. Listen, please don't be offended, but I absolutely have to smoke a cigarette and take a nap. I want to be in good shape when Dad gets home."

He stood up without even touching his second piece of cake, drew a squashed pack of cigarettes out of his pocket, and was already on his way to the kitchen door. "Gary, you can smoke inside, you don't need . . ." Amanda began.

"Just let me get used to being here, Mum," he interrupted

her, and the cheerful façade fell away in an instant, without any warning. He looked young, vulnerable, and incredibly tired. Quickly he disappeared through the door and his outline flitted past the garden window.

We practically jumped to the window to peer out. Gary wandered along the fence, smoking, gazed into our corrugated metal bunker for a long time, picked a leaf out of the hedge. "He's so thin," whispered Amanda, "and did you see his hand?"

"He'll be better in a day or two! And don't you tremble yourself sometimes when you're tired?"

"You're right. Heavens, just look at me." She wiped a hand across her eyes. "A bundle of nerves—just what he needs right now. Promise that you'll kick me if I start to act foolish."

I put my arm around her waist and snuggled up to her. "If you do, I'll think of something else. I'm certainly not going to kick you!"

"My sweetie! I'm so sorry about earlier."

"Me too. It was my fault."

"No. It's just this damned war!"

I let go of her. "What should we cook?" I asked brightly. "I'll put everything away upstairs, then I'll come help you. When Gary's rested, this will be the greatest week ever, want to bet?"

"No. Jewish people don't make bets," Amanda replied, and could finally laugh again, even more so when I countered: "And I'll bet Jews don't say 'damn' either."

We could seat Gary and Uncle Matthew as far apart as we wanted, but at some point the conversation always came around to the war. While Churchill and Lord Halifax ranted against Chamberlain and Lloyd George in the House of Commons, Gary and his father were having the same heated debate in our dining room.

Even Amanda resorted to sarcasm after a few days. "Why don't we invite the BBC to broadcast our dinners? Then the politicians could take a vacation," she suggested.

But it was no use. The war, which had already driven a deep gouge in the European map, now divided the Shepard house as well.

"How can anyone even seriously consider surrendering to these pigs?" Gary ranted. "And especially my own father, a Jew! Do you want to sign your own death warrant, Dad? Yours, mine, and Frances's? Mum they'll at least wave through, and be thrilled by her perfect Irish Catholic pedigree."

"It's not about surrender, it's about reaching a peace agreement with Germany!" Uncle Matthew turned red in the face. "Our death sentence, if you dare speak of such a thing, would be the invasion. If we make a peace treaty, they won't touch us."

"Don't be so naive, Dad. You can't trust those people! They've broken every single treaty they've ever made."

"Have you looked at a map lately? Eight countries around us are in German hands. All our heavy artillery was left in France. The only power that could still save us has decided to remain neutral. It's not a question of wanting to, Gary, we don't have any *choice* anymore!"

"Wrong! Roosevelt will convince Congress. It can't be in America's best interest to have the Nazis ruling Europe."

"Would anyone else like another baked apple?" Amanda

asked. In reply she heard: "Congress?! The entire American public is against the war! Haven't you heard? *We won't sacrifice our American boys to save the Jews!*"

"Okay," said Gary. "Let's just imagine that we do sign a peace treaty with the Germans. Our island remains intact at first. And what happens forty miles away?"

Uncle Matthew bristled with anger. "I've seen what's happening there. I was there myself, you know!"

"Which is why I can't understand you! These tyrants have to be stopped! You may be too old to understand this, but I don't want to live in a world where the Nazis are in charge!" With those words, Gary threw his napkin onto the table and left the room.

"Matthew," Amanda said through gritted teeth, "in a few days our son is going back to his ship to fight! He's lost four mates that he knew personally, and I won't listen for one more minute while you attack him!"

Uncle Matthew turned pale. "You're right," he said. "I at least owe him moral support."

"He didn't tell me that he's lost friends!" I muttered, after Uncle Matthew left the room.

Amanda replied: "It's a pleasure for him to have someone he can still talk to about normal, everyday things."

She was right. As soon as we were alone, the comfortable familiarity between Gary and me returned. For several days we even shared a new secret—though it was one I would much rather not have known about!

Happily, I handed tools to my hero while he dismantled the corrugated metal bunker in our yard. "I hope the Home

Guard is teaching Dad how to build a decent shelter," he teased, after he had exposed the muddy hole that hadn't been sealed off when our shelter had been built the first time. "The shovel, Frances!"

I adjusted my straw hat and moved gracefully to carry out his command. Gary's bare upper body gleamed in the sunlight, and I admired the muscles in his shoulders and arms as he shoveled wet earth out of the hole. "You're incredibly brown," I commented.

"But only to here!" Gary revealed a pasty white stripe below his hips. "Without clothes on I look like someone dipped me halfway in mud."

"So you spend all day on deck in the sunshine," I answered wittily.

"Well, my assignments include a certain amount of scrubbing and mopping outdoors," he replied with good humor. "But did I tell you that I'm going to be transferred to one of the brand-new battle cruisers? The *Princess of Malta*! Sounds good, doesn't it?"

"Fantastic!" I sighed. "Too bad I'm not in Tail's End anymore. I could make them so jealous talking about you!"

Gary laughed and leaned against the shovel. "Tail's End! How I enjoyed your letters!" He took a deep drag on his cigarette. "I'm writing someone," he added casually.

"Oh?" A sharp pang stabbed my heart. "Who is it?"

"Melissa Cole. The sister of Philip, the first of my buddies who got hit—off the coast of Iceland. I wrote to his parents, and Melissa wrote back. Here . . ." He reached into his pocket and pulled out a small photo. "What do you think of her?"

"Nice," I lied to the round-faced blonde and sat down

slowly. The stars that flickered before my eyes, the mounting nausea . . . if I stood a second longer, I would have fallen onto Gary.

Gary took the picture from my hand and looked at it dreamily. "I think she looks a little bit like Mum—around the eyes," he said, which pushed me over the edge.

"Well, I don't think so at all," I grumbled.

"I'll find out soon," Gary announced as he put the photo back in his wallet. "When I leave here I'm going to Henley for three days to visit Melissa's family."

My mouth hung open. He was cutting short his long-awaited visit with us to go stay with a family of total strangers? The afternoon was getting worse by the minute!

"Do your parents know about this?" I asked, outraged.

"Not yet. They know I'm leaving on Monday, but of course they think I'm going straight back to the ship. Keep it to yourself, will you? It's bad enough if they find out on the weekend. Melissa is three years older than me," Gary added, "and she's not Jewish. Seems to run in the family. But of course she won't have it nearly as hard as Mum."

"Wait a minute. You haven't even met Melissa!" The name turned into a hiss in my mouth.

But Gary just shrugged his shoulders. "People can get to know each other through letters too. Is there any other way during the war? Give me the tarp."

I threw the tarp into the hole. Gary unfolded it and began to stomp it into the ground.

"You have no idea how much I've looked forward to see-ing you again!" he said with a smile. "It's hard to believe you just arrived last year! It seems like you've always been here with us, doesn't it? And now," he added, "you can take the other shovel and fill in with dirt from around the edges. I'll stamp it down firm, we'll let it dry, then seal the floor with hot tar and put the bunker back together. Then when the bombs fall, you'll be all cozy and comfortable in here!"

I cried for three nights. By the time it was Amanda's turn to spill tears in secret—not because of Melissa Cole herself, but because of the three days with Gary we were cheated of—I was already feeling better, and even got a certain satisfaction from finally having someone to hate again. It was a good thing I didn't know about voodoo, or I probably would have tried something really nasty! Instead I limited my efforts to secretly wishing that by the time Gary arrived, Melissa Cole would have an enormous pimple.

Gary, who had no clue about the abyss his news had thrown me into, became visibly more relaxed. He slept a lot and ate his way through all of his favorite dishes, which Amanda prepared for him. She had stayed home from work to devote her full attention to him, but the day before he left he insisted on coming along to the Elysée to see how she managed everything.

While the main film was running he said to me, "I couldn't possibly leave tomorrow without showing you my favorite spot in the Elysée!"

Curious, I followed him through the lobby into the back room of the theater. We slipped through a door with a sign that said "No Entrance" into a narrow, unlit hallway that led along the side walls of the theater. The voices and sounds of the film followed us; its flickering lights fell through the narrow openings between the walls and the ceiling and showed us the way.

We turned a corner and found ourselves in the space directly behind the screen, which had a high ceiling but was only a few yards wide. It was used as storage space. I had only been here once, and the sounds of the weekly news reel had washed over me at such an intense volume that I could feel their echoes under my ribs hours later. Now Gary and I found ourselves eye to eye with the friendly face of James Stewart, who strolled through Washington to the gentle tones of a sweet, sad melody.

Immediately, I felt like I had been enchanted. "But what if they see us from the other side?" I asked.

Gary shook his head. "The light falls from the other side onto the screen and breaks there, so no one can see us. Here, take a seat."

Gary turned his chair and mine to face each other and sat down before me with a serious expression on his face. "I want to discuss a family matter with you, Frances," he said.

How strange and unfamiliar he looked. Half of his face was covered by shadows, while bright, flickering light shone on the other half. His one visible eye bored into me. I wasn't listening to the voices coming from the speakers anymore.

"I've been thinking for a long time about whether or not I should do this," he continued. "I mean talking about the future, which no one can know, especially these days. But then I thought, to hell with it, if anyone understands, it's Frances! My little sister with her two lives, with all the decisions and changes she's already had to make without knowing why, she'll understand."

"Of course," I responded encouragingly to his smile, while at the same time asking myself how he could possibly think something so amazing about me.

"I plan to come back from this war," Gary said. "I want to go to college, have a career, be a good husband, and, well, give my mum a pack of grandchildren!" He laughed for a moment and then was serious again. "I fully intend to do all of that, and I believe in it. But what if that isn't the way it goes? It would be foolish to not think about it, wouldn't it?"

I didn't answer. There was no need. Suddenly I knew exactly what he was talking about.

"I have to ask you something before I leave tomorrow, Frances. I've always called you my sister, but will you still be that if I don't come back? Will you be my parents' daughter?"

"Yes, I will," I whispered.

"Promise me you'll take my place, comfort them, make them happy, and be there for them when they get old someday?"

"I could never take your place, but everything else I promise, yes!"

"And your own mother?"

I had to smile. "Mamu will need a new family when she comes too."

Gary turned away and looked at the screen. Light and shadow played on his face and I couldn't see whether he was happy or sad. "I can hardly wait to meet her," he finally said as his face broke out into a wide grin. "And the first thing I'll tell her is that one of the best things I've ever done in my life was to knock her daughter out cold with a car door!"

"Wait a minute! I picked you out, not the other way around!"

"Really? I remember that differently. You just wanted to get out of Satterthwaite Hall, with a huge goose egg on your head and two or three words of English. And the first thing you did was attack my mum! Hey! Stop kicking me!"

The giggling and commotion that suddenly broke out behind the screen couldn't be missed! Confused faces turned toward the projector room—and found it unoccu- pied, because Amanda was already racing through the side passageway like a torpedo.

"Are you two out of your minds?" she hissed, grabbing our wrists and shaking us a little on the way out. "What on earth has gotten into you?"

But neither Gary nor I would have known how to explain it to her.

Chapter 17

Happy Returns

Hitler's ultimatum to Churchill, his "Last Appeal to Reason," came and went. German troops occupied the islands of Jersey, Guernsey, and Alderney in the English Channel. Air-raid alarms became more frequent, and the wail of the sirens every evening cut the films short at the Elysée. The audience calmly filed out, Amanda locked up, and we drove home. Those who hadn't been able to see a movie through to the end could come back the next evening for free.

We were encouraged to collect aluminum for the production of Spitfires, the agile little planes that did much of the defensive fighting against the German invasion. Once again I was knocking on strangers' doors, but this time it was to ask the woman of the house to part with every pot and pan she could possibly spare. "Two thousand cooking pots make an airplane!" went the slogan.

Uncle Matthew started wearing the khaki uniform of the Home Guard. The members of the civil defense—men who were too old for active military duty, but also seventeen-year-olds—kept watch over the skies day and night to identify any enemy parachutes. They used search spotlights and antiair-craft guns, built tank blockades, and held their own drills.

"Ah, good timing," Amanda commented when the air-raid sirens started to howl just as she locked the door to the theater behind her. "Tonight there are movie buffs flying!"

I hooked my arm through hers and we walked toward the Underground, happy that the alarm hadn't sounded fifteen minutes earlier, interrupting the showing. There were still plenty of people out on the street on that warm, humid summer night, coming out of theaters and restaurants and, like us, hardly bothered by the alarm signal. The German planes in the sky that August didn't have their sights set on London. They bombed—despite fierce resistance—the Royal Air Force bases. But the capital city felt secure. Searchlights routinely crisscrossed the sky like bright swords and illuminated our path, which was easy enough to find even though the streets were dark.

Out of nowhere came the rumble of thunder, followed by crackling and bursts of sound that terrified even the Londoners, who were well acquainted with summer thunderstorms. All of a sudden everyone began to run. Laughing, I stood still and looked upward, anticipating the first heavy drops of rain. Even when Amanda grabbed my hand and pulled me along with an exasperated, "Frances, run!" I still didn't understand.

The bombs fell without a sound. There was just the muted rumbling of distant destruction, the cracking and quaking of hits right near us—and the fearful cries of fleeing people. I held tight to Amanda's hand, entirely focused on not letting go of her as we were pulled along with the pack. A penetrating stench fell over us and left a disgusting taste of fire and gunpowder in our mouths.

We were almost at the entrance to the Underground. Air-raid wardens waved us down the stairs, sorting the incoming stream of people between the tunnel and shafts. It was eerily quiet down there; we heard the scraping and scratching of exhausted feet, and here and there someone cried quietly. Hazy outlines of people moved between us and the dim lighting in search of a free spot.

I slid down with my back against the wall next to Amanda. Breathing hard, she leaned against the masonry; she must have lost her hat along the way. I nudged her in the side, filled with an unfamiliar feeling of triumph. We made it! We hadn't let go of each other! We had arrived together! Looking back, it seemed like I hadn't been afraid for a single moment.

A woman staggered past us and cried in a plaintive voice, "John! John! Are you there?"

Her calls faded as she walked farther into the tunnel. "Are you okay?" I asked Amanda, becoming a little concerned.

"Couldn't be better," she said grimly. I put both my arms around her and felt how she trembled. I held her just a little tighter to let some of my newly discovered courage flow into her. The shaft filled with still more people, more quiet calls. Gladys. Emma. Trevor. And the woman still called for John.

"God help us. Now it's begun," whispered Amanda.

But the all-clear signal came quickly. We only crouched on the cold, dusty floor for about an hour and a half, Amanda leaning against the hard wall with me in her arms.

The entire time I listened intently for sounds above us and tried to imagine what might be happening, but aside from the distant rise and fall of the sirens, no other sound made its way through to us. Motionless gray figures waited in a long row that stretched into the darkness; with the all-clear signal signs of life returned to the tunnel. The gray figures rose and took on human form again; trains that had been stopped continued on their way. Most of the people who had sought refuge left the station, while others joined tightly packed lines waiting to ride the train home. I would have liked to see what was going on above us, whether there were fires or even bodies being pulled from rubble. I didn't understand how Amanda could go home without taking at least a quick peek at the damage and knowing what was going on! But she insisted we take the first subway we could, no matter how loudly I protested.

Feeling slighted, I sat across from her with my arms folded and pouted at my reflection in the car window. "I most certainly will not let you go see dead and injured people!" she suddenly snapped at me, as if I had said something.

"All right," I replied angrily. "I didn't know you had such a weak stomach!"

We both stared out the window. It seemed we would never reach our station. Finally the subway rolled out of the tunnel onto the tracks above ground, and I pressed my face against the glass, aghast.

There was only one fire: a thin, black trail of smoke, a shattered roof outlined against flickering orange light. The house stood right alongside the tracks, and as we approached I watched pointed tongues of flame leaping out of the upper story. Behind broken windowpanes, a glowing chandelier swayed gently.

"Those poor people," Amanda murmured. "Hopefully they were able to get out."

Distraught, I walked behind her as we left the station. A fire engine raced past us wailing shrilly. A bit farther, huge clumps of earth lay in the middle of the street, surrounded by agitated people whose yards had been bombed. "If we had been in our shelter, we'd be buried!" exclaimed one woman.

How I would have loved to take Amanda's hand as we walked! I knew that all I had to do was make a small apology, and I didn't understand why I couldn't bring myself to say it. Amanda also kept quiet, probably because she wasn't one to say "I told you so." We went home in silence.

The newscaster on the radio reported that several planes had dropped bombs over London—probably a mistake after part of a squadron apparently lost its way to the RAF airfields. There had been deaths and injuries, especially among people who were just leaving movies and theaters, and in several places gawkers were interfering with rescue efforts.

Now I was even more ashamed, especially since Amanda had also come into the living room and must have heard every word. But she sat down at her secretary to read a letter from Gary. The first one since his furlough, it had to include an extensive report about Melissa Cole, whom I definitely wasn't over yet. Amanda's smile widened as she read; it seemed to me like a betrayal.

"And?" I asked meanly after a while. "Is she going to have a baby already?"

"Most certainly not! That's enough, Frances!" she said, truly enraged.

Fifty-seven nights. When did we stop counting? The sirens kept wailing inside us, even when the nearly constant droning of the planes was absent for a few hours. When the bombers returned, the unused cot above me in our shelter began to rattle quietly; Gary probably hadn't tightened the screws quite enough. But as long as the cot didn't rattle, I knew we were safe.

The gas lights flickered and played with the shadows of our coats, which we hung from hooks in the ceiling in the narrow space between the cots. Amanda, across the aisle from me, turned page after page, reading her way through the blitz. When it got especially bad, when there was howling and crackling and powerful blasts rocked us, she read to me: psalms, detective stories, women's magazines, the newspaper, anything at all. We were alone. Uncle Matthew was constantly on duty and only came home for a few hours during the day to sleep.

Even my thoughts were the same every night: *At least Mamu won't be hit by a bomb, since the Netherlands surrendered. But how is Bekka doing . . . ?*

Because at the same time the Germans were bombing London, British bombers flew toward Berlin. Did Bekka hear the same things at night and see the same things during the day that I did? Planes that looked like a swarm of locusts as they approached, a few in front as the vanguard and then, in their wake, hundreds of bombers and fighter planes. You could spot the tiny black puffs underneath the planes just before the bombs dropped. When they hit, their shrapnel rained down on the street like hail, or shattering glass.

Amanda didn't know about my new theory. She only knew that I followed her everywhere, which was actually a little embarrassing. But what if a bomb fell on our house and only hit one of us?

My theory developed during the long nights of bombing. The Jews believe that people who are dead lie in their graves and wait there for that one day when everyone rises from the dead, but I saw it differently. I was convinced that we go to heaven as soon as we die, and our family is waiting for us! But what about people who don't belong to our biological family? If Amanda and I were struck down at the same time, we would have time on our way to heaven to make a plan. If not, I would probably never find her again. Heaven is big, and the British probably occupy an entirely different part than the Mangolds from Germany.

When the Germans began only attacking at night because they lost fewer planes to us, Amanda forced me to go back to school. All the begging, crying, and angry pleading in the world had no effect. Every morning I set out after a futile argument, the gas mask dangling from my neck and with so much rage in my heart that Uncle Matthew swore he could see a black cloud above my head. I often met him on the way to school, as he was coming home from his night shift. He slept during the day, and Amanda did the shopping, cooked, and cleaned since the Elysée had been closed since the middle of September. Most of the time Uncle Matthew reported back for duty in the early afternoon.

When he was around me, he never talked about what

exactly he experienced. I only knew that he operated spotlights and antiaircraft guns, and sometimes helped dig out
people who were buried in rubble. Thick dirt often clung to
his skin when he came home, and his hair was full of dust
and ashes.

The boys in my class took up a new hobby: They collected
shrapnel, bomb fragments. Some of them even boasted that
they had stayed aboveground during the attacks to get the
best bits when a bomb exploded! The boys didn't even stop
collecting after the home of a girl from our school was hit.
Her name was Bernice; I had seen her at school, and just a
few hours later, she, her parents, and her sister were dead.

A few kids went after school to see the collapsed house
from which Bernice's family had been carried wrapped in
blankets. They hadn't been in the shelter, preferring to bar-
ricade themselves in the tight space under their stairs. Many
of my classmates did exactly the same thing. Only a few of
them spent the nights like I did, with their families in their
Anderson shelters, in the basement, or in another dugout.

At night, while the horror played out above us, the only
way I could tolerate it was by convincing myself that I was
in a safe shelter. When I passed a bombed-out house, I
couldn't bear to look at it, much less gather souvenirs. And
I never went to see Bernice's house, even though it wasn't
far from us.

"You get used to it," people often said. There was even a
popular song with that refrain. But it wasn't true for me. I
hid it as well as I could, but my fear grew. I only prayed that
everything would end as soon as possible: the terrible sounds

at night; the uncertainty of whether we would live one more day, or still have a house; not knowing whether I would see Uncle Matthew on my way to school or have to wait until noon to find out if he was still alive. The exhaustion became a constant. I sometimes left food almost untouched, as if a fist were blocking my stomach. I never got used to it.

It was October before Amanda and I went to downtown London again. The destruction wasn't too bad where we usually went shopping—lots of broken windows, ashes and dirt everywhere, but only a few burned-out ruins stared at us through their blackened window openings. Our regular supermarket had been hit by an unexploded shell that hadn't been removed yet, so the owner had simply moved his business out onto the street. There were even oranges at the makeshift stand under the poster proclaiming *Hitler can't beat us!* We immediately supplied ourselves, if only because they might have been transported to England with Gary's help!

The Elysée was intact. We had protected the glass panes in the entrance with thick strips of tape as soon as the bombardments began. There was a lot of debris, and letters from the name of the last film had fallen down and lay in front of the building. While we cleared the sidewalk, neighbors came over to talk! I couldn't remember ever seeing so many friendly, almost cheerful faces as when our street was half covered in rubble.

The lively mood was so infectious that to my own astonishment I heard myself asking, "Can I go to Café Vienna and look for Professor Schueler?"

Amanda looked a bit relieved—it was probably getting on her nerves to have me tag along with her day and night. "Just make sure you're back in two hours," she replied. "We have to be home in time for tea."

That, of course, had nothing to do with the hallowed British tradition anymore, but was due to the typical start of the air-raid alarms in the late afternoon. "Are you sure you don't need me here?" I asked, having doubts.

"Give him my best!" my foster mother replied with raised brows. If I wanted to maintain my dignity, there was nothing left for me to do but set off.

The farther I walked into the center of London, the more disturbing the devestation was. Entire streets had burned and caved in on themselves, and smoke still rose from the ruins in many places. Other buildings had been hit by explosives; their roofs or exterior walls collapsed neatly, cleanly, without any fire at all. Undamaged furniture was on view for all to see. I saw a bedroom with colorful bedspreads that almost looked inviting—only there weren't any stairs leading up to it. I quickly ran farther and looked away, and had to walk on the street because the sidewalks were buried in debris.

Even more terrible than the destroyed buildings was finding Professor Schueler's usual table at Café Vienna unoccupied. "Don't worry," said the waiter, who recognized me. "He's doing much better!"

"What's wrong with him?" I spluttered.

"Oh, haven't you heard? He had a stroke. He's at Saint Meade Hospital."

Saint Meade Hospital, I muttered over and over like a

mantra on my way back. Just forty-five minutes after I had boldly left Amanda, I was back, and distraught.

"We'll go there tomorrow and visit him," she reassured me. "If he's had a stroke, he may not be able to take care of himself anymore."

"But he doesn't have anyone else! His sister lives in Munich," I protested.

"Let's just wait until tomorrow and see what he really needs, okay? Don't worry. Now that we know what's happened, we can take care of him."

At the Underground station, there was already a crowd of people with bedding and packed suitcases who descended into the tunnel every evening to spend the night there. It must have been anything but comfortable. The trains ran until the wee hours of the morning, the cement floor was hard, and the continual blasts of hot air that blew through the tunnel stirred up stenches and enormous swarms of mosquitoes.

"We have to think of some alternative for the winter," Amanda said a few hours later as we sat on the cots in our own shelter, freezing, and tried not to pay too much attention to the unnerving whine of the dive bombers.

"I don't want to go to the Underground," I said quietly, burying my face in her shoulder.

"And you won't have to. The nursing home asked if I could help out again. They even want to pay me. Now that the Elysée is closed, we could certainly use the money, and if I work night shifts, they'll let us both into the cellar!"

Longingly I thought of the warm basement of the nursing

home, where you could turn off the noises of the air battles with a single push of a button on the radio. "Say yes!" I begged.

"I already did," she admitted, "and I mean loud and clear, even before the head nurse had finished her sentence. I didn't even ask Matthew! I start again on Sunday. Until then we have to make do here."

Four nights, and one of them half over. "We can do that!" I declared with renewed courage.

Amanda's connection to the Jewish nursing home turned out to be a blessing in another way too. Professor Schueler was paralyzed on his right side; he couldn't get out of bed or even feed himself without assistance. The poor man was so ashamed that he started to cry the moment he saw us.

"Why didn't you let us know?" Amanda asked, and sat down on the edge of his bed. Victims of last night's bombs lay next to invalids like Professor Schueler, who were only being kept here because no one knew where they should go. It was incredibly hot, and smelled of medicine and sweat.

"Nah . . . make trouble," Professor Schueler mumbled in a slurred voice.

"You're not making any trouble. The first thing we'll do is get you out of here. I'll arrange a lovely room in the home where I work, and Frances can visit you every evening. They have very good therapists there. You'll be doing better in no time!"

"You're a saint!" he answered in Yiddish, deeply touched.

I nervously shuffled from one leg to the other and desperately wished I could make some meaningful contribution too, but as always, I couldn't come up with anything at all.

"I'll peel an orange for him," I finally announced, and set off to find a knife. It upset me terribly to see my old friend in such a helpless predicament.

When I finally returned with the orange, Amanda was combing Professor Schueler's hair. He looked at me with embarrassment, but already seemed to be perking up. "Don't know . . . can eat," he said, regarding the orange.

"Frances will help you," Amanda said, to my amazement, and gestured to me to come sit next to her on the edge of the bed. "I'm going to talk to the head nurse about his discharge," she announced.

Well. I gathered all my courage and took a piece of orange from the plate and put it in his mouth. "Does it taste good?" I asked a little too loud.

Professor Schueler nodded. Again his eyes filled with tears; one rolled down his cheek into his beard, but I pretended I hadn't seen it. "The waiter at Café Vienna told me where to find you," I babbled. "Maybe it would have been more fitting to bring Sacher torte!"

The one side of his face he could still move twisted into a grin that touched me deeply. "Yesterday was the first time we dared come into the city," I said. "That's why I didn't find you sooner. But now we'll see each other every day. I can read to you. I sing too! At night we're all in the same air-raid shelter. It's warm and pretty quiet, and it even has a radio!"

The head nurse, who returned shortly thereafter with Amanda, said in a friendly tone, "Well, look here! Our patient is already on the road to recovery! Why didn't you tell us that you have family, professor?"

Professor Schueler's English wasn't very good, but he did

understand the word *family*. "I'm an idiot," he answered
unclearly, "and didn't quite believe it."

And the family grew! Just a few days later we received an
ecstatic letter from Walter announcing his and his father's
release from the internment camp. Amanda and I waited
for them at the Liverpool Street station—the same train
station where Walter and I had been separated during
the kindertransport, which seemed like fate to me. Nothing could have prepared me for the joy that filled me from
head to toe when I saw Walter climb down from the train!
I screamed his name at the top of my lungs, shoved my
way through the crowd in a most impolite way, and threw
myself around his neck with the full force of a surprise
attack.

"Uff!" he said, taken by surprise. "What a greeting! I
should go away more often, don't you think, Paps?"

And just like that I was annoyed with him. Herr Glücklich put down their shared suitcase and shook my hand.
He hadn't lost his wheezing and cough, but after so many
months on the Isle of Man, his face had taken on a much
healthier color. Both Glücklich faces lit up even further when
they spotted Amanda, and for the first time I keenly wished
that she wasn't quite so beautiful!

At home the Glücklichs moved into Gary's room and our
recently abandoned shelter. "It's only for a few days anyway," Walter said to me. "We'll look for work in a factory
and try to find a room nearby. They need all the help they
can get, I heard. I'd rather sign up for the Home Guard, but
they don't want foreigners. I can join the army as soon as

I'm eighteen, but not for the home front—it doesn't make any sense!"

"The war will be long over by the time you're eighteen anyway," I chided him.

"You think so? I wouldn't be so sure. In our discussion groups at the camp we came to another conclusion."

"Discussion groups? Just wait until tonight, then you'll see what's going on!"

"Hmm." Walter didn't let himself be swayed by my patronizing tone. "They won't break us with their bomb scares! Göring has already lost a lot of planes and hasn't gotten any closer to his goal. No, this war will be decided overseas."

"Where we're losing one ship after another!"

"But the Americans have offered to lease us an entire fleet! Sure, England is fighting alone, but the British Empire is still strong. Australia, New Zealand, Canada, India, even the Gurkhas from Nepal are fighting on our side! The Germans will have to dig deep," Walter enthused more confidently than I had heard anyone talk about the war in a long time.

"I hope you're right," I answered in a more conciliatory tone. "But it's not as simple as a discussion group. Gary wouldn't tell us anything when he was here. He was awfully nervous and smoked one cigarette after the other."

"I wanted to write to him anyway. I hope he'll give me his honest opinion of me becoming a soldier!"

Walter received a letter from Gary two months later. He carried it with him constantly in the wallet he bought with his first paycheck from the factory, and read it so often he knew it by heart.

HMS Princess of Malta, 20 November 1940.

Dear Walter,

*I'm sure you understand that I can't tell you where we
are, just this: My second winter on the Atlantic has
started and is rattling us through and through. But
I've wanted to go to sea ever since I can remember.
Just look at all the model ships in Frances's room!
Early on my parents taught me that the whole
world was open to me; of course, they were thinking
of something other than the navy, and until I was
about seventeen, the idea of expanding my horizons
through education suited me fine. The things going on
elsewhere in Europe were disturbing, but somehow
beyond my comprehension. They didn't have
anything to do with me until we took in a girl from
Germany—my sister, Frances. She made us look more
closely at the world. She didn't talk about her past
much, she just came alive while she was with us, and
it was amazing to experience.*

*So I actually had two reasons to join the navy:
my old love of the sea, and watching Frances
blossom, which gave me an entirely new idea. You
may think I'm crazy when I tell you this, but I'm
going to anyway: I want to play a part in making
the world "come to its senses"!*

*Please don't think that I always have this lofty
goal in mind while I'm on board here. When ships
in the convoy are hit, burn, and start to sink, and we
know there will be a torpedo speeding toward us at*

*any second, I'm scared to death and can only think:
Shoot, Shepard, hopefully you'll get out of this alive
somehow!*

*Or when the waves crash down over us and we
sail into a storm for days without sleeping, when
nothing matters anymore, life or death, and you
only wish it would finally be over, when after endless
days like that you finally have a chance to think
again, then I sometimes think, What in heaven's
name am I doing here, anyway?*

. . .

Evening, 22 November

Walter,

*I have to thank you for asking for my opinion! The
past few days have been one of those phases when I
almost started to doubt my decision. But writing this
letter to you has gotten me thinking about how I can
best explain to you why I'm here, and it has made it
clear to me again.*

*Would I want to call it off and go home now?
Definitely not! When this war has been won (and I
don't want to imagine anything else!), then someday
we'll forget that we once sat in the cold, filthy and
shivering. All we'll know then is that we were part of
it when civilization was defended—and I'm not just
thinking of us Jews or Brits or the other "good guys."
The more I think about it, the more I can imagine
that even future generations of Germans will thank
us someday.*

Does that help you with your decision? I can't bring myself to say, "Yes, Walter, become a soldier! Try not to get shot and come home a hero!" If everything turned out well, of course, I'd pat myself on the back—but it might not, and before I have to blame myself for launching you on the path to disaster with patriotic slogans, I'd rather say "Sorry, pal, you won't get a straight answer from me."

Walter, I'm curious what your future will bring! You still have just about a year to think about it. But when you decide, please let me know, and give my love to my three at home, Mum, Dad, and Frances!

Your friend,
Gary Shepard

Book Three

Returning Home

1941–1945

Chapter 18

Lightfoot

At least it had stopped raining. The branches and remaining brown autumn leaves still clung to the trees despite the tremendous amount of rain that had fallen in recent days. The grave, in accordance with Jewish tradition, had just been dug that morning. In the past forty-eight hours I had been amazed by the calm, fitting way the burial society of the Jewish community marked the coming and going of Malach ha-Mavet, the angel of death. From the prayers at the deathbed to the vigil, from the cleansing and ritual purification of the body to the symbolic sack of earth from the Holy Land, these men had quickly yet respectfully seen to everything necessary to take leave of life on this earth.

And now that Matthew had spoken a brief but heartfelt tribute to the earthly endeavors of the deceased, the cantor had sung a last shalom for him, and each of the mourners had tossed three handfuls of soil down onto the coffin and prayed the Kaddish, I could rest assured that everything had been done to provide a worthy farewell for Professor Julius Schueler, seventy-four years old, from Munich, Germany.

It would take a while for me to adjust to not finding him in his room, looking up expectantly as soon as I walked through the door: "My young friend! What's going on out there in the world?" The fact that he was bedridden and grew steadily weaker despite daily exercises was puzzling in contrast to his face, which grew happier, more animated, and younger the longer his illness lasted. This last year in the nursing home, he confided to Amanda shortly before his second and fatal stroke, had been the happiest he had known since 1933!

Arm in arm with my foster mother, I walked to the gate of the cemetery, lost in thought, past unadorned graves topped with collections of small stones. "It's too bad Jewish people don't share a meal after a funeral," I said.

"You would have liked to treat his friends at the Café Vienna, am I right?" Amanda pressed my arm.

"That would have been nice," I agreed. "It's funny, isn't it? I went there for my parents and got nowhere, but in the end I gained a grandfather."

"What's so strange about that? You have a talent for gathering a family for yourself, that's all. A family for the war, as your friend Hazel would say."

Just for the war? I thought, but didn't say it out loud. There was a brief moment of tension between us, as happened so often recently when our conversation touched on the future.

I was thirteen, almost fourteen. I had been with the Shepards for almost three years—not so long in terms of a lifetime, but the years prior to that seemed infinitely distant, and faded a little more each day. My foster parents had always made it perfectly clear from the beginning that I was "borrowed," so I'd be given back at some point. Mamu had always been a presence in Harrington Grove. And yet it was Amanda who had formed me. I looked to her, talked like her, took on her mannerisms. I had become her daughter.

When I finally told her about my theory, Amanda's short, astonishingly simple answer was proof of something I had known for a long time. "We aren't blood relatives. If we die when we're not together, I might not find you again in heaven," I explained when she wondered why I didn't join the Girl Guides like the other girls in my class. The Girl Guides took part in all kinds of activities for the war effort. But joining them would have meant being away from home quite often.

Surprised, Amanda listened to my rationale, then finally raised one eyebrow as only she could do and responded: "I wish you had told me about your theory earlier. I could have told you a long time ago that you overlooked something important."

"And that would be?" I asked, puzzled.

"*I* will find *you*!" she said simply.

Being at the funeral had put me in a reflective mood, and I thought about the previous months. Belonging to the Girl Guides and "making my contribution to victory" had made me proud. We gathered materials that could be reused and collected money for the "Spitfire Fund," made bandages from old sheets, and quite enjoyed playing the "victims" in civil guard drills. Our exercises included first aid, recognizing poisonous gases, and putting out firebombs. The older girls served as messengers between the Home Guard and air-raid protection posts, since the phone lines were often down during attacks.

Walter was finally a volunteer now too. The Germans had only allowed us a few chances to catch our breath, and by the end of December half the city stood in flames and the rescue crews were entirely overwhelmed. After that, no one asked whether new volunteers were British anymore! In addition to his work in the ammunition factory, Walter assisted the volunteer fire brigade, which he thought was perfectly fitting: "During the day I put together missiles, and at night I help clean up the mess they make!"

When the air attacks let up for a longer stretch in January, the Elysée opened for business again, and my foster parents and I held daily "breakfast conferences." Would Matthew come home after the evening show, or did he have Home Guard duty? Did I have Girl Guide activities, or would I go help out at the theater and take care of our shopping? Did Amanda have a day shift or a night shift in the nursing home? During that time, there was never a single day when each of us didn't know exactly where the other two were. Being able to rely on each other was the only thing we could depend on; it made everything else bearable.

In April we experienced the heaviest attacks on London yet. I spent "Blitz Wednesday" in the basement of the nursing home with its thick walls and its own small airtight shelter. Three days later, Amanda, Matthew, and I were at home—how could we have known that this particular Sabbath would become infamous?

When the air-raid sirens started up, the usual routine was set into motion: Shut off the gas and water, turn out all the lights, gather blankets, gas masks, thermos bottles, the first aid kit, and the box containing essential valuables, and then single file into the shelter. It was too early to sleep, so we sat on two of the cots and played cards.

"There's an awful lot of action in the air tonight," Matthew said at some point.

The thundering and booming from impacts near us would not quit, the ground shook and rocked, and the loose upper bunk rattled so hard I expected the bed to fall on my head at any moment.

"I win," said Amanda, with her reading glasses on the tip of her nose as she played her last card.

Just then, a gust of wind blew the blanket away from the entrance and scattered the cards, and we immediately threw ourselves to the ground as stones and clumps of dirt rained down on the corrugated metal with violent force. A few moments later we heard a sound through the din outside, a sound I hadn't heard at such close range before: a weak, human sound, calling, screaming, and crying.

Matthew went to the door. "Oh, no," he said, "it's the Godfreys! Stay here, don't move!" He reached for his steel helmet and slipped out. Amanda and I looked at each other in terror. Voices made their way to us, questions and short answers being called out, and already the piercing stench of fire penetrated the blanket in front of the entrance. Now nothing could hold us back, and we jumped up to look out.

Dense smoke immediately filled our noses, lungs, and

eyes. In the blue-white light that bathed the yard next door, shadowy figures were moving around. The crying had stopped, and someone staggered toward us—it was Mrs. Godfrey with her two young children. The three of them were covered in filth. "Your husband sent me. Could the little ones come into your shelter?" she said in a raspy voice. Only then did I notice that the fence between our yards was gone.

As I helped our neighbor and her children into the shelter, the crackling of the fire grew louder; it was apparently finding fuel quickly in the Godfreys' house. "The garden hose," I said to Amanda, "is it working?"

Without another word we both climbed out. While I unrolled the hose, Amanda ran into the house and turned the water on again. Of course the hose didn't reach all the way to the neighbor's house, so she brought tin buckets that had been standing at the ready in our kitchen. A small bucket brigade quickly formed—the two of us and Matthew, Mr. Godfrey, and other neighbors—while from the street we could hear the fire truck approaching. Directly overhead another plane droned and I automatically began to count to six, the usual number of impacts, but we were lucky: There were two blasts very close by, but the rest of the bombs fell a good distance away.

The extent of the catastrophe on Harrington Grove was revealed the next morning. Between protruding remains of walls were mountains of debris, roof tiles, window frames, and some items surprisingly unscathed; trees were charred, utility poles toppled, and a wire still throwing sparks twitched in the street. The Godfreys' house was an eerie, windowless ruin. The force of the blast had shattered all our windows too, and we lived with wooden boards over the openings for weeks.

Making things worse, the second year of the war supplies were noticeably more difficult to come by, and the government had no choice but to ration food. Clothing also had to be purchased with coupons, for which a point system was established. For hours my foster parents and I would plan, laying out the sixty-six points we were each allotted like a card game on the table: ten for a coat, six for a pair of pants, four for a blouse, three for a sweater, two for new underwear.

The rationing made it especially worthwhile to have your own vegetable garden. Amanda waged a bitter battle with caterpillars and beetles for her cabbage and lettuces, and grew potatoes, peas, beans, carrots, leeks, and herbs. On the weekends we would take trips to the forest to gather wild herbs that we dried and steeped when tea was rationed. "Shepard's Delight," our new variety, was such a success that soon my entire Girl Guides troop was traipsing through fields and pastures in search of herbs.

In the fall, Amanda, Matthew, and I had taken up mushroom collecting, which meant getting up at dawn on gray, drizzly days and taking the train out to Surrey. There was a small restaurant on the way where we treated ourselves to a late breakfast once our work was done, our backpacks full of field mushrooms that the waitress looked at covetously.

"If you give me your mushrooms," she said the third or fourth time we were there, "you can have a few chicks."

"Chicks . . . !" I must have exclaimed with such longing that my foster parents broke out into laughter. That day we rode back to London with empty backpacks, but with a small cardboard box on my knees instead that went "peep, peep, peep."

"I hope for your sake there's a rooster in the bunch," grumbled Matthew, who would rather have kept the mushrooms. "Otherwise there won't be any eggs and we'll have to butcher the ladies."

"Don't you dare," I said darkly and put my arms around my carton.

Sadly, my first chick started to fail the very next day. It huddled in a corner apathetically and was dead and buried before I got home from school. When the second one took ill I was determined to fight, and carried it around with me so I could perform mouth-to-beak resuscitation if it came to that—I even took it to bed with me!

In early December two half-grown hens and a rooster moved into the garden shed, strutted around the few square yards of fenced in grass between the shed and the shelter, and eyed Amanda's winter vegetables.

To be honest, we were all pleased to have "Winston," "Victory," and "Queenie" out of the kitchen. We couldn't walk into the room without getting tangled in the dried mushrooms hanging from the ceiling on strings or stepping on chickens. Eagerly anticipating the eggs, Amanda and I were already studying all kinds of recipes, since they had been a rare commodity for some time already.

Walking arm in arm with Amanda after the funeral, my reverie was shattered when someone drove past us on the quiet side street laughing, honking, and waving although we didn't know him at all. "Something must have happened!" Amanda exclaimed.

"He looked pretty happy! Do you think we've won the war?"

We looked at each other. "No," we said simultaneously. The news we had been hearing for such a long time had been too awful! Still, when we reached the main road, there were cars honking, bicycle bells chiming, and people clapping each other on the shoulders.

"What on earth is happening?" Amanda stopped a passerby to ask.

"You haven't heard?" the man exalted. "Great Britain is saved, ladies! The Japanese attacked Pearl Harbor! The USA has declared war!"

Amanda put a hand to her mouth. "Oh God, how wonderful!" she exclaimed. "Finally! Frances, run back, you have to tell Matthew right away! Our prayers have been answered!"

I ran faster than I ever had before. Matthew and the men from the chevra kaddisha were startled and stopped working, asking if something had happened.

"Yes!" I panted. "The answer to our prayers! An American lady was attacked and the USA is joining the war!"

The men looked at each other, puzzled. "Who was attacked?"

"Pearl Harbor," I said. They broke out in cheers.

I didn't understand that Pearl Harbor was the Americans' Pacific stronghold until I heard the radio broadcast that evening. It was the longed-for turning point in this war. For seventeen long months, Great Britain had fought the Nazis alone. Now the cards would finally be reshuffled.

My fourteenth birthday came and went, though I didn't feel the slightest bit more important. In England, fourteen meant the end of compulsory education, and I wouldn't have minded working, if only for the change of pace, but the Shepards wouldn't hear of it. "Your parents would want you to keep learning," they said, and since I knew they were right there was no more discussion. I informed Mamu on one of the telegram-like Red Cross letters we exchanged every few months; from them I learned little more than that she and Aunt Ruth's family were still living at the same address in Groningen, they were "fine," and thinking of me.

Shortly after my birthday we put the soldier Walter Glücklich on a train. To be a member of the Pioneer Corps in North Africa was certainly an honor, and after the long, dreary London winter I could surely understand when Walter said he was looking forward to the desert life in a Bedouin tent. But even this warm outlook couldn't disguise the fact that our troops were suffering enormous losses at the hands of the Germans. This parting scared me.

"Don't let yourself get shot and come back a hero," were my parting words to Walter, and a couple hugging their son good-bye next to us glared at me. They had no way of knowing that I was quoting a friend!

Just as with Gary, it all went too fast. Amanda gave Walter a kiss and he hugged her. He shook Matthew's hand and awkwardly patted his own father, who had tried to change his mind down to the wire, on the back. Then Walter boarded the train, appeared briefly among the other soldiers in the window to give us the victory sign, but when the train started moving we couldn't see him anymore.

Then the train was gone and we stood on the platform, lost in a small crowd of parents and families left behind.

A few days later, a letter addressed to Miss Frances Shepard arrived from the camp where Walter was training for a few weeks before leaving for Africa. The return address listed W. Lightfoot. Why was Walter's superior writing to me? Something had happened to him at training camp! I tore the envelope open right there in the foyer.

Amanda, who had heard my cries, rushed out of the kitchen. I met her halfway and threw my arms around her neck. "They stole his name!" I sobbed.

Astonished, she freed one half of herself from my embrace, squinted her farsighted eyes, and held Walter's letter at arm's length. "He wasn't allowed to join the British army with a German name!" I wailed. "They gave him three choices and he picked Lightfoot. Lightfoot! What an idiot!"

Suddenly I was enraged—Walter had done it again. "Is his English so bad that he thinks *lightfoot* is some kind of happiness?"

Irritated, I pushed Amanda aside to blow my nose. "Well, he could hardly call himself Happy or Lucky," Amanda replied. "Or Frolic, in case that was one of the choices." With growing indignation I saw that she was having trouble holding back her laughter. "Honestly, I think Lightfoot has a certain charm, especially for a man of Walter's stature. Just imagine how he'll sweep through the desert with it."

"That's not funny!" I protested, and took the letter out of her hand to skim it a second time. "That twit is practically delirious because he has an English name now!" I whispered in disbelief.

As I looked up, I was met with the strangest look by far that Amanda, my friend, sister, and mother, had ever given me. It was teasing and tender, questioning and knowing, pleased and a little sad all at the same time, and I could only imagine one reason for such a look: Apparently she had just answered a question before I had even asked it of myself!

"Why am I getting so upset, anyway?" I grumbled.

"Bravo!" Amanda laid an arm around my shoulder and led me toward the kitchen. "That's a very good question! Definitely worth thinking about sometime. But right now let's go raise a glass to our old and new friend, Pioneer Walter Lightfoot, that he not fear the terror of the night, nor the arrow that flies by day, nor his light foot strike a stone—loosely according to the psalms."

"You're right," I said. "He can call himself whatever he wants. What difference does it make to me?"

Chapter 19

Lost

On the day Gary's ship went down, invisible trains traveled through Europe, supposedly unnoticed, and students in Munich who called themselves "The White Rose" distributed flyers urging resistance to Hitler. On the day Gary's ship went down, the World Jewish Congress informed Western governments about a monstrous document that had been signed in a villa at Wannsee. On the day Gary's ship went down, American troops landed at Guadalcanal.

On the day Gary's ship went down, we read *A Midsummer Night's Dream* in school with different people speaking each part. Matthew mounted the letters GREER GARSON IN MRS. MINIVER above the entrance to the Elysée, and Amanda washed and fed old people. That was our seventh of August 1942, and two days later, when the *Princess of Malta* pulled us down into the depths as well, none of us could say what we had done at a certain time.

I would never understand why fourteen-year-old boys were allowed to deliver those telegrams. As soon as they were spotted in the distance in their uniforms, a wave of cold fear preceded them; women who had just been standing at their garden gates chatting fled into their houses, where moments later there was movement at the curtains: *Please go away! Please don't come to our house!*

I had seen the telegram boy go to the Beavers' in spring, the second house just past the Godfrey ruins. He looked serious and afraid. The Beavers were still hiding from him, because they had a second son at the front.

We didn't see our messenger coming. Amanda and I were cleaning up the rest of our lunch; I had vacation and wanted to visit Hazel, who had returned to London in August. When the doorbell chimed, Amanda dried her hands and walked the few yards to the door with a perfectly light step. Amanda moved just the length of the hall, a few steps. The way back lasted almost a year.

I didn't hear a word. When she didn't come back, I glanced into the foyer and saw the house door wide open, and a pale gray sky outside. When I saw her shoe on the bottom step I finally understood. She must have lost it when she crawled up the steps, where she sat halfway up, staring at a thin piece of paper with a furrowed brow.

"Okay," she said in a calm voice. "Now. Call Matthew. Cancel work at the nursing home. Inform the rabbi. They'll let us know about the shiva."

"Amanda," I whispered. "Mum!" Her name wasn't getting through. "Letters to the Shepards, the O'Learys, and the Coles," she continued. "They will want to know, even if . . ."

She must have been trying to prepare herself for this moment for a long time, and gave the telegram another intent look, as if her next steps were written there. Carefully I took the paper out of her hands and set it aside. "Come, let's go upstairs. I can call Matthew. You should lie down for a few minutes."

"But Ziska," she answered, puzzled. "I can't just go lie down now."

"Just for a moment. Please," I pleaded. She had never called me Ziska. She didn't even seem to be sure who I was anymore. "I'll come with you. We'll go together."

"Well, all right. I do feel a little . . ."

"Give me your hand. It's just a few steps."

There had been another time, in my other life, that I felt I had to be stronger than the person who gave me strength and security. Mamu's confusion after Papa was arrested, when she was suddenly alone and had to make all kinds of decisions by herself, was suddenly so vivid that it might have been her I helped up the stairs and tucked into bed. But then the moment passed, and it was neither a dream nor a memory. With an abrupt and very real pain, Amanda balled up, dug her fingers into the blanket, and whispered, "Oh my God." I stroked her cheek, her hair, murmured her name, hoped she would start to cry, but she couldn't yet. I knew all too well how that felt.

There were quiet steps on the stairs and Mrs. Beaver appeared in the bedroom doorway. "I saw the messenger," she whispered bravely. "Can I help?"

"Could you call Matthew? The number's next to the phone."

She nodded and disappeared. I slipped under the blanket at Amanda's back, put an arm around her and my chin on her shoulder, as she had so often done with me. I was always sure she would be there for me. But now, as I wrapped my arms around her stiff body, I wasn't sure anymore. No matter how strongly my love for this, my second mother, might burn . . . it might not be enough. It hadn't been enough for Mamu either.

When Matthew came home, silent, pale, and resolute, and closed the bedroom door firmly behind the two of them, and I had gone down the stairs with stiff, unsteady steps, my concern for Amanda slowly made way for other thoughts. The telegram still lay on the steps. No one had touched it, and I sat on the same step where Amanda had sat earlier.

"We regret to inform you . . ."

No! Desperation, rage, and denial broke over me simultaneously, a hot wave of distress, dizziness, and tears. It wasn't possible. Not him, not my brother, my wonderful, laughing brother, who was the first of the Shepards to love me, gave me my name, and made up "Dictionaryish," our shared language. Not him. Things like that didn't happen! I summoned all my strength and looked at the telegram again.

". . . that Midshipman Gary Shepard has been reported as missing since the demise of the HMS *Princess of Malta* on the 7th of August 1942 off the Portuguese Azores . . ."

Only missing! The Azores! I could see the world map in Mrs. Collins's classroom before me. A whole group of islands lay between southern Europe and the USA—he must have managed to swim to one of the beaches! If not, then he paddled a rescue boat, or floated on a plank.

I jumped up and ran to the phone. "Operator? The Royal Navy please."

"And who exactly would you like to speak to?" The young lady rattled off a list of possible departments.

"The one that's responsible for rescues at sea," I said. There was a short pause on the other end of the line. "It's about my brother. His ship sank the day before yesterday and he's probably stuck on the Azores, near Portugal."

I saw a movement out of the corner of my eye. Hazel stood in the open front door. "Oh, dear," muttered the young woman, flustered. "Then I'd better connect you with . . . let me see . . . can you wait a moment?" she asked helpessly.

I didn't wait. "They've probably already sent boats out," I said. "If everyone called, they'd hardly have time to go out and rescue people." Very slowly I put the receiver down.

"What happened?" Hazel asked with wide eyes.

"I don't know." I looked at the telegram again and forced myself to read it through to the end. "Here it just says that the ship went down and Gary hasn't been found."

"Oh, Frances, how terrible!" Hazel spontaneously rushed over to me, and I took a step backward. "They just haven't found him yet," I repeated.

"But that's still awful," Hazel replied, putting her thin arms around my neck and giving me a kiss—and then I couldn't help it, I cried bitterly, even though I knew this couldn't really be true.

In the next few hours a parade of neighbors streamed through the Shephards' kitchen, all of them bearing pots of soup. Hazel bravely stood by me, after a short whispered phone call with her mother. Sitting at the kitchen table, I was amazed how the soup multiplied. I felt myself overcome by a kind of fog the longer I sat there, and our house was already being subjected to that mysterious transformation that befalls any place where something terrible has happened: No one spoke in normal tones.

The sun already lay deep on the horizon outside the kitchen window when Matthew emerged from the bedroom. His eyes were red from crying, and I would have liked to jump up and throw myself in his arms, but my legs felt like they didn't belong to me. Slowly and heavily he sat down opposite me, nodded a few times, and said, as if to himself, "That was our Gary."

Hazel silently leaned against me. Matthew looked up and seemed to notice for the first time that we were there. "Can Frances spend a few days with you, Hazel?" he asked.

"My mother already suggested it," she replied, taking my right hand in hers.

I immediately wanted to protest. But before I had a chance, we heard steps coming down the stairs and Amanda came into the kitchen.

"What is all that?" she asked sternly, pointing to the pots.

"The neighbors brought them," I said, fearfully searching her face for some small sign of connection, but there was nothing, only a controlled, concentrated expression and tired, dry eyes that glanced at me briefly without any sign of emotion. "Well, of course you can eat what you want, Frances, but Matthew and I won't eat anything until the seudat havra'ah. I hope you know which pot belongs to whom?"

"No," I admitted fearfully, and flinched as she started to

lift the lids with impatient, almost accusatory clattering. She grimaced critically and carried one of the pots to the sink to empty it with the words, "This is certainly not kosher!"

"I'll just pack a few things," I said quietly to Hazel.

The Vathareerpurs must have been counting on my presence that evening. Hazel's sister Jasmine had already moved out of the girls' room to make room for me. And they had also adopted a strategy for dealing with me: Act as if nothing had happened. Hazel's parents hugged me with tears in their eyes, and the next minute everything was perfectly normal. We sat at the dinner table; Hazel's four younger siblings argued and passed around bowls with rice, fish, and samosas. I struggled with Mrs. Vathareerpur's style of seasoning, which she could only have learned from fire-eaters. For a few hours I actually managed to convince myself that I was living a normal life.

But I grew restless. In the middle of the night Hazel peered down from the upper bunk bed and said, "You're shaking the whole bed with your tossing and turning."

"It's not right. What am I doing here? I should be at home. What if they sent me away because I'm not part of the family?"

The bed shook as Hazel climbed down and slipped under the covers with me. "I made a promise to Gary, but I think we made a mistake," I whispered. "I'm not their daughter. How can I comfort them?"

"Frances, right now you couldn't comfort them if you were five daughters! And you'll see them again tomorrow."

"Yeah, at the shiva, with all the other guests!"

"What exactly happens there?" Hazel asked, probably to distract me.

But I just shrugged my shoulders, not only because I had never sat shiva, but because I couldn't think about anything but the fact that I had been sent away. Amanda and Matthew wanted to be alone. I wasn't any comfort. Whatever we had been through together before this . . . in this sorrow that transcended all understanding, I had no place.

They sent Mrs. Bloom. Our rabbi's wife herself, wearing dark clothes and a serious expression, stood next to the delicate Mrs. Vathareerpur in her light blue sari and said, "Your parents asked me to pick you up and prepare you a little."

Timidly I stumbled along next to her, the handle of my suitcase burning in my hand. Fragments of Mrs. Bloom's instructions echoed in my ears: ". . . accept his fate . . . no noise, not the slightest protest should disturb the dead . . . the first meal, eggs and bread . . . for seven days, the mourners don't leave their home . . ."

Did everything she explained apply to me too? Surely not; how could I be one of the mourners when Gary wasn't really my brother? But I wasn't one of the visitors either, because I lived there! And knowing what awaited me at the house by no means meant that I was prepared for it. Mrs. Bloom had told me that "the mourners" didn't wear shoes and sat directly on the floor or on low stools, while "the visitors" sat at the table, but it hadn't sunk in at all that I would find Amanda and Matthew on the floor. Mrs. Bloom had to shove me toward the living room; she deposited me there and took the suitcase from my hand. I was petrified.

One of the women from the chevra kaddisha came to me. I knew her; she had sewn the burial clothes for Professor Schueler with us. She reached for my collar and took a small pair of scissors and made a tiny cut. In the next moment, the woman was pushed aside. I looked up and looked straight into Amanda's face.

How small she was! I was almost as tall as her, but hadn't really noticed. Her eyes had a vacant, withdrawn expression. Very calmly and without any sign of recognition, she took the cut material in both hands and in one quick motion tore it—only a quiet sound, but it seemed to be magnified a hundred times for her, because in that moment I saw a wave of surprise and pain wash over her face.

For me, though, that was the moment when I knew where I belonged. The torn clothes were the sign of the mourners, and it was Amanda, Gary's mother, who brought me into that circle. There was no greater love she could have shown me.

She led me back to her, our, place. Matthew, who was fighting tears, put an arm around me and held me close during the long hours when ever more visitors arrived. Some of them pressed my hand too. No one but me seemed to think that I wasn't Gary's flesh-and-blood sister.

I had crossed the threshold. My arms and legs became heavy and tired and a wholly unexpected, deep peace spread through me. It wasn't like anything I'd experienced before, except maybe the encounter with my father on the beach— a peace that didn't come from within me, but from another place. And without any fear, I realized what Gary must have felt in his last conscious moments, and that he had really left us. I wouldn't talk with him, laugh with him, share secrets, secretly idolize him. I would never see him again. I couldn't imagine how that was possible, but I knew now that it was true.

And yet I couldn't have felt any closer to him. In these hours and days he was honored; the condolences and sadness of everyone who came to the Shepards' was genuine, and I wished Gary could have seen it. He was one of them, a "real" Jew, who was loved and respected, and who would be missed. I felt that gratification for him.

London, 14 August 1942

Dear Walter,

You'll probably get this letter at the same time as the one I wrote two days ago explaining everything, but I'm sending it anyway, just because I wish you were here now.

If only we could do something to help! Matthew can't stop crying after the visitors leave at night, and I'm really worried about Amanda. Nothing seems to reach her. Is she still there at all? We talk about the people who were here during the day, about letters that come.

But we don't talk about Gary. Matthew says she's bottled up her anger and she can't even pray right now. "Don't worry," he says, "she'll come back." But he's not a hundred percent sure either, because yesterday he let slip that if she hadn't married a Jew, she'd have had half a dozen children and not lost her entire future in one blow.

*Last night I dreamed that the nursing home
had been hit by a bomb and collapsed with Amanda
inside and only I knew where to dig for her. The
rescue crew carried Amanda past me on a stretcher
and when she saw me, she said, "Frances, you
saved my life, now it belongs to you!"—"But only in
exchange!" I answered. "You saved my life too, have
you forgotten?"—"I could never take what belongs to
someone else," she said, and I, who sadly only come
up with answers like this in dreams, replied: "In
that case, I would never offer it to you."*

*I wish I could make Amanda's life worth
something to her again. I miss her so much. I miss
her even more than Gary. I want our old life back!
How could God let this happen?*

*I'm sorry for writing you such a letter, but
besides us, there's no one left who's so close to the
Shepards.*

Your Ziska

After the shiva, I woke up to screams in the middle of
the night. Amanda's voice, distorted and distant, came from
my foster parents' bedroom, but not really. I hesitated for a
moment, then peeked in. Matthew stood at the window in
his pajamas; the whole scene must have seemed like a bad
dream to him.

Amanda was outside in the garden and she was on a rampage. In the streaming rain she hacked at her vegetable bed,
so wild and beside herself that the spade kept slipping from
her hand. She trampled and tore down the chicken fence.

Her soaking wet nightgown hung around her legs, and her voice broke.

". . . and don't you think that I'm sorry! You can punish me as much as you want, but I don't regret anything! Not one second of love and caring will be destroyed by anything you can do to me!"

"Amanda . . . don't do this," Matthew murmured to himself.

I ran down the stairs, out into the cold rain that beat down on me. "Laws! Twenty-five years we obeyed, one single time we didn't!" Amanda fell forward onto her knees and ripped the posts of the chicken fence from the earth. "Once, dammit! And I did it, not him! But it was good, and you know what? I'm glad I did it! Nothing you do . . . Go away, Frances! Nothing you do can change that. I don't regret it!"

Matthew stumbled out the kitchen door in a coat and boots, put up an umbrella, and waded helplessly through the muck to hold it above his completely drenched wife. "Get away, Matthew," she said, and plunged the spade deep into the ground.

And then, all of a sudden, it was over and Amanda started to cry loudly. "Oh, God, it's true, it's really true!" she moaned. Matthew put an arm around her and led her into the house.

I stayed and looked around. The garden, the fence, the vegetables . . . completely destroyed. The light from the kitchen fell on a mud-covered battlefield, while the rain fell undisturbed. I put my head back and felt its cold drops on my face until my cheeks grew numb.

"Frances?" It was Matthew, and now the kind man was holding the umbrella over me!

"Come in the house, or you two will both get sick."

"It isn't God, Matthew," I said. "The destruction, losing Gary. It's humans alone that have the power to destroy. I don't know why God didn't plan it differently, but that's the way it is. Maybe he just has too much faith in us."

We trudged through the muck back to the house. "Where is she?" I asked.

"She's running a bath. Are you okay?"

"Yes, I'm fine. Go back to her! We'll see each other in the morning.

"Matthew?" I said to his back as he was already on his way upstairs. "I don't believe for a second that God would punish people like you. If I thought that, I'd stop believing in him right here and now."

Matthew stood still, and it was a moment before he turned around. But then his face softened into a smile. "I don't believe that either," he replied. "If he wanted to punish us . . . would he have sent us you?"

It seemed like the rain would never stop. I didn't know if the garden could be saved in this weather, but it was the only thing I knew to do, so after breakfast I got to work. I rolled up the chicken wire, stacked up the rest of the posts, and gathered the unripe potatoes that were lying around and threw them in a bucket so I could plant them again later. I picked out plants that couldn't be saved, and when Hazel showed up at the fence, I was patching the beans with twine and wire. "No wonder. I've been ringing forever," she said. "Are you alone?"

It was the first time we had seen each other since my night

at the Vathareerpurs'. "Not entirely," I answered. "Matthew is back at work, Amanda is lying in bed. I brought her breakfast, but she said I should leave her alone." My voice quivered. I gestured to our vegetable garden. "That was her doing, last night. At first I was sort of glad. I thought it would do her good to get it out of her system. But I guess I was wrong."

"Do you have another pair of boots? I'll help you." Hazel reached for the garden gate and let herself in. I heard her rummaging around in the shed, and she came out wearing Amanda's boots and rain poncho. "Don't look, but she's standing at the window."

I swallowed my tears and continued working with doubled energy. I hoped Amanda would recognize from up there what that meant: She could throw me out—out of her room, out of her life—but I was still there, waiting, and making myself useful.

We worked until noon, and the results were impressive: Two-thirds of our garden was raked clean, the surviving vegetables salvaged, the rest on the compost heap. The chicken wire was only temporarily fastened, but the fencing was enough to keep Victory, Winston, and Queenie in, at least for the time being. We took off our boots outside the kitchen door and went inside to make ourselves sandwiches.

"Perfect timing," said Amanda, pulling a pie out of the oven. She was completely dressed, pale, but standing—so normal that I could hardly breathe for relief.

With enviable poise, it was Hazel, not me, who crossed the kitchen and gave her a warm hug. "I'm so very sorry, Mrs. Shepard," she said gently.

Amanda smiled. "That's very sweet of you, Hazel," she

said, stroking my friend's hair. "Can you stay for lunch, or is your mother waiting for you?"

"My mother's expecting me," answered Hazel to my surprise, since she had just told me exactly the opposite. "See you tomorrow, Frances!"

It was clear to me that she had only left so Amanda and I could be alone, and my foster mother seemed to figure the same thing, because we exchanged the same tentative, slightly awkward look. She set the pie on the table, sat down, and waited until I had washed my hands.

I slid onto the bench across from her and looked at her quizzically. Would she say the prayer? Should I do it? Would we just not say it from now on? Several seconds passed and I was just about to reach for the spoon to fill our plates when she suddenly put her hand on mine, closed her eyes, and said a short blessing.

"You're not going to go back to work yet, are you?" I asked, almost giddy with relief.

"No, not yet. These are the only two or three hours a day when I feel like I'll make it through somehow." She smiled a little ruefully. "I would just about get to the nursing home and back again. No, I . . . I'd rather get out of bed for you, Frances."

I choked up, and pushed my plate aside.

"I'm sorry about last night . . . I can't explain it. Probably the sum of eight nights without sleep, plus all the food from other people's kitchens—or there were expired antidepressants in the soup!"

For one brief, bright, light moment we smiled at each other, and the spell was broken. Spontaneously I stood up and sat down next to her. We held each other for a long time, without saying anything or crying. Finally she said, "I know that you and Matthew are grieving too. I know I'm only making it harder, but I still can't do anything about it. I can't even say if I'll ever be sane again."

A little later, she asked, "Did you see it? The obituary was in the newspaper yesterday." Silently, she put the page in front of me. I bent over it, and there it was, the answer to my most important, burning question, buried in their last tribute to their son.

Midshipman Gary Aaron Shepard
HMS *Princess of Malta*
12 June 1920–7 August 1942
Beloved son of Matthew G. Shepard and Amanda,
née O'Leary, brother and best friend of Frances.
Lost at sea.

Chapter 20

Revelations

The thin thread that still connected me with Mamu—our
exchange of brief notes, limited to no more than twenty-
five words—was severed in October 1942 after the last
Red Cross letter I received from her. My own letter was
returned several weeks later, stamped with the message that
the recipient was no longer at that address. Surprised and
alarmed, I waited for her to send me her new address, but
maybe there was no Red Cross wherever she was now. The
months went by.

In June of 1943, I met one of the heroes of El Alamein
at the train station with a queasy stomach. I couldn't stop
thinking of all that had happened in the sixteen months
since Walter and I had said good-bye at the very same place.
Walter, whose unit belonged to the Eighth Army, had been
smack in the middle of the nightmarish final battles of the
desert war, from Tobruk to El Alamein to the ultimate victory over the German Afrika Korps in Tunis.

Here with us, there was little to be happy about. His
father lay in the hospital with lung cancer, and it was uncer-

tain whether he would be able to leave the clinic again. And although Walter would stay with the Shepards, in Gary's old room, I was sure he would be affected by the oppressive shadow of sadness that still had a firm grip on our house, even ten months later. No, I thought anxiously, if home leave was supposed to be a time for recuperation, these two weeks would be entirely wasted for him!

When Walter's train came to a stop, hundreds of soldiers streamed into the arms of their overjoyed wives, soon-to-be-brides, or mothers. Walter's arrival committee consisted of a lone fifteen-year-old girl with a stomachache. In the crowd of faces and uniforms, I couldn't even recognize him; he had to tap me on the shoulder.

"Ziska?" I turned around and looked into a sunburned, expectantly smiling face. "I wondered if you would come!"

"Hello, Lightfoot!" I said, feeling shy and overwhelmed. "It's great to see you! I'm sorry I came alone this time."

Walter lifted his duffel bag to his shoulder, offered me his right arm, and I hooked mine through it as we walked to the exit, feeling happier every minute. "Actually, I was hoping you would," he said. "Tell me honestly, Ziska, how are things at home?"

"We've had a terrible year, as you probably have too."

"Do you think I should change out of uniform before . . . ?"

"No, no. At least it's not a navy uniform." I looked at him from the side. "They're very happy that you're coming. They've hardly talked about anything else for weeks."

"Any attacks recently?" Walter asked as we reached the square outside the station.

"You must have heard already. Now we're reducing each

other's historic cities to ruins. Coventry, Canterbury, Exeter, Norwich, York, and on the other side Cologne and Lübeck, and the Ruhrgebiet. I am so sick of this war!"

"It can't last much longer. The time of German victories is over."

"And you? Do you know yet where you'll go next?"

"No idea. Right now it's time for a holiday."

We rode down to the subway. "I hope it will be a holiday!" I murmured. "Your father so sick, and at our house, well, I wouldn't exactly call it relaxing."

"I'll go to the hospital tomorrow and see what I can do for Paps. I can only imagine what the Shepards have been through."

"I thought a broken heart was an expression, or something from a different century. But now I can imagine perfectly well how people die of a broken heart. All your energy drains away."

"How is she doing?"

"Much better. She's dealing with it really well, I think. Matthew fusses about her, but not as secretly as he thinks!" I had to laugh. "No, we'll get through this. I'm sure of it."

"The two of them must be so happy to have you."

"They are. Not as a replacement for Gary, but as a reason to get up in the morning."

Walter smiled. "You've gotten awfully wise, Ziska."

"Don't be so smug! You're only four years older than me, Lightfoot!"

As we sat in the subway grinning at each other, I noticed that my stomachache had given way to a new feeling, like someone was tickling me with a feather.

Back at the house, while Walter unpacked his things I gently opened Amanda's door. "Wake up, Mum! Walter is here!" I whispered.

"And?" she answered sleepily. "Is he well?"

"Looks that way. He seems so grown-up! I had forgotten how tall he is!"

Amanda laughed quietly. "Do you fancy him?" she asked.

"Yes!" I whispered conspiratorially; she gave me a crafty look and countered, "Well, then, I'd better get downstairs right away!"

I put on water for tea and Walter went out in the yard to meet the chickens. He was still outside when Amanda came down, but just as she opened the door to go out and greet him, he pushed it open from outside and they stood face-to-face with a smile and a surprised "Whoops!"

Amanda took a step backward. "So," she said almost shyly. "Private Lightfoot!"

She must have been worried about this first encounter; not everyone got along with her since Gary's death. But Walter wasn't afraid, neither of the misfortune that had befallen her nor of her pain. He simply opened his arms wide without a word, and Amanda practically disappeared in them.

I stood there with my teapot, spellbound, wishing he would never let her go. In my whole life I had never seen a more comforting picture.

The next days were healing. Big, friendly Walter exuded such energy that he brought a breath of fresh air to our entire household. Walter's experiences in Africa captivated us. The hot, dry desert wind, the dust in their noses and eyes, the unfathomable silence when the weapons were stilled, the scamper of little feet and paws outside their tents at night, the glittering sky that seemed near enough to touch. He painted all of that for us, and for the first time in a long time, Amanda, Matthew, and I were in the same place again.

Our recovery may also have had to do with Walter's unabashed delight at being with us. We all remembered ourselves, and instinctively wanted to be near him: Matthew, whom Walter enthusiastically helped out at the Elysée; Amanda, with whom he took long walks and sat for hours; and of course me, who was robbed of sleep by new and confusing feelings. I had been in love with Gary for years and thought I knew all about it, but what I experienced now was disconcertingly different. Again and again I imagined how Walter had held Amanda and imagined myself in her place; my heart felt tight, my whole body hurt, I prayed that it would pass, and at the same time, I hoped it never would!

Fortunately, I managed not to let it show. Admitting to Walter that I had fallen in love with him was out of the question; it would have destroyed everything that bound us together. He confided in me and shared his shock about his father's cancer, and we treated each other as best friends. I wouldn't have jeopardized that for the world.

On Friday evening after we returned from synagogue, Amanda and Matthew made Walter's induction into the family official by asking him to call them by their first names. Matthew said the prayer for all things new, and when he had finished it was quiet for a long time.

I broke the silence by asking, "When you took me in, could you have imagined that you'd eventually have all my friends to deal with too? Professor Schueler, Walter, and Bekka too, if Hitler hadn't invaded Poland."

I had wanted to lighten things up a little, but to my surprise, the laughter was extinguished the instant I mentioned Bekka. "That just shows you how much you've added to our lives," Amanda said, but all of a sudden I had the disturbing, disorienting feeling I'd touched on something awful.

Had there been a message about Bekka that they'd kept from me? I was so appalled by the thought that I didn't dare ask, but I couldn't stop thinking about it either. I began to keep my ears open so I wouldn't miss out on what they talked about when I wasn't around.

I didn't have to wait very long. The little wooden bench Matthew had set out near the kitchen door was directly beneath the master bedroom window. Amanda liked to sit there in the afternoon sun. Walter sometimes kept her company, and when I stood at the window ten feet above them, I could hear them perfectly well.

"They have proof," Walter said. "There are eyewitness reports, and documents that people have risked their lives to smuggle out of Germany. *The Allied politicians say the evidence is 'not conclusively genuine,'* while Hitler and Goebbels talk publicly about the extermination of the Jews."

"It's hard to believe that, Walter. Those labor camps are terrible enough, but not that! No one can just make that huge number of people disappear. There are neighbors, the people who work on the trains and live near the camps . . ."

"Fill them with fear and terror and they haven't seen a

thing. Amanda, you didn't live with the Germans. You have no idea what it's like."

What on earth were they talking about? I leaned forward a little and looked down on them. They sat peacefully in the sun with cups of tea in their hands.

"There's a new resident at the nursing home," Amanda said thoughtfully. "He gets Red Cross letters from his daughter, who's in Theresienstadt. So the Red Cross must have an eye on it."

"I hope they're only rumors too. But the fact is that there were Jewish soldiers among the Free French and Polish troops in Africa who had specific details. The Resistance has helped too many Jews make their way to freedom to not know what they're saving them from."

After a long pause Walter added, "The camps are spread over half of Europe. Germany, Austria, France, Belgium, Holland, Russia, Poland, Czechoslovakia, we know where they are. And another thing—can you explain to me why little children and old people are sent to labor camps?"

I didn't hear anything else, and even his last words weren't very clear, not because Walter had spoken too softly or one of them had noticed me, but because a strange buzzing in my ears began as soon as I heard "Holland." Within seconds, I couldn't hear at all, the walls around me began to sway, and I had the sensation I was lifting off the ground. I slid down the wall until I sat on the floor, and tried to focus on objects in the room until my vision cleared. I broke out in a cold sweat. It lasted maybe two minutes, but when Amanda came into her bedroom a little later I was still sitting there. She glanced at the open window and knew.

"I thought it was about Bekka," I said as she knelt down in front of me without a word. "But it's about all of them, isn't it?"

"We don't know, love."

"But I want to know! I have to know! If what Walter said is right, then the whole world has to know about it, so that it stops!"

"You're right. And even if it's not true it has to be made public so that we know for certain. We can't let up until we've found out what's happening."

"I've known for a long time that I'll never see my mother again," I muttered, as if calling up my deepest fear might lessen the horror.

Amanda replied, "As long as we don't know anything concretely, there's no reason to lose hope. It could be that the Red Cross doesn't know where your mother is because she's gone into hiding."

"I have to talk with Walter," I said. "He has to tell me everything he knows."

If you ask, you'll get an answer. That simple saying proved to be true in the following days, and once we started to ask questions, it wasn't difficult to find answers. It wasn't the great secret I had thought it was that Jews were being transported throughout half of Europe, it just wasn't talked about in public. The author Thomas Mann, who gave radio addresses for German BBC listeners from his Californian exile, had already talked about mass murder of Polish Jews a year earlier. In Holland and France, where Walter's information came from, roundups of Jews were a regular occurrence; in Amsterdam they were taken to the main railway station in streetcars, right out in the open, where trains from the concentration camp at Westerbork awaited them. To single them out, Jews were forced to sew a yellow star onto their clothing.

But what happened to the people after that wasn't clear. There were lots of different claims: forced labor in labor camps, resettlement in ghettos, even deportation to some country in the South Pacific. We heard of camps where the prisoners were left to their own devices until they succumbed to disease, starved to death, or committed suicide.

Other rumors said that entire families simply disappeared; they boarded a train but never arrived anywhere. There was talk of toxic gas. These rumors were so wild and unbelievable that many people we knew in the Jewish community didn't want to talk about it at all. "We Jews shouldn't make too much fuss," people would say, and that Great Britain was already fighting against Germany—what more did we want them to do? We began to write letters to newspapers and members of the Houses of Parliament to draw attention to our questions. Response to our letters was limited. That summer the newspapers were full of grimly enthusiastic reports about the German collapse on the Eastern Front, and if anything was written about the situation of the Jews at all, it was generally preceded by the statement: "Jewish organizations report . . ." It sounded as if these things were only of concern to Jewish people, and no one but us had heard anything.

Once I got over my initial shock, all this information had a sobering effect on me. I weighed everything I heard, hoped that none of it was true, and reckoned with the worst, or what I thought to be the worst at the time—hunger, sickness, mortal danger. I had been living with the loss of my mother for too long to think it impossible that she was dead. After all the fears I had overcome, I became calmer and more distanced, as if I was building armor to protect myself from that final bit of news.

The one thing I couldn't do was relate all of that to Bekka. A train had saved me, and transported me to a new life. Where did Bekka's train take her? I pushed the question far away, because it hurt too much. It was unthinkable that something had happened to her, the one who should have been here safely in my place.

Despite all the uncertainty, we celebrated Gary's birthday, the twelfth of June, during Walter's home leave. I had been dreading that day. Amanda had been slowly but surely improving in recent months, and I was afraid that milestone would set her back again. Helplessly I asked myself how to approach the day. Maybe it was best to just let it come and go.

Finally, I decided to be the first to get up that morning and to set the table nicely for breakfast—not too fancy, but enough to make it special. My foster parents' reaction would show me what to do next.

Secretly I got a little bouquet of flowers and hid it in my room so I could take them apart and use them for decorations. My search for special foods wasn't as successful; after four years at war, the stores simply didn't have anything. There wasn't any honey or sugar, there were no canned goods, no onions, no fruit. By sacrificing all my meat coupons I was able to get several beef sausages.

Amanda also got up earlier than usual, and barged in on my preparations just as I was taking apart my bouquet. "Oh, darn it!" I said, disappointed and a little embarrassed, which wasn't exactly the greeting she was used to. To my relief, she laughed when she saw what I was up to, and let me look into the bag she held in her hand.

The bag contained three small packages. I must have looked a little apprehensive when Amanda placed them on the table.

"Frances, twenty-three years ago today my son was born. This will always be a day of celebration for me, and if I can't give Gary presents anymore, then you'll just get something instead," Amanda explained. It was the first time in ten months that I'd heard her say Gary's name out loud. She held out the smallest package to me. "Let me see if you like it."

Inside the blue wrapping paper I found a little jewelry box. "I thought that might go well with your cross necklace," Amanda said, looking at me expectantly.

I opened it—and resting on cotton was the most beautiful piece of jewelry I had ever seen. It was a tiny Star of David with a red-gold filigree band wound around the points. It was so delicate, I could hardly imagine that a human hand could create something so fine. It took my breath away.

Amanda was pleased by my reaction. "There's an Indian goldsmith in Camden, one of Hazel's uncles. When I told him who I wanted a gift for, he asked me to come back a week later. He made it just for you. The star is quite unusual, don't you think?"

She stepped behind me, opened the clasp on my necklace, and added the star to the chain, which slid down to join my cross. The light, loving touch on my neck reminded me of Mamu and the day we parted, when she had given me the necklace.

"Now I'm wearing both of my mothers around my neck!" I said, half joking, as we admired the perfect harmony of cross and star in front of the mirror.

"Frances, I thank you for this past year. For your love, your patience, your courage. Did you notice that you started calling me Mum when I was least there for you? Instead, you took care of me. I don't think you have any idea how strong you are."

Three days later the war continued for Walter: The Eighth Army landed in Sicily to join the Americans in opening a second front against the Germans. For a short time I managed not to think about what awaited him there, but then the weekly newsreels showed the first images of the invasion of Italy and I noted that love and worry don't take orders.

Herr Glücklich, who was too modest to want visitors other than his son, died in a London hospital in July, alone. At the same time, Hamburg was being bombed and the city was engulfed in a firestorm. I didn't tend to sympathize with the Germans, but when I saw pictures of burned, disfigured bodies of people who had died in an inescapable inferno, I felt sick to my stomach. For the first time it felt like something had spun out of control, that now even the good guys in this fight had stooped to a level that corrupted them, and from which nothing just and pure could come anymore.

Chapter 21

Light

The longer the war lasted, the harder it became to imagine that it would ever end. People were sick of the air-raid cellars, the sirens, the mountains of rubble lining the streets. Almost three years after the Blitz, the Germans renewed their attacks on London—in retribution for Nuremburg, Munich, and Berlin, it was said—and even if they didn't have nearly the same destructive force of the first air battles, their impact was devastating. Maybe the day would come when we wouldn't know how to manage in not-wartime, how to sleep through the night, shop for food and clothing without points and coupons, how to plan for the future—or even what London had looked like before the blackout.

The weak lamp on my bicycle was the only light on the street that night. The streetlights had been dark for five years now, the curtains in the houses firmly shut. My eyes, long accustomed to finding their way at night, couldn't remember it any other way. Not a bad quality for an air-raid messenger, I thought!

Carefree, I stretched out my legs and let the bike roll down a small hill. Something darted across the street in front of me—a cat? The German bombers rarely had enough force for a second round of attacks, and as soon as I delivered my message to the office at the train station, I'd be able to go home.

The sudden dull rumble behind me startled me. Immediately I thought of a dud bomb, instinctively ducked my head under my steel helmet, and pedaled faster, but as I turned around I gasped: An enormous, shapeless shadow sixty yards behind me sank to the ground very slowly, almost in slow motion, and disappeared into the asphalt without a sound.

I stared and must have steered my bike quite a ways without looking forward. Although I immediately knew what I was dealing with, I couldn't get it through my head that it was actually happening to me. In a few seconds I wouldn't exist anymore! I didn't feel fear, only surprise. A bright ball of light flared high into the sky and it was blindingly white, almost beautiful with its two shimmering violet and lavender circles in the middle. Then came the bang of the explosion, and with it a bloodcurdling rumbling and grumbling like a huge dog. Unbearable pain stretched between my ears like a tight rope, the world turned upside down, gray shadows spun around, then darkness.

But how pleasant it was to be dead! I observed how the black surrounding me gradually gave way to a bluish light. Something moved, maybe a face? Before I could recognize it, it was gone, a comfortable exhaustion overtook me, and I fought in vain to keep my eyes open. When I opened them a second time, the face bent over me through the bluish fog, smiling, and my heart leaped. Mum! She had in fact kept her word and found me. Trusting her, I let my eyes fall shut again. We had arrived. Now nothing more could happen to us.

Opening and closing my eyes was like a game: Each time a little more was revealed. At first there was only a face, then the lips moved, and finally I started to understand words. My name, for example, and that I didn't need to be afraid, everything was going to be okay. When I noticed that my voice had returned, I asked, "What happened?"

I was less concerned about myself than why Amanda was here too, but she only answered, "A parachute mine got you, sweetheart. You've been asleep for quite a while." Then her voice cracked and she fought back tears, which shocked me; why would there be tears up here?

"Asleep? You mean we aren't dead?"

"Heavens, no," Amanda said with a shudder, and these two words spoiled everything. All at once I recognized that I was lying in a white bed surrounded by a curtain, and that the slightest movement sent shooting pains through my head and chest that until that very moment I hadn't felt at all. At least as bad, though, was the sight of my left arm, which was covered with bruises and had a needle attached to a plastic tube sticking out of it!

Amanda finally told me the whole story. My eardrum had burst but was healed, I had broken several ribs and my skull, and what I had thought was several hours of sleep had actually been almost six weeks!

"Six weeks?" I gasped in disbelief. "Then it's . . . ?"

"The end of March," Amanda replied, and a muscle in her

face twitched. "But don't worry, you'll be perfectly okay! The doctor says you're a miracle, and you're getting a medal for bravery too."

"I didn't even deliver my message!"

Amanda laughed, pleased. I had almost forgotten what that sounded like. "So what? This country needs heroes, so be quiet and accept it!"

"Is there any other news?" I asked nervously.

"Not that I know of. At home the letters from Walter are piling up. I'll bring them to you tomorrow. Matthew will be ecstatic when he hears that you've woken up! And Hazel asks about you every day."

"When can I get out of here?"

"Well, you'll certainly have to stay a few more days. They have all kinds of tests lined up for you—to see if you're cross-eyed or see double, or whether the little steel plate in the back of your head can receive radio signals."

"Mum!" I protested indignantly.

"Sorry. I'm just so happy, Frances. So unbelievably happy!" Amanda wiped her eyes. "And as far as your head . . . no, take your fingers away! Oh, sweetie. That's no reason for tears. Your hair will grow back. Take it from me, I've been there."

It was mid-April before I was finally allowed to go home, and summer before the hair on the back of my head was long enough to cover the ugly purple scar from the surgery. I didn't realize what had really gone on while I was unconscious until after I got home from the hospital. There were signs everywhere: the neglected garden, the dozens of books carelessly stuffed back into bookshelves after Amanda had read them aloud to me, hoping they would wake me up. Two small books about head injuries and traumatic brain injuries lay on the secretary. I didn't want to think about what I had been spared.

And yet, it soon became clear that I hadn't come away quite as intact as we had hoped. I got tired very quickly, and suffered from vertigo and headaches if I wasn't careful. I wouldn't be the fastest runner anymore, since my head couldn't take the jolting, and I had to wear a hat anytime I was outside to protect my head from the sun. Being healthy was the only thing I'd been able to take for granted in my life, and it was hard for me to accept that I was supposed to be impaired now.

Of course, I tried to tell myself that all of that wasn't important when I had almost died. I might not be able to run, but I could walk normally; I might not be a good student right now, but my brain hadn't been permanently damaged. I could talk, think, feel, I was loved; I had no right to complain! Matthew took me out to the shed several weeks later and showed me something covered with a blanket: a twisted, bent clump of metal and shredded rubber that I only recognized as my bicycle on second glance. "You're allowed to be sad and disappointed and angry, as much as you want," he said, "but when you can't stand it anymore, just come out here and look at this."

"I know. And I don't want to be ungrateful, it's just that . . ."

"Ungrateful! What do you have to be grateful for? That someone launched a mine at you and happened to miss?"

I looked at him, confused. "I'd be bloody angry!" Matthew declared, a statement so out of character for him that I almost had to laugh.

I watched as he spread the blanket over what was left of the bike. "There are a few things I'm grateful for," I said. "That I'm allowed to be with you, for one."

"You can look at that another way too. If Hitler, cursed be his name, hadn't become Reichskanzler, you would still have your own parents."

"True, but then I wouldn't know that I'm Jewish."

"That wouldn't even be a factor. At any rate, it's not a reason to be grateful."

"Fine, how about this: I wouldn't be me!"

Matthew looked at me mischievously. "Now, that is a tough one!" he admitted. "Give me a few days, I'll think of something!"

"I doubt that," I countered, and noticed that my dark mood had passed, at least for the day.

Matthew held the door open for me, we stepped out into the sunlight, and I gave him a kiss. Suddenly he wasn't laughing anymore. "We thought we had lost you."

"You didn't, and you won't either." I said. "I'll always love my mother. I'll never stop hoping and praying until I find her again. But it won't change anything anymore. My life is here, with you."

How simple and clear it was. For years I had tortured myself with this question. It had never occurred to me to make a decision before I knew if Mamu would return—or just to make the decision myself! I always thought it was her answer, her decision. I had always feared them both.

It felt rather audacious not to wait for her permission. I

imagined stepping up to her and announcing: "I don't want my old life back, Mamu. I'd like for you to be part of my new life, and Amanda and Matthew are part of it too."

But that's where my fantasy ended. I started to get butterflies in my stomach, and I couldn't begin to imagine how she'd react. I only knew that this was all I had to offer her.

In May the Germans surrendered Monte Cassino and retreated farther north, followed by the Eighth Army. The Allies invaded Normandy in summer, and within a few weeks, large parts of France and Belgium were controlled by the Americans, the British, and their allies. The Soviets advanced toward Poland. More German cities fell, including Berlin; after months of heavy bombardment it was little more than a ghostly hull of dead walls and half-buried cellars where starving, ravaged people found shelter.

At home we prayed with renewed hope for a quick German surrender. It had to have been clear even to Hitler that he had lost the war. But he chose to let it drag on day after day and be responsible for yet more deaths, not to mention the intrusions into the lives of millions of people. An assassination attempt by his own officers failed, and instead of longed-for peace, there was a new threat for British civilians: remote-controlled rockets that could be launched at us at any time and without any warning, literally out of a clear blue sky. The only defense against them was not to think about it too much.

And yet we began to make plans again, to think of the future. The blackout was lifted—one evening Matthew and I came out of the Elysée and stood in the light, speechless with joy. Mrs. Collins and the kids returned from Wales. I spent time with my books every day to make up the work I had missed, and two afternoons a week Mrs. Collins helped me. She had been the one to offer, and I happily accepted.

She was also the one who planted an exciting new idea in my head.

"Do you remember the foreign affairs conference last year?" I asked Amanda and Matthew excitedly. "When Molotov spoke, someone stood there and translated directly into English. Mrs. Collins thinks I could do something like that: interpret for German and English, and maybe another language too, that I could learn at college."

"A lot of young women are going to college nowadays!" I saw Amanda's face light up as the idea took hold in her mind as quickly as it had in mine. "It's not as unusual as it was when we were young, Matthew."

"You don't have to convince me, dear. Frances as an inter- preter would be logical after the last five years, don't you think?"

They looked at each other almost joyfully, then Amanda said, "We've been setting aside money for Gary's educa- tion since he was born, and now it's lying around in a bank account because we wanted to spend it for something really important. Something that would have meant something to him."

"That's out of the question," I protested immediately. "I won't take money from you."

"You're not taking it from us, it's from him. You can't refuse it, love. He was the first one who translated for you, have you forgotten?"

I shook my head silently. "The lovely Mrs. Collins," Amanda said, and stood up to pour us more tea. "That's the best idea I've heard in a long time. I think I can finally forgive her for putting you in the first grade way back when."

"I can't wait to hear what Walter will say about this!" I blurted out.

But before I could share my news with him, something happened that overshadowed all these wonderful plans and made them fade into the distance. On July 23, 1944, the Red Army liberated the Majdanek concentration camp in eastern Poland. What the world had not dared to think was now thrown in our faces—in pictures that intimated far greater horrors than anything we could have imagined until that day.

"It's the immigration office . . ."

"For me . . . ?" Hesitantly I took the receiver from Amanda. *Yes*, I confirmed, *I am Ziska Mangold from Berlin.*

Did I know a certain Erik Bechstein?

A sharp pain bore into the back of my head. *Yes, I know Erik Bechstein. He's my uncle. My uncle Erik.*

It was several days before we could pick him up. Illegal immigrants were usually sent back where they came from without further ado, but a Jew who had escaped from the Nazis and managed to make his way to England could certainly hope for generosity in the first months after the concentration camps were brought to light. And where would they have sent Uncle Erik?

"You get the room where almost all of my friends have stayed," I said as I led him up the stairs.

We hadn't said much to each other since we had found each other in the hallway at the immigration office. "They're in a safe place," were Uncle Erik's first words. He knew, of course, that there had been only one thought on my mind since I had received that phone call: Where was Mamu?

I had almost expected that we wouldn't recognize each other after five and a half years, but I was wrong, although Uncle Erik was noticeably shocked when I stood before him—as if he had thought I'd be a ten-year-old Ziska after all this time! He didn't look much different at all, just a bit slimmer, and very pale, as if he hadn't seen daylight in a long, long time. As I soon found out, that was true.

It wasn't until I introduced him that I saw he was a different person; the man who shyly shook hands with Amanda and Matthew bore no resemblance to the cheerful, resilient uncle of my childhood. ". . . pleased to meet you," he mumbled in heavily accented English. "Forgive me for being here."

"We are very happy to have you, Herr Bechstein," replied Matthew emphatically. An hour later Uncle Erik set down his threadbare suitcase next to Gary's bed. "Nice," he commented as he looked around.

"This was supposed to be Bekka's," I explained. Uncle Erik promptly looked like he wanted to cry again. "Evchen and Betti . . ." he started.

The horror sliced me like a hot blade. I had never experienced anything like it; a premonition that almost threw me to the floor. "No!" I whispered.

"They were in a convent in Belgium, about two kilometers

away from me. I ran there just as soon as the Americans liberated our town. No one was there, not the children and not the nuns who had hidden them. Someone reported them in the spring and they were taken to Mechelen, the Belgian concentration camp."

"But the Americans . . ."

"Too late. Mechelen was evacuated."

"Evacuated . . . ?"

"Auschwitz. Gassed right after they arrived, like all the children."

Uncle Erik set his suitcase on the bed and started to unpack. I stood there without moving, almost without breathing. "And you?" he asked in a monotone. "Lots of destruction, I see."

"Gary is dead. My . . . my brother."

He looked up. I stared back, caught completely off guard and surprised that anything could shock him, after what he had just told me. He gestured toward the door. "Their son?" I nodded.

Agitated, my uncle rubbed his chin and I heard his stubble bristle. "How terrible. Something like that shouldn't happen to people who help the Jews!"

"They're Jewish themselves, Uncle Erik."

"Still. I have to tell them how sorry I am. Such kind faces! You learn to have a good eye for faces when you're Jewish, Ziska."

I reached past him and gently shut his suitcase. "Let's go outside. The sun is shining and Mum must have tea ready by now."

"That's what you call her . . . Mum?"

I blushed. "It doesn't have anything to do with Mamu," I started, but Uncle Erik shook his head.

"It's all right. It's been more than five years. You had to find some way to survive too, didn't you?"

I looked at him, stunned. Stunned that he understood.

A safe address: In the summer of 1942, that was the only thing Jews in occupied Holland could still hope for. When my mother found a safe address for herself and her sister in a house owned by two older women, there was no time to lose: Aunt Ruth and my young cousins had already received a deportation notice.

But Frau Zaandvort, who was forced to do compulsory labor in the same canned food processing plant as Mamu, had given her something else: contact with a group that hid Jewish children under false identities in Belgian convents and homes. In the same night that Mamu and Aunt Ruth went underground with the old women, who wouldn't have wanted to take in either a man or two children, Uncle Erik set off to bring Evchen and Betti to the Belgian border.

He found a hideout for himself in the back room of a potato cellar on a Belgian farm. From there, he could just hear the bells at the convent that harbored Evchen and Betti chiming in the distance every morning, noon, and night.

I tried to imagine how it must have been after the liberation, his anticipation, the unbearable tension as he ran through the forest to the convent—the first time he had seen the sun in twenty months. And then his disbelief and horror as the last two old nuns tearfully told him what had happened that spring.

Uncle Erik didn't waste many words on something that couldn't be expressed. He picked up his story three weeks later, as if everything in between just hadn't happened. A man arranged passage for my uncle on a boat that would bring him to the coast of England, since he had mentioned that he had a niece living in London.

Had he considered staying and waiting until Aunt Ruth and Mamu were liberated, I asked gently? Holland was still under German control, but the Allies were inching closer and closer every week and were already approaching Arnhem.

Uncle Erik looked at me with tortured eyes. "And then what?" he asked. "Should I tell Ruth that I lost the children?"

That was, in fact, the one question that weighed on him constantly, until after several days he came to the conclusion that he had made an enormous mistake. What was he doing in England? He had to go back as soon as possible and find his wife!

With difficulty we convinced him not to risk crossing the English Channel, which was scattered with mines, until Holland had been liberated—a matter of a few weeks, we assumed. Weeks passed and turned into months. In spring, when the Germans had been driven from all the countries around Holland, and Aachen was the first German city to fall under American control, and Montgomery advanced on Bremen and Hamburg, the Dutch still awaited their liberation.

"This has to be the coldest winter I've ever lived through!" I said to Walter, shivering, as we set off for the city.

The ruins at the lower end of Harrington Grove stared at

us accusingly, as if it was our fault that they were still waiting to be rebuilt more than four years after the Blitz. During the summer, children had climbed among the half-collapsed stairways and exposed beams, gathering together undamaged furniture and creating hideouts for themselves. The expanse of rubble where I had almost died a year earlier was already fading in the gathering darkness when we passed it. At home, the only room we still heated was the kitchen, and we were discussing whether we should cut down the tree in the front yard for wood. At night we took bricks warmed by the embers in the oven to bed with us, wore wool socks and scarves, and still shivered. And just a few days ago I had gone to the shed and found Victory in the straw, frozen to death.

"I don't think we're allowed to eat a frozen chicken, dear," Matthew said, watching as Amanda got ready to thaw my pet.

"I don't intend to ask the rabbi! She's clean, she doesn't smell, she ate nothing but kosher food her whole life. No one's eaten a purer chicken soup in this country for years." Before long, a scent began to fill the house that reminded me less and less of Victory and more and more of Millie and better days long past.

"Victory soup," Amanda had commented amicably as she filled a bowl for Walter, whose home leave had begun just in time for Shabbat. Unsuspecting, he reached for his spoon, tried the soup, looked thoughtful for a moment, took a second sip, and said, "Delicious! Victory is right around the corner, I can taste it!"

The others tried hard to suppress their laughter, and I

bowed my head deeply over my plate. If I was prepared to eat my own hen just to avoid spoiling Walter's appetite, I must be worse off than I thought!

It had been Walter's idea to run the Elysée on Sunday and give Amanda and Matthew a night off so they could spend an evening together. The thought of being alone with Walter at the theater made my heart beat faster. We hadn't seen each other in a year and a half, and I liked to think I had noticed a certain admiration in his eyes when he had greeted me. The previous week it had felt strange to turn seventeen, but now, on the third day after Walter's appreciative look, I felt much better about it!

Amanda and I shared the bathroom and bedroom mirror to try on our meager wartime wardrobe, drawing fake stocking seams on our legs with eyeliner, and generally having a good time. And I wasn't even going out, just to work with Walter! But my excitement about it didn't seem to surprise Amanda in the least. "You look beautiful, dear!" she said when I was finally ready.

We smiled at each other. "You know, don't you?" I asked shyly.

"Don't worry," was all she said. "You didn't give yourself away. If I hadn't been wishing for it for so long, I certainly wouldn't have noticed anything."

"I love you, Mum." I put my arms around her neck. When she pressed her forehead to mine, I could tell that we were the same height, just exactly the same.

"I know you love me," she said quietly. "I see it every day. It's one of the nicest things that's happened in my whole life."

The Elysée had managed to defy all the air raids. With time it had gotten a little shabby; the soft red carpet was worn and plaster trickled from the walls in several places from bombs landing nearby. Settling had left several long cracks through the foyer, and the ceiling in the main theater had water damage in a few spots. "When the war's over, we'll need to close for a few weeks and renovate," Walter suggested when he saw the damage.

We! I thought happily, and once again had another moment I'd be able to twist and turn and ponder the meaning of for hours, even days.

We fell into the typical routine: I swept the theater and opened the ticket booth while Walter changed a lightbulb in the foyer, stood at the entrance to tear tickets, and finally disappeared into the projection room. After I let in several latecomers, I reached for the stepladder to take it back to the room behind the screen.

As always, I thought of Gary as soon as I stepped through the door. This was the place where I still cried for him sometimes, where the sadness was immediate and overwhelming like nowhere else. It hung in the curtain, in the grainy recesses of the screen, in every gouge in the floor. I knew how much his parents suffered because he had never been found; there was neither visible proof of his death nor a grave where they could leave small stones. I was the only one in the family who had a place to say good-bye to Gary.

What would he have said about my feelings for Walter? If I knew Gary, he would have immediately taken things into his own hands. He would have pulled Walter aside and I could almost hear him whispering: "What are you waiting for?"

I laughed. It would have been too perfect to have a big brother right now! My heart felt unusually light, as if something had already changed, and there was more than just sadness in those memories.

I noticed the sounds and pictures of the newsreel on my way out. Out of the corner of my eye I recognized the all-too-familiar motifs: the same expanses of gray rubble and ruins that used to be German cities. Seldom did something stand out that still distinguished one from another—the remains of a familiar dome, a bridge, a church tower. Gaunt, haggard people moved along quickly, as if there was still somewhere to go in the midst of all the destruction. It was more likely that they just didn't want to be filmed in their shame.

But one grubby little girl, about three years old, spontaneously pulled her hand away from her mother's when she saw the camera, stood rooted to the spot, and broke out in a beautiful, perfect smile. The mother grabbed her arm firmly and pulled her along, giving the cameraman an odd look, half mischievous and half accusing, that made it clear how young she was.

The sister, not the mother. My heart stood still. It wasn't only that look, it was the position of her shoulders that made me recognize her. Straight. Unbowed. It took a stronger power than the Nazis to destroy Rebekka Liebich. I had always known it.

"Ziska?" Walter looked at me with surprise as I stumbled up the stairs to the projection room. Outside in the hallway I could have screamed out loud. Now I stood there and couldn't make a sound. "Ziska," Walter said again, coming toward me.

"I saw Bekka," I cried. "She's alive!"

Without a word, he opened his arms wide and I walked into them, without thinking, felt his rough wool sweater and underneath it a heartbeat steadily growing faster, which for a moment I thought was my own. A hand stroked my hair, my neck, then lifted my chin.

Warmth. Surprise. Recognition. Hazel had confided in me that she practiced kissing her own arm. If I could ever think again, I would tell her that wasn't even close to the real thing!

"That's her. I'm sure of it! Of course it's hard to tell, it goes so fast."

"And if I hold the frame?"

It was half past ten, and we stood in the window of the projection room staring over empty rows of seats at the screen. Again and again we played those two seconds of the newsreel.

"What a shame they don't say which city it is," Walter said. "It's somewhere in the Ruhrgebiet, that much is for sure."

"The Ruhrgebiet, why not? It was definitely safer than Berlin, where all the neighbors recognized them and knew they were Jewish. Frau Liebich is as old as Mamu, in her early forties, she could definitely have had another baby. And the little girl looks just like Bekka in our pictures from kindergarten!"

"Is that enough? Are you sure?"

"Yes, I am. We can go home now."

We walked through the sleet to the Underground, the same path we had taken a few hours ago and so many other times before. And yet the street, and all of London, seemed entirely different to me now that my head rested on Walter's shoulder as we walked and he had his arm around me for the first time. We walked more carefully as a twosome. We had to pay attention to each other, otherwise we'd fall out of step or lose our balance.

Even so, I couldn't concentrate entirely on Walter. "Bekka's coming back," I repeated, and I vowed it again as we got into the train. "We're going to see each other again. She's the only one I was completely sure about the entire time."

Chapter 22

The End of the War

"There must be ten thousand people!" Hazel yelled directly into my ear. The enormous crowd that filled the entire length of the Mall pushing toward Buckingham Palace was indescribable. People sang and cheered, traffic had come to a complete standstill, and once in a while I was brushed by one of the Union Jacks that were being waved around.

The Germans had signed the surrender agreement. For people in Europe, the war was over. No more bombs and missiles, no more air raids, no more nights spent in cellars and subway tunnels, no more dread of a telegram boy's knock on the door. It was spring, there was laughter and music. On that day, the Pacific, where the fighting raged on, couldn't have been farther away.

"The king! The king!" The crowd cheered even louder, and indeed, on the palace balcony we could just make out several light and dark spots: the king and queen, the princesses, and the prime minister. "God save the king!" thousands cried. Old men and women placed their right hands on their hearts and wept.

The old empire had withstood the war. It had staggered, suffered, and bled, but it had persevered. The terror had been overcome, and we were free. Church bells rang all over the city, but there were painful absences of chimes that had been part of the city for hundreds of years: St. Dunstan, St. Clement Danes, St. Alban, St. Augustine, St. Mildred, St. Stephen, St. Swithin.

I knew that lots of people in the jubilant crowd would start grieving again as soon as the victory celebrations were over, and that the eighth of May would remain a bittersweet day: the end of the war, but not of the hurting. I had hope for Mamu and Aunt Ruth, and even more for Bekka. But Gary and my father weren't coming back.

The celebration continued on Harrington Grove. Tables and chairs were carried from all the houses onto the street, lamps and flags were hung; someone had even dragged a piano outside. "Can you stay?" I asked Hazel, but she declined. There would be a party in her own street too.

We kissed each other on the cheek when we parted. My friend for the war, which was over now! Our old agreement was so long forgotten that it would have been silly to officially correct it. We knew we'd remain friends.

"Sweet Erik is already upstairs packing." I heard Amanda's voice from inside the pantry, where she was rummaging around. "He'll never get across this week, but he doesn't want to wait another minute. Ah, here it is!"

She pulled a brown notebook down from a shelf and blew a thin layer of flour and dust from its cover toward me. "Your garden notebook?" I asked in amazement.

"Yes! It will be a while before we can get supplies like we used to, but I thought we could make a start."

"And where do you think you'll find flowers?"

Amanda shook her head, opened one of the little packages, and let me look inside. "You didn't really think I had just thrown my most precious treasures on the compost heap!" she admonished, and pulled from the assortment of neatly labeled paper packets one that contained tiny brown seeds. "Darn it. If the Germans had surrendered a few weeks earlier, I could have planted petunias."

I stared at her. "It's over. It's really over!"

Amanda laughed. "I was afraid you couldn't really be happy about it," I said quietly.

She closed the packet again and turned away. "I'm happy for you, Frances," she answered. "For you young people. So much has been taken away from you! If you ask me, there can't be enough celebrating that all of this is finally over."

Amanda had decided to celebrate this day as a new beginning, and no matter how bitter and heartbroken she might secretly be, from now on she wouldn't show it.

Uncle Erik moved around the room that had first belonged to Gary, then Walter, then him and gathered his belongings. "Why are you taking your winter clothes?" I asked in surprise, holding up the gloves I had knit for him at Hanukkah.

"Because I lose my residence permit as soon as I leave England," my uncle replied simply. I couldn't breathe. "The war is over. The island is happy to be rid of her refugees."

"But . . . you have to . . ." I was so shocked I could barely speak. "Mamu . . . how should . . . I thought . . ."

"Let me find them first, Ziska. We can apply for new papers then. Leave it to me to convince your mother that she needs to come here."

"Does that mean"—I sat down on the bed—"you think she wouldn't want to?"

Uncle Erik smiled. He had grown visibly stronger, but his eyes were only rarely without a sad expression. Ahead of him was the prospect of telling Aunt Ruth about their children's deaths. "I'll talk with your mother," he repeated. "I'll tell her that you're the only one of us who still has a home. If we want to start over again together, then it has to be in England."

"How do you think she'll react?" I looked at him anxiously.

"She'll need a little time." He dodged the question. My heart sank. "Ziska, Margot lived to see you again. You're everything she has left. But I don't know if she's prepared for the fact that there are other people in your life besides her."

"You're right. Oh, Uncle Erik!" I hugged him tight. "I'm so sorry about everything that's happened, and that you had to wait so long to go back . . . but I'm glad for every day you were here! And I've never, ever forgotten that you were there to wave at our train that night. You were the farewell they cheated us out of!"

"I haven't forgotten it either." He patted me on the back, and after a moment freed himself from my hug. "And now let's go out and celebrate that the time of good-byes is finally over."

We had known for months that this day would come. One German city after another had surrendered—some without a fight, but in many other cases only after Hitler ordered his last reserves of half-grown boys and old men into senseless, unevenly matched slaughters—before the "greatest commander of all time" shot himself in his bunker. In March Walter had been ordered to Lübeck, where they needed German-speaking liaisons between the British commanders and the residents.

What would happen after that was the subject of continuous speculation—at the Vathareerpurs'!

Walter had become a British citizen on his twenty-first birthday and carried his new identity with pride. Hazel and her mother expected that he would soon ask me "the question," as they called it. I, however, was neither as convinced nor as carried away as my friend. I hoped he would take his sweet time with that question. I missed him terribly, and could easily picture us standing under the chuppah and celebrating an exuberant Jewish wedding. But a wedding meant more than a promise and a party. It meant starting our own household, having our own children, and responsibilities I absolutely did not feel ready for. After I'm finished with school! When I'm nineteen! There was no denying there was something there that wanted to be awakened, but for the time being I clung tightly to my last two years of school.

All the more so when, right after the celebrations, I faced a new and entirely unexpected dilemma. For years we had longed for the end of the war, lived for nothing else; now it had come and gone with breathtaking speed. Londoners went back to their daily lives, everywhere things were cleaned up, built, planned, and the Refugee Committee remembered me again.

"Well, now that the war is over and Germany has been

liberated, naturally we have to consider what should happen to you," Mrs. Lewis informed me.

Unsettled, I sank deeper into the living room sofa. She sat across from me, her purse on her lap. "Have you had news from your mother?" she wanted to know.

I shook my head. "My uncle went to Holland ten days ago to look for her, but we haven't heard anything yet."

"You can also start a search through the Red Cross. I brought the form with me." Mrs. Lewis reached into her purse and retrieved the paper. "Of course, this is only if your uncle isn't successful," she added quickly.

"Of course," I murmured, and "thank you."

"You're finishing secondary school this summer? We're so pleased, Frances. You are one of our success stories! We brought thousands of children out of Germany, but unfortunately not all of them were as lucky as you, I'm sad to say."

"Mrs. Lewis," I interrupted, "why are you here?"

She gave me an unexpectedly hard, scrutinizing look. "You know that your stay in England was meant to be temporary. No one will deport you, even if the danger is past now. You practically grew up here in England. But if your mother is still alive and is waiting for you in Germany, that of course raises questions."

The shock ran through my whole body. "I'm not going back to Germany. Never!"

"Calm down, Frances. As I said, we're not sending you back unless your mother demands it. And that's why we're also eager to find out whether she's alive. We need to know if we are still responsible for you, or whether you still have family."

"I have family," I said with a quivering voice. "The Shepards."

"I believe you know what I'm talking about, Frances," Mrs. Lewis responded. She placed the form on the table between us and pushed it toward me.

"You knew about it, right?" I asked after she had left.

Leaning on the doorframe I watched Amanda cut vegetables at the kitchen table. "That your mother can demand that you return?" she replied without turning toward me. "What's new about that?"

"But don't you think I'm old enough to decide for myself? If Mamu wants to have me back, she has to come to me. After all, she's the one who sent me away."

"Heavens. You still hold that against her?" Amanda finally looked upset, even though it wasn't on my account, but Mamu's. I immediately felt betrayed.

"I don't resent it," I protested. "But she certainly lost the right to make decisions about me when she did. I decide, me alone, and that's exactly what I'll tell her."

My foster mother, the mother I had chosen, looked straight at me and like a flash, the memory was there . . . the seconds of our first encounter, the look of this intelligent, friendly face. Now there was so much more in it, the past six years, the war, Gary's death, our shared history.

"Don't be afraid." I wasn't even sure if she had said it out loud. "Don't plan what you want to say. When you see her, you'll know. Only then."

The Red Cross missing persons form consisted of just a few lines, the first of which was the hardest to fill in. Name of the missing person. My pen hovered above it for several minutes. Days, actually, if you counted the time I had needed to actually look at the form Mrs. Lewis had left, and use it.

Rebekka Liebich. I sighed with relief when it was finally done. The rest was quick. Born on December 8, 1927, last known residence in Berlin-Neukölln, Silbersteinstraße, with her parents, Susanna and Hermann Liebich. There were a few lines for "other information" where I filled in four words that looked like a plea: probably in the Ruhrgebiet, question mark. I stuck the form in an envelope, sealed it, and added a stamp before I lost my nerve.

The other letter lay under the desk blotter, the one we had awaited for such a long time and had arrived the day before yesterday, about three weeks after Uncle Erik left.

Groningen, 26 May 1945

Dear Ziska,

Sadly I don't have good news. The ladies could only hide Margot and Ruth until October due to drastic food shortage. Next stop KZ Westerbork, all else unknown. Don't lose hope. The Red Cross is still listing people who were freed from the camps. Have registered their names and wait for a reply. Will contact you immediately.

Uncle Erik

I had withdrawn to my room with the letter and read those few sentences again and again until I thought I could hear Uncle Erik's voice, and when the tears finally came, they were for him. He can't take this, not again! Don't keep him waiting. Let it have an end.

Since Gary's death I had avoided asking God or Jesus for anything. I would have liked to pray for Uncle Erik to find Mamu and Aunt Ruth alive and well; I would have liked to feel I was doing something for him that way. But I couldn't. What had happened, had happened. I didn't believe in an all-powerful God anymore. He had to watch everything unfold, every evil plan, every single murder. Suddenly I knew what I could pray for.

If you are a compassionate God, then have mercy on Uncle Erik. Don't abandon him. Stay with him and give him strength.

The telegram came a few days later. *Margot lives. Love and hugs. More soon. Uncle Erik.*

Chapter 23

A Phone Call

Mrs. Collins would have to throw away her world map. When the students returned to school after the summer holiday, they would be dealing with different borders, and a few small countries would disappear from the map entirely. Hitler's grip of the countries around Germany had been thwarted, but the victorious powers had their own plans for Europe.

Everywhere, people launched the bitter search for their relatives that might last years, and often in vain.

Groningen, 24 June 1945

Dear Ziska,

At last I can give you the details. On the 9th of June I found your mother in a camp called Belsen in the Lüneburger Heide. The Red Cross had her name on a list of survivors who had been treated in a hospital after the liberation. It was difficult to get permission to take her to Holland, but personal contacts to the British occupying forces—Corporal

Lightfoot!—helped move things along fairly
quickly after all. From Westerbork they were both
taken directly to Auschwitz and in January, just
before the liberation by the Red Army, were put on
a train headed for Germany. Bergen-Belsen wasn't
an extermination camp; the people died of hunger
and typhoid, as did your aunt Ruth on 4 April
1945. Yes, Ziska, your aunt, my wife, is no longer
alive. But she died believing that our daughters
were safe.

I don't know if you and I will ever learn more.
Your mother doesn't talk about it. I definitely don't
see an opportunity to bring up the question of the
future. It does your mother good to be in Holland,
and every day she makes a little progress in eating,
gaining weight, and feeling better on the whole.
Slowly she seems to be coming back to life.

Be patient. I see that she's started a letter to you,
but I don't think she wants you to come right away
and see her like this.

"Why don't you come outside, Frances? I've set out the
little table for you, you can bring your schoolbooks and
study there."

I looked up. As so often since my accident, pains pounded
and bored into my head and it took a few seconds for my
eyes to change focus from the tiny letters in the math book
to Amanda's face.

For days now, my foster parents had been walking on egg-
shells around me, waiting patiently, giving me time. I had no

idea why that didn't help, why it only intensified my feeling of being utterly alone.

Amanda's move with the table was the first attempt to get me to do anything, and it seemed harder to find an argument against it than to just do her the favor. Without another word I packed up my books and papers and followed her.

It was as if my life had been interrupted the moment I read Uncle Erik's letter; as if I had to see my mother, talk with her, receive some word from her before I could inhale again. I had to look at a photograph to remember her face, and even that didn't shut out those other images that wanted to get in the way now. Amanda withdrew to the backyard while I sat on the bench with my books. She had set out juice and a piece of cake for me, but left me alone.

I glanced over at her and saw her quick hands digging, snipping, planting seedlings. The neighbors couldn't get over how quickly our garden was recovering under Amanda's green thumbs. "What's she using, Frances?" Mrs. Beaver pestered me. "Coffee grounds? Something from the toilet?"

"Nothing but love," I said. "That and a little stinging nettle tea."

I squinted at Amanda over my book, wishing with all my heart that she'd come over and take me in her arms—if only so that I could push her away.

I'll go crazy if Mamu doesn't write soon, I thought.

"What would you think of driving to Southend tomorrow?" Matthew suggested on Friday.

We looked at him with astonishment. "What are you talking about?" I asked indignantly. "It's Shabbat. We only drive in an emergency."

"We're going to have an emergency on our hands if we don't lure you away from your books soon! I've already talked with the Beavers. They'll drive us and stay there for a few days; we'll take the train home on Sunday and be back in the afternoon in time for work."

Southend, of all places, across the channel from Belgium and Holland! The barricades had been dismantled, the same little waves rolled calmly and cheerfully onto the beach, and people walked along the promenade as if it had never been otherwise.

No sooner did he step out of the car than Matthew was overcome by his scruples after all. Setting aside that little white lie with the "emergency," Shabbat was expressly not for pleasure, but was reserved for spiritual reflection. Now the fresh sea breeze apparently threatened to be such a great pleasure for my foster father that he didn't dare take off his coat!

Amanda and I stood in front of his lounge chair in our summer dresses and looked down at him doubtfully.

"We want to get postcards and an ice cream—will you come with us?"

"No, I don't want to touch any money on the Sabbath. Just let me sit here and read a little." He squinted under his hat in the sunlight and stretched out his legs to make it look like he was comfortable. I imagined that he was already boiling hot in his black shoes.

"He'll turn the chair around as soon as we're gone," Amanda whispered.

We stopped a short way off and watched with curiosity, and sure enough: Matthew stood up, stomped through the sand with his coat billowing, and pushed the lounge chair into the position with the least attractive view possible. Then he wearily sank back into it and took out his prayer book. As reluctantly as I had come along myself, it was touching that he went through all of this for my sake.

At the postcard kiosk we looked for a card for Walter, but I knew what Amanda was really thinking. "Do you think your mum might like these?" she asked, making her voice sound as casual as possible.

"Mamu," I corrected her. "Try not to confuse the two of you, please!"

She smiled apologetically and held out the card, an image of the famous pier that stretches more than a mile out into the water. On the other side was the coast of Holland. It couldn't possibly have been more obvious. "One of you should finally make the first move," Amanda declared, and paid for the postcard.

I didn't say anything. I knew she was right; I even thought that Mamu probably hadn't written yet because she was having the same trouble with those "first words" that I was. Nothing would be simpler than starting with an ordinary holiday postcard.

Nonetheless, I launched into protest as soon as Amanda pushed the card across the table toward me in the ice cream parlor. "Why do I have to be the one to take the first step?" I blurted. "If I was important to her, Mamu would have gotten in touch a long time ago."

"If there is such a thing as hell on earth, then your mother has been there," Amanda said quietly. "She might still be there now."

"I can't help her," I muttered in the direction of the water.

"I think you can."

"Have I told you why she sent me to England all by myself?" I gave my foster mother a cool look. "Mamu and I could have emigrated to Shanghai; we had all the paperwork in order, including passage for the ship. But Papa was still in Sachsenhausen, and she chose to be separated from me rather than him.

"I was ten years old," I said hoarsely. "I would rather have died than go alone, and she knew that."

"Frances! To be confronted with a decision like that, you can't seriously *blame* her for that!"

"We weren't as close as you think we were. Papa always came first, he was wonderful." My voice failed and for a few seconds I couldn't speak. "It was the best decision she could have made," I finally admitted. "But now I'm here and she's over there."

Amanda folded her hands over the menu and said nothing. I was glad when the waitress came over to our table. But I should have known better—once the topic had been raised, Mum wouldn't let me off the hook.

"Honey, I have a feeling that you're trying to tell me that you're finished with your mother," she said right to my face.

I was shocked. "No . . . How can you say that? I think about her, I'm worried, I . . ."

"That's the problem, isn't it? You can't just go about your business anymore. It's time to settle it."

"To settle what?"

"Whatever it is that stands between you two. What you've been carrying around with you for six years. There are things that become more significant the more you try to convince yourself they don't exist." She leaned forward and looked at me intently. "If I was sure you could be happy without your mother, I would do everything in my power to make things stay just the way they are. But I'm not sure. You're not sure. That can't just be ignored."

"That's true. You'd rather ignore that you're my mother now. You'd prefer to erase the past six years. And I thought we had something special."

"Oh, love. We did. We still do! That's exactly what I was about to say. When you look back on these six years, if you take away the nights of bombing, the fear for your parents, and Gary, and Matthew, your accident, Gary's . . . Gary's death . . ." I could see how the word stuck in her throat. "Wouldn't you agree that it was actually a happy time?" she asked bravely. "You were my daughter, and I was very, very happy to be your mum. We depended on each other, we were there for each other."

Strange. Those were the words I had always longed to hear, but instead of being glad, something hot formed a ball in the pit of my stomach. "We have nothing to feel guilty about," Amanda went on, and I suddenly knew where she was headed.

"No, Mum!" I heard myself say in an entirely foreign voice.

"We love each other enough that we don't always have to be together. No matter where you are, we can't lose each other anymore. That goes for Matthew too."

"Stop!"

"We're not sending you away, Frances. We just want to tell you that you're free to go and win your mother back."

I jumped up. "Be quiet!" I screamed at her, as loudly as I could. Heads turned at the other tables.

But Amanda actually put it into words. "My dear, if there's anyone you're really finished with, it's me and Matthew."

On the last day of secondary school there was a small celebration in the auditorium. We were simply called forward to receive our diplomas, and our teacher spoke a few warm words about each person's plans for the future. Parents I didn't know applauded politely, we crowded together on the school steps for a group photograph, there were hugs and solemn promises not to lose touch with each other. And then the endless wasteland of the long summer holiday before college lay before me.

My foster parents waited with the other parents around the edge of the schoolyard. "That was lovely," Amanda observed. Since we had gotten back from Southend, we had made it a firm policy to be relaxed with each other. To celebrate the day, they took Hazel and me to the Bardolo, a sinfully expensive kosher restaurant in Westminster. My friend met us there, gave everyone a kiss on the cheek, and even as we sat down, the latest hilarious stories from her new life as a telephone operator bubbled forth.

When we were alone, Hazel listened intently as I poured my heart out. I told her what Amanda had done in Southend, that I had been so upset that I ran out of the ice cream parlor and paced up and down the beach and the pier until nightfall. That Matthew, instead of taking my side, had only said how awful it still was for him and Amanda that they had had to break off contact with their parents and families in order to be together.

I told her that I had just walked away from him. And the next day we left right after breakfast and I had to continue pacing in the train so I wouldn't have to sit in the same compartment with people I was through with.

"Well," Hazel remarked when I was finished. "She could have put it more delicately."

"Were you listening to me at all? Amanda dismissed me from being her daughter! What difference does it make how she put it?"

We sat in the late afternoon sun on the terrace of one of the ruins on Harrington Grove that were overgrown with grass and brush. I found the weather-beaten handle of a knife on the ground near me and carved a groove in the stones as I dangled my legs over the wall.

Hazel leaned against the side wall. "I don't think Amanda dismissed you," she said thoughtfully. "I think she just wanted to say that you don't have to feel obligated to them. Does she know what you promised Gary?"

"No," I replied sullenly, and poked around with my knife.

"What did you expect?" Hazel persisted. "That your mother would arrive and move in with the Shepards, preferably along with Uncle Erik and Walter?"

I pressed my lips together. I didn't see what would have been so wrong with that!

"Wake up, Frances," my friend said. "Your problem is that you're stuck between two chapters. One is over, and you're not quite ready to start the next one. But if you just look at the one after that, the whole thing will fall into place. Stop agonizing about your mothers. Your future isn't named Amanda or Mamu, but Walter. What does he have to say about all of this, anyway?"

"Not much. That's part of the problem. He was there when Uncle Erik got my mother out of Belsen, but he's only mentioned it in passing. She was probably in such terrible shape that even Walter doesn't know what to say."

"Wasn't that almost two months ago? Surely she must be doing better. Why don't you go to Holland during the holiday and see her?"

"Because Uncle Erik wrote that she doesn't want to see me yet. And if I leave England, I might not be allowed back in the country." The old knife broke, and I threw it far away into the brush. "She must have gotten my postcard by now, but six and a half years is just too long. Too much has happened. No!" I exclaimed emphatically. "I'm not going to Holland. We would be like strangers to each other. It's better if everything just stays the way it is."

"I believe I had your mother on the phone again," Amanda said when I got home. "That was the third time this week the phone rang but no one spoke when I answered. I could tell from the clicking sounds that it was an overseas call, but the caller didn't say their name and hung up after a few seconds."

"Why would she do something like that?" I asked.

"Because she doesn't want to talk with me. Maybe she's scared."

"Mamu? Scared? Of you? That's funnier than you know," I said, but secretly I was slowly beginning to have my doubts. Could I possibly know anymore what my mother felt and thought?

"It's always late afternoon, just as I come home from the nursing home."

"Maybe you should call her by name," I suggested hesitantly. "Margot."

"That's a good idea. I'll just start talking, tell her about you. I imagine she takes a walk alone every afternoon and passes by a public telephone. Because if Erik were there, he would say something, especially since you probably have to wait for hours for a connection."

Officially we had long since forgiven each other. At the same time, I couldn't forget that Amanda had given me up; I distanced myself from her and hoped that it bothered her as much as it did me.

The following afternoons I stayed within hearing distance of the telephone, but whoever it was that had called had apparently given up. The first week of my holiday passed, the Americans released atom bombs on Hiroshima and Nagasaki, and the war that had begun in Poland found its end in the Pacific. The third anniversary of Gary's death came and went and Amanda decided, "I want to go to the place it happened. Someday, if it's possible, I'll go there."

Hamburg, 13 August 1945

Regarding: Liebich, Susanna, Hermann, and Rebekka.

In response to your search request for the

*above named we have determined that on 19
October 1942 the entire family was deported to
Lettland and perished there. We have forwarded
the particulars to the World Jewish Congress in
London. Should there be any further information
there now or in the future, you will be notified
immediately. We deeply regret that we are not able
to convey more favorable news.*

> *Sincerely,
> The German Red Cross,
> Landesverband Hamburg, Foreign Services*

"Francesfrancesfrances . . ." My name, like a distant echo. In the entrance of the bomb shelter a play of light and shadows, a figure bent forward to peer in, coming toward me as if in slow motion. When we had to spend nights here, this cold little tube of corrugated metal protected me from the bombs. Now it was still and warm inside, it smelled of earth and summer, but there was no protection from a piece of paper.

Deported to Lettland and perished there. Six words, thirty-four letters. The one and only constant hope I clung to. Bekka, who taught herself English, carried around secret escape routes in her shoe, who loved chocolate with nuts, adventure stories, and especially Shirley Temple, without ever once being allowed to go into a movie theater. She had managed to see half of one film at least, *The Littlest Rebel*, before the other children chased her out of the theater. Her eyes had glowed as she told me the end of the story, the ending she had thought up herself. "And when we're in America, I'm going to see if the real ending is as good as mine!"

She knew, I thought. She knew what the kindertransport meant, and what it meant to be left behind. She had braced herself; she had to have been among the survivors. Her world didn't collapse when she was murdered, but a long time before that: When the chance to live fell to me and not her.

I will never understand it, I thought. *If you die and I live, then there are no rules in this world.*

Amanda sat down next to me. "It makes no sense whatsoever that she's dead. It makes all the sense in the world that you live."

I can't remember much about the two days and nights between the letter from the Red Cross and what happened next, but those two sentences remain: the attempt at an answer, if there can be such a thing at all. At the time I didn't have an inkling that they would accompany me the rest of my life; I just clung to the hope that Amanda, who gave me that answer, knew something about it, because a mother shouldn't have to survive her child any more than one friend should live instead of another.

I suspected it wouldn't help at all that my salvation hadn't been my doing. The only comfort was that for a short time, Bekka and I had been allowed to be friends again.

The second morning after the news about Bekka, light came through the window and swept over me and something took shape, sorted itself out. Maybe you can only see the flip side of things very early in the morning, in this other, still new light.

I had two families—it was as simple as that. While many of the young people from the kindertransports were learning that their families had been extinguished, I had two mothers, a father, an uncle, possibly a future husband, and a good friend. Could anyone be any luckier?

But I always wanted to remind myself that at least on that morning I could see something else too. I had lost Bekka, and Gary too, but they had left something behind for me. If I could manage to not let them die within me, to keep something of Bekka's courage and Gary's joy alive, then their lives hadn't been extinguished, and there was nothing that couldn't be overcome.

It was lunchtime when my mother called. Amanda was in the kitchen making something for us to eat, and she was the one who answered. I was already standing at the stairs when she answered the phone: "Shepard residence."

There was a pause. That didn't mean anything; any caller would first state their name and the reason for their call. But I felt it immediately. The absolute silence. The house stopped breathing; it was waiting for the magic word.

Amanda said very gently, "Margot?"

My foot hovered above the first step.

"Please stay on the line. Don't hang up. We've been waiting for you."

I always loved hearing Amanda speaking Yiddish, that warm, cheerful language, our language. A language like a bridge. "How good that you called, especially today. Your daughter is so sad. She had to hear that her friend Bekka died."

The soft wood of the stair railing stroked the palm of my hand, and I felt the familiar little groove in the middle of the stairs.

"Do you remember that Bekka was supposed to come live with us? The war started just two days too soon."

The last step. Amanda stood with her back to me and our eyes met in the mirror, locked.

"Now I can only give one child back to her mother," Amanda said quietly to us both, and only then did I remember that she too had once made a promise.

She closed the kitchen door firmly behind herself after she had handed me the receiver. For the first time in more than six and a half years, I heard my mother's voice.

"Ziska? My Ziskele! I've written almost thirty pages to you, and now I don't dare send them."

Chapter 24

Mamu

Anyone who returns to their mother nearly grown up after last seeing her as a ten-year-old shouldn't count on a joyful reunion—even after talking on the phone every day for two weeks, when their voices have become more familiar to each other again. My stomach knotted as we saw the bright strip of the Dutch coast appear before us; I had remembered the crossing taking much longer. It was still hard to believe I was actually on my way, on my way back.

At the pier in Harwich Amanda had bought a round trip ticket, and only a one-way ticket for me.

"I don't know if I'm still the kind of person a young girl should grow up with," Mamu had objected timidly, who seemed to be much more scared of my return than I was.

"I'm already grown up, Mamu," I reminded her.

"My goodness, I keep forgetting! That big British soldier who put me on the train, thank goodness Erik only told me that he was your fiancé afterward, otherwise I would have fallen over dead one step away from freedom."

"Well, he isn't really my fiancé, but you should get used to seeing Walter again soon. He's stationed in Lübeck and will definitely come by often."

"If you stay," said Mamu, still unsure.

"If I stay," I confirmed.

Uncle Erik's concerns were more concrete. Was I aware that my mother wasn't the same person, that she suffered from panic attacks, eating disorders, sleeplessness, and bouts of deep depression in which no one could help her, not even me? In contrast, I was the only one with a home, with plans and a future; Erik thought it might be stressful for Mamu to think of me giving all that up.

It took a while until he understood that Mamu also belonged to my life, that there couldn't be any future, any plans, any home that didn't include her as well. I wasn't giving up anything, but gaining something.

Since I left Germany, I had been convinced that my mother could only have parted with me because I wasn't especially important to her. While I knew that she saved my life by doing it, there had always been this little barb, even in my happiest moments: My mother had sent me away.

But now my second mother was sending me on a journey too—and everything was different. I didn't doubt Amanda's love; I knew what I meant to her and Matthew. They needed me; it must have been infinitely difficult for them, and yet they let me go. They parted with me for no other reason than that they hoped for my even greater happiness.

And so now, only now, I understood. It's possible to let someone go *because you love them*. Maybe it hadn't been any different for Mamu. Maybe I would know soon. Amanda held tight to her hat, braced herself against the wind whipping about the railings, and squinted her eyes straining to recognize the Continent, as she called it.

Before we left, Matthew said, "No matter what you decide, you'll never be anything but my daughter to me."

"I couldn't go if I didn't know that," I replied.

The train ride from Hoek van Holland to Groningen was difficult. After the Germans had blocked transport of coal into Holland in the last winter of the war, people had torn up railroad ties and burned them out of desperation. There were still stretches that hadn't been repaired, and we had arranged to meet Uncle Erik and Mamu in Rotterdam and then travel farther north together a few days later. My uncle had suggested a certain café that he knew was open as a meeting point.

As we walked the short stretch from the train station to our pension, I was appalled by the damage the war and hunger had left behind. Bombed-out ruins—still from the first summer of war—were certainly a familiar sight to me, but there wasn't a single tree here, emaciated children stared at us, and fake cheeses and butter made of paper stood in the store windows. The people carrying their almost empty shopping baskets through the streets seemed gray and exhausted.

Amanda and I were dressed very modestly ourselves, our coats and skirts patched and mended so often that we had all gotten used to moving very carefully so as not to strain the fabric any more than necessary. But everything we had experienced with rationing in London paled in comparison to the misery that had obviously befallen the Dutch, and when I addressed the woman in our pension in a friendly tone in German, I regretted it immediately. She glared at us with such hatred that Amanda and I were flooded with a long-forgotten, humiliating fear.

"We come from England. We're Jewish," I reassured her quickly, but the damage was done, and the distrustful woman didn't respond to English or French.

"I won't speak another word of German as long as I'm here!" I declared, shaken. "I'd rather they don't understand my English than be stared at like that again!"

We unpacked our few belongings and stretched out on the bed. We had more than two hours until we were supposed to meet Mamu and Uncle Erik, and since we had left England very early in the morning, we were getting tired. But the mounting tension, and probably to some extent the thought that these were the last hours Amanda and I would have to ourselves, kept me awake. Neither of us spoke. We had said everything to each other that was important, and I kept my thoughts to myself: I'll never experience such trust with another person. Something like this only happens once in a lifetime, if at all.

Uncle Erik proceeded very carefully. He had allowed two or three hours for our first encounter, then each of us should have time to go back to our lodgings and relax. The next morning we would meet again—"and then we'll see how it goes." I was glad for his caution. After all, he knew best how much my mother could handle.

The closer Amanda and I came to the designated meeting place, the more nervous I became. When I opened my mouth to announce, "I think that's the café ahead," I didn't recognize my own voice. It was flat and about an octave higher than usual.

"We're too early," I groaned when we had taken a seat at one of the three small tables on the cobblestones in front of the café. An older woman came out, looked at us curiously, and told us she had sheet cake, malt coffee, and tea. With some effort, we explained to her in English that we were waiting for two more people.

"Do you think they have bathrooms inside?" I asked shyly just as soon as the woman had left.

Amanda looked at me with alarm. "My goodness," she said quietly. "Is it so awful? Soon you'll have it behind you. Just a few minutes, love. The end of the journey."

Tears welled in my eyes; I jumped up and stumbled inside the café, where two men sat with newspapers. The old woman approached me, a sweet, round, pale face. Was I all right? Could she bring me a glass of water? I looked at her through my tears and forgot all my resolutions, and said in German: "I'm waiting for my mother. We're Jews. I haven't seen her for almost seven years."

For a moment there was such a silence in the room that I was afraid I'd ruined everything. They were about to kick me out. Terrified, I blinked away my tears . . . and found myself looking into friendly eyes.

"Why don't you sit here, right by the window, then you can see her coming."

She adjusted the chair for me, and through a gray windowpane I had a view of the square. There was a stone fountain, like our old meeting spot in Tail's End. Heavens, how should I even begin to tell my mother about my life?

A few pigeons landed next to Amanda's table and pecked hopefully around her. She sat so still the birds hopped over her shoes.

What am I doing here? I thought with a stab of conscience. *I have to go outside again, I can't just leave her sitting there alone.*

And then: Amanda's smile, the quick jolt that went through her whole body. The pigeons flew away, there was a brief, annoying flurry of wings, and there she was.

Oh, my God. Is that Mamu?

I recognized her because she was on Uncle Erik's arm: an older woman in a light coat, with overly dyed blue-black hair that made the face below it look even more sickly and pale. In spite of the mild weather she was clearly freezing, and her steps were so slow, as if she had lead weights on her feet. As they drew even closer, I saw that Mamu's cheeks formed two little sacks that hung down limply.

A surge of wildly mixed feelings gripped me: pity, love, rage, helplessness. Horrified understanding of what the Nazis had done—my proud mother! She hadn't been killed, but was destroyed nonetheless. Her life had been taken from her too. They had taken everything.

Everything?

No, there had to have been something that made her endure. Something must have moved her to gather her strength, to risk the trip to Rotterdam and come here. Something made her color her hair and re-create an old, familiar trait: the trademark strands of hair that hung in her eyes, giving her haggard face a peculiarly stubborn, courageous, and provocative look. Something seemed to want to urge her to start over again.

No. Not *something*. Me.

Outside on the square, Amanda stood up and did the same thing she had done when we first met: She stretched out her hand and went toward Mamu, and in Mamu's nervous face was suddenly reflected the warmth of this greeting, the smile of my other mother. Mamu's hand still held in hers, Amanda turned around and pointed in my direction, said something, she and Uncle Erik laughed . . . and the loose ends of my life were woven together, Ziska and Frances, Mamu and Amanda, yesterday, today, soon.

I felt myself being pulled through the room toward the door.

"Is everything okay?" asked the woman in the café.

"Absolutely." Then I stepped outside. "Everything is fine just the way it is."

That would have been a good ending, I suppose.

Epilogue

The captain watched silently as the passengers helped each other on board. There were five—two couples and a little girl about three years old sporting a red life vest. They had found him through the owner of the pension in Ponta Delgada, as was often the case. The older of the two couples would be around fifty, a tall, serious man wearing a long coat and a hat, the woman slim and introverted with a delicate, attractive face and a warm smile.

The young woman was practically still a girl herself, not more than early twenties, and her partner—clearly the father of the little girl, who had inherited his brown curls and round cheeks—wore a uniform, but probably only for this occasion, because it was hard to overlook that it was already tight across the chest and stomach. One of Monty's boys! The captain saluted when he recognized the insignia of the Eighth Army.

The coordinates they had shown him were those of the HMS Cole or the Princess of Malta, which weren't far away. Three hours on a calm sea, he guessed. He didn't ask which one: Sometime in the next hour the first of them would come over and tell him, and be grateful and relieved that Captain Swanson was familiar with the story of "their" ship.

Looking out over the water, he was glad the day was calm. It made it so much easier on the relatives to see a peaceful blue sea, feel a warm breeze, and experience absolute calm in the place where "it" had happened. Those would be their memories from that point on, and they wouldn't know how it had really been.

The elderly captain of the small charter boat glanced over his passengers at short intervals. The men stood at the railing with the child safely between them, and the women had started to weave a wreath on a table in the rear of the boat. He saw what they were tying into it, and was amazed.

But the younger of the two wasn't concentrating on what she was doing. She kept looking at him, as if she was mulling over how he came to be making such a trip with them! The captain met her gaze, held it for a second, then looked forward again and discreetly went about his own business.

"Isn't it a wonderful day?" Amanda asked me.

She leaned back for a minute, breathed in deeply, and I knew her cheeks were touched by more than just the wind.

I never went to college. Three and a half months after Amanda brought me to Mamu and Uncle Erik, I returned to England together with Walter, finished my schooling, and got married right away—at nineteen, and more than ready for it! Our chuppah stood in the garden on Harrington Grove, which could just barely accommodate the wedding party: Amanda and Matthew, Mamu and Uncle Erik, all the Vathareerpurs and Mrs. Collins, Bekka's brother Thomas Liebich, who had come from Cambridge, and Millie, who had traveled from Kent, as well as a few friends from school.

From Walter's side came three friends from the army and a whole contingent of fire brigade colleagues, who enthusiastically tried to do the dances.

But when Walter placed his ring on my finger and Rabbi Bloom ceremoniously read the ketubah out loud, my thoughts suddenly flew to all those who should have been there, and I tried not to think of them all by name, otherwise I probably would have started crying bitterly at the happiest moment of my life.

Walter and I also had to overlook the fact that it wasn't Mamu's best day. She followed the entire ceremony, which was unfamiliar to her, with cool discomfort, and later that evening I heard her say to Bekka's brother, "Now my only daughter has really turned into one of those absurd orthodox Jews."

By then I knew how she could be, but some days it was just more difficult to bear than others.

The changes had begun already during my stay in Holland. The stronger and healthier Mamu became physically, the more violently things seemed to be churned up inside her, until in the end almost all her interactions were clouded by anger and suspicion.

Mamu went out in the streets every day. She didn't have any particular goal except to look strangers in the face and ask herself what this one or that might have done during the occupation. She brushed away the good years with an impatient sweep of her arm, as if it had been nothing but a sham. We hoped her rage would wear itself out over time. But the neighbors started to find her unnerving. Finally, the van Dyck sisters, with whom she lived and who had made a small room available for me, tearfully asked Uncle Erik to find a different place to live. Mamu had hurled back at them that she hoped Aunt Ruth's death, for which she held them responsible, would haunt them for the rest of their lives.

I wasn't there to help with the move. When I left for England with Walter, it was clear that my staying wouldn't have changed anything. If there was anyone who Mamu felt understood her, it was Uncle Erik, with whom she shared the majority of her experiences and losses. But me? As painful as it was for both of us, the longer I stayed, the clearer it became that I hadn't grown up as her daughter.

I went to the synagogue on Fridays, observed Shabbat, didn't eat pork or shellfish; that alone was fodder for countless arguments. At first she accepted it with wonder, but after several weeks it burst out of her: How could I worship a God who had allowed his own people to be annihilated? Did she really have to remind me again how my father had died, or my aunt Ruth in Mamu's arms? Had I forgotten Evchen and Betti, and did I want to defile the memory of Bekka, my own dead friend?

I lost all control. Mamu had shown so little reaction to Bekka's death that I had only mentioned it a single time; I understood that her own awful memories were more than enough to deal with. But to be accused of betraying Bekka— that was the one accusation I could least bear. "Leave Bekka out of it!" I snarled at her. "Don't act like you suddenly care about her!"

My mother recoiled, slapped me across the face, and ran from the room crying.

From then on, each weekend brought the same discussions, beginning with accusations on Friday afternoon and dragging on smoldering and sullen until Saturday evening. My offer to go to church with Mamu only made things worse: My mother *really* felt betrayed when I declared that on top of everything else, I still believed in Jesus!

If Walter hadn't come to visit at regular intervals, I would have been frantic.

Mamu and I had our nicest and most honest conversations only after I gingerly shared with her that Walter was returning to England and had asked me if I wanted to go with him.

Mamu said immediately, "I think you should do it."

"And you?" I asked quietly. "I always imagined we'd live together in England one day . . ."

"Maybe," she answered evasively. "Maybe Erik and I will come later. But you shouldn't wait that long."

"Mamu, do you know why I came to Holland to be with you?"

"Well, I think because . . ." It was clearly difficult for her to say this out loud. "It had to do with love, I assume."

"Exactly."

"Ziska, every single day, whether in hiding or in the camp or later here, every single day I thought of you and wished . . ." Her voice cracked. "I'm so sorry. It has nothing to do with love, that this isn't working. You have to believe me."

"I know." Now I was crying after all.

"You're a good girl. I'm so glad you came; it means a lot to me. But now go back and be happy. I can't do it anymore."

When I went home to England with Walter, I went for

good. Mamu and I phoned each other at least once a week, she came to our wedding, and once in a while I told her—half in jest—about apartments that were available nearby. But in spring 1948 she and Uncle Erik announced they were not coming to England, but going to Israel, the recently established nation of the Jews. Despite Mamu's religious beliefs, she felt the Jews were the only people who could understand what she had lived through.

Mamu knew her grandchild only from photographs. Rebecca Lightfoot was born on September 10, 1948, and it was her grandmother Amanda who placed her in my arms. Walter and I often joke that Becky's first, all-important bonding can't have been with me; she and Amanda love each other dearly, have special nicknames for each other, and since our daughter has been able to walk we've had to lock our garden gate to keep her from toddling halfway through Finchley to "Amma."

Of all the stories we and her grandparents tell her, there's one Becky wants to hear over and over again: "Amma, tell me why Ziska wanted to hide."

And Amanda tells her about the little girl who always had to run away from scary people and hide, until her mother finally sent her to a foreign country to live with strangers, all by herself, where the scary people wouldn't find her. But the girl couldn't believe she was safe, and the first thing the girl asked her foster parents was where she could hide in this new country. Her foster mother explained to Ziska that she would never need to hide again, that she was quite safe now, and that her new parents would do everything they could to make sure nothing bad happened to her.

The story always ends with the same little ritual.

"And Ziska, that's my mummy, right?" Becky asks, smiling.

"That she is," Amma answers. "And I should know, because I was there."

And so Amanda makes me a heroine in my daughter's eyes, but she doesn't yet tell her that there was a second little girl in that story. I want to do that myself one day, because I want Rebecca to know whom she's named for.

Walter returned to the fire brigade after his discharge from the army and is in charge of his own rig, and I write subtitles for foreign films. We still rent a basement apartment near my old school, but one of the plots with ruins on the other end of Harrington Grove is for sale, and Amanda and Matthew have offered us the money that was intended first for Gary's college and then mine. We haven't agreed yet, but Walter and Matthew are already busily planning and drawing a little two-story house with children's rooms, a garden, a sandbox, and swings.

The captain, who has been observing us so intently, would surely be surprised if he knew how this family on board his ship today was patched together! He was certainly surprised when Matthew and Walter put on their teffilin and started to pray quietly after he told them we'd soon reach our destination. There probably weren't very many Jews in the navy.

The man's eyes grow wide and round when Walter takes the Military Cross off his uniform and gives it to me so I can weave it into the wreath.

"Are you sure?" Amanda asks softly.

"Quite sure," he replies with a smile. "I've been looking forward to this for years."

Now Becky has to touch everything one more time and ask questions, even though she already knows the story behind them: the one about the worn-out little dictionary, for example, that her mummy brought with her to England a long time ago, or the delicate strip of white lace from her bridal veil. Then there's the key to a certain room in the Elysée and a pacifier with a little hole from Becky's first baby tooth. And all the colorful, hand-picked fall flowers come from Amma's own garden; she kept them moist in a box during the flight, and held her breath while going through customs, hoping she wouldn't have to open her suitcase!

But when we finally reach the spot, Becky forgets all about the wreath. She stands on her tiptoes with a furrowed brow, holding tight to the railing, and peers into the water without a sound, serious and steady, as if she could make out the ship that lies thousands of feet below us. It's perfectly still out here; little waves lap against the sides and I hear how Matthew's soft voice becomes one with the expanse of the ocean and the breath of the wind: "Glorified and sanctified be God's great name throughout the world which he has created according to his will. May he establish his kingdom in your lifetime and during your days . . ."

I see Amanda bend over and whisper to Becky, just two words, but she already understands. Together they lift our wreath and let it glide over the edge of our boat into the water. Immediately Becky reaches for her Amma's hand and holds it tightly to her, as if she wants to share her sadness.

"This is for you, Gary, my sweetheart," Amanda whispers, which isn't exactly what she was supposed to say.

Matthew says it for her. "Gary Aaron Shepard," he states in a loud, clear voice.

"Paul Glücklich." That comes from Walter, somewhat more softly.

"Lotte Glücklich."

"Franz Mangold.

"Ruth Bechstein.

"Evchen Bechstein.

"Betti Bechstein."

For a moment I don't think I can continue. But Walter steps over to me and I feel him behind me, like a long time ago, when we made our first sea voyage, a stormy crossing when we were children.

"Rebekka Liebich.

"Susanna Liebich.

"Hermann Liebich.

"Julius Schueler.

"Frank Duffy.

"Ruben Seydensticker.

"Chaja Seydensticker."

My voice grows stronger. All these names that want to finally be spoken! There will never be another trace of the Seydenstickers and their entire family, whose history stretches back into the seventeenth century, except my voice.

"Benjamin Seydensticker.

"Jakob Seydensticker.

"Beile Seydensticker.

"Herschel Seydensticker . . ."

Our little wreath bobs away on the waves, comes back toward us a little ways, as if it was looking for just the right spot, then begins to sink quickly. Out of the corner of my eye I see that the captain has taken off his cap, and just as at the start of our trip, I suddenly feel very close to him.

We belong to those who live with the dead. They depend on us. As long as I have a voice and as long as there is someone listening, I will name them, and tell our story.

I would never find another friend like Rebekka Liebich. She crouched on the narrow windowsill, one hand holding tight to the frame, and held the other hand stretched out in front of her, as if that would somehow shorten the distance of almost five feet between her and the trunk of the birch tree.

Afterword

Anyone who reads a novel based on historic events is bound to ask themselves: How much of it is really true?

The kindertransports are real. The first one left Berlin via Hamburg on December 1, 1938, and the last on August 31, 1939. Another train with 250 children from Prague wasn't allowed to depart because of the outbreak of the war, and these children really experienced what happened to Ziska's friend Bekka in the novel: Their transport was too late by a single day.

Apart from the many familiar personalities whose names and deeds have been recorded in history books, all the characters in this story are entirely fictional. What they experience, however, is based on true events: the hopeless, inescapable situation of the Jews in Germany and the occupied countries; the evacuation of hundreds of thousands of British children from the cities to the safer countryside when war broke out; the terror of the German bomb attacks; the consequences of years of war on the life of the island population. Without the seamen of the Merchant Navy and the Royal Navy, who provided protection for the supply ships on their dangerous passage through the Atlantic—men like

Ziska's brother, Gary—England couldn't have withstood the war.

Walter's wartime experiences lead him to be interred in May 1940 with other "enemy aliens" on the Isle of Man for several months. Two years later he is a soldier stationed in North Africa and then Italy, where he follows the actual route taken by the Eighth Army under General Bernard Montgomery ("Monty"). For dramatic reasons, I have sent him overseas nine months earlier than was actually permitted to a native of Germany who joined the British Forces.

In Holland and later in Belgium, Mamu and Uncle Erik's family are overwhelmed by events that unfortunately really did happen. Also accurate is the dramatic rescue of about 370,000 British and French soldiers from a beach near Dunkirk in Belgium (May 26–June 3, 1940) that brings Matthew Shepard back to his Amanda. The radio program through which Ziska learns about it didn't exist in exactly that form.

I hope the Jewish community in Finchley, London, will not mind that I set the main stage for this story—the Shepards' cozy little house on Harrington Grove—in their neighborhood. Any parallels to actual people, places, or events there are purely coincidental and not intentional.

Berlin, July 2006
Anne C. Voorhoeve